The window beside him explod
his face as the glass shrapnel
hands reached in, grabbed him b
thing Ethan knew, he was jerked through the busted window
and thrown.

Ethan didn't think he'd been knocked out, but he was somehow on the ground with no memory of landing. His vision was
blurred as he looked toward the Blazer. He was shocked by how
far he'd been launched. It looked as if they were on opposite
ends of an empty swimming pool.

The big man started moving.

ALL WILL DIE

by Kristopher Rufty

Dedication

For Kristopher Triana

1.

That was a scream.

Gale dropped the true crime book she'd been reading onto her pillow. Her heart had already been racing from the horrid details she'd gleaned from the story and now it was a fist trying to punch through her chest. Living in the mountains, spooky sounds were a common occurrence she'd grown used to. But not this time. That was a person.

Shit!

She tightened the belt on her robe and shuffled away from her comfortable bed. On her way to the bedroom door, she paused by the dresser to grab the double-barrel shotgun she kept leaning against the wall. Though she knew it was loaded, she checked anyway. The copper tops of the shells gleamed in the meager light from the bedside lamp.

Her compact living room was dark, save the silvery light filtering in through the curtains. She left it that way. She didn't want anyone to know she was approaching the door. Her movements were hushed, the only sounds were the soft scratchy sounds of her bare feet on the wood floor.

Another scream ripped through the night outside. Gale froze in place. She thumbed back one of the hammers on the shotgun.

That sounded like it was right outside!

Gale took a few deep breaths. Her chest felt as if it were shrinking around her breasts. Her heart sledged. Sweat began to dribble down from her hairline.

It was a girl. The scream had been close enough that she'd been able to decipher that much. Sounded like she was making her way up the driveway. Probably be at the front door at any moment.

Gale wasn't taking any chances. She'd watched plenty of horror movies in her day. Usually, people in these situations opened their front door to find out what the ruckus was about, only to receive an ax in their face for their trouble. Nope. Gale was not going to do such a stupid thing.

Gale grabbed the cordless phone from its cradle on the small table by the couch. She had a cell phone, but reception was spotty out here. The device was only useful in town, closer to the towers. It was better to have the cell working there in case she ever had any trouble.

But now the trouble was outside her home, and the cell phone was useless.

Gale called 911. Someone with a monotone voice answered before the first ring had even finished. Gale told the uninterested woman her name and address in a voice that wanted to shout but emanated in a loud whisper. "Send cops! Now! That's three times I've heard the screams."

"Do they sound like they're hurt, or just fooling around?"

"Sounds like they're being *murdered!*"

Gale hadn't once thought about that, but now that she'd said it, she realized that was exactly how that poor girl had sounded.

"Are you there?" Gale asked. There had been no response for longer than what made her feel comfortable.

"Yes. I'm dispatching the authorities right now."

"How long before they're h—*shit!*" Gale flinched at the scream. It was in the woods just outside the border of her yard and filled with an agony Gale had never heard in real life. "Did you hear that? Did you fucking hear that?"

"Yes, ma'am, I did. Twenty minutes. They'll be there in twenty minutes. Do you have something to protect yourself?"

"I have all I need…" Gale saw her hand rising in the dark, reaching for the slide-bolt lock on the door.

As if sensing the idiotic effort she was making, the dispatcher said, "You need to stay inside, ma'am. Do *not* go outside, no matter what."

"That girl's not going to last twenty minutes."

To prove Gale's statement, another scream resonated from outside. It was weaker in valor but just as strong in volume.

Gale took a deep breath and slowly let it out.

The dispatcher cleared her throat. "Don't. Sit tight. Help is on the way."

Gale knew the sensible thing was to stay inside. After all, she'd just told herself that what she was planning to do was stupid horror movie bullshit that would see her head severed from her body and launched into the air like a blood-spewing kickball.

But Gale could never live with herself knowing she'd "sat tight" while a poor girl was being killed. There was no doubt at all that was happening outside her home.

Gale couldn't go outside with the phone clutched in her hand and expect to handle the shotgun as well. She thumbed the button to end the call, then tossed the phone toward the dark shape that she assumed was her couch. She heard a muffled thump when it struck the cushion.

I'm doing this. I'm really doing this! Shit!

Gale opened the door. Expecting the sounds of wildlife and insects to greet her, she was met with the unusual silence of the night holding its breath. Gale realized she was as well and slowly let it out. Her lungs felt as if they were being squeezed by icy hands.

Standing on her porch, she raised the stock to her shoulder. Though she already had one hammer prepped to fire, she was tempted to pull back the other. She decided against doing so. One was enough, for now.

She had no flashlight, nor did she need one. Her eyes were used to the dark now. Plus, the flashlight would announce she was outside. As far as she was concerned, keeping herself as inconspicuous as possible would be wise. That way, she could move about undetected. And if she needed to, she could make a speedy retreat inside her house.

She gently pulled the door shut behind her. The hinges made no sound, nor did the porch when she crossed the wooden boards and headed down the steps. Her slippers weren't the best protection for her feet on the gravel and dirt, but they were fine when she reached the grass. She'd gone only a few steps before feeling the dampness of the dew seeping through. She ignored it as she made her way to the tree line.

Right here. This is the spot.

She was sure of it. She stared at the tree trunks, at the deep shadows packed between them. Tendrils of fog swirled between the black spaces like beckoning fingers. She could smell the sweet, damp smell of the woods. A smell she normally relished, tonight it held a strange odor. Something had caused the usual smells to shift. The air around her also didn't feel right, like it had somehow spoiled.

She suddenly wanted to be back inside.

Sorry, girl. You're on your own!

Gale spun around, prepared to run.

A screaming girl launched at Gale as if the night had vomited her into Gale's path. Gale glimpsed a lot of bare skin slicked in dark muck before the feral girl rammed into Gale's stomach.

Knocked back, Gale managed to throw up an arm, catching the girl around the waist as she started to drop to her knees. Gale pulled her back to a standing position. The girl's eyes were big and round inside a mask of dripping crimson. Her teeth looked very white inside trembling lips.

"Help me! Help...!" The girl began to drop again.

Gale's fingers slid over the gelid sheen of the girl's skin. She couldn't get the grip she needed to hold the girl up and watched her drop at her feet. Gale held her hand up to the moonlight.

It was slicked in blood.

Gale gripped the shotgun in both hands. This time, she thumbed back the second hammer.

"Where are you? Huh? I can smell your crazy ass!"

The girl moaned at Gale's feet. This surprised Gale because she thought the girl had just died. Gale started to bend down to help her up when she heard the thin cracking sound a stick might make if it had been stepped on.

It was very close.

Gale didn't take the time to properly aim. She fired once into the woods. The night was blown away in a flash of brightness as the silence was overtaken by the boom of the shotgun. Gale waited a second, heard another crunch from the woods, and fired at it. The blast of the second barrel knocked her shoulder back. She felt a stinging flash of pain from the recoil. Her shoulder was no longer built for two rounds of buckshot.

And both barrels were now empty.

Gale wasn't about to linger out here in the dark without any means of protection. She crouched, scooped the girl up, and leaned her against her side. The girl's whole body was slippery. It looked as if she'd been swimming in syrup. Her hair was glued to her face and neck like a matted veil.

Gale spotted the wounds on her chest. They were easy to see because the girl wasn't wearing a shirt. Her breasts bounced and swayed, knocking against Gale's arms as she pulled her along. Gale saw the deep gashes like stripes that added more blood to the tacky suit she already wore. One of her nipples was gone, leaving a ragged point as if it had been chewed off.

"Come on," said Gale. "Almost there. Move your feet!"

The girl either couldn't hear her or was no longer conscious. Gale was dragging her, using all her strength to keep her upright while she moved as fast as she could.

Reaching the front door, Gale turned to the side and slammed the door open with her hip. Then she spun around and flung the girl onto the couch. The girl's rump hit the cushion. Her feet shot upward, dumping her onto the couch. Gale cringed inside at the amount of blood getting on her furniture, then felt awful about her thoughts. That should have been the last of her worries.

Gale swung the door shut, bolted the lock. She dropped the gun, ran to the kitchen, grabbed the table, and dragged it with her, wedging it against the door. She was about to grab the gun, then decided to pile the chairs on top first to add as much weight to the barricade as possible.

Gale stood there a moment, hands on her hips, catching her breath. Finished with that, she rushed into the bedroom. She opened the nightstand drawer and grabbed the box of shells. She saw the book she'd been reading where she left it. Just minutes ago, she'd been in bed, reading about murder and blood. Now, she was covered in it and fearing for her life.

Back in the living room, she checked on the girl. She was alive and still awake, albeit barely.

"Stay with me, girl. Don't conk out after I did all that to get you in here."

"I'm...trying..."

Gale smiled, though she doubted the girl could see it. Then she grabbed her shotgun.

By the time she'd reloaded it, she could hear the faint wails of sirens. It would take them several minutes to reach them. Her house was far back in the woods, at the end of a two-mile driveway. Seclusion she'd wanted, but right now, she wished she was closer to the road.

Gale, both hammers cocked, sat down beside the girl on the couch.

2.

Ethan Bowers had a hard time finding a parking space at the ER. Even so early in the morning, the tiny lot was brimming with cars. Some were normal, everyday vehicles that he'd see in any other parking lot. The rest were cop cars. Seeing so many made his stomach cramp.

She's okay. You know she is. They told you she was.

Ethan had been watching a movie with Liz, a damn horror movie, when his cell phone began to ring. He'd ignored it, thinking nothing about it. Besides, his plans had been to take to Liz to the bedroom when the movie was over. He'd even washed the sheets and squirted them with a scented spray that was supposed to trigger arousal. It was a lonely, lowlife thing to do, he knew. But he been a lonely guy for years and Liz was the first woman he'd actually had feelings for in a very long time. He'd figured that should grant him a shred of slack in the creep department.

But the phone had kept buzzing. And buzzing. Finally, he'd decided somebody really needed to talk to him. The number was one he didn't know. The voice was another mystery until the man introduced himself as Detective Paul Wilcox.

"You need to get to Meyer Memorial Hospital right away," Wilcox had said. "It's in Mountain Rock. Do you know where that is?"

"Yes. I have a cabin out there. Is something wrong?"

"It's your daughter. She was...attacked. They're bringing her in. She'll be rushed straight into surgery. I'm heading there now from the scene. She's been airlifted and will beat me there."

Emily had gone to the cabin with her friends for the weekend. They had left yesterday and weren't planning on coming back until sometime next week. Ethan wanted her to stay home. He'd even told her he thought she was too young to go on such a trip, but she reminded him that she was eighteen now and would be starting college in September. She claimed if she was old enough to live off campus, she was old enough for a weekend away with her friends. Besides, it would be the last time they would be able to do anything like it for a long time, maybe forever.

Ethan had agreed with that, though he hadn't wanted to, and agreed to let her go. Soon as she drove away from the house, an odd feeling latched itself somewhere low on his spine and hung there. He knew why as soon as he answered the phone.

"Attacked?" His throat felt like it was being squeezed. "Emily...?"

He turned to Liz, who was watching him with a handful of popcorn paused an inch from her mouth. Her eyes were wide. She was ten years younger than him, but right now, she looked like a child who'd just been told her puppy had died.

"Everything okay?" she asked when he hung up.

"I have to go..."

Liz had insisted she come along, though Ethan had tried to talk her out of it. After all, they'd only been on a few dates. Only one kiss had been exchanged in all that time, a soft peck on the lips while standing on Liz's doorstep after a movie. But there had been a lot of conversations throughout the rest of the days. They had gotten to know each other which, he supposed, made Liz feel comfortable enough to accompany him to the hospital.

Ethan unfastened his seatbelt and stared at the big building. From the way the lights glowed all over in the dark, the medical center looked more like an airport. It had taken him almost two hours to drive up here. It would have been much longer if it were daylight hours, but the roads had been mostly empty.

The building was small. The mountains were like black fangs behind it. He figured in about an hour, the sun would begin to spill light across the peaks.

He needed to get in there, but his legs felt like solid, unmovable steel. Ethan gulped. That was where Emily was. She needed him. He wanted to be the first person she saw when she woke up. But he was afraid to find out what had happened to her, to learn how bad her injuries actually were.

So bad the detective wouldn't say on the phone.

He took a deep breath, trying to calm himself.

If he went in there and received news that she didn't make it...

Knock it off!

Ethan flung the door open and stepped out. The glacial air caught him by surprise. When he'd left the house, it had been muggy and warm. Now, the air felt cool and thin, a breeze sliding through the parked cars that ruffled his hair.

Liz stepped around the front of the car, taking his hand. She put her other hand on his cheek. Her fingers felt cold and smooth. She turned his head to look at her. "I'm with you on this."

Nodding, Ethan said, "Thank you." He began to walk on legs that felt weak and trembly. He could hear the claps of their footsteps all around them, hollow and repetitive like nails being driven into wood.

The closer they made it to the entrance, the more dread he began to feel inside.

He saw uniformed officers on the other side of the glass, huddled together around a small group of adults. Looking as if they'd driven straight here from their bedrooms, he recognized them. Most were still in pajamas. Others were dressed in wrinkled clothes that had probably been thrown on in a rush. He spotted Cole Dwireson, his friend of many years, and his wife Tina. They were also Kali's parents, who had been Emily's best friend since birth. Born a month apart, they'd been inseparable throughout their lives.

Cole glanced over as the automatic doors opened. The rattling whir hushed the voices that were running together.

"Ethan!" He ran over to greet him, leaving Tina to deal with the officers. He put his arms out and pulled Ethan into a strong hug. "Was the drive up all right?" Cole was easily a foot taller than Ethan, and broader with wide shoulders and firm arms. He'd played football all the way through school before leaving for the Army after graduation. He'd managed to hold on to the essential physique, even in his forties.

"Yeah..." He pulled away from his friend's embrace.

"I've been trying to reach you on your phone, but it keeps going straight to voicemail."

"It does?" Ethan tugged his phone from his pocket. He swiped the screen. There were no notifications of any missed calls. Then he noticed he had no signal. "My shit phone..." He put it away, looking Cole in the eyes. "What the hell's going on? What's happened to our girls?"

"I don't know. We got a call telling us to get here as fast as we could. There was an attack. That's all we know. I have no idea what kind of attack, if anybody was seriously hurt. They won't tell us anything!"

Heads turned toward them at the recoil of Cole's shout reverberating off the hollow walls. A blond female officer started walking toward them. She was much shorter than the others and, Ethan realized, much younger.

"Mr. Dwireson," she said, approaching. "Please, try to control your voice."

Nurses at the stations were now watching them from their perches behind the glass. They had gathered together in their own pack.

This must be really bad.

"Sorry," Cole said. "It's not intentional."

The officer nodded. The name pinned to her shirt said *Reese.* "I understand. Please, just wait here and as soon as we have all the details, we will be able to share them."

A man stepped into the room from a door across the hall. Dressed in a worn trench coat, his face was pale, making it hard to guess his age. The short gray hair made Ethan think he was probably in his sixties. His eyes were filled with an unknown knowledge that made Ethan uneasy. But more than anything, he looked weary with a hint of dismay. Ethan could tell this man knew more than anybody else in the room.

The man held up his hands. "Okay, listen up. We're causing more problems out here than helping. Please, everyone, just take it easy." He looked toward the officers. "Take the parents to the private waiting areas. I'll be along shortly to address each one personally."

Ethan stepped forward. "You're Wilcox?"

"That's me." The man didn't even look at him.

"I'm Ethan Bowers. You left me a message—"

Wilcox's head shot up, his eyes filling with an alertness that hadn't been there moments ago. "About time. Come with me." Ethan turned to Cole, shrugging.

Cole cleared his throat. "Why just him? We're all here for the same reason."

"I need to talk to him right now," said Wilcox. "Please, go with Reese. I'll be along shortly."

The group had moved toward the far side of the room where a nurse waited, the door held open by her hip. Her eyes were grim. Ethan suddenly realized it was probably best he wasn't going with the others.

Cole stood there a moment, maybe even starting to realize the same thing, before turning around and following the blond deputy back to the group.

Ethan looked at Liz. She stood there, hands clasped under her chin. "I can't go with you."

"You can."

"I'm not a parent. I have to…wait here."

He remembered Wilcox's order and nodded. "Right." He looked into her eyes. The blue haloes glimmered under a sheen of tears.

"I'm not going anywhere," she said. "I'll be here."

"Thank you." He didn't know what else to say, so he added, "Really."

Wilcox grabbed his arm. "Come on, please. We *need* to talk."

Ethan walked with the old detective. The man moved a lot faster than Ethan had anticipated. They reached the other door. Wilcox rapped his knuckles on the smooth wood. A moment later, the door clicked. Wilcox pulled it open, stepped back, and ushered Ethan ahead of him.

Ethan stepped into a hallway. It was long and quiet and dim, with doors on either side. A desk was at the far end, where a nurse sat, working at a computer. She glanced up, saw Ethan, then went back to her work.

"Come on," said Wilcox, stepping past him.

He motioned Ethan through a doorway on the left. Chairs lined the walls inside. A small couch was to the right of the doorway. A TV, mounted in the corner, played an episode of *Gunsmoke* on mute. With the furniture and the dim lighting, the room had been designed as an artificial living room. Ethan knew it was their attempt at creating a comfortable environment. He'd been in one before, years ago, waiting on Claire's surgery to end. Nobody else was inside.

Wilcox followed him in, leaned down, and pulled the peg that held the door open. When it clicked shut, Wilcox let out a breath that rattled his cheeks. "This is a damn mess," he muttered, more to himself than Ethan.

"What the hell's going on?"

Wilcox removed a cigarette from the pocket of his coat. He clamped it between his teeth.

"I don't think you can do that in here," said Ethan.

"Are they going to throw me out?" Taking off his coat, he tossed it into an empty chair.

Ethan shrugged. "Probably not."

Lighting the cigarette, Wilcox took a long drag. He held it in a moment before letting the smoke ease out through his nostrils. "That's better."

"Look," said Ethan. "I know you're a...man of the law, or whatever, but I'm not going to ask nicely again. What the *hell* is going on?"

Wilcox grabbed a Styrofoam cup from the small table beside the sink. He ran some water in it, then flicked the ashes inside. They made soft sizzling sounds when they landed in the water. "Your daughter was still somewhat conscious when I got to the location. The medics were tending to her while we waited on the chopper. She told me everyone else was dead."

Ethan felt cold slither through him. "Dead?" He thought of Cole, and his heart ached.

Wilcox nodded. "We're still counting bodies, but I would have to predict that she's correct. She wasn't making a lot of sense, but she said five of them went out there. Is that right?"

"Um..." Ethan thought about it. "Was it five? I thought it was six. Three couples."

"She said five."

"Oh, wait..." He remembered Alec Hansel's girlfriend, Paula, had dumped him right before graduation. "Yeah, five. Two girls and three guys."

"Then we've found them all. And nobody, but her, survived."

Jesus Christ.

Wilcox was relaying the information in an emotionless tone, as if reciting a grocery order. Ethan doubted it was because the guy was being rude, and figured it was more of his "work voice" shining through.

They're all dead.

He thought about Cole again. Poor guy didn't know his daughter had died. None of them out there knew they were suddenly without children. Ethan felt moisture building in his eyes. "Who did this?"

Wilcox shrugged. "Like I said, Emily wasn't making a lot of sense. Shock and loss of ..." He paused. "Well, her injuries, I believe made her a bit confused. But she said a monster of a man just came out of the woods. She found the bodies of her friends here and there and fought the man off and on throughout the night. She tried killing him multiple times, but he just kept coming. Said she got him good and bit off his nose."

"Bit off his nose?"

Wilcox nodded. "Right. Before she passed out, she described him as the size of Bigfoot, wearing a mask, and reeking of the tomb."

"She said 'reeking of the tomb'?"

"She did."

Ethan felt a smile tug the corners of his mouth. "She's a writer. Going to school for an English degree. Wants to write cozy mysteries. She's always using metaphors like that."

"Ah."

Ethan didn't know why he'd felt the need to share that, but he thought it was important Wilcox know. "How bad are her... injuries?"

"I'm not going to lie to you...they're really bad. Had she not wandered up on another cabin where someone resided, I have no doubt she wouldn't have made it. She's been in surgery ever since arriving. I have no updates on her condition."

Ethan's legs folded. His knees pounded the hard floor. When he looked up, the room was spinning. He felt hands tugging him upward. He tried to assist by working his legs, but they wouldn't cooperate. Then he felt himself being lifted and slammed down. There was now support under and behind him. He realized he was in a chair.

"Drink this," he heard Wilcox say in a voice that sounded like it was coming through a funnel.

A cup was shoved into his hands. With Wilcox's assistance, he raised the cup to his lips and drank. The water was cold and refreshing. It took a couple minutes, but the room began to clear and resemble a normal room again. His hearing no longer sounded like it was being muffled by earplugs.

"Thanks," he muttered.

"No problem. I should have had you sit down before I started talking. I unloaded a lot of shit on you."

He looked over and saw that at some point Wilcox had sat beside him and lit another cigarette.

"I..." Ethan didn't know what to say. "Did you catch who did this?"

"No. We have officers combing the area. We also have help from the fire department and local volunteers. Choppers are doing full sweeps. If he's out there, we'll get him."

"Do you believe her?"

"What?"

"That somebody 'reeking of the tomb' did this?"

Wilcox opened his mouth to answer but a soft knocking on the door stopped him.

Before anyone could acknowledge the knock, the door swung open. A petite woman entered, dressed in scrubs. A hairnet concealed her hair and showed her plain, smooth face. Her eyes looked like crystal and seemed to reflect the room in their glossiness.

She tried to smile but her nose wrinkled. She sniffed. "Wilcox? Smoking?"

He dropped the cigarette in the cup of water. "My apologies.

This is Ethan Bowers, Emily's father. Mr. Bowers, this is Dr. Maxine Chambers."

"I see. Are you alone or is her mother coming?"

"Claire died when Emily was little." He saw the embarrassment begin to form on the doctor's pleasant face. "Don't be sorry. It was a long time ago." He stood up. "How is she? Can I see her?"

He noticed that her facial expression began to shift to something else, a subtle grimness that was heavy with remorse. She took a deep breath, preparing to speak.

The realization crashed on Ethan so quickly, his mind tilted. *She's dead...*

"Can I have a moment alone with Mr. Bowers?" asked Dr. Chambers.

What little bit of color that was in Wilcox's face drained away. Nodding, he began to stand.

"Don't," said Ethan. "God...no...don't you dare tell me..."

He dropped back into the chair as tears began to spill down his face. His throat closed, making it hard to pull in air. This was how they'd told him Claire hadn't survived her heart surgery. The same goddamned way. Pulled him into a room that offered artificial comfort, made everyone but him leave so the surgeon could be alone while explaining about the unexpected complications. Told him he would now be a widower, a single father left to raise a little girl all on his own.

And now he no longer had the little girl, either. Just as she was about to embark on her own adulthood, most likely marrying Steve in the future, and would eventually make Ethan a grandfather. It had been all snatched away by a psychopath. *That reeked of death.*

"She's dead, isn't she?" he heard a voice ask. He realized it was his own, though it sounded nothing like him. This voice was blubbery and choked by sobs. "Isn't *she?*"

There was a brief pause, then Dr. Chambers said, "I'm afraid she didn't make it, Mr. Bowers. We did everything we..."

This time when Ethan fell to the floor, he was no longer awake to try and stop himself.

3.

A year later

Ethan tore down the caution tape stretched across the wood railings. At the front of the cabin, it blocked the way from the steps to the porch. The plastic faded to a piss-yellow with dull gray lettering.

He flung it aside.

More birds began to chirp as the sun rose above the valley. The cabin, blocked by trees, was submerged in deep shade. But the heavy shadows did nothing to hide the large bloodstain on the porch. Nor did it conceal the large chunks missing in the doorframe. Half the door had been chopped down and now resembled a maw of sharp wood points. A piece of plywood covered the opening from the other side. He supposed somebody with the police had added that meager addition of security. Maybe the insurance company. He wasn't sure which.

All Will Die.

Ethan stared at the skinny red scrawl on the plywood. No doubt it had been put there by some smartass trespasser and a can of spray paint to scare people. *Mission accomplished*, Ethan thought. He felt pretty scared looking at the highlighted warning. A jittery chill slid down his back.

He heard his Jeep's door thump shut. Turning around, he spotted Liz standing beside the passenger door. Arms crossed, she watched him through her sunglasses. A frown caused wrinkles on her brow and the glasses to dip on her nose.

It was the same look he'd been getting from her for months, ever since he'd first pitched his concept to the group. He knew she didn't like it, but she'd still come along for him. They'd been together for a year now, and he supposed they were a legitimate couple, though neither had said as much. She'd stayed with him that first night after the hospital and hadn't stopped.

A small part of Ethan wanted to get in the car and drive back home. Liz would be just fine with that decision. But the bigger part of him, the part that had turned bitter and cold, was more convincing.

And that part wanted to stay and see this through, no matter what.

Ethan turned around and faced the front of the cabin. This was the first time he'd been out here since *it* happened. His father purchased the cabin when Ethan was barely ten years old. They spent many summers out here. When his dad passed, he'd willed the cabin to Ethan with the rest of the estate.

Emily loved the cabin. It was her favorite place to go. A lot of times, the two of them would pack up the car and drive out for an unplanned weekend of fun. Whenever they were here, Ethan usually hung around close to the cabin while Emily hiked all over. She knew the area even better than he did, and he'd practically grown up out here.

Not one time had they ever crossed paths with somebody who "reeked of the tomb."

Ethan stepped closer to the door, or what had at one time been the door. His eyes slipped back down to the red graffiti.

All Will Die.

Ethan gulped. In a low voice, he said, "Don't think so, pal."

"You need the hammer?" Liz's voice sounded overly loud in the morning's stillness.

Ethan shook his head. He swallowed the dry lump in his throat. It felt as if it hung somewhere in his upper chest. Stepping back, Ethan raised his foot. He'd been taking jujitsu classes and had become pretty decent at it. Not great, by any means, but he was better equipped at self-defense than he used to be.

He threw out his foot, catching the plywood on the corner near where the door would have latched. It splintered with a loud crash that sent the thin sheet of wood spinning inside the cabin. The warning was obliterated into a cloud of wood dust and splinters that floated in the dark entrance. Knowing he'd destroyed the cautionary writing made him feel better.

Scuttling noises came from the woods to the left of the porch. He turned, trying to gaze past the barrier of tall trees and shields of green.

"A squirrel," said Liz. She removed the flannel shirt she'd been wearing. Underneath, she had on a white tank top. He could see the smudges of her black bra through the fabric. The morning had been cool, almost nippy, and now it had burned off and the heat of the day was rising quickly.

He stared at the woods a few moments longer. The sound didn't repeat. He turned away from the trees and the sweet smells they provided, then entered the cabin as Liz made her way to the front door.

It was cool and stuffy inside. A slight odor of mildew and dust hung in the air. There were dark stains on the floor, the walls, and even a corner of the stone fireplace was coated in it. Most likely, that was the cause of Trevor's awful head wound. He hadn't seen the wound himself, just heard it described in graphic detail by Cole, whose daughter, Kali, had dated the boy all through high school. Ethan had met the boy a few times when the kids had gotten together. Seemed nice enough, he supposed. But he'd always been glad Emily hadn't been dating him.

"Jesus," said Ethan. His voice sounded flat and weak in the empty room.

"Those poor kids," Liz whispered, probably more to herself than Ethan.

He left Liz in the living room and entered the kitchen. Pots and pans were scattered across the floor among shards of glass from busted plates and drinking glasses. Acorns and leaves were sprinkled along the tile, debris left behind by the wildlife that had gotten in. He saw shattered beer bottles strewn here and there. He felt a tug of anger that the kids had been drinking, but it didn't last. At least they'd been able to misbehave some before everything went to shit.

For all he knew, the beer cans could have been left behind by trespassers.

He stepped over the litter, making his way to the other side of the kitchen to another doorway. He stepped into the hall.

And saw somebody standing there.

Gasping, Ethan jumped back, hand reaching for the hunting knife in the sheath on his belt.

Liz stared at him, eyes wide. "You scared the *shit* out of me!"

"Me?" Ethan let out a wavy breath. "*Me?*"

"Sorry. I figured I'd wait here for you."

Heart pounding, Ethan let out a low breath. "It's fine."

Her eyes moved to the knife. "It makes me uncomfortable that you carry that around everywhere now."

Emily had picked it out at a flea market and talked him into getting it because of the blade's size. Not that she thought he would ever use it. She thought the blade was humorously exaggerated for somebody like him.

"In case you have to fight a bear," she'd said.

"There's always that possibility," he'd said.

He moved his hand away from the knife. "Emily thought it would be funny. Told everyone she got it for me, when actually I paid for it. She never could afford anything with the shitty pay I gave her at the restaurant."

Liz rubbed her eyes. "I understand that. That's sweet, really. But you're always ready to stab somebody with it now."

"Why do you think we're here?"

"So you can stab somebody?"

"You know what I mean."

"I…" Liz paused, mouth open. She slowly closed it.

Ethan figured she didn't want to get into it again. He didn't, either. It would be the same as yesterday and all the days before it. A suggestion from her that would turn into a debate that led to a terrible argument. "I'm about to head upstairs," he said.

"Want me to come with?"

Ethan kind of wanted to be alone, but he also didn't relish the idea of going up there by himself. "Sure."

They checked all three bedrooms without speaking, saving Emily's for last. Other than some serious cleaning and dusting, the first two seemed fine. Approaching Emily's door, Ethan saw it had been knocked down. The hinges hung askew in the cracked frame. The top of the doorframe had a jagged crack leading to the ceiling, where it had begun to stretch farther up. Eventually, the whole thing would need to be replaced.

The floor was buried under the rubble of clothes and various other clutter that had been spilled all over. Emily's dresser was broken in half, as if a giant hand had chopped it through the middle. The mattress was on its side, the bed frame angled outward toward the smashed window. Blankets had been tied together in knots, formed into a rope that led toward the window. It was coiled below the sill in a bundle of colors.

There's how Emily got away the first time.

He could picture his daughter, frantic but still thinking clearly, tethering the sheets together. He didn't see the small footstool anywhere, so she must have used it to break the window. While she did this, the psychopath was pounding on the door, busting it open bit by bit. He saw her chuck the makeshift rope out the window and use it to climb down.

Smart girl.

He felt something like pride knowing she hadn't made it easy for the son of a bitch. He'd had to work for it. Feeling his throat tightening, he turned around. Liz stood just inside the doorway. Her eyes were shimmering.

"Let's start bringing in everything," he said.

Liz nodded.

They returned downstairs.

Ethan was on his way to the front door when he sensed somebody else was in the room. Before he could point this out to Liz, the stranger spoke.

"You're trespassing," said the unfamiliar female voice.

Ethan turned and spotted a woman standing off to the side of the doorway. Her hair was pulled back in a tight blond ponytail, smooth on top as if it was silk. She wore a tan uniform, a golden star above the breast gleaming in the dim light. She was short but fit, the uniform clinging to her.

"The hell I am," he said. "I own this place."

The woman stared at him, her eyes moving from Ethan to Liz as she took them in. The hand that had been slowly progressing toward the gun at her hip lowered. "Mr. Bowers."

Ethan nodded. He remembered the deputy but not her

name. She'd been at the hospital that night.

"Sorry I didn't recognize you at first," she said. "I thought you were another ghoul coming to get a glimpse of the murder shack."

Ethan grimaced at her choice of words. "That's what they call it?"

"Sorry," she said. "Bad analogy. I'm Deputy Reese. Don't know if you remember me or not."

Liz cleared her throat. "What are you doing out here?"

"The cabin is on my rounds. I work the night shift, so I always check it when I first go on and when I get off. Been doing it every day for almost a year now."

"Seen anybody out here that doesn't belong?" Ethan asked.

Reese lifted a shoulder a subtle shrug. "Here and there. Usually just tourists wanting to snap some pictures. Nothing too serious. I wouldn't be surprised if some stuff is missing, though. You out here to fix it up?"

"Something like that," said Ethan. "Going to sell it."

The pretty deputy looked surprised, then nodded. "Best of luck to you. If you notice something has vanished, make a list. I'll file a report and you can contact your insurance."

"We have some friends joining us," said Liz. "They'll be by a little later to stay the weekend with us. We'll probably be out here every weekend for the next few weeks."

Reese nodded. "Noted. I'll still ride by, even on the weekends I'm on. Kendall rotates with me. I'm sure you'll be fine, but…" She shrugged, letting the understood silence finish her statement. "But I'll let the station know that you're out here."

"Appreciate it," said Ethan.

Reese let out a breath that puffed her cheeks. "Well, I'll let you guys get to it. If you need anything…" She reached into a shirt pocket and brandished a card. Holding it out to Liz, she said, "The station's number is on there, so is my cell. I can swing by in the morning, just to check in, if you'd like."

Liz took the card. "Thanks, that would be wonderful. We appreciate it."

"No problem. Be careful. And I'm still sorry for your loss. I wish I could do more."

Before Ethan could produce the generic response he saved for moments like this, Reese had turned and stepped through the busted doorway. A short while later, he heard a motor start, followed by tires crackling as they rolled over gravel. Soon, silence returned and all he could hear was the constant chirps of birds all around. Feelings of guilt began to trickle through him, but he shoved them aside and didn't allow himself to feel anything at all.

"I guess she drove up while we were upstairs," he said.

"Shouldn't we have heard it?"

"You would think. That might be a problem, but we'll worry about it later. Let's get started."

Liz nodded, then followed him out to the Jeep. The day was already starting to turn hot. He removed his flannel shirt, tied it around his waist, and opened the back of the Jeep. Inside was the new door. An artificial shell of wood paneling covered the thick steel underneath like the brittle butterscotch on a dipped cone.

Liz helped him carry it onto the porch. Then, while Liz went inside to get started on the clean-up, he brought all the tools he'd packed to the front porch. There were probably more than he really needed, but he wanted to be sure he had plenty. He removed the busted door, taking out the frame and replacing it with a perimeter of metal. It didn't take as long as he'd expected it to.

Then he set up the door, adding new hinges and a reinforced locking mechanism that was secured by a thick tongue of steel that inserted into a matching steel mouth. It took him almost an hour to complete the job. When he was through, he tested the durability and was pleased.

He'd do the back door next. Then he was going to take a ride over to Gale Rinehart's place, on the other side of the ridge. He could hike there, but driving would be much quicker.

The others would be here after lunch, and he wanted to be back before they arrived.

4.

"I don't even see any restrooms," said Tina.

Cole, in the driver's seat, put the gear in Park. He looked over at his wife. She was leaning forward, as if putting her nose closer to the windshield would somehow make one magically appear. Her hair hung by her face like a wavy curtain. She'd let it grow out over this past year. He liked it better this way.

"I told you I didn't think this place had one. It's a junkyard. A huge one at that." Cole stared at the tin paneling in front of them that acted as the main gate. It was positioned between chain-link fencing that was topped with spirals of barbwire. The sign read: *Otis's Salvage and Tow.*

Beyond the junkyard was a barrier of thick woods that rose into faint shapes of mountains in the distance obscured under wispy clouds.

"Has this place always been here?" asked Bill. He yawned. "I don't remember it, at all."

"Sure," said Cole. "I mean, look at it. Looks like it's been around longer than any of us. Combined."

"Aren't we close to the cabin?" Ramona asked. "I can't remember. It's been years since we've been out there."

Ramona was Bill's wife, and probably the youngest of the group, next to Ethan's girlfriend, Liz. She'd given birth to Adam when she was only nineteen. Bill wasn't Adam's biological father, but he'd been the only dad the kid had ever known since the frat house scuzz-bag that knocked up Ramona had run off. Bill had a bond with Adam that Cole wanted to have with his own daughter, but one he could never quite pull off. Maybe it was because she was a girl, and there was a part of him that always worried people who thought he might be trying to molest her if he was too close to her. He'd shared these fears with Tina, who pointed out how close Ethan and Emily were, and nobody thought that about them.

"Less than an hour," said Cole. "We have to take that dirt road up the mountain, and it's a bit rough at times. But nothing this tank can't handle." He patted the dash of his Blazer. He'd had the bulky vehicle since the early Nineties and never planned to get rid of it. More than once, he'd almost lost her to age, but he always replaced any part of her that wore out with something newer and better.

"I don't think I can hold it an hour," he heard Ramona whisper to Bill.

That would be three stops in the last two hours. Each time, Ramona had apologized and explained how her new medication made her need to pee a lot more.

"You can't hold it?" asked Tina, turning in her seat to look back at Ramona. "There's not a lot of options for restrooms out here."

"The office is right there," said Ramona, pointing at a ramshackle structure to the right. It looked as if the entire assembly was shifting to the right. There was a door, and one window that was obscure behind a layer of dust. The wood was old and warped, looking as if it was giving the poor nails holding them in place a fight.

"Don't think the owner's in," said Cole. "Doesn't look like he's been in for a long, long time."

"There's probably a bathroom in the back," said Ramona, starting to squirm in her seat. "Or one of those portable toilets, you know?"

"If there is," said Cole, "I wouldn't want to use it."

"And if there's not?" Tina asked Ramona. "What are you going to do?"

"Then I'll find a place in the woods. Unless you *want* me to ruin your seat…"

"Okay, okay," said Cole. "Let's *all* get out. You do that, and we can stretch our legs. This last little bit of the drive will have my nerves a wreck anyway."

Not really. He'd done the drive up to Ethan's many times.

It no longer worried him driving around those narrow curves that allowed him to look out his window and see the bumpy ridge that led to the bottom of the ravine far below.

They all climbed out. The tranquility of the day was interrupted by the bangs of the Blazer's doors being shut. Standing at the front of the SUV, Cole held out his arms and stretched. The tingling he felt rushing through his muscles was nice. He looked over and saw Ramona scrambling toward the rickety office, and Bill trying to keep up behind her.

Snickering, Tina joined him. "If I didn't know any better, I'd think she was pregnant."

Cole snorted. "You think maybe she is?"

"No. She can't have any more babies. But the way she's acting..."

"What kind of medication makes you have to pee as much as she's had to?"

"I don't know. Probably a lot to do with bad nerves, making her like that. I guess it's better than the alternative."

"What's that?"

"Having to do a number two that often."

Grimacing, Cole nodded. "I agree."

He pulled his wife into his arms. He was a foot taller than her, so he could rest his chin on top of her head as she nuzzled her face into his chest. "*Everyone's* nerves are probably pretty much shot."

He felt Tina nod against him. "What are we *doing* here?"

Cole took a deep breath. He didn't know what to say.

"Door's locked!" Bill said, coming down the wobbly steps. "She's checking the back."

Ramona appeared at the back corner of the office, arms held out. "Can't get back there because of the fence! I'm finding a bush."

"Jesus," Cole muttered. "This is taking forever."

"I'll go help her find something," said Tina.

"You have to pee, too, huh?"

Tina pulled away, winking. "So?"

"Knock yourself out."

Tina jogged toward Ramona. "Hold up. I'll join you."

"Thank God," she said. "This place is creepy."

Cole couldn't help agreeing with that. He watched the women walk along the tree line, pausing at a dirt path etched between two large trees. They said something to each other, then hurried onto the path.

They'll be okay.

He spotted Bill standing on the front porch under the shifting roof. His head was tilted down, a slight frown on his face while he thumbed through his cell phone. Though the office might have been on the brink of collapse, it offered plenty of shade. He decided to join him.

Bill saw him coming and lowered his phone. "Found this place listed online. Apparently, it's still open for business. Just not sure why it's not open today."

Cole stepped up onto the porch. He felt the wood sagging beneath him. Pausing, he gave the floor a moment to decide if it wanted to break. After a few moments, he figured it was going to hold. He stared at the lifeless cars on the other side of the fence. Weeds and things that looked like purple stalks were growing all around them, as if trying to conceal their damage from onlookers. Cars stretched onward for a long way. "How are there so many cars here?"

"Who knows?" His fingers worked on his cell phone. "The kids are in position, but they haven't moved from the spot in a long time, though."

"What about Group B?"

"Checking now."

Bill's fingers worked. Within seconds, he'd pulled up another screen and was reading the coordinates. "They're where they need to be. Since yesterday afternoon."

"Good. Any contact from them?"

"No."

Cole began to say something, then stopped himself. "Right. Ethan's idea. Radio silence."

"Right. Like he said, it'd look weird if people are supposed to be camping but constantly contacting other people."

Cole nodded. He agreed with that aspect of the plan, but it didn't mean he had to like it. He was sure Ethan also didn't like it, though it had been his idea from the start.

At least we have the GPS trackers. We know they're there.

"And the kids didn't check in? No texts?"

"Nope."

"They're still supposed to check in. Look, we'll give..." He checked his watch. They'd wasted too much time here. "We really need to get going."

"Right."

"Go ahead and contact the kids. Make sure they're okay. They were supposed to let us know when they reached the trail marker."

"They reached it. I can see it." He held up the phone. Their location was a red dot on the map displayed on the screen. It pulsed but remained still.

If you're supposed to be hiking, that means you walk. Not stand around for an hour or so.

"Still," said Cole. "I'd feel much better if we knew for sure."

"I guess I would, too."

As Bill began working at his phone again, the sounds of leaves rustling and voices drifted from the trail. Cole looked at the dirt path and spotted his wife. She was smiling, her cheeks pushed wide and showing a lot of teeth. Seeing the expression on her face made a tingling spot open in his chest. God, he loved her smile. He fell in love with her the first time he saw it at the library back in high school. She'd been reading a *Garfield* book alone at a table and was laughing so loud, the lazy tabby could have been sitting beside her telling jokes.

"Here I go," said Bill. He held up the long-distance radio. It was supposed to have an expansive range and operated off the satellites. There was no way it shouldn't be able to reach Robbie and Trish where they were in the mountain.

He knew the kids were probably fine, but he also wouldn't be able to stop worrying about them until he heard their voices.

5.

Trish raked her fingernails up Robbie's back, leaving lines of fire on his skin. Tilting back his head, Robbie nearly cried out. Though it hurt like hell, he loved it when she got rough. She was underneath him, laying on the spread sleeping bag, bare legs parted wide, ankles hooked behind his back. Their clothes were strewn all over the clearing. He saw her panties dangling from a tree branch.

Trish's breasts bounced with each hard thrust of Robbie's hips. When their skin connected, it sent a smacking echo around them that sounded like applause. Robbie pretended it was, an audience gathered to watch while Robbie pounded Trish's brains all over the woods.

Both were coated in sweat. He watched perspiration drip from his forehead and plop when they hit Trish's cheeks. Teeth bared, she whimpered and moaned. Her hair shook, falling into her face and sticking to it from the sweat.

He could feel his release building.

"Robbie?" Bill's voice crackled from his backpack leaning against nearby tree. "You there? Talk back."

The swelling he felt in his crotch tried to withdraw back inside.

Still moaning, Trish shook the hair out of her face and looked around. "Is...that...?"

He shushed her. "Ignore it."

"But..."

Almost there!

Trish looked at his backpack a second longer before letting her head drop back onto the sleeping bag. She hugged him tighter, squeezed her thighs against his sides harder. He knew this meant she was almost there as well.

He lunged and shoved a few seconds longer, about to burst, when Bill's voice shot from his backpack again.

"Answer me, damn it! You were supposed to check in an hour ago."

Trish opened her mouth to say something, but Robbie slapped his hand across it. At first, Trish acted shocked by this. Then she got into it and began throwing her hips outward, matching his pace. Within seconds, he was spurting and pumping. This seemed to trigger the same response from her, and she began to buck and thrash beneath him.

Robbie collapsed on top of her. He moved his hand away from her mouth and listened to her gasping.

"Far out," she said.

"I'm the best."

"Damn right, baby."

"*Robbie!*" This time, it was Cole's voice booming from his backpack. "Talk back, you dumb shit!"

Robbie shot to his knees. He could ignore his neighbor, Bill, all day long and not feel the slightest bit of anxiety about it. But Cole scared him. The man seemed nice enough, but just like with Ethan, there was an intensity below the surface that made him uneasy.

Naked, he jogged toward his pack. His penis flapped against his thighs, feeling sticky and wet when it touched his skin. He crouched by the pack, reached in, and pulled out the radio. It was so big, he needed to hold it with both hands.

He squeezed the button on the side. "H-hello?"

"Damn it, kid. What the hell took you so long?"

"Sorry, I was…" He looked over at Trish. She lay on her side on the sleeping bag, her back to him. His eyes landed on her plump ass. "Indisposed for the moment."

She wiggled her rump for him. He felt a little twinge in his penis that made him throb. He moaned.

"You better get to the picnic tables at Marker Eighteen by four. Are you going to be able to do that?"

"Huh? Oh, yeah. No problem."

He had no idea for sure. He wasn't even sure how far away it was.

"That's where you're supposed to run into Group B, pretend they're just campers you stumbled upon. You're looking for a place to pitch a tent and—"

"—they offer me a spot at their campsite," said Robbie. "I got it."

"George will be at the picnic area, setting up one of those grills for dinner. If he's out there for any other reason, it won't look right. So don't fuck this up. Got me?"

Robbie gulped. "I-I-I got you. Got you, big time."

"We're going to make our way to the cabin. Radio silence from here on, unless absolutely crucial. Copy?"

"Yeah."

"Good. Be careful. You see anybody trailing you, or somebody that just doesn't seem right, let us know." The radio hissed for a moment, then went quiet.

Robbie waited until he was sure Cole was finished, then dropped it back in the pack. The relief and good feelings he'd had moments ago were gone. All the stress and worry were back and even stronger than before.

They'd been hiking along the trail all morning, reaching the clearing ahead of schedule. Trish had been able to detect the anxiety in him and had thrown herself at him. They'd torn off their clothes in an aroused frenzy. It had been nice, much needed, and probably one of the best screws they'd ever had.

"Man," said Trish. "They're really serious about this, aren't they?"

Robbie looked over his shoulder. He saw Trish had slipped on her socks and hiking boots while he'd been talking. Wearing only that, she walked around the clearing, gathering their clothes. He liked watching her walk, how the movements made her breasts sway.

"Yeah," he said. "Obsessed."

"I get it," she said. "They lost their kids, you know?"

Robbie nodded. "I understand that part of it. But not all this."

"Then why are we here?" she asked. She turned around,

hugging the collected clothes to her chest.

"Money."

Trish's lips pressed together. Then she sighed. "There's more to it than that. You knew Adam, liked him, didn't you?"

"Yeah. He was all right. We were better friends when we were younger."

"But you still got along with him."

"Yeah. We used to hang out a lot, but that feels like a lifetime ago."

Before Robbie got into metal and began playing guitar. He'd shifted away from sports and activities that most the other kids his age thrived on. He formed a band called Night Hiss and had been working hard to get to the point he could take the band on the road. His original plan had been to leave right after graduation, but things had changed. The main thing was Trish. They'd started dating back in the fall, and he had never felt like this about anyone before her. She'd complicated things, made the band seem like less of a need.

She was what really mattered.

And that was why they were here.

Money.

They'd been offered five thousand dollars to spend some weekends hiking. Robbie had agreed to it without even considering what they were asking of him. Two days with Trish in the woods for a few weekends in a row had felt like a dream come true. But after he concentrated on it for a bit, he realized why he and Trish were here.

The *real* reason.

We're fucking bait.

But, he thought, they were bait for a mission that would never be finalized because it was completely bonkers to begin with. That was fine with him. They would be five thousand dollars richer, either way. That was money they could use toward a deposit on a small house or an apartment to live in while they worked and went to school. Neither of them was going on a campus anywhere. Their college education would be achieved the community route.

That would also leave him time for the band.

"Here," said Trish, walking over to him. "Get dressed."

Robbie groaned.

"I know. It stinks. But we made a deal. We're good people, so we honor our commitments."

"Yeah, I know." He took his Exhumer shirt and pulled it on. Then he grabbed the rest of his clothes. "This whole thing is just…"

"Stupid. I know. To us. But not to them. You heard them. You saw the same pain in their eyes that I did. This is like…a coping mechanism for them or something."

Robbie remembered the meeting a couple weeks ago, when this whole plan had been presented to him. They needed young people, and Bill Kisner, his neighbor, had referred him. Robbie had been mowing the Kisners' yard since Adam was no longer around to do it. He'd like to say the kind gesture had originally been his idea, but his mother was the one who'd set it all up.

"Earth to Robbie. You seem to be orbiting the conversation with your girlfriend."

Robbie blinked, then looked over at Trish. She was dressed in her denim cutoffs and green tank top. Her hiking boots had been laced. A strip of sock showed above the tops. Hands on her hips, the straps of her backpack pulled her shirt taut across the mounds of her breasts. Seeing her like that made him want to tear her clothes away another time.

But he knew she wouldn't go for it right now.

"Sorry," he said, sticking his feet into his boots. "I was zoning."

"You were gone, kiddo."

"Yeah. A part of me wishes we hadn't agreed to this."

"Oh?"

"Yeah. Not that I'm having a lousy time or anything."

"I was hoping you'd say that."

"I am. This—us, has been great."

"And we could use that money."

"Exactly. It's just that I guess I feel guilty or something." He grabbed his pack by the straps, hefting it up.

"What do you mean?"

"Well, they're counting on this weekend to go a certain way.

If not this one, one of the others. You and I both know it won't."

"I know."

"Don't you feel bad about that?"

"Like we're encouraging it."

"I guess." He slid his arms through the straps, tightening them. "Or stealing their money. Just because they're giving it to us doesn't make it right. We know they're basically throwing it away. Does that make us shitheads?"

"I don't think we are. I mean, they asked *us* to do this. We didn't volunteer. We didn't participate in any of the planning or anything like that. We're just here, hiking. For money."

Robbie smiled, though he didn't feel any better. "You're right."

"Now, let's get moving. If we don't reach that camping spot in time, Cole's going to shit a golden egg."

"Then beat my ass with it."

"Right. So let's get to it."

Together, they found the trail again and got back to walking. It was a hot day, but the canopy of tree limbs above them provided a lot of heavy shade that isolated them from the heat.

On any other occasion, Robbie would be having a great time.

But there was something causing his stomach to feel like it was trying to digest a chunk of lead. He didn't know why he felt so weird, but he did know that he didn't like it. As much as he would enjoy all this alone time with Trish, he was ready to be away from it all.

And have five grand in his bank account.

6.

Gale was sitting on her porch, enjoying a glass of sweet tea when she heard the crackling sound tires made when they rolled across gravel.

Who the hell is this now?

Since that poor girl had showed up at her house that night, she'd received many visits from a wide array of folks. Police mostly, but there had been others ranging from reporters to nosy townies to visitors just wanting to see the area where it all happened.

My home's a horror movie location.

And now somebody else was paying her a visit, uninvited and unannounced. She wondered if she'd have to run them off like some of the others. Usually, the curious visitors were polite and almost bashful about it. Others acted as if she should be serving them punch and cookies or something, like they were doing her a damn favor for showing up out of the blue and disturbing her day and ruining her peace.

Sometimes they'd ask: *"Still have the gun?"*

She did and would tell them so.

"Can we see it?"

If they were nice about it, she'd drag it out. If they were assholes, she'd point it in their faces. Either way, she wasn't timid about breaking out the shotgun.

An SUV appeared from the other side of a stand of trees that her driveway curled around. A cloud of dust trailed the vehicle as it made its way closer.

A Jeep.

I'm not in the mood for this shit today.

Sighing, Gale rose from her rocking chair and walked over

to the steps to wait for her guest. When the Jeep turned to park beside her truck, she saw into the open window.

Ethan Bowers.

He raised his hand in something like a wave. She nodded at him. He shut off the engine and climbed out. His face was brushed with the early stages of a beard, and he'd lost weight.

Not quite, she realized, looking him up and down.

He's in shape.

She could tell by the way his shirt clung to his chest that he'd been working out. She could see the muscle lines through the fabric. Though he was a little shaggy, he looked better than the last time she saw him.

"Morning," he said, attempting a smile.

He probably thought it had been a convincing one, but she could tell it was forced. "Morning back. Wasn't expecting to see *you* driving up."

"I bet not." He wouldn't look directly at her. His eyes were aimed just to the right of her, as if avoiding making eye contact.

"You okay?"

He shrugged. "I really don't know."

Gale understood what he meant. Probably hadn't been all right in a year. "Want to come in?"

"You don't mind?"

"Not at all. I'll throw on some coffee."

"Oh, that's okay. Don't do that on my account."

"I want some, too. It's no trouble."

Ethan nodded. "Fine."

She opened the door and held it so Ethan could enter first. She didn't know why, but she knew this wasn't a casual visit. He was here for a reason. And she could tell he was having trouble with how he wanted to present it. His body language gave him away. Even when she told him to sit down, she could see the tension in his movements as he sunk onto the couch, moving like somebody afraid they might blow shit all over the cushions.

Gale got to work on the coffee. She'd already added more scoops into the filter after her morning cups. So, she added the water, then turned it on. Within seconds, the machine began to gurgle.

"Want any creamer?" She looked at him from over the counter, the only object that separated the compact kitchen from the living room.

"Sounds great."

"I have vanilla, hazelnut, some weird birthday cake bullshit, and the powdered kind."

Ethan thought it over a minute, then answered, "Hazelnut."

"That's what I like to hear."

"Your drug of choice, too?"

"Yep."

"Same. I had it years ago while visiting some friends in Wisconsin."

"Changed your life, didn't it?"

"Completely."

"When I'm making coffee, hazelnut is my go-to. But when I used to go to New Orleans in my younger days, I would get a small kettle of cream and pour it into the coffee. Damn, if that wasn't the best coffee I'd ever had."

"Sounds amazing."

"It was. I've tried to replicate that myself, even going as far as looking up recipes online, interrogating coffee shop baristas and all. Nothing ever comes close. So, it's hazelnut for me, I guess, unless I get back to New Orleans one day."

Ethan chuckled. She could tell it was another forced response. She had to nearly bite her tongue to keep from asking him why he was here.

Wait till the coffee's done.

They made more small talk about nothing of particular importance while the coffee pot filled with hot, murky liquid. After a few minutes, she determined it was good enough and began to pour the cups.

"Need any help?" he asked.

Gale shook her head. "I've got it. You're my guest. That makes me the hostess."

Ethan nodded.

Gale put the mugs on a tray, adding a cup of sugar, the bottle of creamer, and two stirring straws. She grabbed some napkins from a drawer and put them in a stack next to the mugs. Then she slid the tray up onto her hand, balancing it while she headed into the living room.

"You're really good at that."

"Used to wait tables in a bar in my glory days."

"Wow."

"Wasn't anything to brag about, but I picked up a few tricks." She placed the tray on the coffee table. "Soup's on."

Ethan laughed softly while he grabbed a mug. Gale sat in her chair on the other side of the coffee table. Clinks and scraping sounds filled the room while they mixed their preferred blends.

Leaning back on the couch, Ethan sipped his coffee. He gave an approving nod. "Good stuff."

"Thank you, Ethan. Now tell me why the hell you're here."

Ethan choked on the next sip, nearly dropping the mug. Gale made no move to help him while he apologized and set the mug back on the tray. He grabbed some napkins and dabbed his chin.

"Burned yourself?" she asked.

"Surprised I didn't melt the skin right off."

"Coffee's hot, Ethan. Take it easy." She sipped. The coffee left a hot trail down her throat and warmed her belly. "You're here for a reason. What is it?"

He shrugged. "I came to suggest you leave for the weekend. Actually, the next several weekends."

"Oh?"

Ethan nodded. "Yeah. You don't need to be around here."

"Why's that?"

"Just trust me?" He phrased it as a question. A question that Gale smirked at. "Please?"

"Get real, kid. I'm not going to let somebody, even you, tell me when I can come and go in my own place without a good reason."

"It's a lot to explain. And you would just think I'm crazy, anyway."

"Look at me. I'm an old hag living alone in the fucking mountains. The only thing I'm missing is a cauldron and a horde of black cats. I'm not going to judge anybody for anything."

"You haven't heard why I'm here."

"You want me to leave. Said that much."

"I don't want you to get hurt. And if my theories are accurate, I'm going to be luring a potential nightmare right to me. Good chance a lot of us will be hurt, or worse. But we've all accepted this possibility, no matter what happens to us. But you haven't. It's not fair for me to expect you to. But you're a part of it, sort of. And you should have the choice."

"What are you talking about, Ethan?"

"I figured out what draws him in to kill."

"Who?"

"The maniac that killed my baby girl."

Gale's throat tightened when she saw the shimmer rise in his eyes. On the verge of tears, he managed to somehow prevent them from spilling down his face.

Clearing her throat, Gale put her mug on the tray beside Ethan's. She didn't want the coffee anymore. "I'm smart enough to follow what you mean. But I don't know the how and why."

"You really don't need to," he said. "You were the reason Emily was able to make it to the hospital and tell the police as much as she could. You did that. You risked your life for her. And I don't want you caught in the middle of this."

"Ethan..."

"You've heard about those campers? Up on Haaga Hill?"

"The family? Parents and kids."

"Teenage kids. Right."

"Like yours."

"Right. And a couple months ago, those hunters? Two guys, their wives waiting for them back at a campsite. Hunters' bodies were found, decapitated. They never found the wives."

"What's this have to do with anything? I'm pretty sure we can both agree it's most likely the same guy doing it. But what are you getting at?"

"The circumstances generate the results. My daughter and her friends, partying for the weekend. Group of campers just hanging out, having a good time. Two couples out in the woods, together, hunting and spending time together. All scenarios with legitimate explanations for their activities."

Gale nearly trembled at the dark intensity she saw in his

eyes. She wasn't sure how his ramblings fit together, but she was certain he'd already convinced himself whatever it was he wanted her to understand was accurate.

Ethan took a deep breath, prepping for the next part. "Now we have circumstances. I'm fixing up the cabin after a tragic loss with the help of some friends. We're Group A. Group B, other parents, have set out on a camping trip, trying to get over the losses of their children. We also have two recent high school graduates, hiking together. They'll eventually come across Group B, and they will join up with them. We've created the scenario, set the stage, painted the scene."

"And you're expecting your *star* to show up right on cue?"

"I have no idea. Honestly." The almost mad determination that had been on his face dropped away. He dropped back against the couch as if he deflated. "Probably a big waste of time, but we're giving it our all. If it doesn't happen this weekend, we're coming back next. And then the next. If it doesn't happen any of these times, it probably never will."

"Ethan, it's probably a *good* thing if it doesn't happen. Doesn't matter what kind of paper you use to wrap this box you're in, what's inside is still the same: Revenge. You want to kill this guy, right?"

"Of course I do."

"Ethan..." She looked up at the ceiling, spotting a cobweb dangling in the corner. She'd have to knock that down later. "What you're saying is absolute insanity."

And somehow, she saw all the logic in his theory. It was absolutely crazy, and she knew it. But buried somewhere deep in that insanity was a certainty that couldn't be ignored.

"I know it is," he said, his voice lifeless. "But it's all I've got. Been so focused on setting all this up, I kind of stopped processing exactly what it is I plan to do. It's not going to change my mind, though. I'm seeing this through, even if it is a big failure."

"I hope, for your sake, that it is a big failure. What would Emily think about all this?"

Ethan looked at her. He shook his head. "Don't do that."

"Sorry. That—I shouldn't have said that. But you need to

really listen to yourself. When you're driving back to your cabin, say all this out loud to yourself. *Listen* to its meaning."

"You're not going to leave, are you?"

"What do you think?"

Ethan nodded. "Didn't think you would, but I had to try."

"So your conscience is clear?"

Sighing, Ethan stood up. "Thank you for the coffee."

She looked down at his mug. It was nearly full. "You seemed to really like it," she muttered.

Ethan headed to the door, pausing just as his hand gripped the knob. He looked back at her. "I'm going to do what you said, play it out again for only me to hear. But I suggest you do the same. Think about the victims, their situations before they were killed. Think about everything else. Think about how, if I'm right, that my coming here to warn you put you in it as well."

She felt a cold snake slither up her spine.

"And if I don't leave," she said, "I'm pretty much opening myself up to a maniac's attack. Is that what you're saying?"

"Think about the setup, then think about the execution."

"This isn't one of those splatter films I used to watch at the drive-in. This is the real world."

"Right. But it's a real world through the logic of a slasher movie. Nothing else makes sense."

Gale stared at the handsome man, shaking her head. His daughter's murder had really torn the rational side of his brain to shreds. Here he was, trying to convince her that the rules of a low-rent genre of horror movies applied in the real world. That somehow fiction had blurred into reality.

The man's nuts.

But was he? Sure, he *sounded* crazy. But there was that nagging tingle in her brain, urging her to pay attention. Something wasn't right, and it just wasn't Ethan's new sense of logic. Though she would never admit it to Ethan, she was damn terrified that he was right.

How could he be right? How was any of this possible?

But if he was, then he was also right that his being here dragged her right into the mix of it. Maybe she *should* leave, at least for the weekend.

And go where? A hotel? No, thanks.

She would sit tight. Keep the gun nearby in case she needed to use it.

Listen to yourself!

Ethan huffed through his nose. "Be careful, Gale." He opened the door and stepped out.

"You, too."

Then the door closed.

Gale sat there for a few seconds before getting up. She went to her bedroom, crouched by the bed, and slid the double-barrel out from underneath. She dropped it on the mattress. Then she walked over to her dresser and dug out the two boxes of shells from the drawer she kept her nightgowns. She placed them next to the gun.

"What are you doing, Gale?"

She wasn't sure, but she knew the next thing that needed to be done was a quick sweep of her property, then make sure all the windows were locked. She couldn't shake the feeling that she might be in danger, but she also couldn't bring herself to leave. Somehow, doing that made her feel that she would be encouraging Ethan's paranoia.

She loaded the gun.

I'm not taking it with me. That'd be too much.

She'd leave it here for when she returned from the quick scan of her property.

Gale made it all the way to the front door and was putting on her boots when she decided to go back for the shotgun.

Carrying it by her side, she walked out, locking the door behind her.

7.

Liz hated being alone in the cabin. She sat in the recliner, staring at the lifeless fireplace. She'd cleaned out the charred wood and tossed it outside. Then she went through and scrubbed up the bloodstains. She wanted to make sure that was finished before Ethan returned. Plus, it was awful seeing how much carnage had happened. There was still a lot of work to do, but at least the violent evidence was gone.

She'd always wanted a cabin in the mountains. Now, she had a guy who owned one, but it had become the scene of his daughter's grisly murder. It was a lovely place, though. Overall, the scenery was gorgeous and very isolated.

Liz sighed.

It was too damn quiet in here.

Should've gone with Ethan.

No, she knew she was right in not going. Though she was here to be with Ethan, here *for* Ethan, she couldn't jump on board with riding to some lady's house to tell her she needed to go away for a few days. If Liz was on the other side of a conversation like that, she'd have looked at Ethan and said, "Who the fuck you think you are telling me this shit?"

Liz snorted. She could never say that to anyone. She'd never been the kind of person to spout off a retort like that. Sure, she would think it, but could never actually say it. Ethan was better at that. He could somehow convey his point without the need for foul language. He could be damn convincing when he wanted to be.

If anyone ever needed proof of that, they would have to look no further than Liz. She'd been seeing him for only a year and yet here she was, ready to do anything for him. She'd come out to these mountains to assist him in his mad quest to slay a slasher killer.

"I've lost my damn mind."

Liz stood up and padded to the kitchen. She grabbed the broom where it was leaning against the wall and got back to work. The floor was still a mess covered from one side to the other with dirt, debris, and broken glass. The broom did okay, for the most part. Some sections she had to sweep multiple times before she was able to see the hardwood again.

She liked to joke with herself that she was the crazy one of the relationship. She'd barely gotten to know Ethan when Emily had died. He'd told her that he understood if the situation was just too much for her to bear, giving her a clean opening to bail. Though she'd been tempted to, she couldn't bring herself to do it. She liked him, a lot. Even back then, when she had so much to learn about him, she wanted to stay with him. Their age difference didn't matter to her, either. She was barely thirty, and he was forty-one. Her mother nearly screamed when she told her, but when she found out how much money Ethan made, he was suddenly the perfect guy in her mom's eyes.

The money had nothing to do with Liz's decisions. Liz didn't even find out about his wealth until after Emily's funeral.

Until two months ago, he'd acted normal. Well, as normal as someone who had gone through what he experienced would act. He'd been seeing a therapist for months. Reluctant at first, he'd grown to appreciate the weekly appointments. Liz could even tell the talks with the doctor were starting to work.

Then he'd called for a spontaneous meeting at his house. Liz hadn't been invited. Hadn't even known about it until she'd stopped by his place to surprise him with a home-cooked meal. Pulling up to his house, she'd seen all the cars right away, parked in a line on the sidewalk by his front yard.

Tempted to come back later, she decided to ring the doorbell. After all, she was a bit curious to know what he was doing. To her surprise, he let her sit in on the meeting. All the parents of the kids that had gone to the cabin with Emily were present, seated around the living room on the couch, recliner, and chairs brought in from the kitchen. Turned out this wasn't their first time assembling like this. It had been going on for weeks, meeting like this to discuss the murders and what they planned to do it about themselves, since the police had been unable to solve it on their own.

Ethan had created a PowerPoint presentation and had set up a projection screen in front of the fireplace. His laptop was connected to a projector. On the screen was a news article about some hunters found brutally murdered in the same mountains the kids had been killed in.

Ethan told her she could wait in the kitchen if she wanted to. She decided to join them.

Martin Kelly held a bottle of beer in his hand while he pointed at the screen. "What about that massacre that happened in Mountain Rock a few years ago?" He was Steve's father and, Ethan had explained to Liz, Steve had been Emily's boyfriend since their freshman year.

Nodding, Ethan held out the pointer and thumbed the button. Slides clicked and changed until stopping on another newspaper article.

FOUR WOMEN SLAIN!

"This one?" Ethan asked. "A guy murdered some women in a cabin, or something. Claimed they raped him. Unrelated."

Martin nodded. "Right. I knew there was something like that."

Martin's wife, Gina, wiped her eyes. Her mascara was smearing, making it look as if her sockets were half an inch larger than her eyes. "I still can't believe Steve lied to us."

"Hey," said Martin, putting his arm around his wife. He pulled her to him. "He was a kid. He wanted to go on that trip with Emily, so he did whatever he could to be with her."

Cole, leaning back against a kitchen chair, folded his arms over his chest. "That's right, Gina. You can't hold yourself responsible for that."

"I know," she said. "I just hate that...that the last thing he ever said to me was a damn lie."

Liz's throat tightened. She couldn't even begin to try to understand the hurt that poor woman was feeling.

Ethan gave her a few minutes of peace before launching

back into his presentation. He spoke slowly, but with a serious tone she'd never heard in his voice. There was almost a coldness to it, but not quite. She realized she didn't like it. He spoke like a general, briefing his soldiers before a big mission.

And it was a big mission for them all. One they'd all previously agreed to.

They were going to construct their own slasher movie scenario. Why? Because Ethan believed the only way they could lure out the maniac that had butchered their children was by doing something similar to what their children had been doing.

"We'll split into two groups," Ethan had said later. "Group A will join me at the cabin to help me go through it and fix it back up. I'm planning to sell it, anyway."

That had been the first Liz had heard about his plans to sell the cabin. She hated that she did, but she felt herself getting angry at him for it.

"I'll be in Group A," said Cole. "Makes sense, since I own a damn construction business."

"Right," said Ethan. "We're going to rebuild it, all right, but we're also going to set that place up like a fortress. We'll be there, working, like anybody else in a situation like that would be, all the while preparing ourselves for the attack."

"What's Group B?" asked George Portman. He was bald except for a crescent of bushy gray hair that wrapped around the back of his skull. Short and rotund, he sat beside his plump wife, Wilma. She had short hair that was like a dark cloud of curls. They looked like they could have passed for siblings instead of husband and wife. They'd barely spoken at all during the meeting.

"Old friends on a camping trip, looking to heal."

"I'll head up that one," said George. "We used to go camping all the time. I have plenty of gear we can use. Nobody has to bring anything except for their own essentials."

"Excellent," said Ethan. His mouth twitched, a smile trying to form on his face.

"Who's going in what group?" That was Gina Kelly, speaking behind a tissue pressed to her nose.

"Well," said Ethan. "Cole, Tina, and myself—"

"—And me," said Liz, interrupting.

Ethan looked surprised. "Liz, I don't expect you to participate in this."

"Why not?"

"Um...well..."

"Don't you dare say because she wasn't my kid."

"I wasn't..."

But she could tell that he was going to say exactly that. Maybe not in those words, but the meaning would have been the same.

Liz sat there, silent while they devised the groups. They agreed Group A needed to be larger, since renovating the cabin was a large project. Two couples on a camping trip made more sense. That was when the plan to add the teenagers had been born. That way, both teams would be even in terms of numbers. The more they talked, the more Liz felt disgusted and a little frightened.

At the end of the meeting, Ethan stood by the front door like a generous host at the end of a swinging party while his guests filed out.

Cole and Tina paused at the door. Cole turned to Ethan, holding his fist up to him. Ethan raised his and bumped his knuckles against Cole's knuckles. "We're doing this, brother," said Cole. "All the way."

"The only way," said Ethan. "It's all I've got."

"It's a good plan," said Cole.

Liz studied Tina, trying to see if she could sense any kind of wariness or unease. She saw none. Tina was a wife truly devoted to whatever her husband wanted them to do. She didn't seem eager or joyous about the plan, but she didn't seem to be dreading it, either.

"I don't know how good of a plan it is," said Ethan. "But it's something. Better than doing nothing."

"That's all the cops have been doing," said Tina. "Nothing. I'm tired of nothing. So if this is 'something', then I'm all for it."

Ethan nodded. "Can't hurt to try."

For some reason, Liz cringed inside when he'd said that. It reminded her of those poor fools uttering, "*What's the worst that could happen?"* moments before jumping off a bridge, expecting deep water below them only to shatter their legs on a mound hidden inches below the water.

When they were alone, Liz helped Ethan clean up. So many things that she wanted to say went through her head. Instead, she kept her mouth shut.

In the cabin, a bird smacked the window above the sink, jarring Liz away from her thoughts. She looked over just in time to see the bird bobbing in the air as it tried to fly away. It looked as if it wasn't going to make it, then suddenly shot off as if it had been launched from an air gun.

Heart pounding, Liz looked down at the floor. Without realizing it, she'd swept up a large pile of mess by the door. There was still a lot of work to do, but she was almost done with this part. She could move on to the counters next. Mopping would come last. There was no point in doing it this early.

Wood groaned outside.

Liz paused. The sound repeated. Somebody was on the porch, trying to be quiet as they tiptoed toward the front door.

Now, her heart was sledging hard enough to make her throat cluck. She leaned the broom against the wall, hurried into the living room, and sank to a crouch at her carry bag. Unzipping it, she reached in and grabbed the Glock she'd owned for years. Her father had taught her how to shoot and appreciate guns at a young age.

Liz stood up, keeping the barrel pointed at the floor. Her finger, stiff and extended, hovered near the trigger. She moved in quick, silent strides toward the front door. Ethan had done a great job replacing it. She had no idea he was able to do any kind of carpentry until he began shopping for the supplies. That was when he told her he spent summers working with Cole for a local construction company, doing whatever they were allowed to do.

Always finding out something new about Ethan.

Right, and now somebody's outside. Focus, you idiot!

Liz clamped her mouth shut and concentrated on breathing through her nose. Doing it this way forced her to slow down, to take longer breaths, which helped her heart rate to decrease and release a welcomed sense of ease.

Lowering her ear to the door, she listened. She could hear the soft sounds of talking. Sounded like a female, maybe two, doing their best to keep their voices low.

Liz took another deep breath, gripped the doorknob, and jerked the door open. She flung herself through the doorway, raising her arm. She knew she should probably shout something cool, but all that came out was, "Hah!"

A girl, barely older than eighteen, threw her hands in the air with a sharp gasp that sent the cigarette in her mouth into the air. The girl next to her dodged the burning projectile while trying to get her hands up as well.

Both had hair the color of night and skin that looked pale and smooth under the torn fishnet sleeves. Both wore black shoes, with black socks that reached their knees, split by the white stripes at the top.

The smoker was tall and slim with plump lips painted in dark red. She stared at the gun. "Don't shoot! Jesus, we didn't know anyone was here!"

Her shorter, curvier friend, nodded. "It didn't say anything about *that* on the Facebook page!"

"Facebook page?" said Liz. "What the hell are you talking about?"

The tall one gulped. "We're members of the Facebook page for unsolved murders in North Carolina."

Liz knew nothing about the page the girl had mentioned. "Who the hell are you? What the *hell* are you doing here?"

The taller one looked at her, mouth a wide grimace. Compared to the rest of her, the girl's eyes were the brightest blue she'd ever seen. "I'm Viv," she said. "That's my friend Clare."

Clare, hands up and trembling, nodded. Her dark hair had twinges of red streaked in. It looked cute, and the way it was styled near her shoulders and layered by her face worked really well for her.

It was hard to tell how long the taller one's hair was from the way it was pinned into a messy bun on top of her head. Neither had weapons that Liz could see, other than long fingernails tipped in glossy obsidian. She noted the small synch-sacs hanging over their shoulders. Filled with water and snacks, most likely. Maybe a camera.

These girls aren't threats.

Liz lowered the gun.

Viv let out a long breath that puffed her lips. "Thank you so much." She lowered her hands.

Clare dropped her hands as well. "I nearly shit myself."

Liz almost laughed. "What are you girls doing out here?"

"Nothing bad," said Viv. "Honest." She grabbed the bottom of her short t-shirt and adjusted it so the faded monster on front was facing Liz. From the way the bottom furled, it was obvious Viv had cut it to the short length herself. A narrow slit of pale skin showed between the shirt and top of her shorts. She saw the wink of a navel under the furled fabric.

"She means," said Clare, "that we just wanted to see the place where it all happened. You know?" Though Clare's shirt clung to her, it was longer than Viv's and reached over the top of her shorts. A red devil was on the front, winking with a smile that dinged. The red hue of her bra was bleeding through.

"Oh, I see," said Liz in a cold voice.

A pair of damn vultures.

"Sounds awful," said Viv, "I know."

"Well, that's because it *is* awful." Liz shook her head, clucked her tongue. "A lot of kids your age were butchered here. You better be glad it was me you ran into and not my boyfriend. His daughter was one of the victims."

Clare bit down on her bottom lip.

Viv's mouth hung open. "Ethan Bowers? Yeah, we kinda already know that. His daughter was the one that lived the longest and gave the description of the killer. I have a picture of the artist's rendering that I printed off the internet." She started to reach for the sack hanging between her shoulders.

"I don't want to see the drawing," said Liz. "I've seen it enough."

Ethan had it tacked to a pushpin board above the desk in his office at home. Whenever she was over there, she avoided looking at the monstrous man rendered on the page. Wasn't that the image really showed much, other than a big hairy man wearing a mask.

"Oh, right," said Viv, lowering her hand. "You probably have."

"What did you expect to see out here?" Liz asked. "The bodies still lying around? Blood splatters all over the walls and the floor. Because I already cleaned up most of the that. We might be able to find more, if you really feel like it's something you want to see."

Viv shook her head. "Uh...well, um..."

"Why would you want to see that? Huh? Why is someone else's tragedy your fucking Graceland?"

Clare held up her hand, patting the air. "Chill, lady. We do a podcast. It's on YouTube and Pod-Tower Podcasts. We talk about true crime, the supernatural, and all things horror and recipes."

"And makeup tips," Viv added.

"Right, makeup tips. Wings and lashes and stuff. Anyway, our viewers asked us about this case. We hadn't even heard of it until then. So we did some research and decided it was something we wanted to feature on the show. No big deal. We're not the first to do that."

"You girls are what? Investigative journalists or something?"

"Not exactly," said Clare.

"Then what are you?"

"Like we said, we have a channel on YouTube and..."

"So you're no different than anyone else. You just have an outlet for what you like, and people enjoy watching. Since you're doing a 'show' about the murders, then I should be fine with you being here?"

Viv said, "I don't expect you to be, but it gives us a legitimate reason for it. We just wanted to see it with our own eyes and conduct our own investigation. We parked our car at the end of the road because there was no way in hell my little Nissan was making it back here. Then we hiked two hours up the mountain to your front door. We meant no harm. Just wanted to get some pictures and video for the show. We're doing an entire episode about it."

Clare said, "We're not trying to be disrespectful. We just

do reports on cases like this while we do our makeup, talking to the viewers about it while they watch us do our thing. And since this case remains unsolved, it's gotten a lot of our attention the last few months. We drove all the way here from Maryland just to see it."

Liz was still frustrated with these girls, but she could feel her anger starting to fade. They seemed like decent people, even with the weird hobby Liz didn't understand.

They picked the wrong damn weekend to make a trip out here.

"All right," said Liz. "Take a few pics, then go."

Viv smiled. Clare clapped her hands, letting out a high-pitched squealing sound.

"But just the outside," said Liz. They looked as if they wanted to protest, but Liz held up her finger. "That's the deal. Get the pics and scoot before my boyfriend gets back. I doubt he'll be thrilled about your being here."

Nodding, Viv swung the sack around to her front. "Right." She pulled out an SLR camera with a very long lens. "Let's get this done, Clare."

Liz monitored the girls while they walked around the cabin, snapping pictures at every step. They vanished around back, reappearing on the side. When they reached the front porch again, Clare stood on the steps, folding her hands in front of her while Viv snapped a few more pics. Then she passed the camera to Clare, and they switched places so Clare could take some of the taller girl standing with her fingers formed into a pyramid under her chin. She tilted her face to the side, bright eyes aimed upward as if something on the eave of the porch had caught her attention.

To Liz, they looked almost professional until the end. Then they blew it by posing like Instagram teenagers.

Liz checked the time on her watch. Ethan had been gone almost an hour. He'd probably be back any minute. "All right, ladies. Wrap it up."

The girls didn't try to convince her to let them stay any longer. They put the camera away and walked back over to her, thanking her repeatedly.

"You're welcome," said Liz. "Now, hit whatever trail you

walked in on and get out of here. My boyfriend's probably on his way back now."

"Sure thing," said Viv. "We're going to make our way to Gale Rinehart's place now. Want to talk with her before it gets too late in the day and we have to walk back to my car in the dark."

Liz was glad they'd come here first. Ethan would have lost his mind had they showed up while he was playing the role of the foreboding doomsayer. "Be careful out there," she told the girls.

They both thanked her, then started walking toward the woods on the far side of the driveway. She watched them until they slipped between the trees, looking as if they were slowly sinking in a sea of thick green.

Liz looked at the time on her phone again. She couldn't believe it wasn't even lunchtime yet. She was so exhausted that the day felt as if it should be almost over. This was going to be a long weekend—a slew of long weekends.

She already couldn't wait for them to be over. Maybe then, Ethan would revert to the guy she'd known before all this insanity began. At least, a version that was somewhat close to that guy. She understood that he was still grieving. There was no time limit on how long somebody should be able to. But the way he was handling it was terrible. Did that make her even worse for supporting it? Was she an enabler? She hoped not. The books she'd read about the subject all suggested you must be supportive in these times, no matter how far your loved one slides away.

Patience, Liz. Just be patient.

Nodding to herself, Liz headed back to the cabin.

Was it too early to break out the booze?

8.

Ethan made it back to the cabin just minutes before Cole's Blazer came rocking around the jut of trees in the driveway. Standing on the porch, Ethan sipped a can of Pepsi. Seeing them made Ethan feel a tad better about all of this.

"The gang's all here," said Liz. She leaned against the front door, hands tucked in the pockets of her shorts. All her weight was planted on one foot, while the other leg was bent at the knee. Ethan kept sneaking peaks of her. He liked her legs, her dusky skin. When the sunlight hit it just right, she looked as if she'd been painted in butter. If she knew he thought that, she would probably have a few smart remarks to say about that as well.

He pretended not to notice the irritation in her voice. He'd purposely overlooked her complete lack of empathy through all of this so far because she was trying to look past the absurdity of it. That was better than anybody else would do in a similar situation. He appreciated that more than she'd ever grasp.

Just don't leave me because of this.

He'd almost said that to her many times. Instead, he spoke it silently and hoped she could pick up on it. The way she always acted as if she were a mother trying to support her son's decision to quit school so he could focus on an acting career made him think she was not picking up the message. Still, he couldn't bring himself to say the words aloud. Something always stopped him. Fear, most likely.

He liked her, a lot. Maybe even loved her.

And the thought of possibly losing her scared him. He felt sweat break out through his hairline.

"You okay?" Liz asked.

"Huh?" He blinked.

Looking over his shoulder, he saw Liz was watching him. Her hair was pulled back, save a few strands dangling by her cheek. The way her arms were folded at her chest caused her breasts to jut upward. She really looked good in the gray tank top and khaki-colored shorts. He wished the two of them were out here for other reasons. He suddenly felt a strong sense of loss that they weren't.

"You seem off," she said. "Even more off than you've already been."

He almost admitted he was starting to reconsider what they were doing. He felt the words starting to form in his mouth and quickly swallowed them back down. He had to do this. They'd put too much work into it already.

Besides, it was the only plan they had.

Ethan shook his head. "Nothing to worry about."

Liz frowned so hard her brow creased. If he kept causing her to make that expression, she'd have a permanent set of wrinkles there.

"Do you think I'm an idiot?" he asked.

"What do you mean?"

"This." He waved his hand to indicate everything around them. "All this."

Liz stared at him a minute. "It's not all this that makes me think you're an idiot."

"Wow, thanks."

She smiled. "I'm kidding. No, I don't think you're an idiot."

"Then why am I doing this?"

Liz let out a long breath. "I think your mind's made up, and you have to see this through." Then Liz puckered her lips while she thought something over, and said, "I just hope you're wrong as hell."

"Why?"

"Because if you're right..." She shook her head, not wanting to finish it.

He was able to finish it in his head for her. Those words didn't need to be spoken. He set the Pepsi on the porch rail, reached out, and pulled Liz to him. She wrapped her arms around his back, nuzzling her head against his chest. Chin on top of her head, he closed his eyes.

"I'm glad you're here," he said.

He felt her smile through his shirt. "I wouldn't want to be anywhere else. Well, maybe somewhere else. But I'm fine being with you."

Ethan was surprised when he felt a chuckle escape him.

"Yo!" Cole's voice bounced off all the trees. "You ready to rebuild a cabin? Put in some hard work because we're going to be working a lot. Swear to God."

"Jeez," Ethan muttered. "There goes the award for overacting."

Liz laughed. "Big time."

They separated from their hug and turned to face the oncoming "crew." Tina and Ramona were carrying luggage while Cole and Bill began to untie the straps on top of the Blazer that had been securing a bulging tarp. Bill tossed the bungees aside while Cole climbed onto the sidestep. He unwrapped the tarp to unveil the lumber stacked underneath.

Ethan saw how Cole's bicep bulged when he slid a board from the pile. Ethan had been working out a lot the last few months and had managed to put on some muscle. Not much, but a lot more than he'd ever had before. He couldn't compare to Cole, though. Years of construction had given Cole a hardened tone that probably would never soften.

"Heads-up," said Cole, angling the board downward.

From the strained worry on Bill's face, it was obvious he didn't know what he was supposed to do once he had the lumber.

"I better go help them," Ethan said.

"Go get 'em, tiger."

Ethan gave her a wink, then trotted down the steps. He greeted the wives in passing on his way to the guys. He stepped beside Bill, assisting him with the wood. They set it on the ground beside the Blazer.

He looked up. Cole, standing on the bumper, gazed down at him. "Anything suspicious yet?"

Ethan shook his head. "Nothing. Liz said some girls that

run a podcast showed up shortly after I went to talk with Gale."

"Podcast?" asked Bill, face scrunching around his sunglasses.

"Some true crime podcast, or something."

"That's just what we need," said Bill. "People nosing around."

"Might improve our chances," said Cole.

"But we don't want anyone to get hurt," said Ethan. "More people out this way, those chances are improved as well."

Cole nodded. "No, we *don't* want that. I don't want that. But..."

Bill cleared his throat, apparently wanting to change the subject. "How'd it go with Ms. Bedford?"

Ethan cleared his throat and looked up at Cole. "She's staying."

He could tell by Cole's expression that his friend was wondering if Ethan had done what he said he would. Ethan gave a slight nod, hoping Bill hadn't been able to pick up on it.

Cole winked in response. "Our chances are getting better and better," he said.

"Jesus, Cole," said Bill.

"I want to get this guy's ass," said Cole.

"We all do," said Ethan. "We all do."

They finished taking down the boards, then hauled them over to the cabin and stacked them on the porch.

Cole stood straight, breathing hard. "Door looks good. I don't know if I could've done a better job myself."

Ethan wiped the sweat from his face. He could hear the women talking from inside, their voices muffled but vigorous. "Thanks. I just followed your instructions."

Cole pushed on it. "Sturdy. Glad you went ahead and did it. Looks like you didn't have any trouble from a maniac, but this door is good to have if one *had* shown up."

"I hope so. It cost enough. Let's head inside and check the GPS, see how everybody's doing."

"Plus," said Bill, "it's cooler in there."

"Damn right," said Cole.

Ethan opened the door. The voices were louder, coming

from the kitchen. It sounded as if Tina and Ramona were doing most of the talking.

Bill and Cole stepped past him. As he turned to shut the door, he thought he saw movement in the woods beyond the driveway. He stared at the line of trees, noticing a single branch swaying as if somebody had pulled it back to clear a spot to see through and let it go.

Ethan studied the woods. He looked for any subtle movements or glimpses of clothing, but saw nothing. A crow squawked. Ethan let out the breath he'd been holding. Most likely, that was what had caused the branch to move, but it didn't help him feel any better. After a couple more seconds of staring, he turned away and entered the cabin.

Pulling the door shut, he twisted the deadbolts into place. They locked with a firm clicking sound. Ethan turned around and sighed, enjoying the cool air. It glued his shirt to his back. He reached behind him and plucked it loose.

Bill grabbed a carry bag amongst the luggage against the wall. He carried it over to the coffee table, sat down on the couch, and opened it. Removing a laptop, he set it on the table.

"Why not use our phones?" said Cole.

"Just easier that way. It'll also run off the Wi-Fi and stayed logged in the whole time. Did you set it up, Ethan?"

Ethan nodded. "It was never off. But yeah, it's still going."

"Good."

Ethan watched Bill work. He glanced over at Cole, catching his longtime friend staring at him. "What?"

"You sleep at all last night?"

If Ethan wanted to be honest, he would have told Cole that he hadn't slept in two nights. But if he admitted that, he'd have to endure another one of those Cole lectures about taking care of himself and needing to be as healthy as possible. Instead of putting himself through all that, he only nodded.

Cole frowned. He looked as if he wanted to say something, but the beeping from Bill's laptop stopped him.

"All right," said Bill. He lifted the laptop, folded the screen over, and set it down so it now resembled a hybrid of an easel and a tablet. Using a stylus, he began tapping a series of buttons.

Ethan was thankful they had an IT person on the team. Anything that dealt with technology had been handled by Bill with help from Martin on Team B. They'd been able to set up a dependable GPS and other tracking apps, synced them all and made them operational. Ethan didn't understand the technical aspects of it all, but he was grateful for it.

"Team B is at the campsite," said Bill. "See?" He tapped a blue blot on a screen filled with green and brown. They've been there a couple hours from the looks of the timestamps.

"Any contact with them?" asked Ethan.

"We're about to right now. Figured we'd wait until we were all accounted for."

"What about Robbie and Trish?"

"In route right now." He pointed at a blinking dot with the tip of the stylus. It was moving at a lethargic pace toward the blue smear.

It's all coming together.

Ethan felt a smile tugging the corners of his mouth. He sat in the chair as Cole grabbed a seat next to Bill.

Cole slipped a cigar from the front pocket of his sleeveless T-shirt. "We *have* had contact with Robbie and Trish within the last two hours. They were lollygagging around but seem to be moving in double-time now." He unfurled the plastic and plopped the cigar in his mouth. He used a Zippo to light it.

On a normal day, Ethan would have asked Cole to smoke outside. He guessed it really didn't matter. It was strange how the trivial things no longer felt important to him.

Bill hooked a device into the laptop with a USB cable. Twin antennas jutted from the top. He adjusted them, then connected a microphone. After flipping a switch, the square device began to softly hum. Using the stylus, he swiped the screen, pulling up a smaller screen from the bottom. Ethan saw it had green, red, and yellow buttons. Bill tapped the green button, then leaned down to the microphone. "Team B. This is Team A. Over."

Ethan pointed at the screen. "Can we only see *them* or is there a way to also see everything around them."

Bill snorted. "I wish. We'd have to either have some serious clearance for satellite access or the ability to hack into it. No, we can only see the trackers, running off the towers around us, which are scarce."

Ethan nodded. In movies, people filled a small room and viewed satellite feed before initiating a massive assault or something. All they had to work with was what they could get from Amazon.

The speakers on the laptop crackled, then George's voice said, "Team B here. You guys hanging in there?"

Ethan and Cole nodded at each other.

"We are," said Bill. "We're at the cabin, all accounted for. Anything weird to report?"

"Nothing. Just another day in paradise. Seem to be a lot of critters scampering around. We can hear them everywhere. Martin's going to head to the cookout area in a few minutes to wait for the kids. They're doing okay?"

"Yep. I'm watching them now. They're right on schedule. Maybe a few minutes behind."

"Wow. Guess I lost the bet. Figured they wouldn't show at all."

"They want the money," said Cole.

George chuckled. "I would too."

"George," said Ethan, leaning forward. "Don't ignore those sounds that you think are animals. Don't take anything lightly. Confirm everything."

A pause. "We're not. Martin went to do a quick check of the area. He took a gun. I'm here minding the radio. The wives are keeping the fire going. We're all set."

Ethan felt something inside. It was a subtle twinge that seemed to ooze through his bowels. It was barely there, but he didn't like it. "Keep your eyes and ears open."

"Will do," said George. There was a hint of annoyance in his voice.

"All right," said Bill. "We're signing off. Going on strict radio silence unless it is a matter of urgency. Remember where the SOS button is?"

"Martin showed all of us."

"Good. Signing off."

"Roger that," said George, trying to sound official. His laughter distorted the speaker.

"Glad you're enjoying yourself," said Cole.

"I'm bored off my ass," said George. "I hate camping. I wish I would have taken the cabin instead."

Cole stood up, making his way toward the sliding glass door on the other side of the room. He tugged it open, stepped out, and began to pace while puffing the cigar. Ethan thought about joining him but decided to stay put.

"Just make it *look* like you're there because you want to be," said Bill.

"Sure."

"All right," said Ethan. "You guys be careful."

"You, too. Holler if you need us."

"Same to you."

George paused before saying, "I think Martin's making his way back now. I'm going to send him toward the grills."

"Sounds good," said Ethan. He could hear the crunching leaves on the speakers. "Take care."

"Later," said George.

The red button blinked dark. Bill began unhooking everything from the laptop. "Want me to leave this open?"

Ethan thought about it. He wanted to keep it open. That way, he could always see the others' location. But he decided against it. "Better not. If anybody tries to look in on us, and they see that?"

"Right. Might look a bit odd. I'll leave the apps open, but just close the laptop."

"That works."

Ethan checked the time on his cell phone. Before long, Robbie and Trish would be stumbling across Martin setting up the grill for their meals.

"Martin's going to be grilling hot dogs," said Bill. "What's on the menu for us?"

"Hot dogs," said Ethan. "Liz got them in bulk. She said she'll handle the cooking while we do the grunt work."

"Guess we should get started."

"Right," said Ethan, standing up.

"Where *do* we start?"

Ethan pointed toward the glass door. "Outside. I need to talk to you about something."

Bill paused as he was starting to stand. He looked from Cole to Ethan and back. "This doesn't sound good."

"Everything good?" said Cole.

"Not until we're outside," said Ethan.

"I already don't like this," said Bill.

But he still followed Ethan outside. Ethan hated this part, the secrecy. He almost regretted what he did, but he also felt it had to be done. Admitting it to his friends was almost as stressful as coming clean about a secret addiction.

When they were on the porch, Cole slid the glass door shut.

"Okay," said Cole. "What gives? What's with all the mystery?"

"There's been some changes to the plan," said Ethan. "More like some additions made on the fly."

"And you have to tell them to us out here?" asked Cole.

Ethan nodded. "Don't want the women to know. Not yet."

Bill rubbed a hand over the smooth skin of his scalp. "You're not making any sense."

Ethan took a deep breath and prepared to tell the guys what he did while he was at Gale's cabin.

9.

The view was much better walking behind Trish. Robbie liked the way her hips swayed, hiking the shorts up bit by bit to show the lower curves of her buttocks. Her legs looked very bare and tanned as they flexed with each step. When the sun glinted through the trees, it caused the sweat droplets on her skin to sparkle.

She glanced back at him, caught where his eyes were focused, and smirked. "I feel like a piece of meat when you look at me like that."

Robbie smiled. "A *fine* piece of meat."

"Well, that's something, I guess." She faced forward again. Gasped. "Look." She pointed to the right.

Robbie didn't see it at first. He took a few more steps and saw where the trail led around a tree. A wooden sign had been hammered to a post in the ground. He couldn't make out what was engraved on the front, but he figured it was a marker for where they wanted to be.

That must be the cooking area. Past those trees.

"Finally," he said. "I'm ready for a break."

"Same." She slowed down so he could catch up. "Do you feel cheesy about having to act like we don't know these people?"

Robbie, walking beside her, shrugged. "I don't know. A little, I guess."

"I haven't done any acting since drama class. I don't know how good I'm going to be."

Good enough to be a pro in porno.

"I guess we just nod a lot," he said. "Smile and nod. Like tourists."

Laughing, Trish hugged his arm. He felt the heat of her body through her shirt. "Right. Same way you talk to my parents."

"Hey."

Trish's laugh reverberated around him, bouncing off the trees like squeaky gunfire. It sounded unnaturally loud in the quiet woods. Robbie realized that other than their footsteps, it was all he could hear. Where were the birds and all the other scuttling creatures of the forest?

"Hold up," he said, stopping. He tilted his head upward, listening.

Trish snickered. "You're so cute."

He shushed her. "Hear that?"

Trish bit down on her bottom lip to hold back another laughing fit. She shook her head. "I don't hear anything."

"Right. Shouldn't we, though?"

"Shouldn't we what?"

He groaned. "Hear something? We're in the woods, so we should hear noises. Lots of them. Scampering sounds that freak us city people out. But we don't. That bothers me."

"Calm down," she said. "You're just getting spooked."

"Duh!"

"If you get spooked, I'll get spooked. That won't be good. Let's go, tough guy." She nudged him toward the right side of the trail where it split.

Now, he could read the sign just fine: *Camping Ahead.*

Robbie was thrilled to finally make it. He wasn't looking forward to spending the weekend with a group of adults he barely knew, but he was glad to be done walking for a while. It would be good to be around people and not feel so isolated.

But fooling around with Trish would be much harder, if not impossible. They'd have to make up for it while hiking back to the car on Sunday morning.

We'll have the whole day for that.

With nowhere to go but home, there would be no rush. He liked the idea of that.

"There's a grill," said Trish in a voice that didn't quite sound like hers. Robbie supposed it was her "acting" voice. He remembered how bad she'd been in the school plays. So bad that many of the students thought she was doing it on purpose.

Robbie now knew that she had been displaying what tiny bit of acting range she had.

"Sure is," he said, trying to sound interested.

He expected to smell either woodsmoke or cooking meat, but all he smelled was the satisfying scent of the woods with a hint of what he thought might be wild animal shit. He glanced over at Trish and saw the goofy smile that had been on her face moments ago was dipping. When they reached the grills, it dropped away entirely.

There were four grills in a clearing, two on each side, with a flat patch of dirt between them. Wood benches had been assembled in front of each one. There was a rusted drum to the right that had been put there for a trash can. It looked empty.

Other than that, the place was deserted. Nobody was around.

Trish plopped onto the first bench they came to. Her head swiveled this way and that. In a quiet voice, she said, "Where are they?"

Robbie shrugged out of his backpack and let it drop to the ground. He slipped his phone out of his back pocket to check the time. He whispered, "We're a couple minutes early."

"Ah."

"I figured they'd already be here, though."

"I guess not."

"Where do you think they are?"

Trish shrugged. "Maybe they're just slow walkers, or they lost track of time."

"Maybe." On his way to the bench, Robbie tried to ignore the cold feeling swelling in his lower back. He dropped down beside Trish. Sighed. It felt wonderful to be off his feet. When this whole operation was over, he was done with nature for a long time.

They sat in silence for a few minutes. Robbie waited for a bird or anything to make any kind of sound but heard nothing. He half expected any moment to hear footsteps heading their way. Again, there was nothing but the sound of their breathing.

At least they were in shade. A lot of it. The entire area was cloaked in a comfortable dusk thanks to the big trees. Though they were in a higher elevation, the heat had been horrendous all day, but he could feel the temperature dropping since they were no longer moving.

Trish dug water bottles out of her pack and offered him one. He took it, thanked her, and twisted off the cap. He had to force himself not to guzzle every drop. If he did, he'd either throw it all back up or have such a bad stomach cramp he wished he would.

Trish put the cap back on her water bottle, then set it on the ground between her boots. "What the hell?" She held out her hands.

Robbie shrugged. "I don't know."

"We've been here long enough. How late are they?"

Robbie didn't want to check the time to see. He kept his phone in his hand, turned over. "I know we've been here long enough that it's past three."

Trish looked at her phone. "Almost twenty minutes past."

Shit. Longer than I thought.

"They knew to meet us here at *that* time, right?"

"I assume so. You heard the way Cole made sure *we* knew the time. No way they don't know it with the way he is."

Trish nodded. "So what, then?"

"Hell if I know."

Trish nibbled at her lip. It was a habit she displayed whenever she was anxious. He wondered if she even knew when she did it. "Should we wait a little longer? I mean, what if they told us three, but told them four."

"Why would they do that?"

"To make sure we got here on time."

Robbie thought about it. He supposed a trick like that was possible. It wouldn't surprise him. "Yeah. We'll hang around a bit."

"What if they still don't show? Should we call Cole?"

Robbie didn't want to do that until it was absolutely necessary. But maybe it had already reached that point. The preparations had been precisely planned. And there was no way the other group didn't know they were supposed to meet here at precisely 3:00 pm.

Unless they had been told a different time, like Trish said.

Robbie sighed. "Ten more minutes. We'll wait that long."

"Then what?"

"We decide the next part."

"Okay."

Trish rested her head on his shoulder. Robbie leaned his head against hers. He stared out at the trees, listening to the deep quiet that seemed to stretch all around them. Darkness began to spread around the outer edges of his vision, closing in bit by bit and shrinking the brightness while doing so. Confused at first, Robbie realized it was his eyelids drooping. He blinked a few times, and the darkness was gone.

He needed to lift his head, but it felt impossible. The way Trish's hair was pulled back had created the perfect pillow for his cheek. He wondered why factories couldn't recreate such comfort and sell it in the stores. He'd buy two pillows if they were this soft.

Then Robbie thought he was falling and jerked to catch himself, only to find he was still sitting on the bench. Trish let out a little yelp and flew backward, her rump slamming the ground.

"Oh!" she said through a grunt.

Even in the shade, the sun seemed brighter than a thousand flashlights shining in his eyes. He blinked away the tears and looked down at his girlfriend. She looked around, her eyes wide and confused.

"Sorry," Robbie said. "Did I knock you off the bench?"

"*Threw* me off is more like it."

"Sorry. I thought I was fall—"

"Wait. Were we asleep?" she asked.

Robbie shook the fog out of his head. "Couldn't have been more than a couple minutes." He checked his phone and saw how incredibly wrong he was. His throat dropped into his stomach, making him gulp. "Shit."

"How long?"

"It's five after four."

"Fuck!" Trish shot to her feet. "Come on."

All the grogginess drained away as Robbie stood up. "Where?"

"We're going to the campsite. That's where *they* are, so we'll just change the plans a bit. Actors call it improvising."

"I know what improvising is. *Shit!* Cole's going to be pissed."

"It's not our fault. I'd rather do that than radio him about it. Right now, anyway."

"What if something's wrong?"

"Then we need to get over there and see for sure. Could you imagine how mad everyone will be at us if we call for their help, only to find out they lost track of time? It would ruin everything for them, and they would be pissed. At *us*. I can hear them blaming us for messing everything up."

"And there goes our five thousand."

"Exactly. Believe me, I don't like the idea of us going to the campsite, but I don't like just sitting here, either. And I really don't like the idea of radioing Cole if it turns out we didn't need to."

She was right about that part. Still, he didn't feel that going to the campsite was the right idea, either. But he supposed it was better than anything he could think of.

He picked up his backpack and pulled it on. His skin felt sore where the straps rubbed him. Trish grabbed his hand, her grip tight and sweaty. He put his phone in one pocket and his water bottle in the other. Trish slipped her bottle in her side pocket. The top half jutted next to her hip.

Together, they made their way to the trail. The campsite was a short walk through the trees ahead. He could see the main trail, a dark chasm between the tall, leafy trees on either side. His stomach tried to tremble, but he sucked it in to keep it still.

"Ready?" Trish asked.

Robbie nodded. They passed through the opening. Deep shade swallowed them. The temperature seemed to plummet. It must have rained within the past day or so, because the path was slightly damp. Small puddles were placed here and there.

The path shifted downward. Robbie's foot skidded. Trish's hold on his hand tightened and jerked back, preventing him from dropping onto his ass.

"You okay?" she asked.

Nodding, he said, "Thanks for that."

"Always here for you, babe."

"Good to know."

Her smile was a pale arc in the heavy shade all over them. It looked like evening under these thick trees. The cooler temperature felt nice to walk in. He was looking forward to the cool night, sitting around a campfire.

If that's even going to happen.

Robbie resisted those thoughts from taking over. If he allowed his worry and paranoia even a tiny margin in his mind, they would consume his thoughts. He always worried. Didn't matter what the situation was, he dwelled on every possible angle of it until he was sick with grief. He needed to be the man this time, for Trish. She needed to see that he could handle situations no matter how the plans shifted.

She needed to know she was safe with him.

"See that?" she asked, killing the silence.

At first, he didn't. But then he saw the trees to the left. Bright blue showed between the gaps in the branches.

Tents.

"Yeah," he said. "There they are."

"Come on," she said, picking up the pace. "Follow my lead."

Robbie was confused by her comment. What was she planning to do?

"Oh, honey, look! Campers!"

Robbie began to smile at that direct-to-video acting of hers. It was quite adorable, really, though nearly dreadful in performance.

"I see them," he said in a stage voice that wasn't any better than hers. "Hello there! We are hikers, making our way through the woods."

"Dial it down," Trish muttered.

Robbie knew his performance was bad. Clearing his throat, he said, "I'm doing my best."

Trish rolled her eyes. "You're no actor, babe."

He wanted to point out that neither was she, but figured it wouldn't be a good idea to do so.

They stopped walking when they reached the top of the campsite, brandishing big smiles. Their bogus expressions didn't last as they looked around at the tents and empty camping chairs. There were two large tents, placed on opposite sides of the clearing. A mound of sticks had been assembled in the center of a rock circle. Metal skewers were leaning against the sticks, probably in preparation for roasting marshmallows.

"Hello!" Trish called out. "Is anyone here?"

No response came.

They looked at each other.

"Let's check it out," he said, slipping the backpack around to his front. He unzipped it, reached in, and gripped the radio. He wanted it nearby, just in case.

Just in case of what?

Something was wrong. What it was, he had no idea. But this campsite should have some type of activity in it. Instead, the area looked like a camping display at Bass Pro Shop. From the shine and gloss, he could tell the camping gear was new. Even the camping chairs were all in good shape. One still had a tag dangling from the arm.

Trish stepped closer to Robbie as they began to walk. The blue tent was closest, so that was where they went. It had been placed between two large trees, the thick branches reaching over the top. A wall of green and brown was behind it.

"Hello," he said. "Anybody in there?"

Robbie pulled out the radio, handing over his backpack to Trish. She nodded, granting him permission to use the radio if needed.

He walked on legs that felt soft and stringy. His stomach felt as if it were slowly twisting. A cold prodding worked in his lower back. "Please," he said. "Answer me. It's Robbie."

He stopped outside the tent. A breeze came up, rustling the leaves around him. With it came a new odor he hadn't noticed before. It smelled...raw and cold.

When he was a kid, he'd gone to his cousin's house for a sleepover. His uncle had just killed a deer while hunting and had the carcass strung up outside the shed. When Robbie had arrived, his uncle was spraying the dead animal with a hose, rinsing the blood away. The stink that had emanated from the deer smelled a lot like what was filling the air around them right now.

"What is that *smell?*" Trish asked.

Robbie turned to tell her the story of his uncle's deer.

Then a body dropped from the tree branch above him.

Robbie spun away as limp arms swung at his face. Trish screamed. When Robbie stopped moving, he looked back at the tree and saw George Portman wrapped in rope, dangling upside down from the tree. Blood poured down from the wide gash in his abdomen.

Robbie realized an error had been made in his first hasty assessment of Mr. Portman's predicament. Rope hadn't been used to tether him in an inverted position.

It was his intestines.

Stretching from the crater in his gut, they looked as if they'd been coated in pink mucus. Blood had drenched his shirt, gluing it to his body, so Robbie was able to see his pale face, twisted in a death grimace. His tongue, purple and bloated, hung from his mouth, touching the tip of his nose.

Robbie heard Trish scream and turned to see what had caused it. He bumped into Portman's shoulder, which threw him off balance. Twirling, Robbie stumbled over to the tent and fell against it. Robbie's weight easily crashed through the weak sturdiness, ripping the vinyl wide as he dropped inside.

And landed on a pile of bodies and various body parts that had been piled inside. His arms sank up to his elbows in a heap of messy skin and gore. His eyes came within an inch of a protruding chunk of ragged bone. Had he fallen a bit farther in, the sharp tip would have ruptured at least one of his eyes. The gray sliver jutted from the meat of a severed arm that had once been attached to a woman's body. Robbie figured this was so because of the quick glimpse he got of the manicured and painted fingernails on the blood-spattered hand attached to the other end.

Trish's shrieks tore Robbie away from the cold blanket of shock that had been covering him. Rolling over, he kicked the ruined walls of the tent out of his way and sat up.

Trish was still in the clearing, her legs thrashing back and forth. The way she moved, she should have been sprinting, but she remained in place, her boots kicking up dirt as they swished across the ground. Her eyes were wide and frantic, mouth hanging open as her lips trembled around her teeth.

Robbie saw thick fingers spread around her face, palming the top of her head. The large hand's grip mashed down her hair. Sprigs of yellow twirled out between the gaps in the spread of the fingers.

The reason why Trish wasn't moving anywhere was because the hand was holding her just a couple inches off the ground.

"Oh, fuck me," Robbie said through a gasp.

Cole. He needed Cole right now.

He moved to radio for help and saw his hand was empty. He'd lost his only connection to the others in his fall.

Shit!

He needed to search for the radio, but he also needed to help Trish. He only thought about it for a moment, then jumped to his feet. He dashed out of the ruined remains of the tent, almost tripping over a vinyl flap. Regaining his composure, he picked up speed. He grabbed a log from the top of the pile and ran toward Trish.

The large man was behind her, shielded by Trish's body. He couldn't see much of him at all, save his wide shoulders and massive frame.

Robbie was almost to Trish when she was suddenly raised even higher. Robbie's feet skidded across the dirt as he tried to stop. It didn't work. They kept going out in front of him, leaving the earth and dropping him. His ass whammed the ground. The jolt of his landing caused his body to lock up. He dropped the log he'd intended to use as a weapon. He didn't think to look for it, as his focus was on Trish, her kicking legs and wild screams.

A beefy arm extended, moving Trish outward as another arm rose so the other hand could grip her chin. The fingers on her scalp started to flex, triggering Trish's screams to rise in fervor. They were cut off when her head was wrenched around, her face being replaced with the back of her head. It looked as if Trish had put a wig on the wrong way.

Now, it was Robbie's turn to shriek as he watched Trish's body get tossed aside. Moments ago, she'd been alive and beautiful and in love with him. What smacked the ground hard enough to dent it was no longer Trish, but the empty corpse of what she had once been.

She's dead!

This time, Robbie really began to wail. He didn't even notice the large man had approached until he saw the ax rising in front of his face. He glimpsed his reflection in the dingy blade, the frightened face staring back.

Jesus…it's real. The whole thing is real!

Robbie's last thought before the ax came down and split his head into halves was that Ethan had been right all along.

And he wished he and Trish had stayed in town.

10.

Staring at the two girls on her porch, Gale started to regret she answered the door. Dressed for Halloween, the young pair were decked in all black, with makeup caked on their faces. Pretty, overall, but way too much black around the eyes. And in their hair, and all over their bodies.

How they hadn't dropped dead from heat stroke was a mystery to Gale.

The shorter one was a tad thicker than her tall friend, but both were well developed, much more so than Gale ever had been. They seemed to be proud of this because they wore shirts that accentuated the twin mounds God had given them on their chests.

"You want to do what?" she asked the spooky girls.

They shared a look that Gale could read quite well. They were wondering how much clearer they needed to be to the poor, dumb old woman in the cabin. She understood what they wanted, why they were here. Just like many before them, they'd come to see the place, to see the woman they'd read about online or seen on the news.

But the difference with these girls was they wanted to record her for an interview for their web show or some shit like that.

The shorter of the two, Clare, cleared her throat. "Um…just wanted to ask about that night. You know what night we mean. Ruh-right?"

Gale rolled her eyes. "For fuck's sake."

The taller, thinner girl's eyes widened. "We won't take up much of your time. Honest."

"What's your name again?"

"Vivian—Viv. Call me, Viv."

"Viv. Got it. Do you know how many people have come here saying the same shit and asking the same questions?"

Viv looked hurt by the question. "Um…no."

"A few?" asked Clare.

Gale glanced at the shorter girl. Her plump lips were bowed. She must have understood the annoyed look Gale was conveying because her expression changed into a pained grimace.

"I'm sure you can find all my answers online," said Gale.

Viv stepped forward, placing her boot in the doorway. Gale realized she'd done this in case Gale decided to swing the door shut. Her foot would block it. Probably wouldn't hurt her, either, since the boot looked like it had been built for trenches.

"Please," said Viv.

"Oh, well, since you said please."

A corner of Viv's lip curled. "I know you must be tired of this sort of thing."

"You don't know the half of it." Gale sighed. She thought about her visit from Ethan Bowers earlier. It had left her feeling odd all day. At first, she'd been genuinely disturbed by his admonitions. As the day had worn on, however, she'd gotten over it. Now, she was just tired. And a visit from two tragedy-obsessed dark lords was something she didn't need.

But she knew she would feel lousy if she turned them away. They'd traveled a good distance to talk to her, and she supposed she could let them in for a few minutes to get out of the heat, at least.

"How much you willing to pay me?" Gale asked.

"Wha—?" Clare blinked. "Pay?"

"Yes." Gale rubbed her thumb and forefinger together. "Fee for my interview."

Viv cleared her throat. She swallowed. It made a wet clucking sound. "Well, we don't usually…well…"

Gale held out her hands. "You're going to make money off this, right? I mean, if you get enough views and all, you'll probably stand to receive quite a payout. And this story, well, you know people like to hear it. You wouldn't be here if they didn't. Am I right?"

Viv closed her eyes. When she opened them again, the

charm had left her. She seemed to be on the verge of tears. "I guess we could give you the money we were going to use to pay for a hotel room on the way back." Her voice lowered. "We can sleep in the car, or something."

Gale laughed. "Damn. You two can't take a joke. Make me feel like shit. I'm just messing with you." She took a step back, pulling the door wide so they could enter. She waved them in.

"You're *not* charging us?" asked Clare.

"No," said Gale. "I'm not a leech or anything."

Smiles split their pretty faces as they rushed in, spouting their thanks as they walked by. Once they were inside, Gale shut the door. She took a moment to engage all the locks. When she was finished, she turned around and noticed how the girls' playful demeanor had faded to something like worry.

Shrugging, Gale said, "Can never be too careful."

They nodded their understanding.

Clare plucked the front of her tight shirt, fanning it as she leaned back her head. "Feels good in here." She looked at Gale, then her smile turned to a gasp when Gale snatched up the shotgun that had been leaning against the wall. She stepped back when Gale walked to the fireplace, giving her plenty of room. She leaned the gun against the wall, then sank down in the recliner with a sigh. Her legs began to throb. This might have been the first time she'd sat down since Ethan was here earlier.

Gale grabbed her thermos of water from the coffee table. She'd just finished filling the large aluminum cup when the girls started knocking on the door. Leaning back in her chair, Gale raised the thermos, adjusting the tiny straw to her mouth. Ice sloshed and clacked as she drank. Her chest began to ache from the cold water flowing down.

She set the thermos between her leg and the arm of the chair. While the girls set up the camera, she smoked a cigarette. Usually, she liked waiting until later in the evening to start smoking. But she figured it was close enough. It was suppertime already, though Gale wasn't that hungry yet.

The camera was on a tripod and pointed at her by the time she leaned up and stubbed out the cigarette in the ashtray on the table. She lit another one when she leaned back.

Viv stepped in front of the camera, taking slow steps backward until the juts of her rump were right in front of Gale's face. "Good?" she asked.

At first, Gale thought she was talking to her. Then she realized she was actually speaking to Clare when the shorter girl nodded. "Yep. No shadows. The fading light coming through the window makes for a nice, soft glow. Natural."

"Well," said Viv, "it is natural, so that's good."

Clare chuckled. "True."

"Ready to get started?"

"Ready if you are."

Nodding, Viv turned around to Gale. "How about you?"

"Ready as I ever am when it comes to this." She let out a deep breath that sent a runnel of smoke into the air. "Are you going to try a few test-runs on the questions, or are we just going right into it?"

"We'll just go right into it. Even if we do a test, we'd still record it in case the answers you give are amazing. So there's really no need to practice if we're already recording."

Gale shrugged. "It's your rodeo."

Viv smiled. Then she walked around behind the camera and stood beside Clare. Bending over, Viv studied the small screen that Clare and flipped out from the side of the camera. A small crease formed above her nose as she observed the image displayed in the small box. Then her eyes widened, and her skin smoothed back out. The smile returned to her face.

"May we sit?" she asked, gesturing to the couch behind her.

Gale nodded. "Of course. Would you like something to drink before we get started?"

Though Clare looked as if she were about to accept the offer, Viv spoke over her. "We're good. For now, anyway. I want to get started before we lose more of that light. It's perfect right now. We'll have to fake it somehow if it gets much darker in here."

"Gotcha," said Gale.

The girls settled onto the couch, heaving sighs of relief to be off their feet as well.

Clare used a remote to start the camera. It beeped, then a

red light appeared on the front. "We're recording," she said.

Gale nodded. For some reason, she felt a nervous flutter in her stomach. She lit another cigarette and waited for them to begin.

11.

Officer Lori Reese spotted Kendall's matching SUV cruiser in the parking lot of the old junkyard. Except for the dim glow from the screen of his computer, the whole area was covered in growing darkness. Fog had started drifting out from the chain-link fence, parting as it surrounded the car and swirled upward into the sky.

Reese drove onto the lot, the gravel crackling under the tires. She came to a stop next to his SUV, the front of hers beside the rear of his so their driver's windows were side by side. She put the SUV in park, leaving the engine idling.

As she rolled down her window, she saw Kendall was doing the same. He was almost fifty and tonight looked it. His silver hair, usually brushed back, had fallen over his brow. Stubble was spread across the lower part of his face. The half-moons under his eyes looked like bruises from the shadows inside the car. He gave her a lazy smile. "Morning."

She smiled. "Evening."

He feigned surprise and looked around. "What? Oh, yeah. It's time for the nightshift."

"Yep. And that means you get to go home."

"Joyous time for me."

"How's it been today? Anything?"

"Nothing. You'd think it was the winter. No visitors, other than that party that checked in this morning. No calls. Not even any speeders. It's been dead."

"That's fine with me. I plan to do some slow patrol anyway."

"What for? There's really no need right now. You're the first car I've seen."

"Better than sitting still all night."

"Says you."

Reese smiled. "Did you swing by the Bowers' cabin at all today?" She'd told Kendall about her interaction this morning.

"I started to but decided against it."

"Why?"

Kendall shrugged. "Figured they would want their privacy."

Reese checked the time on her phone. It was nearing seven. Not too late to do a ride by.

Kendall must have known what she was thinking. "Just leave them be, Reese. They don't need us bothering them. Especially not now. Let them be in peace."

"I offered to check in."

"Well, do what you want. But I better not hear we received a complaint about a loitering officer. I'm sure the last thing they want to see is you. No offense."

Reese smiled. She understood his point, but he also hadn't been there this morning. The woman had genuinely acted as if she would appreciate Reese checking up on them. "No offense taken."

"That's better." His arm moved. She heard the keys jingle as the ignition was twisted. His SUV hummed to life. She didn't know why his sounded quieter than hers.

Probably because he spends so much time parked here.

"Enjoy the rest of your night," she said.

He nodded. "You, too. Going to get home in time for some late supper and catch up on how the Braves did today."

"Sounds good."

"Keep your nose clean and try not to die. Of boredom." He gave her a salute, then drove off. She watched his taillights in the rearview float away like twin red orbs, crooked in the swirling fog. They shrank until vanishing around the bend in the road.

Reese leaned back, letting her head fall back against the seat. Her shift was just starting, and she already felt exhausted. She stared out her windshield, her headlights carving a bright tunnel through the darkness that spread against the privacy fence of the junkyard. On the other side, she could see the husks of dead cars spread all over. The moonlight painted them in faded gray.

Reese shivered.

"Creepy out there," she muttered. Her quiet voice felt like a shout in the stuffy car.

Knock it off.

She couldn't allow herself to get spooked. She rubbed her eyes and felt some of the tension fade. She'd felt odd ever since seeing Ethan Bowers this morning. She had no reason to be bothered. He'd been polite, albeit short with her in his conversation. Somehow, she felt like he'd been lying to her. She was always able to tell when somebody was being dishonest and Ethan had been holding something in, though he hadn't really said anything. As if he didn't want her to know what he was up to.

Of course not. He's selling the cabin. His daughter was killed there. Did you really expect him to be skipping around the place and throwing candy all over?

Still, he was acting strange. And whenever anybody acted strange, there was a reason for it.

She told herself to let it go. She couldn't hold his behavior against him. How else would she expect him to behave being back in the place where it had all happened? She remembered seeing the bloodstains. That alone must have been enough to make him not feel like talking to anyone. She remembered when her father died a couple years ago, she didn't speak to anyone for months. It had been hard to even leave her house.

Maybe Ethan's attitude was exactly how it should have been.

Reese decided that she would leave it at that. Let Ethan Bowers do what he needed to do to get on with his life and stay out of his way.

She reached for the ignition, ready to shut it off. She figured she could hang out here for a little while before driving on. She'd probably take some of the backroads just to make sure there had been no rockslides or no felled trees anywhere.

Her hand froze just before she twisted the ignition. She already knew what she was going to do.

I don't have to go in. I can just ride out there, be nearby.

That seemed like a good idea. She would be close if they needed her, and she could drop in tomorrow morning on her way home just like she'd done this morning. She'd even take the longer route there, so that way it didn't feel like she was purposely driving out there to see what they were up to. Check on things along the way as well. Nothing wrong with that.

"Nothing at all," she said.

She dropped the gear into Drive and pulled away from the parking lot. She was glad to leave the junkyard behind. She'd never liked that place. When she was a kid, she'd ride with her father out there when it had been under a different owner. She loved spending the time with him but wouldn't leave his truck once they were there. He never forced her to, and she was grateful. She used to imagine getting lost amongst the old cars, becoming trapped in a world that was somehow hidden deep in the wreckage. A few times her mind produced images of broken cars coming to life and gobbling up her father as if their mangled hoods were mouths.

Reese laughed at herself. She thought she would be over that stuff by now, especially since she was a cop. It looked like those dumb fears would stay with her.

She saw her turn up on the left. Slowing down, she took the turn and started making her way up the mountain.

She'd be there soon.

12.

At first, the questions were not anything Gale hadn't heard many times before. But here and there, a response from Gale would trigger another series of questions. Some Gale hadn't been asked only a handful times, but others she could spout off a response as if it had been scripted for her.

Then came one Gale hadn't been asked.

"Do you think it might happen again?"

Gale started to laugh. Remembering Ethan's earlier visit, the laughter died off. She didn't have an answer right offhand. What could the answer be?

Yeah, Gale. What do you really *think? Will it happen, again?*

She noticed Viv and Clare were both staring at her, hanging on to the silence as if their blinking might send Gale running like a spooked deer. Gale realized she really was spooked. Out of nowhere, she'd begun to feel scared. "I think this interview is over," she said.

"What?" said Viv. "Come on."

"We were just getting to the good stuff," said Clare.

Gale sighed. "Right. The good stuff. Maybe that's where you should've started because you're out of time."

She pointed to the window. The sun had descended behind the trees. Cracks of burning red were splitting the sky, spreading a bloody layer over the streaks of clouds. Everywhere else was black.

Viv looked at the window, groaned. "Damn. She's right."

"It's dark," said Clare.

"Nothing gets by you," said Gale.

Ignoring the remark, Clare stepped over to Viv. "We have to get back to the car in the dark."

"We brought flashlights."

"I know, but..." Clare wrinkled her nose. "It'll still be dark. Mountain dark. We've never walked in mountain dark before."

Rolling her eyes, Viv stood up. "So dramatic. Dark is fucking dark, no matter where it is."

"Wrong. Mountain dark is a different kind of darkness. It's deeper. Darker."

Viv groaned. "Jesus, Clare." She walked over to the camera and switched it off. Then she flipped the screen. It closed with a *thump*. "We'll walk straight down the driveway. Then head over..."

"Wait, wait," said Gale. "Where the hell *is* your car?"

Clare turned to her while Viv removed the camera from the tripod. "On the turnoff down by the path."

"The old bike trail?"

Clare shrugged. "I guess."

Gale rubbed her eyes. She could feel the early tenderness of a looming headache. She wanted to ask the girls why they parked all the way over there and walked the long hike through the woods to get to Ethan's and here when they could have just driven up the driveways.

Probably didn't know what they were doing.

Gale let her hand drop into her lap. "Nobody uses that bike trail anymore. Not since the murders. You basically took the long way around in both directions. I don't know how that's possible, but that's what you did. Walking down my driveway and walking back to your car? You'll probably be walking on the main road for the better part of an hour in the dark once you finally get to the main road. Uphill part of the way, too. And all grandparents hiking to school jokes aside, uphill out here can be a real bastard. Not to mention the coyotes and other wildlife."

"Shit on me," said Clare through a sigh. "Probably bears, too?"

"This *is* the mountains," said Gale. "You said so yourself."

Viv carried the camera in one hand and the tripod in the other to the couch. "Well, nothing we can do about it, is there?" She looked at her friend, not addressing Gale. "I mean, we can't spend the night here. Even if we could, we have to be back to do the show tomorrow and still need to upload and edit the footage."

Clare held out her hands. "Yeah, I get that, but..." She nibbled her lip. "Two girls. Walking alone. In the dark. Where murders happened. The killer still at large..."

Viv dropped the camera into the case, then began breaking down the tripod. "I get what you're saying." She held up a hand to her throat, fingers tapping her chin. "Oh, no," she said in a high voice. "What are we going to do? The slasher man is out there and widdle ol' us will be all alone..."

Clare stomped her foot. "Yeah, make fun of me. Cute. But you know as well as I do that's slasher movie formula bullshit. We're the two characters that are introduced partway through the story, only for the audience to get to know them right before they die."

Ethan. She sounds like Ethan.

Gale felt heat between her forefinger and middle finger and gasped.

The girls looked at her.

Leaning forward, Gale rubbed out the cigarette in the ashtray. She'd been so focused on their conversation that she'd forgotten she was smoking. It had burned down to the filter. "Sorry," she muttered. "Burned myself." Gale stood up, stretching. "Just stop arguing. I'll drive you to your car."

A goofy smile appeared on Clare's face. "You will?"

"We can't ask you to do that," said Viv.

"You're not," said Gale. "I'm demanding. And I'd hate myself in the morning if something did happen to you. I'm not saying I think it would, but I'm not taking the chance."

Clare clapped her hands. "Thank you so much."

"Just get your shit together so we can go."

They packed up in less time than it took them to unpack. Within a couple minutes, the girls were standing by the front door like kids ready to go on a trip while Gale grabbed her cigarettes. When she had them, she walked over to the wall beside the door and grabbed her keys from the key pegs. "Car's off to the side of the cabin. Go on out, and I'll be right behind you."

She thought about grabbing the shotgun but decided not to. She would probably feel better having it with her, but it would be too much to carry in her compact SUV with the two girls and their gear. It'd have to go in the back, where she couldn't get to it quickly if she needed to, so there was really no point bringing it. Leaving it behind was probably the better idea, though not one she liked.

Gale stepped away from the wall, moving behind the girls as Clare pulled the door open.

There was a quick strike of wind, followed by two gasps. Gale looked up in time to see Viv throwing herself to the left while Clare threw herself to the right. Parting like a curtain, they unveiled the large man standing outside.

She noticed the spear's curved blade a moment before it pierced her stomach. It felt as if a sliver of ice had penetrated her and unleashed a cloud of frost inside her.

Stumbling back, Gale brought the spear with her, jutting from her stomach like a flagpole. Though the blade was long, she saw it wasn't very deep.

Deep enough...

Her feet tangled together, tripping her. She shook when she landed on her back. The wind might have been knocked out of her. She wasn't sure because the pain from the spear already made it hard to breathe.

Trembling, Gale tore her eyes away from her injury to focus on the large man in her doorway. She could only see him from the shoulders down because his head was blocked by the top of the doorframe. Instead of ducking down to enter, he stepped forward. His head smashed through the thick wood as if it were the consistency of a paper flag.

Now she ogled him in full and barely had the wits about her to focus on his appearance. In her terrified vision, she saw his face was covered in a pale mask that looked too small for his face. There were no facial features, other than surface cracks here and there. Thick straps held it in place over his head. It sunk in, causing the flesh rimming it to bulge. Tufts of wild hair dangled like a veil in his eyes. He wore a long, dark shirt over filthy pants that ended in tatters over scruffy boots.

A sour, rotten stench began to fill the cabin, spreading out like an invisible rancid cloud.

Gale glanced over to the shotgun, still leaning against the wall by the fireplace. She could reach it in seconds, a quick sprint. But even attempting to get up seemed impossible.

Viv screamed.

Gale looked over and saw the tall goth girl sliding backward on her stomach. Her fingernails grated along the floor, snapping, ripping loose as she tried to find purchase on the hardwood. A beefy hand gripped each of her ankles as if the maniac was using her as a wheelbarrow.

Clare, on her back, grabbed for her friend to no avail. Viv was too far out of reach. "Leave her alone!" Her voice was shrill, reminding Gale of the sound her brake pads made when they needed to be changed.

You lay here much longer, you'll never get up again.

That voice had been Jack's, her husband. He'd been dead almost ten years now from a heart attack that neither of them saw coming.

"I'm trying," she said.

Get up. Get the gun.

Viv's wild screech called her attention back to the melee before her. Gale gasped as she watched the big man heft Viv into the air by her ankles, twist so he faced Clare, and bring Viv's flailing body down on her friend just as she blocked her face with her arms.

It wasn't enough. Viv crashed into her, knocking Clare's crossed arms away. Their heads connected with a *thunking* sound like an ax splitting wood. Viv's screams died. Her arms stopped swinging and hung limply as she was hoisted back up.

Clare moaned. Blood slid down her face, into her fluttering eyes. It looked as if her forehead might have been slightly dented.

"Stop!" Gale cried. Before she realized she was about to do it, she sat upright. The pain it caused made her growl deep in her chest.

If the man heard her, he gave no indication. He brought Viv back over and down. Her hair flapped back, exposing her split face. Gale glimpsed a cracked skull where her brow should be. Then Viv whacked Clare again. This time the sound was juicier, like an egg from a giant chicken dropping onto rocks.

Now, Clare was also silent.

When the man raised Viv a third time, her head was a gloppy mess of hair and shattered skull dripping thick beads onto Clare's broken face. He saw the ruin that was Viv and Clare, then flung Viv's lifeless body aside. It smacked against the far wall, leaving a wide red streak as it slid down to the floor.

The maniac, pleased with his work, turned to face Gale again.

What he hadn't realized was that while he'd been occupied, Gale had gotten onto her feet. She'd pulled the blade from her stomach, biting into her bottom lip to keep from screaming. The wound was a slanted slit that bled freely now, spilling down the front of her pants. To her relief, the flow wasn't heavy. Still hurt like hell, though, each time she took a breath.

She didn't wait for the maniac to process what she was about to do. She stepped forward, thrusting her arms. The blade shot toward his chest.

It came to such a sudden stop that Gale stumbled. She managed to catch herself before she fell. Just as she started to realize she hadn't stabbed him, the spear was wrenched from her hands. The maniac held it up, eyes boring down on her from inside the dark holes of his mask. His shoulders rose and dropped with a huff.

Oh, now you've done it.

Jack's voice was back. And she didn't need him telling her how much she'd just pissed off the psychopath. She saw it in the way he gripped the spear's staff. Filthy and stained, black fingernails protruded from the fingertips. Some were longer than others, jagged and chipped on the tips. But the knuckles were white from how hard his hand was clenched.

Gale took a step back.

Should've gone for the gun like I told you.

Gale wanted to tell her inner voice, Jack's voice, to shut it. She couldn't. Her mind didn't seem able to do much other than shut down. She could feel it, bit by bit, closing out as it accepted the fate that was surely to come.

No way would she reach the gun in time.

She wished she would have bled out on the floor. At least that way she wouldn't have to endure what was coming to her.

The big man turned the spear outward, her blood tacky on the curved blade facing her. It caused a trembling glow on the floor from the light.

"If you're gonna do it," she said, "just do it!" She slammed her fists on her thighs. "I can't stand this drawing-it-out bullshit!" She'd expected her voice to sound authoritative and sincere. Instead, she sounded like a whiny child.

The man's head tilted as he studied her. She wondered what he was thinking, then decided it didn't really matter.

Her back bumped the wall, causing her to let out an involuntary squeal. She'd been walking in reverse this whole time and hadn't realized it. Maybe because he'd matched each of her steps, moving as she did until there was nowhere left to go.

He lowered the spear so the blade was level with her chest. He wouldn't miss a vital spot this time. Wherever he put that blade, it would be a position that would kill her.

I'll see you soon, Jack.

She closed her eyes.

"Hey, asshole."

Gale flinched at the voice. At first, she thought the maniac had been the one to speak. But she quickly realized the voice was one of an ally. She knew this because she'd just heard it earlier today.

Cracking an eye open, Gale saw the maniac turning slightly to look behind him. His shoulder moved slowly aside, unveiling the person who'd entered her home without her realizing it.

Ethan stood there, a high-powered rifle trained on the masked man. His finger was over the trigger, ready to squeeze. "I've fucking got you," he said.

Gale let out a long breath. "Thank...God..."

Ethan was here. How he'd known she needed help, she had no idea. She was just thankful he'd shown up when he did.

Whenever she watched movies and a scene like this happened, she would scoff and yell at the screen that no way would somebody show up in just the right time to save someone else.

But here she was living it. Thank you, God, she was living it.

Footsteps to her right nearly made her scream. She saw a bigger man enter her living room, an AR-15 to his shoulder. She recognized him from the news and papers. He was one of the dead kid's dads. She had no idea which one, but she recognized his handsome, rugged face.

The taller guy let out a humorless chuckle. "Holy shit. It's him."

"Yeah," said Ethan. "We got the son of a bitch."

13.

"Why don't you drop that?" said Cole, lifting his chin toward the spear. He'd never seen one like it, so he figured the bastard had constructed it himself. The blade looked as if it had once been attached to the handle of a scythe.

The maniac made no move to discard the weapon.

"Now," said Cole. "I've got you dead to rights. You look tough, but I doubt you're so tough a slug to the brain wouldn't put you down. For good."

The tallest in the room, the man wasn't overly huge. But he was buff and lean with arms that filled the long sleeves of his shirt. His wide shoulders rose and lowered as he let out a long breath. It was muffled inside the mask. Cole wondered how long he'd been wearing the disguise. He was probably hideous underneath it, horribly scarred or disfigured. That was why these guys wore masks, wasn't it?

Finally, the big hands relaxed.

The spear fell to the floor with a clamor.

"That's better," said Cole. He kicked the spear away. "On your knees."

Only a slight hesitation, then the maniac's legs folded. His knees struck the floor with two solid thuds like sledgehammers. Cole kept the rifle trained on him, ready to start blasting if he even hinted at not following the commands.

"You okay, Gale?" Ethan asked.

"Been better, but I'm okay. Can't say that for the girls."

"I know. I'm sorry. We tried to get here as fast as we could. I was afraid we would have been too late to help at all."

"How'd you know to come?"

Ethan sighed. "I bugged your place while you were making

the coffee earlier. And before I left, I put a tracker outside that let us know if anything was snooping around out there. I didn't want to leave you out here..."

"It's fine," said Gale. "I'm glad you did."

Cole was thankful he'd done it too. When Ethan first admitted to leaving the tap at Gale's, he'd thought his friend had been wasting his time and some good equipment. Now he realized Ethan might be the only one who knew what they were truly up against. He'd *known* the bastard would come here. They should have been here waiting for him, as Cole suggested, but just like Ethan had told him, if they'd done that, the killer would have struck at the cabin instead.

This had been a surprise to the killer. Finally, the good guys were one step ahead.

Ethan shrugged. "A lot of good it did. Those girls..."

"It saved *my* ass, so I'm grateful."

Ethan nodded. Lowering his rifle, he looked at Cole. "You got him?"

Cole nodded. "If he tries anything stupid, I'll blow off his kneecap." A big part of Cole wanted to shoot and watch pieces of the bastard explode. But that would put an end to what he and Ethan planned to do next. This part of the plan was devised in secret without the others' knowledge. Now that they'd made it this far, Cole wondered if Ethan would still want to carry it out.

Ethan slung his rifle over his shoulder, using the attached strap. Then he walked over to the sack they'd left by the door and dug out the manacles. They looked even bigger and sturdier in Ethan's hands than they had in his own when he'd packed them this morning.

"What are you doing?" asked Gale.

"Making sure he can't use his arms. Cole here made these."

Cole knew that Ethan was in this as much as he was now. His friend was not turning back, either. He nodded without taking his eyes away from the maniac. "Yep. Steel clamps and chains. I wanted to make a pair of cuffs that even God couldn't break."

"Shouldn't you be calling the police...?" Gale moaned. "And an ambulance."

Ethan crouched behind the maniac. "Give me your arms. Slowly."

The maniac offered no assistance, nor did he resist when Ethan pulled his arms behind his back. Ethan was out of sight behind the killer, but Cole could hear the chains rattling and clanking. There was a clack, then another. Both cuffs had been locked.

"Now his ankles," said Cole.

"I still think we can do that in the truck."

"Not taking any chances."

Ethan nodded. "Right." He walked back to the sack, reached in, and removed the other steel pair. They looked like robotic crab claws. Crude handiwork, Cole knew, but he'd built them piece by piece. He was proud of what he'd constructed.

Ethan crouched behind the man again, snapping them on his ankles. "And now..." Standing, he pointed a gun at the maniac's back.

"What are you doing?" said Gale in a voice nearing panic.

"Putting him out."

"Wait!"

Ethan pulled the trigger. Instead of a loud blast that Gale had probably been expecting, the gun made a hissing spit sound. Gale still let out a squeal, though the gun hadn't made a sound louder than a sneeze.

The dart stabbed into the man's bulging shoulder. He turned his head to look at the tranquilizer's fuzzy tip jutting from his dark shirt. He turned his head even more to look back at Ethan. His breathing started to increase as a palpable rage began to flow through him.

"What the hell, Ethan?" said Gale. "What are you doing?"

"One should have done it," said Ethan. He looked up at Cole. "He's not fazed."

"Do it again."

"It might kill him."

The maniac began to strain, arms flexing through the shirt. Cole could see the shapes of natural muscle undulating underneath the soiled fabric.

"Shit," he muttered. "Do it, now. He's not messing around."

Ethan fired another dart without argument. It smacked into the killer's neck, quivering as the juice was injected. The maniac pulled at the manacles a few more times with a surprising force that shouldn't have been there at all. But as the seconds ticked by, his struggles became less and less intense. He gave the chains one more yank before pitching forward. He slammed the floor hard enough to rattle the frames hanging on the walls.

"How many more darts do we have?" Cole asked.

"Two."

Nodding, Cole said, "Might want to have them ready. One should have been enough to put him down for the night within seconds."

"Right."

Gale staggered over, slightly bent over with a hand to her stomach. It was slicked in red. "Gentleman, this has been fun. I understand all the precautions you're taking and, believe me, am thankful for them all. But I need a hospital, and we need cops, pronto. Those girls there probably have families..."

"We have a nurse back at the cabin," said Ethan. "Her name is Ramona. She'll take care of you."

"She won't like it," said Cole. "None of them will."

"She won't have much of a choice. I'll help Gale into the Blazer, then I'll be back to help you carry this son of a bitch out there."

"Sounds good."

"Ethan," said Gale. "What the hell are you doing? I need medical attention."

"And you'll get it. At my cabin. We're not calling the police. Not yet. We're not finished with him."

"You can't do this," she said. "I get what you want to do, and I understand it. But you can't. I..."

"You should've left when I told you to," said Ethan. "I wasn't joking around about what I said. I said if you stick around, you'll become a part of it. So now you are. Had you been gone, then he wouldn't have come here. *They* wouldn't have come here." He pointed at the dead girls on the floor.

Gale's shoulders slumped as the guilt crashed down on her. It had been a cold thing to say, Cole knew, but he also didn't care. She had been warned, more than once.

And two more people were dead.

Though it looked as if Gale wanted to say more, she didn't. She lowered her head. Her graying hair fell over her face. She looked defeated and weak. Her wound had a lot to do with that but not all of it.

"Let's go," said Ethan. He held out his arm. When Gale reached him, he let her lean against him as he escorted her outside.

Cole looked down at the maniac. Seeing him curled up on the floor made Cole realize he really was a big monster. Cole had never seen such a tall person in real life. Sure, he'd seen them in movies and on basketball teams, but this guy was like Goliath from the Bible—large and nasty. He reeked of death and rot.

It felt like Ethan was gone for hours before he returned, when really, he'd only been away for a couple minutes. Cole felt as if any moment the killer would leap up with a surprise vitality that was supernatural, a strength granted to him from Hell.

He didn't.

Though it wasn't easy work, they were able to carry the heavy man to the Blazer and get him loaded up. Ethan waited with him while Cole went back into the cabin and made sure they had everything. He couldn't shut the door because there no longer was one. When he returned to the Blazer, Ethan climbed into the back with the killer, keeping the rifle close and the tranquilizer gun pointed at him.

Cole glanced up at Gale in the front. She sat leaning against the door, her head resting on the window. He knew she didn't like this. He also knew that he shouldn't like it, either. When Ethan first pitched this part of the plan to him over beers one night, he should have told Ethan he was crazy. Instead, he let the idea percolate in his head while he drank. The more it lingered in there, the more he began to love the idea. A year ago, Cole would have never agreed to it. But there was a darkness that had started to spread through him, blotting out everything that seemed to possess even a shred of sensible thinking after he buried his only child. And it was this fucker who'd put her in the ground and caused the change that had grown in Cole.

Now, it was his turn to return the favor. His turn to inflict pain and torment.

And just like Ethan said—they didn't have to get to that point quickly.

"*Cole! Come in.*"

Cole jumped, nearly yelping. "Shit!" He took a deep breath and held it in a moment.

Gale sat up, looking around. "The hell was that?"

The radio crackled and Bill's voice came through again, more urgent this time.

Even in the dark, Cole saw the worry in Ethan's eyes as he looked at him.

"What do you think he wants?" Cole asked.

"I unhooked the tap before we left. I know he couldn't have heard anything..."

"Answer me now, damn it!" Bill sounded on the verge of shouting.

Cole had never heard his friend like that, even when they were at the hospital. Bill was always the calm one. Hearing the hysteria in his tone made Cole uneasy. He hurried to the front as Ethan pulled the gate down and shut it.

Climbing in, Cole grabbed the radio from between the sweats. He thumbed the button down. "I'm here, Bill. What's wrong?"

"Been radioing Team B since you two left. Nobody's responding."

Cole felt a cold tingle slither through his chest. "Maybe they just..."

"I even used the SOS button. They should have responded then. We all agreed that if that button is activated, immediate response is required. I think something's happened."

"We don't know that for sure," said Cole, feeling stupid for it. He already knew. Soon as Bill had told him he hadn't been able to reach them, he had no doubts the others had already been killed.

"Come on, Cole," said Bill. "You know as well as—"

"We'll look into it," said Cole.

There was a pause. "You'll...what? What the hell does that mean?"

"It means we'll look into it. We're heading back now."

"Did you get there in time? I tried to listen, but—"

"Everything is secure," said Cole. "Don't do anything until we get back."

Another pause. "You're not making any sense, Cole."

"We'll explain everything when we get back. We'll be there soon."

"I'll alert the police and have them meet us all here."

"Don't you do that. Do nothing, and I mean *nothing*, until we get there. Everybody better be hanging out in the living room when we walk in the door."

Before Bill could respond, Cole dropped the radio. Bill's voice continued, but Cole couldn't understand what he was saying.

"I guess we're going to ride by the second location," said Cole.

"No. They're dead. It's too late for them."

"You don't know they're all dead," said Gale. "You could be leaving injured people out there to die."

Cole turned in his seat, gazing back into the darkness of the Blazer. He saw a subtle black shifting against the darker black behind it. "She knows about the others. I told her the plan earlier."

Cole nodded. "Gotcha. We should go out there..."

"No," said Ethan. "I hate it just as much as you do. But it's too late for them. When we get back to the cabin, we'll figure out who's going to go check on the others. I doubt everybody will be so anxious to take part in what we plan to do. That can be where they go while we do what we do."

It almost scared Cole how easily this was all coming to his friend. He'd never known Ethan to be so...cruel. But he supposed the last year hadn't only changed himself. Ethan had been affected nearly as much, if not more, than Cole.

He didn't like the idea any better than he assumed Ethan did. But it was all they had right now. Cole cranked the Blazer and pulled away, leaving Gale's cabin behind them.

14.

Liz sat in the chair, using the nail of her thumb to pick at her other fingernails. Leaning forward, she couldn't sit still. Her legs bounced, knees going up and down as she watched Bill continue to shout at a tiny microphone attached to his laptop.

"Just stop," said Tina. "Nobody's answering."

"I'm not giving up on them," said Bill. He pointed at the laptop screen. "See? Shows they're right there. They're in trouble." Squeezing the button on the mouthpiece, he said, "Answer me. This is Bill. Come in. Somebody. *Any*body!"

Ramona entered the living room carrying two glasses of wine. She handed one to Tina, then joined her on the couch. "Bill," she said. "They're not answering. And I don't like that they aren't. The more you try to reach them, and they still don't answer, it makes me very nervous and very sick to my stomach."

Bill's head sagged. He'd opened the laptop in front of him and then hooked up other equipment to it. The box he'd connected last, the SOS button as he'd called it, still flashed from when he'd pushed it. He'd said that it would stop when somebody on the other end pushed it to show the SOS call was received.

It blinked a bit longer before Bill shut it off. He leaned back in the chair, sighed. His eyes looked watery.

Tina emptied her wine glass in two gulps. She put it on the coffee table, then rubbed her eyes. "I didn't like that."

Bill sighed again. "There's no point letting it flash if they're not responding."

"Not that. Well, not just that. Did you hear how Cole sounded?"

"I did," said Ramona. "Very short."

In a quiet voice, Tina said, "Didn't sound like himself."

Liz wanted to add that Ethan hadn't been *acting* like himself since he got back from Gale's. He'd eaten in silence, constantly checking his phone. A few times, he and Cole wandered off, dragging Bill with them. She'd spot them away from the everyone else, talking in hushed voices. It hadn't sat right with her.

"What's with you and Cole?" she'd asked Ethan when they were in the kitchen together. They'd worked out a system on dishes. Each night would be somebody else's turn. They'd taken the first night. There hadn't been much to wash, since they'd only boiled some hot dogs and used paper plates and plastic cups.

Ethan, drying a pot with a towel, said, "What do you mean?" He put it on the drying rack, waiting on Liz to hand him another dish.

She finished rinsing the chili bowl before passing it over. "Your little secret meetings. Like it's a club and only the boys are the members. I've been waiting on you guys to put up signs that say no girls are allowed."

Ethan smiled, though she could tell he didn't find her comment amusing. "We're just going over things. Making sure we have everything the way it needs to be tonight."

"You're not telling me something," she said.

Ethan put the dry plate next to the last one. The look on his face showed she had been right. He was keeping something from her.

"What is it?" she said. "You told me you trusted me."

"I do."

"Not enough to tell me everything, apparently."

That was when he admitted to bugging Gale's house. He'd set up a sensor outside when he left that would alert him whenever somebody approached her cabin. Then he could tune in to the tap he'd left under her couch.

After he finished telling her all he'd done, Liz didn't feel any better. Something was still being purposely left out. Something he was keeping to himself. She assumed Cole was the only person who knew whatever it was that Ethan was holding in.

When the alarm on Ethan's phone had gone off again after

the girls reached Gale's cabin, he'd known it was the killer. He and Cole had left within seconds, telling everyone else to stay behind.

It was Bill's idea to reach out to the other team. She felt bad now for trying to talk him out of it from the fear that Ethan and Cole might be angry about it.

As it turned out, Bill had been right to do so. Now they all knew.

"Do you think the others are okay?" Ramona asked. It didn't seem to be directed at any particular person, just a question to the room.

It was a question that went unanswered, though everybody probably already knew the answer to it.

Bill grabbed the handgun he'd brought along and set it in his lap. Liz hadn't seen it up close, but from where she sat, it looked like a .22. Nothing powerful, but if fired enough at close range it could do some real damage. It seemed like the kind of gun that Bill would have.

"Anybody want something to drink?" asked Tina, standing. "I'm getting a refill."

"I'll take a beer," said Liz.

"Right back," said Tina.

"I'll join you," said Liz, standing. "I feel like if I don't move around, I'm going to lose my mind."

"I know the feeling."

They left Bill and Ramona in the living room and headed into the kitchen. Ramona hadn't shut off the light when she left a few minutes earlier. The contrast from how clean the kitchen was now compared to what it had looked like this morning still shocked her. It didn't even smell like a room that had been abandoned for a year.

Tina opened the fridge, first grabbing the wine bottle. She held it to the light and shook it. Liz saw how it was nearly empty. Frowning, Tina set it on the island. Then she grabbed a full bottle from the fridge and placed it beside the other. "What beer?"

"Huh?"

Tina smiled. "What beer do you want?"

"Oh." Liz shook her head. "Duh." She and Tina laughed. It felt good, yet odd to be laughing right now. "Um, I'll take a Coors."

Tina grabbed a can of Coors Light and passed it over to Liz, who used her index finger to pop the tab. Before Tina had finished pouring her glass, Liz had chugged half the can. She let out a quiet belch, sighed, and guzzled the rest.

She crushed the can.

Tina, pausing with the glass at her mouth, looked at her from over the rim. "Thirsty?"

"Yep. And stressed." She tossed the empty into the trash and took another can from the fridge. She opened it. This time, she didn't drink as fast.

"What's on your mind?" asked Tina. "Besides the obvious."

"I feel like this will be our last normal moment before our lives go to shit."

Tina's nose wrinkled. "What do you mean?"

Before she could answer, the low grumble of an engine drifted into the kitchen.

The boys were back.

15.

Liz felt her stomach drop the moment she saw Cole help Gale out of the Blazer. "What the hell?" she muttered. Staring out the living room window, she stood off to the side, blocked by the curtain.

"What is it?" said Bill.

"Cole's got Gale with him."

"What?" Bill marched across the room, his gun pointed at the floor, and flung the front door open. Standing in the doorway, his face scrunched up as he stared into the darkness. "What's going on?" It sounded as if he was asking himself more than anyone else.

"Does Cole look okay?" Tina asked from somewhere behind them.

"Give them some light," said Liz.

"Right." He reached over and flipped the switch. Light burst onto the porch. "She looks hurt."

Liz realized she looked more than "hurt." She looked seriously injured. Cole assisted her, holding her up because the poor woman could barely walk. Bill stepped aside so they could enter.

"Where's Ethan?" Liz asked.

"Waiting on me to get back out there," said Cole.

"Why? Is he okay?"

"He's fine."

Liz felt a hint of relief until she looked at Gale. Doubled over, a hand pressed to her bloody stomach, the older woman's skin was the same shade as wet cement. Her cheeks looked sunken, and her eyes had a hollow texture to them.

Bill watched them walk by. His mouth hung open, eyes

blinking. His lips trembled a few times before he was finally able to say, "What the hell is this?"

"Get Ramona to bandage her up."

Ramona stood against the wall, her arms crossed and hands up to her mouth. She shook her head. "I..."

Cole spotted her. "Now, Ramona! There's a medical kit in my bag over there." He gestured with his chin to the left.

Liz turned around and saw the tote bag in the corner. "I'll get it."

While she fetched the med kit, Cole guided Gale to the couch and helped her sit. Gale let out a groan that turned to a cough.

"She needs a doctor," said Tina. She stood in the doorway that led to the kitchen. "Cole. She's hurt pretty bad. She..."

"Ramona will have to do," he said, cutting her off.

Tina looked as if she wanted to say more but did not. Shaking her head, she gnawed on her bottom lip.

Liz carried the red tin over to Cole. He looked down at it, then back at her. "Not me. Ramona."

She looked over and saw Ramona hadn't moved from where she stood by the wall.

"Ramona!" Cole yelled, making everyone in the room flinch.

"Damn it, Cole," said Tina. "Scared the shit out of me!"

Cole closed his eyes. He looked as if he'd just swallowed something with spikes on it.

"Don't yell at her like that," said Bill, stepping forward. "That's my wife, and I'm not going to allow you to speak to her that way."

"Not now," said Cole.

"Don't talk to me like that, either."

Liz had never seen Bill stand up for himself or anybody like he just did. She could tell by the way he stood with his arms tense and straight by his sides and his trembling jaw that he was nervous to be doing so.

It was probably the gun that gave him the courage he normally lacked.

Cole let out a long breath through his nostrils. He opened his eyes. "Fine. *Sorry*. Go grab a chair from the kitchen."

"What?"

"You heard me."

"I did," said Bill. "But why?"

"No time to explain. Do it."

Cole started for the door.

"Cole?" said Tina.

He paused without looking back.

"What have you done?" she asked.

He let out a sigh. His shoulders slumped but only for a moment. Raising his head, he marched out of the cabin.

"What the hell is this about?" said Bill. "What the hell...?" He turned to Tina as if she might have the answers. Her eyes were spilling tears as she shook her head. "Tina? What's he up to?"

"I don't know!" Her fingers twisted together as she wrung her hands. "I don't know what he's doing!"

"Knock it off!" Liz shouted. "Knock off this yelling at each other bullshit." She turned around. "Ramona. Get over here and help her. She needs your expertise."

Ramona looked as if she might throw herself through a window to get away from here.

"Oh, the hell with it," said Liz. Dropping to her knees in front of Gale, she set the tin on the couch beside her. She opened it. Inside, it was stuffed full of medical supplies. She found a package of gloves and tore it open. They felt a little tight as she pulled them on, but she figured they would be fine.

"You doing okay up there?" asked Liz.

Gale made a wheezy sound. "Dandy."

"What happened?"

"That bastard showed up, just like Ethan said...he would." She took a deep breath. "Killed those girls. Damn near got me."

"Shit," said Liz. "The goth girls?"

Gale nodded. "Got them both."

Liz's throat tightened. *Damn it.* Those girls should have never come here. Now they were dead before their time, just like all the other kids that died out here.

"Ethan wouldn't let me call for help," said Gale. "I tried to get him to call the police, or an ambulance. *Somebody.* He wouldn't do it. Made me come here instead."

"He what?" Liz looked up at her, shook her hair out of her face. "The police aren't coming?"

"No," said Ethan, behind her.

Liz looked over her shoulder. She saw Ethan and Cole standing just inside the doorway. They were on either side of a large man stretched out between them. Ethan held the stranger under the arms while Cole had his ankles. Their prisoner's wrists and feet had been cuffed with some type of contraption that looked as if it had been constructed for a bear. His masked head was canted to the side, bobbing as they carried him into the living room.

You've got to be kidding me.

"I told you to get a damn chair!" Cole's voice was like thunder in the small room.

"Cole," cried Tina. "Stop..."

Cole didn't acknowledge her. Instead, he stared at Bill. The anger caused his face to flush.

Without argument, Bill ran toward the kitchen. Tina barely moved out of his way before he plowed through her. She stood off to the side, looking around in shock. Tears had turned her face shiny, causing dark lines to spill down from her mascara. Liz wished she could go over there and hug her. She wished Cole would at least say something to help ease the hurt and betrayal she was probably feeling. She also wished Ethan would say something to her. Anything at all that might make her understand why he was carrying a killer into his cabin.

Banging sounds emanated from the kitchen before Bill emerged with a chair in front of him. Holding it up, he ran into the living room.

"Where?" he said.

"In front of the fireplace," said Ethan. "Make sure it's facing outward."

"Okay," said Bill. He walked over and placed it right where Ethan had instructed. When it was in place, he stepped back.

"Oh," said Gale. "If you haven't noticed, they brought the bastard with us."

Liz found a small bottle of antiseptic rinse. She twisted the cap open, then reached up and tore the gash in Gale's shirt wider. There was a slit above her naval that looked as if it had been added there for credit cards.

A hand grabbed Liz's shoulder. Though it had been a soft, gentle grip, Liz still let out a small yelp.

"Sorry," said Ramona.

Huffing, Liz nodded. "Fine."

"Let me take it from here."

Another nod, then Liz stood up. Her knees felt sore and tight from being crouched for so long. She was thankful that Ramona decided to finally take over. Liz knew a little bit about first aid, but she wasn't a nurse. That was Ramona's area.

Liz looked over and saw Bill was pointing his handgun at the unconscious nightmare while Ethan held him up by the shoulders so he wouldn't slide out of the chair. Cole was nowhere in sight. Before she could ask where he'd gone, she heard stomping coming from the open front door. She didn't like how it had been left open all this time. Where the light spilled onto the yard was intercepted by a trembling wall of fog.

Cole stepped out of it, carrying another tote bag. This one jangled with his movements. As soon as he was inside, Liz hurried across the floor and swung the door shut. She locked it, feeling a little better with the additional security features this new door offered.

"He still out?" Cole asked.

"Seems to be," said Ethan. He looked up at Bill. "Remember, if he so much as twitches, fire a dart into him."

Bill nodded.

Liz realized that wasn't Bill's gun. It was too blocky. Plus, the barrel was too skinny. From the way Ethan was talking, she assumed it was some type of tranquilizer gun. "Ethan, now can you tell me what's going on?"

Ignoring her, he turned to Cole. "Start back here."

Cole reached into the sack. When his hand lifted out, a length of chain came with it. The rattling links continued to grow until finally the other end came free and swung back and forth. These chains looked like something that might be used to tow large machinery.

Watching them work at connecting the chain to the cuffs

on the killer's wrists and ankles, what they were up to became clearer. "No." Her voice came out as a throaty whisper. No way they could have heard it above the harsh clamors of the chains. They ran the length up his back, looping it once before snapping the wrist and ankle locks to it. If the large man tried to stand up, he would turn into a human wheel and drop to the floor.

"No," she said, louder this time.

Ethan stood up from behind the man. His face was slick with sweat, his hair plastered flat. "I know what you're going to say."

"Do you?"

Ethan nodded. "Same thing Gale said."

Liz glanced over at Gale. Ramona had cleaned the wound and was placing a compress against it. Then she faced Ethan again.

Ethan stepped out from behind the chair. "You're going to say we need to call the police."

"We do."

"Why?"

"To report this. To report what happened to those girls and to Gale. To report the others...the kids..."

"This mother fucker," said Cole, stepping forward. He had a cigar in his hand. His rifle hung behind him from a strap over his shoulder. "He killed my daughter. Killed Ethan's daughter. Killed Ramona's son. He doesn't get to get off that easy."

"Guys," said Bill. "Adam was my son, too. Just because..."

"Right," said Cole. "Right. Sorry." He used a Zippo to light the cigar. "That was horrible of me to exclude you like that."

Bill held up his hand to stop him. "Drop it. So what's the deal with this?" He pointed at the man chained to the chair. He turned and looked at Liz as if she might know.

Liz shrugged.

Ethan returned to the room. She hadn't even noticed he'd left. He carried a hammer, the wooden handle in his hand, the head swaying by his leg.

"Try the smelling salt," he said to Cole.

Nodding, Cole dug out a small packet from his pocket.

Cigar clamped between his teeth, he ripped it open and put it in front of the mask where a nose was probably hidden behind it. He waved it from side to side.

Nothing happened.

"Hmm," said Cole. He squinted behind the smoke. "I wonder if I should've pulled off his mask first."

"Not yet," said Ethan. "He can get air through it. He'd die of suffocation if he couldn't."

Cole shook the packet now, smacking the mask. It made soft tapping sounds against the front of it. Shrugging, he tossed the packet aside. "Nothing."

Ethan sighed. "Guess he's snoozing too hard from the tranqs."

"Damn it," said Liz. "Ethan! Look at me!"

Ethan turned, eyes blinking. He held up his free hand, patting the air. "Calm down, Liz."

"Calm down! You're telling me to calm down? You don't get to tell me that. Not after all this."

"All what?" he said. The serious, confused tone of his voice angered her even more.

"*This!*" She waved a hand around the room, pointing at Gale, then the unconscious maniac. "So your big plan is a little payback torture? Is that it? Going to torture him some to make you feel better? That's what you boys have been planning?"

Ethan glanced at Cole, then back at her.

"I said we should just kill him," said Cole. "Bury him out in the woods and be done with it."

"Cole," said Tina. She put a hand to her mouth. "Cole..."

He shrugged.

"So now it's torture?" said Liz. "You know, you'll go to jail for this. Right? Doesn't matter what he did anymore. Soon as you hurt him one time, you become an assailant. You will be arrested. It's not self-defense when he's chained to a damn chair!"

"He took our babies," said Ethan. "He should pay."

"I agree," said Liz. "I do. Let him *pay* in prison for the rest of his life. You've got him. Just leave him there, call the police. Let them handle it from here."

"Not taking the chance," said Ethan.

Cole shook his head. "Nope. This is how we wrap it up for us. Torture his ass until he dies. Here. Not in a cell somewhere at old age, getting fed three meals, a weight room, library, cable, and internet. He'll have fanboys and girls flocking to him. You've seen how they come out here. This place is all over the internet. He'll be like a god to them. No. It stops now."

His argument made so much sense to Liz that she felt as if she were arguing with herself as much as him. "And what about all those other parents whose children he took? Huh? What about George and Wilma and Martin and Gina? All the others? You'll rob them of their closure. You kill him and bury him in the woods, the murders will just stop. Nobody will know what happened to him. Nobody will know the…"

She saw the way Ethan and Cole were staring at each other. They looked like two villains in a movie when the hero had just put a damper in their plan, only to learn that the villain had been expecting it.

Bill moaned. He put his hand to his eyes, using his thumb and forefinger to rub his temples. "That's why you told me to bring the camera. Isn't it?" He lowered his hand. "You're going to film it for them. A damn snuff movie."

Ethan nodded. "It's only fair. We'll give them the option. They can watch if they want. If not, that's okay too."

"Jesus Christ," said Liz. "Ethan…? I…" She didn't know what to say. Not only did he sound like a stranger to her, he suddenly looked like one.

"That's right," said Cole. "Set it up."

"I already did. Just needs to go on the tripod."

"Get it."

Bill opened his mouth to say something, but the look Cole flashed at him scared away any protest he might have had. Without speaking, he turned and headed out of the room.

Liz looked around for any kind of support. She saw Ramona taking her time with Gale to avoid getting involved. Gale's eyes were closed, mouth in a tight line. And Tina was useless at this point. She stood off by herself, hugging her waist and sobbing quietly.

Liz was alone in this. "Ethan. Cole. Just think about it for *one* second."

"We have," said Ethan. "We've been thinking about it for a whole year."

"No. *Really* think about it. Team B? Remember them? Martin, Gina, George, and Wilma?" She counted the names on her fingers. "Robbie. Trish."

Though Ethan didn't say anything, she could see the grimness in his eyes.

"Bill hasn't been able to reach them. If they're…" Pausing, she decided to reshape what she was about to say. "If something's happened to them, something…bad…" She let out a breath that rattled her cheeks. "Do you get what I'm trying to say?"

She hoped he did because she wasn't so sure she knew how to say it.

Cole puffed on his cigar, tilting his head. Ethan wouldn't make eye contact with her. She figured they both understood and just weren't admitting it.

"I get what you're saying." Bill's voice. He entered the room, carrying a large video camera by the attached handle. An extended tripod was in the other. He set the tall stand on the floor, spreading the legs. "If they're hurt in any way, and we're here torturing the guy that did it, then how's that going to look? Wouldn't it be odd that the killer would only go after them and not us?"

"And what if one of them needs medical attention like Gale? What if somebody's hurt and can't tell us?"

"We don't know anything's happened to them at all."

That voice had surprised everyone in the room. All heads turned toward Tina, who no longer stood consoling herself by the wall. She had grabbed a tissue and was using it to wipe her eyes. Her eyeliner and mascara were smeared like fingerpaint, making the vibrant blue shade of her eyes look almost supernatural.

And wicked.

"They're just not answering the call," said Tina. "Doesn't mean they're hurt. Could be anything. Faulty equipment or something. Maybe you bought cheap stuff."

"I never buy cheap stuff," said Bill.

Tina shrugged.

Bill sighed. "The SOS button..."

"How do we know it even works?" she said. "You guys were so adamant about not testing it out of fear of your little ruse being exposed to...to him." She pointed at the chained killer.

"What are you saying, babe?" Cole asked, eyes narrowed behind a plume of cigar smoke.

"I'm saying somebody can go check on them. Since the killer's here, whoever goes will be fine."

"And that somebody should be Liz," said Ramona, standing up. She turned around, removing her gloves. "She's the only one who'll have a problem with this. Well, I'd say we send Gale also, but I don't think she's up to moving around just yet."

Liz realized she hadn't taken off her own gloves. She peeled them off as if they were a layer of skin. Sweat had soaked the inside of the latex, leaving her fingers slippery. She wiped them on her shirt. "So you two are on board with this?"

Tina and Ramona shared a quick glance before looking at Gale. It was Ramona that said, "He killed our kids. When would we ever get a chance like this? You can go out to the campsite and skip all this since you're so against it."

Liz felt a sneer forming on her face. "I'm not going anywhere."

Ramona gave her a pitiful look as if she'd accidentally peed on the floor. "Oh, Liz. You won't like what you're going to see."

"What *will* I see?" She looked at Ethan. "Huh?"

Ethan looked down at the hammer. "If you stay, you'll see what I do to him. And if you see that, I just hope you won't hold it against me."

Bill attached the camera to the tripod. "You all sound like you've lost your minds."

"Watch it," said Cole.

"No, I will not. We came here to catch this son of a bitch. Mission accomplished. We can turn him over and be done with it. Healing, true healing, can finally begin."

"My healing will begin when this shithead is begging me to stop," said Ramona. "I bet he made sure Adam begged for his life. Probably makes them all beg."

"We don't know that," said Bill.

Ramona continued as if he hadn't spoken. "And if that makes you hate me, Bill, if it changes how you look at me, then so be it. I want to hurt him. Plain and simple. I want to hurt him, a lot. Then I want him to die. I won't ask for you to forgive me because I really don't care if you do or if you don't."

Bill looked as if her words had manifested into a physical being and walked across the room to slap him.

Tina looked at Cole and Ethan. "You guys had planned it this way from the start, hadn't you?"

Ethan shook his head. "Not the start."

"But for a little while," said Cole.

"Oh," said Liz. "You hear that, Tina? They put this foolproof plan together that quickly. Strap him down and torture him. Kill him. Bury him. And now your friends are probably dead. You get that, right? They are probably out in the woods, dead. So are those kids. Two more kids that are dead because of you. *You.*"

"They didn't have to come!" Ethan shouted. He slammed the hammer against the wall, cracking the wood paneling.

Liz flinched. She took a step back.

"Nobody forced them to come. I pitched this idea and explained the risk. Did I not?" He looked around. Everyone but Bill was quick to agree with him. He faced Liz again. "You heard me yourself. I laid it all out. All of it. And..."

Liz threw the soiled gloves. She hadn't expected them to go very far but, to her surprise, they soared across the room. One bounced off his chest while the other smacked the front of his face. "Asshole," she said. "You knew this would happen. And you don't care."

"Liz...?" He said, reaching out to her, though he was too far away to touch her. For a moment, she saw something like regret flash across his face.

Liz stomped to the front door, keeping her head up and not looking back. She had trouble with the locks, which ruined her dramatic exit. When she finally had them turned back, she yanked the door open.

For a moment, she expected the maniac to be standing on the

other side ready to swing at her with a large, blunt instrument.

Nobody was there. Only bugs that flittered around the light and a swirling mass of fog. She marched outside, slamming the door behind her.

Tears filled her eyes, making her vision blurry. She used her arm to wipe them away.

Asshole. I can't believe him!

That wasn't the Ethan she'd grown to know this past year. Something had changed in him, even more so than when he buried Emily. She'd expected that personality change, the grief to alter him in a way that would take time to heal from. But what he was displaying right now was something completely different.

There was anger, sure. But more than that, he was a man consumed by rage.

How long had he fantasized about this? How long? He probably spent good blocks of time each day just dreaming about inflicting tremendous pain on that maniac. That was normal, she supposed. If she were in his situation, daydreams like that might even help her feel better at times. But acting them out? Isn't that what serial killers do? Fantasize until the need to do it for real becomes unbearable?

She waited on the porch a few more minutes, expecting Ethan to come out any moment to talk to her. She wanted him to, prayed he would, because there was no way she was going back in there. She wanted no part of what they were about to do. She'd sleep in the damn car if she had to.

She doubted it would come to that, though. Ethan would come talk to her. He'd apologize. She was certain of it.

She could hear voices inside but had no idea what was being said. She thought she recognized Bill's voice as being the loudest. At least he'd somewhat taken her side. Showed that he slightly understood where she was coming from.

Bad thing was, she appreciated why they felt compelled to do it. A part of her even agreed that it was the right thing to do. But the rational part of her, the place where her conscience dwelled, reminded her how bad of an idea it was.

How wrong it is.

The worst part had been seeing Ethan look at her with such anger. That had hurt her more than anything. He'd never acted that way around her before. This was all new to her. She'd never seen him hit anything, so when he'd bashed the wall with the hammer, she'd wanted to cry.

The doorknob turned, snapping Liz out of her quarrelling thoughts. Liz stepped back as the door opened, ready to see Ethan. She felt a nervous flutter in her stomach as she prepared herself to talk to him. Should she speak first, or wait for him to start talking?

The uncertain feelings fizzled out when she saw Bill. He stepped outside, pulling the door shut behind him. She saw he had two flashlights in his hand and a backpack over his shoulders.

She stared at him. "What the hell, Bill?"

"Looks like it's the two of us." He held out a flashlight. "We're supposed to radio back to them when we get there."

Liz snatched the proffered light from his hand. "This is ridiculous."

He held up a set of keys. "Ethan said to take the Jeep."

"Oh, that's so thoughtful of him." She grabbed the keys. "I can't believe this."

Bill lifted a shoulder. "Nothing we can do about it." He walked down the steps. "Beats being here."

Liz watched him for a moment. "There's plenty we can do."

He let out a single, "Ha." He didn't laugh, just said it to show he didn't find her comment to be amusing.

Liz hurried to catch up to him. "We can just call the police ourselves. Get them out here. I have my phone."

"You'd do that to Ethan?"

"What? What do you mean by that?"

"Because I wouldn't do that to Ramona. We call the police, they'll come here and arrest them. Sure, they might understand their reasons for doing what they did but..." He shook his head.

Liz wasn't sure what the authorities would do. She did know that she didn't want to risk it. Maybe not yet.

You're going to let them do...whatever to that guy in there?

He was a murdering psychopath. He was probably getting off easy.

Still, Liz didn't like how it made her feel knowing Ethan was going to be inflicting pain on someone, even if he had killed a bunch of people. Maybe they would come to their senses before crossing that line.

And maybe a meteor will crash in front of me and spew liquid gold everywhere.

She cleared her throat. "Do you know where to go?"

"Yeah. I think so." A screen lit up, painting him in bright light. Squinting, he tapped the screen and the glare dimmed. "I'll just let this lead our way."

"I have a feeling," she said. Then she stopped. She didn't know how to finish that statement. It wasn't anything she'd planned to say, but now that she had, she couldn't stop the dread from coming on.

"A feeling about what?"

"Nothing. Let's just get this over with."

Bill took a deep breath. "I think I know the feeling you're talking about. My stomach feels like it's being pulled from my ass."

Liz almost laughed. Then she realized he was exactly right in his crude description. "You're putting it mildly."

Together, they headed for the Jeep.

16.

"I think he's faking it," said Cole. "Bastard's just playing possum."

Ethan looked over his shoulder. His friend stood back, puffing on the cigar. He hated the way the damn things smelled, but he decided to ignore it for Cole's sake. He probably needed the cigar for his nerves. Hell, he could go for something right now himself. Anything to ease the tension he felt twisting his insides.

He couldn't believe how he'd spoken to Liz. He regretted what he'd said and done, but there had been no other way. He didn't want her here for this part, didn't want her to see what he was willing to do. And the only way he knew to get her away was by being mean.

I was cruel. Worse than mean.

Hopefully she'd understand later. He somehow doubted it, though.

"Do something," said Tina.

Ethan wished she would clean the makeup off her eyes. It made her look as if she'd just come from the nuthouse.

"Like what?" said Cole.

"Anything," said Tina.

"I don't want to see this," said Gale in a groggy voice. "I don't want to be an...accessory."

"Jeez..." Tina rolled her eyes.

"Take her upstairs," said Cole.

Ramona sighed. "I'm not. I got her the water."

"You and Tina both do it," said Ethan. "She can rest in my room. I'm not going to be using it any time soon."

"No," said Tina. "We're not here to run your little errands.

You're not going to keep us away from this. I will..."

"Just do it, huh?" said Cole. "Okay? Help her up there and then come back. Nobody's asking you stay up there all night. It'll go quicker if you both are doing it, anyway."

"How do we know she's even going to keep quiet about all this?" said Ramona. "What if she sneaks away while she's upstairs and calls the police?"

Gale angled her head so she could stare up at the short woman as if she were speaking a language she couldn't understand. "What did you just say?"

"Jesus, Ramona," said Ethan. "She's not a damn prisoner. We'll call the police ourselves when we're done. If we need them."

"I'm just saying," said Ramona. "We don't know what she might do."

Cole rubbed his temple with his finger. Eyes closed, he said, "Just take her upstairs."

Gale looked over at Ethan, her tired eyes staring directly into him. "Ethan? You're not going to hurt me. Are you?"

Ethan shook his head. "Of course not. Nothing like that's even crossed my mind. If I were going to hurt you, why would I make sure you got patched up? Why would I make sure you're safe?"

"Safe?" Snorting, Gale pointed at Ramona. "She's not going to do anything to me. Right?"

"No," said Ethan. He looked at Ramona. "See what you're causing with the bullshit you keep saying?"

Ramona held up her hands. "Sorry for just wondering."

"She's got a point," said Tina.

"Oh, shit," said Ethan. He was getting annoyed with this. Maybe they should have kept the guy at Gale's house. They were already wasting too much time. "Not you, too. Nobody say anything else about Gale. Just help her upstairs so she can rest."

"We'll worry about that later," said Cole. "Help her upstairs."

Tina pointed at Cole. "Are you going to let him talk to me like that?"

Cole looked as if he wanted to bang his head against a wall. "Just get her upstairs, Tina. Damn."

Tina's mouth went slack. "You better watch that tone, buddy." She moved her finger to Ramona, jabbed at the air, then pointed to the stairs. "Move it."

Ramona put an arm behind Gale. Then, moaning the whole way, Gale stood up. She staggered a bit, but Ramona was there to keep her from falling.

Tina came around to the other side and slipped an arm around Gale's waist. "Going to be able to walk?"

"Oh, sure," said Gale. "No problem." The sardonic tone of her voice was easy to decipher through the obvious pain she felt.

Tina looked over her shoulder. "Don't start without us," she said as they made their way to the hall.

Ethan and Cole watched them start up the stairs. Tina stepped behind Ramona and Gale, following them one step below.

"This is already becoming a problem," Cole said when they were out of sight.

"You're telling me."

"Maybe we should just slit his throat or something. Get it over with. I can't handle everyone snapping at each other."

"We agreed that..."

"Do you know how long it would take him to die like that?"

"No. I don't know, Cole. How do *you* know?"

Cole sighed. "Tina is all about that humane slaughtering of animals bullshit. She reads all these articles about the savage nature of slaughterhouses and processed meat. You know, that tree-hugging bullshit. Anyway, she said it can take up to ten minutes, maybe more, for something to die from a slit throat. That would be ten minutes of agony for that bastard."

Ethan only briefly considered the possibility. "No way. That would be like mercy for him. He doesn't deserve that."

"True."

The ceiling groaned from the ladies' footsteps upstairs. They were making their way up the hall to Ethan's room. It shouldn't be much longer before they were back downstairs.

"We should have a system," said Ethan.

"Meaning?"

"A system, you know. How long we go about this? Should we take turns? Or just everyone goes all at once."

"I think a system isn't going to matter much. We can start off that way..." He shrugged. "I doubt it'll last, though. Not with the way Tina and Ramona are acting."

Ethan figured Cole was probably right about that. The wives were treating this like some sort of couples' game that they didn't want to be left out of, though Ramona's husband was missing from the action, as well as Ethan's own partner.

Listen to yourself. Plotting out how you're going to torture somebody.

It did seem odd how relaxed he and Cole were discussing such morbid matters, talking about them as if they were about to embark on a special bonding project or something.

In a way, Ethan realized, they were. What they were about to do would either make them all closer than family or tear them apart for good. The saddest part was, Ethan didn't care which, so long as it meant making this bastard suffer.

The maniac twitched. It was a subtle motion, a slight tick of his finger.

"See that?" asked Ethan.

"I did."

They studied him in silence, looking for any other movements. The only sounds were the faint voices of the ladies and the soft thumps of their moving around upstairs. Ethan could hear his heartbeat in his ears, a steady drum knocking in his head.

The maniac didn't move again.

Ethan's chest began to hurt, and he realized he'd been holding his breath. He let the breath out, slowly.

Footsteps clamored from the stairs. A few seconds later, Tina and Ramona entered the room.

Ethan's stomach quivered with either apprehension or excitement. It was a similar feeling to the first time he'd slinked a girl into his room as a teenager while his parents had been sleeping. There was something good about it, yet everything surrounding the situation was wrong.

Cole looked over at Ethan, nodded. "It's our show now."

Ethan nodded back, then held up the hammer to look at it. He'd purposely chosen this one at the store because it had the longest handle and biggest head of all the available hammers. The claw end was like two large hooks curving behind it. It felt heavy in his hand. The hilt slid against his sweaty fingers, so he gripped it tighter. He took a deep breath.

Am I ready to do this?

He was.

Am I sure?

He looked over at the bound killer, eyes scanning the dirty mask. He saw what looked like old bloodstains on the solid surface. More was on his shirt, turning the dark material darker in certain spots. Then he noticed what looked to be fresher blood on his sleeves, more on his fingers. His blackened fingernails were crusty with crimson smears.

Evidence of what he'd done to Group B, most likely.

He was suddenly very sure.

"Let's get started," he said.

Tina and Ramona began to cheer and clap, their own cheerleaders in this morbid game that was about to begin.

Ethan stepped back, revved his arm so the hammer was high above his head. Then he brought it down.

The blunt end connected with the killer's right kneecap, shattering it upon impact with a sound like exploding porcelain.

The killer snapped awake, howling behind the mask. Didn't matter if he had been faking comatose or not. He was awake now.

And in a lot of pain.

17.

"Up there on the right should be an off-road," said Bill. His face was washed in pale light from his phone.

"We're off-road now," said Liz. She held the steering wheel with both hands. The high beams were on, blasting bright light ahead of them that still didn't seem to penetrate the thick blackness enough for her liking.

"This is *more* off-road."

"Great."

Liz squinted as if it might make the road easier to spot. It must have worked because she saw the decrepit marker to the right—a wood sign with an arrow carved into the center.

Pointing right.

She slowed the Jeep down to a crawl. She didn't see the entrance at first. As they approached, she thought she could make out a narrow gap between the drooping limbs and thick shrubbery pressed tightly against the road.

"Is that it?" she asked.

"Should be."

"Bill, if I drive us off the side of the mountain, I'm going to kick your ass."

"I'll kick my own ass."

Biting her bottom lip, Liz steered the Jeep onto what she hoped was an actual road. The limbs squeaked as they rubbed against the doors. She hoped they weren't scratching the paint. Then she felt bad for worrying about that in a time like this.

I'm sure your friends would understand you're worried about an expense instead of their lives.

Remembering how Ethan had spoken to her earlier, she began to hope the limbs were peeling the paint off in layers. She hoped they wouldn't stop and would tear away the Jeep bit by bit.

"How close will this cow path take us?" she asked.

"Right up to the crossing. The park's website claims there's a parking area. Then we'll go by foot the rest of the way."

"How far will that be?"

"Not far."

Liz was about to ask him to elaborate when she glanced up in the rearview mirror. She glimpsed a patch of light through the trees behind them, beyond the dim red glow of the taillights. She stomped the brakes.

Though she wasn't going fast, the Jeep still jerked to a halt. Bill let out a gasp and tried to catch his phone before it bounced off the dashboard. "Shit," he said through a gasp. His head snapped in her direction. "What the hell was that about?"

Liz continued to stare into the rearview mirror. The engine idled, exhaust and dust combining into a curtain of fog behind the Jeep. "I thought I saw a light."

"What?" Bill turned to look. After a beat, he said, "I don't see anything."

"I don't either. Not now. I swear it was there."

"A car?"

"Bigger. Truck or something."

"Following us?"

"It looked like it." She let out a deep breath. Maybe there hadn't been anything at all. Her nerves and fear and worry could be making her see things that weren't there.

"I think we're okay," said Bill.

"Yeah." She nodded. "Seem to be."

She eased her foot off the brake and let the Jeep roll into motion.

Bill leaned forward, reaching between his legs to the floorboard. He grabbed his phone and turned it over. "You've got to be kidding me."

"What's wrong?"

"Well, when you panicked and the hit the brakes like that, I dropped my phone. And…it's busted." He held it out to her. "See?"

She saw. The screen was a network of cracks and colorful lines. "Sorry."

"I'm not worried about the phone. I'm worried about tracking our way to the campsite."

"I thought you knew where it is."

"Thanks to this," he said, holding up his phone. "Now, I'll have to guess... *Wait!*"

Liz stomped the breaks again. And again, Bill's phone flew from his hand. This time, it bounced off the windshield, slid across the top of the dashboard, and fell off on Liz's side.

Bill held out his hands. "What the hell, Liz?"

"You said to 'wait'!"

"That was just my way of—never mind." He turned in the seat again, reached into the back, and pulled his backpack into his lap. "Please be in here. Please be in here."

"What?"

"My GPS tracker. I have it synced to the laptop. It's the match to Cole's. See, my phone was only guiding us to the location. But this will guide us to Martin's tracker."

Liz understood none of what he said. "Ah."

"Yes!" He let out a shrill whistle. "Got it."

"That's good?"

"Yes. We're lucky it got put back in here when I got the laptop up and going. Ramona probably did it. I doubt I would've thought about it."

Bill turned it on. It beeped a few times, then made static whistling sounds until the screen clicked on. She watched a map load onto the small screen. Then red lines appeared. She saw dots in the upper corner.

"Is that them?" she asked.

"Yeah, but..." He shook his head. She saw the confusion on his face in the glow of the instrument panel. It made him look much older than his actual age.

"What is it?"

"The campsite should be in this area. This is where Martin checked in at, see the timestamp?"

She saw a star symbol in the center of a green patch. "I think so."

"This is where this dot should be." He pointed at a dot far on the right, away from the green patch. "But it's over here. So is Robbie and Trish's tracker. It's moved right along with it."

"How far from the campsite?"

"I can't really tell."

"Maybe they're okay, then."

"Well, they made it over there somehow. They still weren't answering the calls, though."

"Maybe they were taken?" Bill moaned. "Taken. Damn. I didn't think about that. Captive?"

Liz ignored the question. "So, that's them?"

"Yeah. Should we radio Ethan and Cole?"

Liz thought about it. What good would it do? All Ethan would do was tell them to go check it out themselves. They wouldn't want to leave all the fun torture they were doing anyway. "Forget the radio." She pointed at the screen. "That's where we'll go. Can we get there in this?"

"I have no idea."

"We're going to try. Just tell me which way."

"Um...straight. For now. They left the campsite about the time we left the cabin."

Liz followed the instruction.

Bill hummed while he looked at the screen. "Looks like we would have originally pulled off to the right, like I thought. Now, we'll go straight at the crossing. It should be coming up in a couple minutes.

Just as Bill predicted, Liz saw the crossing a couple minutes later. The trees thinned out around a graveled intersection that led in different directions into heavy woods. Each one looked ominous and scary, stuffed with shadows and darkness. A flat patch of ground was to the right, vacant except for a rope cordon that surrounded the small area.

"You notice that?" said Bill.

"What?"

"No cars. Shouldn't their cars be parked in the little parking area over there?"

A cold uneasiness slithered through Liz's insides. "Maybe they parked somewhere else."

"Where?"

"Beats me." She kept going straight, looking each way as if a car might suddenly appear and crash into them. They made it to the other side without any incidents. She hated this, hated how wrong and foreboding it all felt. It was the kind of feeling that somebody might get before boarding a plane and suddenly believing it would crash.

What seemed like an hour passed without either of them speaking before Bill finally said, "There has to be a trail or a road or something to the right that would take us to where they are." He stared at the screen, then looked up. Should be coming up soon.

Liz looked around, keeping the speed slow. She saw nothing but trees and dark. Heard nothing but the low hum of the engine, the tires crackling over gravel, and crickets.

She was beginning to think there wasn't anything around when she spotted a recess in the woods. "What's that?" She nodded toward the alcove between a thick patch of trees.

"You might have just found it."

Liz brought the Jeep to a stop without breaking any of Bill's equipment this time. She saw the barricade blocking it. *Keep Out* was printed on a sign attached to the center of the metal bar that stretched across the road, blocking their way in.

Liz drove the Jeep right up to the metal arm and put it in Park.

Bill sighed. "Guess this used to be an access road. Looks closed now."

"Try to open it?"

"Give me a second," Bill said, unhooking his seatbelt. He set the tracker on the dash, then opened the door. Bright light burst inside the Jeep, blinding them both. He quickly shut the door, throwing the interior back into comfortable darkness.

Through the windshield, Liz watched him walk around the front. Squinting against the headlights, he looked around a few times before trying to push the bar. It didn't budge. Then he tried pulling it. Still nothing. He turned to her, held out his hands, and shrugged.

Liz killed the engine. She put the keys in her pocket, then shut off the lights. Opening the door, she hung her head out. Bill was a pale shape in the dark. "Guess we're walking," she said.

"Shit."

"I agree."

18.

Cole stood back while Ethan bashed the other knee. The killer's screams rose in pitch, piercing his ears like a dagger. "Jesus," he said. "Not so tough, huh?"

Ethan stood there, panting. "Nope." He'd only made two swings and he sounded winded. His good friend had gotten into great shape this past year, so it had nothing to do with overexerting himself. He recognized the heightened breathing for what it really was.

Ethan's adrenaline had kicked in to hyperdrive and his lungs couldn't keep up.

Tina and Ramona hooted and whistled as if Ethan had just hit a grand slam in the last inning of a tied game. He thought he saw tears in Ramona's eyes.

The killer's legs sagged where his knees should be, feet wagging with the jerks and shakes of his thighs. Nothing but bone gravel connected them anymore.

Ethan, holding the hammer in his left hand, slapped the killer's face with the right. Though it was a hard swing, the man's large head barely moved. Ethan shook his hand, hissing through his teeth. "Hit that damn mask," he said.

"That's an easy fix," said Cole. "Let's yank the damn thing off."

The killer's screams had turned to low moans, his head sagging. Now he whimpered with sharp cries, shaking his head as Cole stepped over to him.

"You got something to say?" Cole asked.

Head continued to shake, breaths coming out in shrill gasps.

Cole reached out to his mask. The killer leaned back his head, trying to keep out of reach.

"Do it, baby!" Tina called. "Do it! Tear his mask off! Show his ugly fucking face!"

"For you, dear," said Cole.

An expression of teenage adoration appeared on his wife's face. He hadn't seen her gaze at him that way since his glory days playing school football and she'd been on the sidelines, leading her squad in cheers and support.

Kind of like she was doing now.

It's like the old days.

Tina nudged Ramona's side, then started to lead her in a chant of: "*Show his ugly face! Show his ugly face!*"

Ramona looked confused at first, but her mouth began to curl into a wicked grin. Then she joined in, matching Tina's volume and spirit. Then, to Cole's surprise, Ethan pitched in as well.

Cole held up his hands, making a dramatic display of flexing his fingers. This only seemed to rile up the cheers even more. Then he extended his index and middle finger.

He took the cigar from his mouth and jabbed it into the left eyehole of the mask.

He was met with glorious cheers from his peers and horrible shrieks from his daughter's killer. Cole didn't stop there. He began to twist the cigar back and forth where he figured the man's eye was. Sizzling sounds emanated from the dark chasm of the eyehole as smoke eddied out. A sour, burnt smell drifted around that reminded Cole of singed hair.

Cole tossed the stubbed cigar aside, then used his thumb and index finger to hook both eyeholes and pull. He expected the mask to plop right off, but it didn't move. It felt like he was trying to dislodge a rock that had been imbedded into the soil.

The cheers began to dissipate behind him.

"What is it?" said Tina.

"The damn thing's really on there."

"The straps," said Tina. "It's the straps. I'll take care of them." She jogged into the kitchen.

The killer yanked his head from Cole's grip, slicing the tip of his middle finger on the rim of an eyehole. "Ow!" Cole said, snatching back his finger. He looked down at it, saw the line of blood, and felt his skin tighten with anger. "Bastard."

He swung his left arm, whacking the killer with the back of his hand. The solid blow sent a tingling jolt up Cole's arm, but the hit had been hard enough to knock the killer's head to the side.

Cole let out a low growl at the new pain he felt.

"You okay?" asked Ethan.

Cole nodded. "He's not going to be, though."

"Good."

Cole clenched and unclenched his hand a few times to work out the ache. His elbow felt tight and there was pain in his shoulder. Felt like he'd backhanded a tree.

Tina emerged from the kitchen. She carried a pair of kitchen shears. Holding them up, she moved her fingers, making *snick-snick-snick* sounds with the blades. "Hold his head up."

Cole stepped back over to the killer. No longer was their captive screaming or moaning. He was looking at Cole through the dark holes of his mask. Cole ignored the shiver he felt lodged in his spine.

Smiling, Cole said, "You're going to die tonight."

The killer held his stare, peering deep into him. Cole figured if the man would have spoken, he might have said, "So are you." Cole could hear the whispery voice in his brain, like an intruder that shouldn't be there.

He shook his head to jar away the thoughts, then looked at his wife. "Do it, already."

"*Hold his head,*" she said again.

Cole put his hands on either side of the killer's head, which felt like squeezing a small boulder. His finger was slicked in blood from the cut he'd suffered a few minutes ago. "Just keep still," he said. "Don't want you getting cut or anything."

Tina snickered as she stepped up behind the killer. She opened the shears, slid the blades around the top strap, and squeezed. The material bent but didn't split. "Damn," she said in a strained voice. "What's this made of? Kevlar?"

Cole tried to avoid the killer's stare. Though he couldn't see his eyes, he could feel them boring into him.

Eye. I took out one of them.

Cole felt better about that. But he could still feel the hateful leer of the other one, looking into him, past his confident veneer to where that scared little boy still hid inside, the one that had returned after Kali was murdered. For years, Cole had forgotten what fear was—true, paralyzing fear. After his daughter's death, he remembered. Now, he was haunted by it, afraid of everything. Something he'd never admitted to anyone, including the shrink he secretly visited behind Tina's back every two weeks. He'd never tell anyone about the kid he used to be, the kid afraid of his mother. The kid who was afraid of the dark.

Tina tried to pull the strap away from the killer's scalp. It was too tight, like trying to stretch steel cables. She angled the shears differently, using the tips to cut. This time, the material split. Not all the way, but she followed the path it started with another snip.

The strip sprung in two different directions, dangling like parched party ribbons.

Huffing, Tina looked up, smiling behind the hair that had fallen into her face. In that moment, she was the sexiest woman Cole had ever seen. He liked how winded she was, the way her breasts heaved with her heavy breaths. The way her hair was mussed and wild. He even liked how the smeared makeup on her eyes made her look a little feral. He felt a stirring in his pants.

Tina must have sensed his carnal thoughts because she winked at him, then ran her tongue over her lips. Cole nearly moaned. Instead, he only smiled.

Smiling back, Tina went to work on the other straps. It didn't take her nearly as long with the remaining two.

But when all the straps had been severed, the mask was still lodged in place.

"Well, shit," said Tina. She ran a hand through her hair. "That didn't work." She made a face. "Whew. He *really* stinks."

Cole had become nose blind to the pithy stink that wafted off the killer. He thought about trying to pry off the mask again. If he used both hands that might yield better results.

He felt a tapping on his shoulder. Turning his head, he spotted Ethan off to the side. He held out the hammer, flipped around so the claws jutted. "Use this."

Cole felt a corner of his mouth curl. "Good idea, pal." Taking the hammer, he turned back to face the big man in the chair. "You might want to be still. Don't want to me to slip..." He waved the hammer around as if he were having trouble holding it. "Might accidentally jab you."

His little joke got laughs from Tina and Ramona. Ethan remained quiet behind him.

"Let's unmask this fucker," Cole said, putting the claw tips against the killer's brow.

Though the rim of the mask looked to have sunken into the calloused flesh from how much it had been worn, surely it hadn't been on constantly. The guy had to eat at some point. And unless he was sucking his meals through a straw, the mask had to come off from time to time.

Cole slid the claw ends back and forth along the thick hair above the mask, looking for some type of rift that he could slide the claws into. The tip of the left claw slipped behind the edge of the mask. He paused. He worked the claw back and forth, forcing it to dip deeper. The mask lifted, granting room for the other claw.

With both claws behind the mask, he heaved as if he were trying to dislodge a nail from lumber. The mask groaned like strained plastic before tearing away from the face with a squelch. Cole reached out with a hand and caught the mask. Stringy goo tarnished the back of it, stretching to the killer's face like chewing gum on the bottom of a shoe. From the looks of it, it was a congealed combination of blood, sweat, and mucus. An odor like dead fish and rotted sores puffed in his face, gagging him, making his eyes water.

"That smell..." said Ramona, gagging. She turned away, coughing a few times before the wet splats of her vomiting drowned her hacking.

Cole stepped back, bringing the mask with him. The fetid adhesive stretched until finally breaking apart and spattering the floor. Holding the mask by the top strap, Cole looked up at the killer. He'd expected to see a hideous, mutant-like face riddled with open sores and scars.

But he was wrong.

A young man that could have worked on a farm sat before him. Almost good-looking, in an uneducated backwoods rugged kind of way. He also hadn't gouged the killer's eye with the cigar as he'd thought. Instead, he'd smeared a line of ash back and forth above his eye, singeing off most of a thick eyebrow. The cigar left behind a ruddy burn that was already blistering.

"Why isn't he ugly?" asked Tina. "He wears the mask...and he's...normal?"

Cole snorted. "Hardly."

"Normal-looking. He's a damn kid."

Cole had noticed that as well. Probably not much older than Kali. If Cole had to guess, the boy was probably twenty, or just shy over that.

"Can you talk?" Ethan asked. "Got a name?" He tapped on Cole's shoulder, holding out his hand for the hammer. Cole gave it to him.

The killer lowered his head, averting his stare. Without the scary mask, he seemed so...pathetic.

"Do you think he's mute or something?" said Tina.

"I'm fine, by the way," said Ramona. Back turned, she glanced over her shoulder. Frothy drool clung to her chin. "Thanks for checking on me. I'm going to go clean myself up."

Ethan nodded. "Bring something to clean up...that." He pointed toward the chunky puddle on the floor.

"I was born for it," said Ramona. She shuffled toward the hallway, then vanished down it. The sound of a door closing soon followed.

Cole focused on the killer again. "My boy asked you a question. What's your name?"

The killer's eyes glanced up and down, skimmed here and there without making any kind of contact with anyone. Cole figured he could probably speak but just didn't want to. If he wasn't some hideous mutation under the mask, then he probably knew how to articulate verbally.

"Let me see that," said Ethan.

"Huh?" Cole turned as Ethan stepped forward and grabbed the mask. "Oh, take it."

Ethan, holding the mask up, walked over to the coffee table. "This yours?"

Cole wasn't sure why he'd asked such an obvious question. He figured his friend was going somewhere with it, though.

"Right?" said Ethan. "You were wearing it, so it must be yours. And from the looks of it, you've been wearing it a long time." Holding the mask up by the strap, it slowly swiveled this way and that as he stared into it. "Was this what you had on when you killed my daughter?"

Cole studied the killer for any kind of reaction to the question. There was nothing. It was as if the disheveled kid wasn't even listening. "He's ignoring you," he said.

"I see that," said Ethan. He placed the mask on the coffee table, the face pointing upward. "You must really like this mask. Doesn't look like any I've ever seen before. I've seen a lot of slasher movies, you know. Not all, but many of them, have an iconic mask that the maniac likes to wear. Something to trademark for Halloween costumes and movie memorabilia to sell to kids and collectors. This right here, wow. It's pretty good. If I was at a horror convention and saw this..." He clucked his tongue, shook his head. "I'd want to buy one."

He tapped the face with the flat end of the hammer. It clacked as if Ethan were nudging hardened clay.

The sound arrested the killer's attention enough for him to tilt his head toward Ethan. And when Ethan saw that, he smiled an evil smile that Cole had never seen on his friend before. The cold, almost delirious appearance that had taken over his friend's face caused the hairs on the nape of his neck to go erect.

Damn, he looks crazy as hell.

"Like I said, I've never seen a mask like this. So, I'm thinking it's an original. One of a kind. You made this yourself, right? This is something you put time into, getting it just right. You've worn it so long, it's become an actual part of you. Am I right? More than a mask. It's who you are. This is what you want the world to see you as. And we are what you see through the eyeholes. A reflection of the beast lurking inside you. Right?"

Cole was impressed by Ethan's analysis. He'd always known Ethan was smart, but to speak in such a way like that made

Cole think of a prosecutor talking to someone on the stand. But all his creative and introspective words fell flat as the maniac continued to stare, saying nothing.

Ethan sighed. "Tell you what. Just tell me your name, and I won't smash it with this hammer."

Head raising, the maniac peered at Ethan. His dark eyes widened, stretching the burn above his left eye.

Ethan stared back, his eyes intent and mean. His face was emotionless now, ashen and almost sickly. His hair shined from sweat. "I'm not in the mood to give you any chances. You killed my baby girl. And if you don't speak right now, I will shatter this fucking mask and stuff the pieces down your throat. You got me?"

The maniac began to shake in the chair, twisting and turning against the chains holding him in place. Cole kind of hoped he would just say anything so it would make Ethan stop making those facial expressions.

"Time's up," said Ethan. "Tell it 'Bye-bye.'"

He brought the hammer up and swung down.

"*Noooo!*"

The cry tore out of the maniac as his head lashed from side to side.

The hammer halted right before it struck the creamy face of the mask. Ethan turned around, mouth gaping. "Wha...? You...?" He looked at Cole. "He speaks."

Cole was still in shock from it. The cry had sounded almost youthful in its fright. Now, the large maniac's head sagged while he...sobbed?

He's actually crying.

Both knees had been bashed to bits, and he'd only hollered. But the thought of his mask being destroyed had turned him into a blubbing child.

Cole couldn't believe it. "Holy shit," he said through a gasp.

He looked over at his wife and saw the way she stared at the tied kid. She'd managed to hold on to the anger and almost maniacal glee from earlier, but it had taken a hit and was starting to crumble. It was the sobbing that was doing it, how it humanized the monster and made him just as vulnerable as the rest of them. Seeing him this way was a complete contrast to the emotionless killing machine they built him up to be.

It's a mask. He's crying over a mask. That doesn't make him human.

He pointed at Tina and spoke his thoughts out loud.

Tina shook her head, as if only coming out of the haze because of Cole's voice. "What did you say?"

He repeated himself. "Don't look at him with...with sympathy like that. He killed Kali. He killed her. Doesn't matter if he cries us a fucking river we can swim in, he's still a damn murderer!"

"I know that!" Tina shouted back. "You don't think I fucking know that, you stupid prick!"

Cole blinked as Tina's words sank in. Not only had she never shouted at him before, even when she was in the throngs of her overpowering depression, but she had ever called him a name. And the one she'd chosen, though almost funny, hurt just as much as if she'd told him she wanted a divorce.

Tina must have sensed his hurt feelings because the scowl on her face softened. "Sorry, Cole. I really am. Just don't talk to me like I'm soft."

"I didn't mean it," he said.

"Guys," said Ethan. "Enough."

Cole nodded. He walked over and stood beside Tina. After a moment, she reached out and hugged his arm. It felt good to have her there.

Ethan focused on the boy. "Your name. What is it?"

The killer sniffled a few times before saying, "Zeb...Zeb Gorley. Please...not my mask."

"Zeb-fucking-Gorley." Ethan turned to survey the room. He paused. "Glad you made it back."

Cole looked to his left and spotted Ramona slowly making her way over to them. She held a roll of paper towels in one hand and a bottle of cleaner in the other. "I heard his scream."

"Don't let it affect you," said Tina. "Nothing's changed."

Ramona nodded.

"Zeb Gorley," said Tina. "That's your real name?"

The killer nodded.

"Our friends," said Cole. "Are they okay?"

Zeb made a face. "W-what?"

"Out at the campsite. Our friends are there. Have you hurt them?"

Zeb closed his eyes, bared his browning teeth as he thought about it. "I..." He opened his eyes. "Give me my mask back and I'll tell you."

Ethan and Cole shared a look that showed each other they both already knew the answer. Ethan saw the same anger in Cole that he felt building inside himself. Were they dead? They would know soon enough, after Liz and Bill had confirmed it.

But Ethan figured that was a verification they wouldn't need.

Zeb sniffled. "Can I have...my mask back?"

Ethan lowered the hammer, sighing. "You did tell us your name, so I guess a deal's a deal."

Zeb began to relax in the chair, though his eyes never moved away from Ethan.

Ethan started to reach for the mask, then suddenly spun around with the hammer swinging down.

It shattered the mask in one hit. Shards and bits flew all over.

A few sharp pieces flitted across Cole's face, stinging as they nicked him. "Ah, shit, Ethan! You almost got it in my eyes."

Tina also let out a small yelp as she dodged the flying debris.

Another cry tore loose from the killer. He continued to scream while Ethan scooped up a handful of mask shards.

"I told you I'd give it back," said Ethan. "I'm being true to my word. I'm going to give it back to you, piece by fucking piece! Right down your throat!"

Ethan marched over to Zeb and rammed his fist into the killer's open mouth. His screams turned to stifled chokes as Ethan began shoving the fragments down his gullet.

Cole almost went to stop him, but Tina gripped his arm tighter. He could have easily torn free of her if he wanted to. Instead, he just stood there and watched while Zeb jerked and bucked against the chains, gagging and choking on the chunks Ethan stuffed down his throat.

19.

Ethan stood at the kitchen sink, washing the vomit, blood, gooey morsels, and mucus off his hand. The blood wasn't his. It came from the shards shredding the inside of Zeb's throat. To Ethan's surprise, he hadn't cut himself. He'd tried to hold the killer's mouth shut while he choked on mask scraps, but Zeb had started projectile vomiting. The frothy spray was filled with shrapnel as if a grenade had detonated in his mouth.

He finished rinsing off the soap and checked his hands. This was his fourth attempt to get them clean. There were still some stains on his fingers, and the undersides of his nails were black. This was as good as it would get for now.

Zeb unleashed another howl that was cut short by a solid crunching sound. Tina's wild laughter followed.

She's lost her mind.

Tina had been skipping around Zeb, whacking him with the hammer in random places on his body, when Ethan had headed for the kitchen. The blows were hard, but not so hard they did any real damage. That last one had sounded a lot harder than the others.

Another whack and Zeb howled.

It was music to Ethan's ears.

Drying his hands with a dishrag, he grabbed a beer from the fridge and quickly chugged it. He tossed the empty can in the trash, then walked through the kitchen and exited out the back doorway to his study. They hadn't made it to this room yet in their cleaning and reorganizing, so it was still a mess. But it took him no time to find where he'd put the bag this morning.

Crouching, he unzipped it, flinging aside the flaps. He smiled at the contents inside.

"What to take, what to take."

He grabbed the machete. The blade was long, curving at the tip, and very sharp. He put it aside, then selected the hatchet. He thought about getting some nails for the hammer to nail the bastard's hands together or bang a nail through the head of his dick. But he decided against it. Not only would the task be too time-consuming, he also recognized how close to crossing a line he was getting. Make him hurt, yes, but try not to become sadistic while doing so. Besides, he wanted to be wrapped up and have all the evidence removed by the time Liz and Bill made it back.

Liz.

The memory of the hurt he'd seen in her eyes flashed in his mind. He wished she were here right now. But he knew she would never participate in anything like this. She hadn't endured what Ethan had, what the others had. Everything that had been wonderful about her world hadn't been destroyed by Zeb Gorley. She hadn't spent the past year imagining what she would do if ever given the chance to enact retribution on the bastard that took his little girl from him.

He never once thought he might actually be granted his wish. But here they were, Zeb at their mercy. Fate had for once given him something he'd asked for. He hated that more innocents had to die for it. And there was also the definite possibility that some of his friends had also lost their lives just to get to this point.

That's how it works. You get something but you have to give so much in return.

He may also lose Liz, once this was over. He doubted things would ever be the same between them. Most likely, she would leave him. And that was something that scared him just as much as a life without his daughter.

You can fix it.

Ethan knew that wasn't true. Nothing could fix this. And he was too far in now to stop.

Besides, he didn't want to stop.

Ethan carried the machete and hatchet into the living room. Tina was leaning against the couch, head tossed back while she caught her breath. Her hair hung down between her shoulder blades in a tussled mess.

Ramona now had the hammer. She stood behind Zeb, who sat with his head hanging, taking long, measured breaths. Welts had formed on his semi-handsome face. Some abrasions had split open and were spilling crooked lines of blood down his face. There was a large lump rising on the back of his head, forming a tent shape in the dark hair.

Cole had lit another cigar and stood off to the side, puffing on it while he watched. His face was shiny with sweat, his dark hair nearly flat with dampness.

Ramona was lifting the hammer and slowly lowering it, as if rehearsing her first hit. She glanced over, saw Ethan's hands, and gasped. She dropped the hammer. Eyes rounding, she snapped her fingers. "I want the hatchet."

Cole turned and smiled. "Ah. New toys."

Tina waved her hand. "None for me, thanks. I'm taking a break. I need something to drink. Anybody else want anything?"

"I'll have a water," said Ramona, taking the hatchet from Ethan.

"Ethan?"

"I'm good."

Tina looked over at Cole. "What about you, honey?"

Nodding, Cole said, "Yeah. I'm parched. I'll help you."

Cole joined Tina. Together they headed for the kitchen.

Ramona looked at Ethan. "Should I wait for them to come back?"

Ethan shrugged. "If you want. We're running low on time, though." He walked over to the camera and looked at the screen. He saw the counter displayed in the lower corner. It had been filming for over an hour and had enough disc space to record an hour more.

Jesus. That long?

Ethan felt odd realizing how much all of them had become absorbed in this punishment. Would they ever be able to revert back to the people they'd been before chaining Zeb to the chair? He wasn't so sure. Maybe they could, though nothing would ever be right again. Nothing would ever be normal.

He just hoped the pain he'd felt inside for the past year would at least soften.

"I want to chop off his arm," said Ramona.

Zeb raised his head with a gasp.

Ramona looked at Ethan. "Robbie had one of his arms severed, below the elbow. I think it's only fair that I get to do the same to Zeb here."

Zeb groaned.

Ethan shook his head. "You can't. If you chop off his arm, it'll throw off the tension in the chains. He'd be able to slip out of them."

"Look at him, Ethan. He's not in any condition to try anything. Both his fucking knees are like a package of Pop Rocks."

"You saw what he did to our kids, what the cabin looked like. You know the damage he's capable of. I'm not taking any chances."

Ramona groaned. "Fine. Then what do I get to do, if I can't do that? Huh?"

Ethan shook his head. "I don't know. Cut off an ear or something."

Ramona seemed to think about it. "Both ears. It's only fair."

"Fine. Both ears. It's going to be hard with the hatchet. Want to use the machete?"

Zeb whipped his head back and forth, grunting with each lash. Neither of them paid him any attention.

Ramona clucked her tongue. "Remember, I was the hatchet-throwing champion at the County Fair three years in a row when we were teenagers. I can handle it. That's a skill you don't forget."

Ethan didn't remember that at all. But he hadn't really known Ramona all that well back in school. Though she'd always been pretty, she was mostly a loner in their younger years.

Ramona held the hatchet up, angling the blade so it pointed toward the side of Zeb's skull.

"Don't stab him," said Ethan.

"I know what I'm doing."

"Hold up," said Tina, her shoes clacking over the hardwood.

"We're back." She carried a glass of wine in one hand and a bottle of water in the other. Her face was flushed. Ethan saw a blemish on her neck that might have been a hickey.

Were they making out in there?

A glance at Cole's red face told him that was exactly what they'd been doing. He thought about reminding Cole that this wasn't the time to be fooling around, then decided to let it go.

Tina set the water on the coffee table, then took a heavy swig from her wine glass. "I'm ready."

Rolling her eyes, Ramona returned her focus to Zeb. The young maniac tried to lean away from her hand. The chains held him in place, only allowing his neck to swivel a bit. Ramona gripped him by his thick hair and jerked his head in place. "Hold still," she said through gritted teeth. "Time to take your medicine." She spoke in a low whisper, probably to avoid anybody hearing her.

But Ethan had, since he was standing the closest to her. He frowned at her comment. Was she doing one-liners? He didn't think so. That must have been something she'd heard herself before being administered a form of punishment.

Then he remembered Barry, her first husband. There had been rumors he'd abused her and Adam for most of the marriage. Ramona never admitted as much, but that could have been something the old husband had said to them.

Zeb began to hiss as if he'd sat on something hot. Ethan looked up to see Ramona pull off his right ear, using the blade of the hatchet to slice. She held up the jiggly flesh, smiling. A bloody nub was all that remained of his ear, trickling lines of red down the side of Zeb's neck. He didn't cry out, only breathed hard, puffing his cheeks as he fought to hold it in.

She raised the ear to her mouth. "That hurt?" Laughing, she blew into the ear a couple times. "This thing on? Helloooo?"

Tina cackled as if Ramona was on stage delivering an amazing set of comedy. She raised the glass to her mouth, laughing as she tried to sip. She managed to slurp more wine between the trickles spilling down her chin.

Cole shook his head. "Jokes?"

Ramona shrugged, then tossed the ear over her shoulder.

"Please keep it contained," said Ethan. "To this area. Don't want to have to clean the whole damn room again."

"So sorry," said Ramona in an annoyed voice. "I'll do better, sir!" She gave him a salute.

"Give me the hatchet," said Ethan. He stepped forward.

"What?"

"You heard me." He held out his hand.

"No," said Ramona. "You're not taking it from me."

"You're acting ridiculous. This is serious. We're not having fun here."

"We're not?" said Ramona.

"I sure as hell am," said Tina, raising her glass. She spoke in a thick voice, slurring words. "I'm having a ball. A great Friday night in the mountains."

Cole gave her a look, then shook his head again.

Ramona pointed at Ethan with the hatchet, then moved it in Cole's direction. "Don't try to say you're not. This is the best night you've had since—well, in a year. At least."

Ethan wouldn't tell her that she was right. He couldn't. But if he told her she was wrong, he'd be lying. Cole must have felt the same way because he also remained silent.

Ramona coughed a laugh that sounded cold. "I don't care what you think about me, but I'm as pleased as a peach right now. Know why? Because I have the bastard that killed my son right here. And I'm giving it back to him. That should be enough for me to sing from the rooftop if I want to."

"All right," said Cole. "Just get to it."

"Don't rush me," said Ramona. "You don't get to rush me. Nobody does. This is *my* time."

She popped Zeb on the back of the shoulder with the hatchet. The blade sunk in less than an inch. Zeb let out a groan and tilted back his head. Wincing, he took a deep breath to stifle his pain.

"See?" said Ramona. She pulled the hatchet out. Blood dribbled off the tip of the blade. "He's no superhuman. He's not indestructible. Tough, maybe. But he's just a bitch in a mask that killed our babies. And I'm having the time of my life hurting him back some. So, sue me."

Ramona didn't wait for anybody else to say anything. She turned around, pinched his left ear, and hacked it off in one brief swing. The severed lobe bounced off his shoulder and landed on the floor where Ramona stomped it. Grinding her foot, she mashed the ear into a flat smirch of flesh.

Before Ethan could say anything, Ramona held up her hand. "I'll clean it up, so don't start fussing at me again."

Ethan patted the air, keeping quiet. He guessed each of them had their own way of dealing with this. He wondered how bad she got in the private moments with only Bill to witness it. How could he blame her for any kind of spiteful behavior at all?

I can't.

So Ethan decided he wouldn't say anything at all.

"My turn," said Cole. He turned and put his cigar on the edge of the coffee table, so the burning end hung off the edge. He tilted back his head and drained what was left of his beer before setting the can beside his cigar.

Ramona stepped back, letting out a whine. "I'm not ready to stop yet."

"Tough. It's my turn. You got his ears. I get a go at him for a bit."

"Fine. You want this?" She held out the hatchet.

"No. I'm using these." He held up his fists.

"Macho," said Ramona.

"Kick his ass, baby," said Tina.

"I plan on it, darling." Reaching into his back pocket, he brandished a pair of brass knuckles. He slid the fingers of his right hand into the four holes.

Tina gasped. "The knucks? I didn't think you had them anymore."

"Oh, I've got them. Figured since my bouncing days were over, I'd never have need to use them. But here we are."

"They always looked good on you, baby," she said.

Cole gave her a single nod. "Appreciate it, darling."

Ethan rolled his eyes. What was happening here? It was like Cole and Tina had turned into teenagers themselves again. Ramona too, for that matter. Ethan wanted to hurt Zeb, make him suffer for as long as possible. The more he hurt, the better.

But he couldn't let it become a game to him. This was personal business, and he needed to keep it that way.

Cole bent over, putting his left hand under Zeb's chin. Cole lifted his head without any resistance from Zeb. "Do you even remember my little girl?"

Zeb took heavy breaths, closed his eyes. "I remember all your kids."

"Oh?"

Zeb opened his eyes. Gone was the fear and pain. In their place was a black hatred that made him look demonic. "Your little girl cried for you when she was dying. Begged for your help." Rising his voice in pitch, he said, "*Daddy! Help me. Where are you, Daddy? I need you! Please, Daddy!*" Zeb smiled. "My dick's getting hard thinking about it."

Tina choked on a gasp. The wine glass slipped from her hands, shattering on the floor. "My...baby..."

Cole's jaw was clenched so tight, his teeth made sounds like scraping stones. "She did, did she?"

Zeb's eyes fluttered as he savored the memory. "Her fear smelled so sweet. She lost her virginity that night. You probably didn't know that. I could tell. I could smell the blood in her panties. The blood of her innocence dying." He turned to look at Ramona, who stood there, staring at him. The color had drained from her face. "Your son took it from her. I watched them in the car, the back seat. She hadn't wanted to, but your son made her feel so guilty. After all, they had graduated and would be going away to college in the fall. They should be doing it—"

"Mother fu—" Cole's shouts were cut off by the crack of air from his violent punch. The brass knuckles connected with Zeb's jaw, knocking it sideways with a horrible crunch. Teeth flew from his mouth, scattering across the floor.

Zeb's head whipped to the side so hard that Ethan wouldn't have been surprised if it tore loose from his neck and bounced off the wall. His chin was now pointing the wrong way, the flesh under his ear torn to show gray jawbone slicked in blood.

As Zeb started to raise his head, Cole shifted his position and made a short jab in the center of his face. The brass shattered Zeb's nose, flattening it to a rumpled strip and two crooked holes. Blood spurted, splattering Zeb's eyes, which Cole destroyed with two quick punches. If Zeb could see out of them at all now, it would be a miracle.

As much as Ethan wanted to see this, he couldn't let it go on. "Okay," he said.

Cole punched him on what remained of his right ear hard enough to cause blood to splash out the other ear. Zeb's head sagged and didn't move.

Cole stepped in to deliver another blow, but Ethan grabbed his arm. He needed both hands to hold him back. "That's enough. You've made your point."

Huffing, Cole looked back at him. "Getting soft now, Ethan?"

"Oh, fuck yourself, Cole. You know that's not it. The deal was we kill him together."

"I say we do it now, then," said Cole. "I can't stand the thought of him taking another breath."

"Agreed," said Tina.

"He was trying to turn us against each other," said Ramona. "Wasn't he? Making up those lies about my Adam. Adam would never..." She shook her head. "Not my Adam. He was too good. Too good."

Tina stepped over the scattered bits of her wine glass. Gripping Ramona's shoulders, she gave her a hard, quick shake. "Snap out of it, Ramona. Look at me."

Ramona's eyes blinked a few times. She shook her head and was back in the room. The focus had returned to her eyes. "Don't do that." She pulled away from Tina's hands. "Don't touch me."

Tina looked as if she wanted to say more, then decided not to.

Ethan walked over to Zeb, staring down at him. His head was tipped to the side, jaw askew, blood dripping from his mouth. His eyes were two swollen hillocks that had already turned purple. His nose was mashed back into his skull, leaving only the tip and nostrils that flapped with his heavy breaths.

How this guy was still alive, Ethan had no idea. Maybe he'd die soon. They could just leave him there and wait for it to happen.

No, Cole was right—it was time to wrap it up.

"Let's get this done," said Ethan, raising the machete. "Each of us gets one final blow."

Cole still had his brass knuckles. Ramona still had the hatchet. As he was about to ask Tina what she wanted to use, he saw she was already picking up the hammer from the coffee table. She patted the meat of her hand a couple times.

They joined Ethan, standing around him and ready. His team. His friends. All of them had their special weapon. They'd lost some of their numbers, but they would make sure those deaths weren't pointless. Zeb would regret them all, right before Ethan granted him his death.

20.

"What was that?" said Bill.

Liz spun around, following the path of Bill's flashlight. It sliced through the darkness, spreading over the trees as he swung it back and forth. She shone her light in the same direction. There was nothing to see but shadowy woods.

They'd been walking for a long time now and Liz was ready to be done. She knew it was selfish to be complaining about sore legs and tiredness when others were in danger, or worse. She couldn't help it. She was scared, tired, and wanted to be far away from this place.

But she already knew that no matter how far away she managed to get, how much time passed, she'd never be free of its hold. This night would stay with her forever.

I shouldn't have come here.

She'd wanted to be there for Ethan. He was her boyfriend, and she hoped that someday, he'd be her husband. Did she still want that? After all this, would she even be able to look at him again?

Probably.

Liz was hooked on Ethan Bowers. She loved him. She'd loved others before him but never had she loved anybody as *much* as him. It was different with Ethan. It made her understand how characters in those romantic comedies would drive across the country to confess their feelings to somebody in another state. She could see herself charging into a wedding chapel to stop Ethan from marrying somebody else because she knew they should be together. Ethan had brought something to her life that she never knew she even wanted.

An owl hooted nearby, nearly making her cry out in fright.

Keep it together. Stay calm.

Easy to think but hard to accomplish. She'd never seen such spooky woods in real life. This was stuff she would expect to see at the kind of haunted attraction people paid to walk through. She could feel the eeriness on her skin like fusty moisture, making her feel clammy all over.

She noticed Bill was staring at her, waiting on her to say something. At first, she couldn't remember why they'd stopped walking. Then it came back. Bill had heard a noise behind them, a cracking sound that a foot might make when stepping on a stick.

"Probably an animal or something," said Liz, though she hadn't heard anything.

"Think there's bears out here?"

"Don't they sleep at night?"

"How should I know? Do they? Or are they nocturnal?"

"Beats me. Maybe that's what you heard, a deer."

"Who knows?" Bill waved his light another time across the trees and the path behind them. Sighing, he turned around. "Guess it was nothing."

"You're making me paranoid."

"Well, you started it by claiming you saw headlights following us."

Liz still wasn't entirely convinced she *hadn't* seen that. But there had been no sign of vehicles or anything that could have caused such a light. Far as she knew, it was just her and Bill out here.

"Let's keep moving," said Liz. "The longer we stay here, the more it might make us be too late."

Nodding, Bill started walking. "I think we're already too late."

"Don't think that. We don't know. Not for sure."

"You think so, too. I can tell."

Liz nibbled on her bottom lip. She didn't want to tell him what she thought. "How much further?"

Bill raised the tracker. He'd decreased the brightness of the screen, so now the light was a meager glow and didn't spray brightness like a light grenade. He studied it while he walked. "Damn. We're not far away."

"Oh?"

"No. We have to go off trail, probably."

"I don't like that."

"I don't either. But it's not like we would find them just hanging out on the service path, waving at us."

"Of course I didn't expect *that*. But they have these trails for a reason. We go trotting off into the woods, in the dark, we're liable to hike our asses right off the mountain. There are ridges all over the place. A friend of mine's boyfriend stepped off a trail one time to piss and dropped a mile into a gorge. Took two days to find his body."

"That makes me feel better."

"I'm just saying that going off into the woods is a bad idea."

"Well, there's no other way. Do you have a way to fly us over there? A magic carpet, maybe?"

Liz could tell Bill was as frustrated as she was. He was right, though, and she knew it. If the only way to get to them was by going off the trail, then that was what they would have to do.

"How long before we have to do that?" she asked.

"Not long at all. I bet when we get over this hill."

Liz pointed her flashlight upward, the beam fading into the darkness at the top of the slope. It looked like a solid black wall was beyond the crest of the hill.

Or nothing at all.

Liz saw herself stepping over the top, expecting to feel solid earth beneath her feet again but finding open space instead and plunging into an abyss of unending nothingness.

Liz shivered at the vision.

"Are you okay?" Bill asked.

"Oh, sure."

"You just made a noise like you got in cold bath water."

"You heard that, huh?"

"Yeah. Sorry."

"I just don't like this. Any of this. We shouldn't be the ones going out here. We should report this to the police. *They* have a way to fly out there, and we wouldn't have to worry about plunging to our deaths."

"We can't report anything. And you know that."

"What if...?" She stopped talking. She wanted to ask Bill something, but she didn't want to actually ask him.

Bill sighed. "I know what you're going to say."

She really hoped so because she didn't want to just come right out and say the words.

"You're wondering what we're going to do if we are...too late."

Liz nodded. "That's something we can't just hide, you know. We won't be able to pretend were dumb about that. The police will have to be called if that happens. They'll want to know why they were out here camping while we were at the cabin. And Robbie and Trish..."

"I imagine we can tell the truth about that. Say we'd come out here in hopes of luring out the killer. And it worked."

"Okay. Sure. And then there's Gale..." Liz raised her hand and let it drop. It smacked her thigh. "She'd have to go along with it. I'm not so sure she will. They're not thinking at all."

"No. You're right about that." Bill stopped. He pointed with his flashlight. "I think this is our turn."

Liz aimed her flashlight into the trees. A narrow path etched through the trees as if somebody had used a pocketknife to carve it through the brush. "Well, there's a trail, at least."

"If you can call it that."

"It's better than nothing."

"Is it?"

Liz sighed. "Let's go. How much further?"

"Twenty minutes or so."

Liz's back felt as if it was being scraped with an icy fork. Wouldn't be long now and they would know exactly what had happened to their friends.

Gale flung the blankets aside. She sat up, swung her legs around, and set them on the floor. The movement caused hot pain in her stomach. The gauze tape pulled at her skin, stretching it.

Got to get out of here.

She hadn't had any trouble hearing what was going on down there. They were about to kill that man. She had zero qualms about whether he needed to die or not. The man was evil. She'd seen him in action, lifting one girl and beating her to death against another girl. He behaved as if he were superhuman or something.

Inhuman.

"A monster," Gale whispered.

But she wanted no part of this morbid spectacle. She had no idea what their next move would be. Gale was a witness and, even if she promised to keep quiet about what transpired here, she figured Ethan and his pals would never fully trust her. She had become a liability to their plan by surviving the attack at her cabin.

And that meant she needed to get away from this place. What she planned to do after that, she had no clue.

Getting to her feet, she bit back the groan that wanted to come out. She felt sore all over, especially where she'd been stabbed, but she expected this. What she hadn't expected was the sudden tilt of the room, the way it blurred and streaked as she nearly lost consciousness.

She stood there a moment, taking measured breaths. After a few moments, she finally managed to regain her bearings. Though the room looked as if she were viewing it through an old, cracked lens, it no longer seemed to be sloping and twisting.

Gale took a cautious step. No dizziness. She tried a few more and seemed to be fine. She grabbed the water the women had left her from the nightstand and chugged it until the bottle started crackling. Forcing herself to stop, she set it back down. Though the water tasted amazing, she didn't want to make herself sick.

Another howl of pain resonated from downstairs.

Gale nearly cried out herself. They were about to commit a murder down there. A murder that they would try to cover up. It didn't matter if it was a warranted kill or not. It was in the first degree, premeditated. They would be punished for it. Made no difference who the rat bastard was that they killed.

Unless they all lied.

And how would Gale be able to lie about those girls at her house? Plus, she'd been injured. She could see Ethan and his friends coming up with a good story for the police that would probably clear them. All they had to do was hide the body. All of them could say the killer was still out there somewhere.

And that still leaves me. Ms. Liability.

It left what happened at her house needing to be explained. How could Gale have made it back here? Why would they have patched her up and waited so long to call the authorities? There would be more questions than she, and probably the others, would have answers to.

That would mean the easiest route to take would make it look like she'd been killed at her house, too. While Gale had been lying up here in this very comfortable bed, she'd been playing the problem and possible resolutions over and over in her head.

She'd come up with plenty of problems, but no solutions.

What if we just tell the cops that Ethan came out there to check on me? Found me wounded like this. The maniac had left me for dead.

Why didn't they call the police right away? Why didn't they get Gale medical help as soon as possible? There were phones. Cell phones and a landline.

A good cop could rip that story to shreds.

There was a chance that the police wouldn't even think twice about whatever story they told them. The evidence that it was the same killer from last year would be easy to recognize, the pattern and signature would be a perfect match.

Sure, Gale thought, that was easy enough. But the reasons for why Gale hadn't received any help when Ethan found her wounded put a damper on any plan they might come up with. The reason for that was because the girls would have been dead for so long.

Gale realized she sounded like somebody in one of those true crime books she liked to read. People liked to tease her about her fascination of those gruesome accounts, but they had helped her tonight. She'd looked at this situation from all angles, saw where each possibility would lead her.

And what she'd determined was they wouldn't get her anywhere good.

She had to leave.

But how?

Her original plan had been to sneak downstairs and out the back door while they were distracted. Now, she wasn't so sure that was going to work. One of them was bound to see her. There was no getting around that.

Then she looked over at the window.

Bingo.

The front porch was right underneath the window, and the porch was covered. That meant the roof should be right below the windowsill.

Making her way over to the window went slower than she would have liked. She opened the curtains, unlocked the window and pulled up. The window slid open without any difficulty. Now she had to worry about the screen. There were latches on either side. It took a few tries to get her shaky fingers to work right.

Finally, she slid the screen upward, giving herself enough space that she should be able to fit through.

So long as she didn't slip and fall off the roof, she should be okay.

21.

Ramona sunk the hatchet's blade into the back of Zeb. She ripped it back out, moving to the side so Tina could bring the hammer against his shoulder. There was a vicious crunch as his shoulder was knocked out of socket. Zeb let out an agonized howl that sounded slurpy thanks to his broken jaw.

Cole stepped forward and punched him in the throat, turning those howls into choked quacks.

Ethan stood back, watching them. He felt sick to his stomach and didn't understand why. He enjoyed watching Zeb buck and thrash in the chains as he tried to get air. He liked seeing him hurting, seeing him bleed.

But he did not like how much the others seemed to be enjoying it. They weren't like themselves at all, smiling and laughing while they inflicted their payback. There was no way that could be healthy for them. Or maybe Ethan was the one doing it wrong. Perhaps he should be in that same lunatic daze they seemed to have slipped into. If he succumbed to it like they had, maybe he could enjoy himself just as much.

Another hatchet strike, this time on Zeb's thigh. Blood spurted onto Ramona's face when she wrenched the blade out, leaving a wide slit in the meat that filled with blood. Standing straight, Ramona wiped the blood on her face, smearing her cheeks in red. Ethan thought she might lick her fingers, but instead she let her hand drop.

Tina went to the other shoulder, held the hammer above her head with both hands, and brought it down. Zeb's shoulder was knocked lower, a sound like wood snapping following. Zeb tried to scream. Couldn't. All he could muster were hacks that sounded as if they were being compressed with a brick.

Cole stepped in front of Zeb, grabbing a handful of hair. He unloaded on Zeb's face with a series of punches. The sounds quickly went wet and juicy, sounding as if Cole was beating up a bag of ground beef. When he stepped away from Zeb, the killer's face looked as if it could have been ground beef. The skin was serrated and torn away in several places showing glimpses of skull and sinewy matter. His left cheek had been torn open. His teeth shone through the tattered flesh.

Now, it was Ethan's turn.

He stepped forward, raising the machete. He looked Zeb all over, trying to find a place to get started. There wasn't much left of the young man now, only a battered body that looked to be barely hanging on.

The fact that he was still alive at all shocked Ethan. He knew the killer's time was limited either way. But the games were over. It was time for everything to be wrapped up.

Ethan stared at the ruined face, made even uglier by Cole's recent beating. The eyes were swollen, looking like two hardboiled eggs pressed together over both sockets. He noticed a small slit in the right one, barely wider than the tip of pencil lead.

The eye underneath the puffy rims watched him. It didn't flinch, didn't glance away. It stared straight into Ethan, as if daring him to do what Zeb knew he wanted to do.

And Ethan decided to give him that, to show him that he wasn't afraid of anything anymore. Zeb had taken all that really mattered to him. And now, Ethan was going to take the last thing Zeb had.

His life.

The warning on the plywood in red paint flashed in his head. He remembered the chill he'd felt after reading it, the renewed sense of fear that had taken hold of him and remained until they finally captured Zeb. It was gone now. In its place was a brutal confidence that pushed away any fear and doubt. This was why he was here—to put a stop to Zeb and avenge not just Emily but every other person who'd lost their life or a loved one because of this sick bastard.

All Will Die.

Ethan shook his head. "Not all," he said. He put the blade under Zeb's chin. "*You* die."

Zeb stared up at him, the corner of his split, swollen mouth curled upward. "Nuuuh…"

Ethan tilted his head, eyes narrowing. He thought about trying to decipher the mangled dialect, then decided it wasn't worth the time it would take.

Pressing the blade to Zeb's throat, Ethan prepared to do a single, slow slash and let the kid bleed out as Cole suggested earlier.

Then Zeb titled his hips. The chains that had been holding his arms in place dropped to his waist. Ethan jumped back just as Zeb lurched, making his dislocated arm swing out. The hand smacked Ethan, spinning him around. The machete flew from his grasp, stabbing into the floor where it wobbled just out of reach.

Cole pushed past Ethan. The women were starting to scream in alarm and panic. As Ethan fell to the floor, he turned to see Cole reaching Zeb too late. Somehow, the maniac was standing on legs that shouldn't be able to support anything at all. As Cole approached, Zeb flung his head forward. His forehead connected with Cole's nose, busting it open. Blood spurted into Cole's eyes, blinding him. He made a wild swing, missing Zeb completely before crashing into Tina as she had begun to approach to help.

Both hit the coffee table. The wood crumbled underneath them, letting them fall to the floor in a pile of debris.

A thought registered somewhere in Ethan's mind. A thought he should have had much sooner than now. It had been seeing Cole's nose busted open that had conjured it. The thought took him back to a year ago, to that uncomfortably serene room at the hospital with the detective.

She said she bit off nose.

Right, Ethan remembered. The detective had said Emily claimed she'd bitten off a chunk of the killer's nose.

But Zeb's nose had been fine when the mask came off, normal until Cole flattened it.

Ethan shook his head, trying to clear his mind of those

thoughts. Most likely, Emily had been wrong. Maybe she had bitten him, like she said, but it hadn't come off.

Screams pulled Ethan's attention back to the ruckus in the room. He saw Ramona, squealing through harsh breaths, stepping back while lashing her head from side to side. She still held the hatchet, though she acted as if she had forgotten all about it.

Ethan pushed himself to his knees. He tasted blood, felt it trickling down from the corner of his mouth. How this had gone so bad in an instant was almost bewildering. He realized it was Ramona's hammer hits to his shoulders that had given him the advantage. It had allowed him to slide his arms loose of the chains behind his back. Just as Ethan had feared would happen.

Zeb lifted his left foot. A sound like a bag of rocks came from where his knee should be. Groaning in pain, Zeb swung it out and put his filthy boot on the floor. Then he lifted the right foot. Though the knee looked three sizes too big, it moved well enough and without sounding like a bag of marbles.

Now Zeb was free except for the manacles around his ankles. He didn't bother to mess with them, didn't bother with Ramona. Instead, he shuffled toward the fireplace mantle. As he neared it, he reared back a shoulder and slammed against the chunky wooden corner. There was a harsh cracking sound which caused Zeb to howl. Before giving himself a chance to reconsider, he repeated this motion with the other shoulder to similar results.

Still crying, Zeb turned around and faced Ethan. He lifted his arms, flexing his fingers.

"Oh, shit," said Ethan.

Ramona rushed over to Ethan, helping him to his feet. His cheek burned. The skin felt too tight on his face, so he figured a welt was already forming from the hit.

Ethan glanced down at the machete, jutting from the floor like the mythical sword in the stone. He was much closer to it than Zeb, but it still felt like going for the machete was too risky.

Zeb turned, grabbed a fireplace poker from the stand, and flung it at Ethan. The throw went wide and struck Ramona on the shoulder with a dull thud. She let out a grunt before falling backward. Ethan went to catch her, then snatched the hatchet from her hand.

As she dropped to the floor, Ethan turned, ready to face Zeb one more time. Then he only stared at Zeb's back as he hobbled toward the window next to the fireplace. The chain clanked and rattled between his feet as it slid along the floor.

Ethan wasn't sure what Zeb had planned, but the maniac wasn't slowing down. He hopped on his right leg, dragging his left behind him. Though his gait was constricted because of the manacles, he moved much quicker than Ethan would have expected otherwise.

As he reached the glass, he suddenly threw himself forward and crashed through it.

"Shit!" Ethan yelled, running toward the window.

He watched the boots and chain vanish over the sill as glass rained down on the floor. "Damn it!"

Ethan dropped the hatchet. He gripped the machete's hilt, yanked it from the floor, and ran for the front door. He fumbled with the locks. "Come on!" Finally, he unlocked them all and jerked the door open. On his way out, he flipped the switch for all the outside lights. Then he ran over the porch and down the steps. He turned left, sprinting alongside the house. His shadow stretched over the front, contorting like a specter. Reaching the corner of the cabin, he tried to make a sharp turn. His upper body turned just fine, but his feet kept going. They swished across the grass, yanking him down to the ground. His side smacked the damp grass as he slid a couple feet.

Ethan felt rattled. The dew soaked through his clothes. He'd lost the machete in his fall. Sitting up, he looked around. He noticed the machete was within reach. Leaning forward between his spread legs, he grabbed it and pulled the large weapon close.

Then he checked over at the window. He saw the light from inside spilling out, the jagged maw of glass in the frame. His eyes moved down to where he figured Zeb had landed. He'd expected to find the ground empty, the killer long gone.

Instead, he saw Zeb.

What's he doing?

Sitting on his ass, Zeb was tugging at his boot. He'd already removed one. Ethan saw a ragged sock, pocked with holes. The big toe, tipped with an angular, rotted nail, poked through a tear at the top of the sock.

Zeb pulled off the other boot, letting it drop beside him. He looked over at Ethan, his jaw pointing the opposite way. Ropes of drool dangled from the crevices around his mouth. Grunting sounds emanated from Zeb, making his shoulders shake.

It only took Ethan a moment to realize what those sounds were.

He's laughing at me.

And Ethan understood why when Zeb slipped the manacle over his foot, freeing it.

"Oh, no..." Ethan moaned as he got to his knees. "No..."

They'd put the manacles on him when he'd been wearing the boots, clamping them around the upper half where they'd been laced. Without the boots, the manacles were too big. Zeb further proved this when he slid off the other manacle with no trouble.

Now both feet were free.

And Ethan needed to hurry.

He stood up with a groan, wobbling on his feet. His body felt sore and achy as he started moving again. The fall had hurt, but he didn't think all the soreness had come from it. No, he was exhausted. Fatigue had set in, and it seemed to be even stronger than the adrenaline that was pushing him along when he didn't think he could.

Zeb pulled on a boot.

Come on, Ethan! Move your ass!

He was only a few feet from where Zeb was parked on the ground, tugging his other boot onto his foot. He got it on, started to stand. Ethan knew if the big man got upright, he didn't stand a chance. He had to keep him down on the ground.

Ethan threw himself into Zeb just as he started to rise. Both went down, sliding over the slippery grass. Ethan scrambled on top of Zeb, dropping all his weight onto the killer, pinning him to the ground. Bringing up his knee, he rammed it up into Zeb's crotch. He felt testicles mash under his kneecap. Another scream tore loose from Zeb's damaged mouth. Ethan brought his knee up and down several more times, pounding Zeb's crotch until his leg could no longer move.

Ethan collapsed onto Zeb's torso, panting. He was so tired. His arms felt as if they had been strapped to weights. He started to wiggle away from Zeb.

Then Zeb's hand gripped Ethan's throat, squeezed. The air going into his lungs was pinched off. Ethan tried to suck in a breath, but nothing came in. His chest felt as if it was starting to shrink, pressing against his lungs the same way Zeb's hand was pressing his throat.

Ethan felt himself being lifted, pushed upward as Zeb sat up. His mangled face was turned toward him, that bit of eye gazing at him through the swollen slits on his face. Ethan remembered he still held the machete, but his arm was too weak to use it.

Ethan swung his other hand. It bounced uselessly off the side of Zeb's head as if he'd tried to brush some strands of air away from the kid's face.

His lungs felt hot and cold at the same time, and somehow felt as if they were shriveling. He tried to catch another breath and got nothing. He continued to rise with Zeb, then he was going upward more, higher than Zeb, gazing down at him. Zeb's arm was extended upward, holding Ethan by his throat.

The pressure began to tighten even more.

I'm going to die.

Ethan saw movement by the backside of the cabin where the outside light met the darkness. There was a subtle shift as someone slinked through the shadows, a lighter black than the black behind it. He wondered if it was Liz, returning from the campsite.

Too little.

This was a small person with dark hair.

When Ethan recognized who it was, tears formed in his eyes.

Emily stood over by the cabin. She was little again, wearing the purple shorts and white shirt with the unicorn on it. She was seven years old when he bought that outfit before the trip to the cabin. She'd loved the clothes and had worn them the entire time they were there. It was probably the best vacation they had at the cabin. One that they always looked back on fondly.

Now, she stood at the rear of the cabin, half hidden by shadows as she watched him. She looked just as adorable now as she had back then. She noticed him watching her. A smile appeared on her face, a soothing smile that seemed to radiate warmth across the cool night to reach all the way over to him. He felt it whirl all over, enveloping him with a form of peace he hadn't felt in a long time.

Without being told, he somehow knew he would be with her soon.

And that was okay.

His head felt as if it were swelling like a balloon ready to pop. His eyes bulged as if they wanted to plop free of the sockets holding them.

He was done fighting back. It was time to let go. He made peace with his looming demise.

Emily was waiting for him.

Something boomed. It was a faint popping sound that Ethan could barely hear through the rushing of blood in his ears. Something wet pelted his face. The pressure on his throat went away.

Then he dropped at Zeb's feet.

He pulled in a breath that made a sound like squealing tires. Air gushed into his lungs, feeling like tiny razorblades all the way down his chest. Hand to his throat, he looked between the gap of Zeb's legs, back to the edge of the cabin.

Emily was gone.

A sense of loss washed over him that would have caused him to cry out had he been able to find his voice. Then he remembered he'd been dropped. He could breathe now. How had that happened? Looking up, Ethan saw Zeb towering over him. A hole was in his throat, spurting blood while Zeb held his hand against the wound as if trying to hold the blood inside. Ethan looked around Zeb's leg to the window.

Cole, standing in front of the window, aimed his rifle at Zeb through the jagged rim of glass. A thin runnel of smoke curled from the barrel.

Ethan struggled to his feet.

"Stay down, Ethan!" Cole yelled. "Don't want to hit you!"

Shaking his head, Ethan stepped around to Zeb's side. Though he was glad his friend had saved him, he also was furious with him for doing so. He'd made Emily go away. That warm serenity he'd felt moments ago had gone with her.

And in its place his anger and need for retribution had returned.

He shoved the machete into Zeb's stomach, pushing until the hilt touched the kid's shirt. There was a sodden ripping sound as the blade tore through Zeb's back. Blood dumped onto Ethan's hand. It felt like hot soup on his skin, quickly cooling into a tacky substance. Zeb reached down with his other hand, gripping Ethan's wrist to shove it away. There was no strength there to apply any pressure that might hurt him.

"You killed…" Ethan's voice sounded thick and warbly. He cleared his throat to rid it of the prickling taps he felt. "You killed my little girl…" He ripped the machete from Zeb's stomach.

Then Ethan stepped back and swung the machete, aiming high. The blade chopped into the side of Zeb's neck. Ethan only felt slight resistance as the machete sliced all the way through. The head lopped off while Ethan brought the machete around. Zeb's head spun through the air before it smacked the ground and bounced a couple feet away.

Blood spurted from the stump of Zeb's neck. Ethan could see Cole on the side of the crimson geyser, watching. He nodded to Ethan and Ethan nodded back.

Zeb's hands reached out, gripping the air as they seemed to hunt for Ethan. He took a step back, out of their reach. Zeb's body surprised Ethan by stepping forward, still searching for Ethan as if the last command the body had received was to make sure Ethan died.

But he knew Zeb wouldn't. Couldn't. Even as Zeb's large hands patted his chest, his shoulders, he could tell the force guiding them was fading fast. Fingers brushed Ethan's neck again as if they wanted to squeeze it one last time.

Then Zeb's body pitched over, landing beside the head that been attached to it moments ago.

Ethan peered down at the body in silence, taking deep breaths. The pressure in his skull was fading fast.

Finally, Cole spoke. "We got him, partner."

Ethan nodded. "We did."

"It's over."

"Yeah."

Ethan felt no different than he had when they'd arrived at the cabin. There was no great release of his torment, no feeling of victory that he'd craved. It was as if they had accomplished nothing at all. What surprised him the most was how he felt even worse, somehow even deader inside.

This grisly affair had done nothing to help him at all.

22.

Bill was the first to see the dilapidated, two-story house, just as they stepped out from under a canopy of thick branches. The trail went down a short hill, then up again where it ended on a set of rickety steps. The house was shrouded in darkness. Limbs dangled over the roof, raining leaves down as if trying to bury the ramshackle structure in dead foliage. Where windows had once been was now covered in skewed planks. Gaps between the boards showed even murkier darkness inside. The house could have been here since the beginning of time.

"They're in there," said Bill, holding up the tracker. "They haven't moved in a while."

"Guess we better go see."

Bill nodded. "Yeah." He looked at Liz. "Should we radio Ethan now?"

Liz shook her head. "We're in this by ourselves."

Sighing, Bill said, "I was afraid of that."

He pulled his backpack around to his front, opening it. He dropped the tracker inside, then held out something to her. She recognized the shape of her Glock.

Smiling, Liz took her gun. It felt comfortable in her hand, reassuring. "Thanks for grabbing it."

Bill nodded. "Ethan made sure I did."

Liz's throat tightened.

So what? Oh, he's all forgiven for making sure you took a gun?

He wanted her to be safe. That should account for something.

If he wants me safe, I should be there with him. Not out here.

Liz shoved away her thoughts and aimed the light at the house. The bright disc moved along the rotted, warped walls.

Vines slithered here and there, looking like the gnarly string used to tie beef.

Without speaking, they made their way over to the misaligned porch, shining their lights this way and that. Acorns and leaves crunched under their feet. Reaching the steps, they climbed up without stopping. The porch floor felt jittery under Liz's feet as they crossed to the front door.

"Should I kick it in?" Bill asked.

"Check if it's unlocked."

"No doorknob."

"Then we should be good."

"Right." Bill gave a terse nod. "Right."

Liz hoped he was going to be okay. He seemed on the verge of panic. She could hear his fast breaths, almost whistling.

He reached out with a palsied hand, keeping his light pointing at the hole where a knob had been broken away. He pushed on the door. It swayed inward with a low creak that reminded Liz of a squawking crow. Stepping up behind Bill, she aimed her flashlight around his side, into the house.

The twin beams split through the dark, highlighting dust motes swimming in the bright funnels. The beams swept over old furniture that was caked in mud and dust. Springs poked through the cushions of a couch. There was an old rocking chair near a crumbling fireplace. Holes were spread across the hardwood floor as if landmines had been detonated under the boards that blew away chunks.

Liz's beam reached to a hallway next to a set of stairs that rose into shadows. At the far end, she noticed a meager glow, writhing against the back wall.

Candles, maybe a lantern.

"Light," she said.

"Where?"

"Back there."

Bill stared ahead. "I see it."

"Think that's where they are?"

"It's a good possibility."

"Only one way to find out."

"That's true." His voice choked off at the end.

Liz sighed. She almost felt bad for him because he was so frightened. "Wanna trade?"

"Huh?"

"You take the gun, and I take your light?"

Bill was quiet for a moment, then shook his head. "No. I don't...I don't think that would be a good idea."

"Are you sure?"

"Positive." He cleared his throat. "You're not going to accidentally shoot me, are you?"

"I hope not."

"Same here."

They stood in the doorway, gazing toward the back section of the house. There were a lot of murky areas to pass through before reaching it. Plenty of places for somebody to be hiding.

Who would be hiding? The killer's back at the cabin. There's nobody here.

Shouldn't be, anyway. No one except for their friends. They could be alive, for all she knew. Could be back there, waiting, praying for somebody to come help them.

And we're standing here, waiting on one of us to make the first move.

"I'm going in there," said Liz. She entered the house. The floorboards sagged under her with each step. Felt like the floor was made of puddy.

"Damn, it's dark," said Bill, entering behind her.

"Just watch your step."

"Right."

They started moving toward the hallway. Each time they took a step, they stirred up musty dust that Liz could feel on her tongue. There was an odor of decay and mildew and mold all around them. Bill swung his light all over while Liz kept hers trained in front of them. She noticed Bill pause long enough to shine the light up the stairs. The beam swept over old, framed photos, covered in dust. It was impossible to see the pictures inside. Cobwebs were strung all along the railing as if it were a Halloween spook house.

It is a spook house.

Liz gulped.

Bill brought the light down and added it to Liz's in the corridor beside the stairs. They kept walking, moving at a lethargic, yet prudent pace. They passed the kitchen to their right, the doorway filled with darkness. Liz didn't like walking in front of it, not knowing what was on the other side. Bill's light pierced the heavy black, showing there was nothing there except an empty doorway. A table was just inside, covered in dirty plates and pans. Then they were moving past it, continuing down the hall.

The final doorway to their right glowed with a carroty flicker. Liz saw part of the wall coming into view, lined with cracks in the plaster. What she could see of the floor was hidden under leaves and other debris.

Their already sluggish walk slowed to a crawl. Liz assumed that, like her, Bill had no desire to see what was in there.

A few seconds later, they reached the doorway, standing just on the outside. The putrid stench was much stronger here, overpowering any of the musty odors that she'd been able to smell before.

"The hell is that smell?" whispered Bill.

Liz shook her head. She had no idea, didn't want to know. But she knew she was about to find out. There was no way getting around that.

Liz pushed herself away from the door frame, stepped around, and faced inside the room. Her light pushed into the dim luminosity, grazing over a slew of discarded bodies along the floor. Looking past those, another corpse grabbed her attention—decayed and rotted, its skin pruned and the color of old wood. It had no eyes, only vacant sockets inside a grinning, filthy skull draped in dingy, yellow curls. It had been propped up in an old, padded chair in the corner, like the guest of honor at this grotesque party.

Choking on her scream, Liz averted her eyes and noticed Trish. She seemed to be on her stomach, yet her face was somehow pointing upward. A lumpy column of flesh bulged from her neck. Beside her was Martin, his stomach fileted and hollowed out. She saw ridges of spine and the tips of his ribcage inside the flaps of skin. What she thought was George's face had been stretched around a lantern so that the glass showed through his open mouth and scooped eyes. Piss-colored light wavered from the orifices.

Then Liz was turning away, a scream tearing through her lips as she heaved vomit all over the wall. Somewhere behind her, she thought she heard Bill screaming as well. It was hard to understand much over her own shrieks that seemed to be coming so close together she couldn't take a breath between them.

Another light clicked on, exposing them in a tunnel of brightness greater than their combined flashlights. Liz saw the dark shape of a person formed below the glare. She glimpsed twinkling metal, the shape of a star.

Then she saw the blond ponytail, the gun drawn, and realized who she was looking at.

The deputy.

As if to confirm her theory, Deputy Reese stepped forward, lowering the gun. Her mouth was clenched into a grimace while her eyes, narrow and focused, flicked back and forth from Liz to Bill before landing on Liz.

Deputy Reese managed to relax her jaw before saying, "What the hell is going on here?"

23.

While the women started cleaning inside, Cole helped Ethan spread out the tarp on the ground. They each picked a side of Zeb and lifted the carcass. Zeb's arms bounced as they carried him, his hand smacking Ethan's thigh. When they were both on either end of the tarp, they let him drop. His body smacked the tarp, making it rattle.

"How long have Bill and Liz been gone?" asked Cole in a winded voice.

Ethan checked his phone and saw how late it was. "Pretty long." He felt a cramp in his gut. He assumed they would have heard from them by now.

"Want me to go look for them while you're handling this?"

Ethan wished he could. But he needed Cole to stay here and supervise and make sure the mess inside was cleaned up. He told this to Cole. Then he said, "When I'm done, I'll see if I can track them down."

"How much longer until daylight?" asked Cole.

"Couple hours."

"Think that cop's going to stop by?"

"She said she would, so I imagine so."

Nodding, Cole said, "We'll have this place sparkling by then."

"Good. Help me wrap him."

Ethan grabbed a corner of the tarp and folded it over Zeb's right shoulder. The edge draped over the nub that was his neck. "Damn," he said. Looking up, he saw Cole was starting to fold the opposite ends over Zeb's legs.

Cole paused. "What?"

"His head."

Cole looked over, winced. "Damn. Forgot."

Ethan had forgotten too. He was surprised he was able to remember anything at all from how exhausted he was. It was like his body was handling everything while his mind was in sleep mode. "I'll grab it."

"Nah, I got it."

Cole walked over to where the head rested on the ground, gazing up at Cole. The jaw was still cocked to one side, the skin of his cheek stretched farther than it should have been. Staring down at the head, Cole said, "Damn, partner. We did a number on this bastard."

"Yeah." Ethan sighed. "We did."

"Feel guilty about it?"

"Do you?"

Cole seemed to think about this. "No. That's not it. I'm not sure how to express it."

"I don't think I feel anything at all."

Cole looked over at him, nodded. "Yeah. Same here. What about the machete?"

"What?"

Cole tapped the hilt of the machete with his boot. Ethan had left it on the ground near where Zeb had fallen. "Want to keep it? A trophy or something?"

Ethan shook his head. "No. I don't want any reminders."

"Gotcha." Bending over, he grabbed a handful of Zeb's hair with one hand and the machete with the other. As if the head was a bucket and the hair was his handle, Cole started back toward Ethan. The machete blade swayed by his other leg. "You know, when the mask came off, I expected him to be damn hideous under it."

"He wasn't gorgeous."

"No. But I expected him to be gross. Deformed. Like in the movies. Sure, he wasn't going on any magazine covers, but he really just looked like a guy."

"Yeah."

Cole dropped the head in Zeb's lap, followed by the machete. "I'll be honest. It pissed me off that he wasn't ugly." He looked up at the stars. "I don't know why it did, but it did. I was already furious by that point. But when the mask came off, and he was just somewhat normal-looking, I..." He shook his head, looked back down at Ethan. "I wanted to rip his face off."

"Was that why you went at him with the brass knucks?"

Cole lifted a shoulder in a slight shrug. "Part of the reason, I guess. I didn't think he deserved to be an almost average-looking guy. He needed to be ugly because of what he was—a killer. But he wasn't. He was just a kid, huh? Probably not much older than our girls. And I guess that bothers me some. He was a kid, too."

Ethan didn't know what to say. He continued to stare at Cole. He'd never heard that tone in his best friend's voice before: vulnerable and a bit ingenuous. It reminded Ethan of the first time they went deer hunting together as kids. They'd gone with Ethan's grandfather and had been so excited about it they hadn't slept at all the night before because they were too busy predicting all the deer they were going to slay. Neither of them shot anything, but Grandpa got a nice buck. It had actually cried out when the bullet struck its neck. They'd watched from the deer stand as it wobbled this way and that, its head sagging lower and lower until finally it dropped onto the ground. It still didn't die right away. Several agonizing minutes went by while the poor animal suffered.

They acted as if they were proud and enthusiastic about Grandpa's kill, but both boys had been so traumatized by it that they swore to each other they'd never hunt a living creature again. Sure, that pact only lasted until they were teenagers, but the cold shame they'd felt over the deer's death had stayed with them for a long time.

Ethan didn't think he felt any regret over what they'd done tonight, but he knew something had changed inside of him. Maybe it was knowing that he could take a life, even if he felt it was justified and would only be consumed by a blank emotion afterward. What if the kid version of him had somehow known this day would come, and he had been mourning the loss of his morality instead of the deer?

Too tired for such deep thoughts.

He needed to stop.

"You all right?"

"Huh?" He looked up at Cole. "Why do you ask?"

Cole stared down at him. His face was blocked by shadows, but his sympathetic eyes were easy to see. "You zoned out."

"Thinking."

"About?"

"Nothing, really."

Cole was quiet a moment. "Yeah."

Ethan sighed. "I think it might be best if neither of us think too much about this. We should just do what we know we have to do and not let the rest of it get to us."

Cole nodded. "Sure."

So they got back to work. By the time they finished wrapping Zeb's body, he looked like he'd morphed into a tarp cocoon. Cole used rope to tie it all down, interlacing the rope in different directions so it wouldn't come undone. With that finished, they grabbed their chosen ends and hefted. Somehow, the body felt even heavier than before. With Ethan in the front, his back to the driveway, they shuffled toward Cole's Blazer. Cole had already lifted the gate, so it hung open like a hungry mouth. Ethan stepped aside, placing the upper half of Zeb on the edge of the cab. Then he joined Cole at the back as they shoved him in.

Ethan fetched a couple shovels. The blades clanged when he added them to the back. He stepped out of the way as Cole reached up and gripped the gate. He swung down. The gate banged shut, its retort resounding like a rifle blast in the quiet night.

Cole let out a breath that puffed his cheeks. "You're sure you don't want me to go with you?"

Ethan shook his head. "I'm sure. You need keep an eye on things around here."

"That's a lot of digging to do by yourself."

Ethan didn't want to get into this again. He sighed. "I want to do it."

Though Cole acted as if he wanted to say more about it, he only nodded again.

"Be careful out there."

"I will. If Liz and Bill get back before I do, let me know."

"Got your walkie?"

Ethan nodded. It was in his backpack, which he'd put in the passenger seat before they'd mummified Zeb. He'd packed some water, snacks, the walkie, and his gun.

"Radio me when you get there," said Cole. "And don't mess up my ride."

"Sure thing, dear."

Cole smirked. He patted Ethan's shoulder. "See you soon."

Ethan watched Cole walk back to the cabin. As he started up the steps, the door swung open. Tina stood in the doorway, arms spreading. Cole hugged her, then guided her back inside so he could close the door.

Watching their affection filled him with a sinking feeling. He thought about Emily before his mind turned to Liz. He wondered if it was over between them. He didn't want it to be, but he also didn't see how they could move past this. He wasn't even sure they were going get away with it at all. If legal trouble came from this, Ethan didn't know what he would do. He also supposed it didn't matter either way.

He'd have to worry about that later.

Ethan climbed in the Blazer and cranked the engine. All the exhaustion he'd been trying to resist finally conquered him, spreading through his muscles like lead. His arms felt heavy and weak. He let his head drop back on the headrest. He knew if he closed his eyes, he would fall asleep and still be sitting here when the sun came up.

Out of nowhere, he started to sob. He'd meant to take a deep breath, but his lip had started to quiver, and that was all it took for the tears to pour out. His throat clucked as he cried, shoulders bouncing. He rubbed his eyes, wiping the tears away, only for fresh batches to take their place. It went on like this for a couple minutes.

Get it together. Cole's going to come out here and check on you if you don't get moving.

Sniffling, Ethan tried to settle himself. It didn't work at first. He tried a few more times before catching control of his breathing. Once he did that, he was able to stop the tears. He used the bottom of his shirt to dry his face.

"There," he said, his voice jittery. "There. You're better now."

He almost started to cry again. This time, he swallowed it back down. Held his breath. After a minute or so, he let it out. Though his chest felt sore and quivery, that seemed to do the trick. He seemed to be okay now.

He let out another long breath through his nostrils. His hands were no longer shaking. His vision had cleared. He was good to drive now.

Get it over with.

Nodding to himself, Ethan switched on the headlights. Light burst in front of him.

And exposed the large man standing in front of the truck.

Thick arms hung by his sides. Ethan glimpsed a bushel of long hair, wide shoulders and overalls before the hairy giant turned and dashed to the left. Ethan tried to follow where he was going but lost him in the darkness outside the span of light.

"Son of a bitch," he said through a gasp.

He turned to reach for his bag. He needed the walkie. And his gun.

The window beside him exploded. He felt nicks and slits on his face as the glass shrapnel was flung all over him. Beefy hands reached in, grabbed him by the shirt, and pulled. Next thing Ethan knew, he was jerked through the busted window and thrown.

Ethan didn't think he'd been knocked out, but he was somehow on the ground with no memory of landing. His vision was blurred as he looked toward the Blazer. He was shocked by how far he'd been launched. It looked as if they were on opposite ends of an empty swimming pool.

The big man started moving.

Ethan tried to scream, but his voice was stuck in his lungs, unable to break through.

Instead of coming toward Ethan, the man walked alongside the Blazer, making his way to the back. He gripped the handle on the gate and swung it upward with such force the hinges screamed.

The man stood in the spill of cab light, peering into the cab. He reached in. Rustling sounds came from inside, followed by a quick ripping as the tarp was torn. The man jumped back with a pained moan. His large hands went up to his face that was covered with crudely patched cloth. Ethan saw the straps leading into the nappy hair where it tied in the back. The lower half of his face was covered, connected to a patch that masked the left side as well. All that was exposed was the section around the tears spewing from his right eye.

Ethan couldn't lay there any longer. Each second that ticked by was another second he couldn't afford to lose. But moving seemed like an unfeasible fantasy because his whole body felt as if it had been dropped from an airplane.

The enormous man shook his head as if he were trying to shake away the moans and sobs. It must have worked because when he turned to face Ethan again, all that was in the visible eye was hatred. Ethan could see the evident rage even in the heavy darkness cloaking him. A thick arm lifted, hand reaching behind his back. When it came back, it held a double-edged ax with blades that would have made Paul Bunyan envious.

"God Almighty," Ethan managed to say through his stammers.

The man took a step toward him. The boot that pressed down on the ground looked as if it had been constructed for Frankenstein's monster. Ethan had nothing to defend himself. His only weapon was inside the Blazer.

That wasn't true, he realized. He still had his knife. The one Emily had selected for him. Had she not done that, he would have nothing to defend himself with right now. But what good would a single blade do against a tree-killer like the one the man held? At this point, it didn't really matter. One knife was better than being empty-handed.

Ethan gripped the hilt, tearing it free of the sheath. Scrambling to his knees, he held the knife out in front of him. The blade pointed at the giant monstrosity, the tip quivering as he loomed closer. This maniac was related to Zeb. No doubt about it. The streaks of gray in the wild hair made him think he was staring at Zeb's father—Mr. Gorley.

"Stay away from me," Ethan tried to say. All he managed to produce were strained croaks.

The ogre kept coming, one menacing step at a time. His fingers were like sausages, curled around the thick shaft of the ax so hard they made crackling sounds. He came closer still, and Ethan swung out with the knife. The blade whooshed through air, missing the man's legs by almost a foot.

Ethan stared up at the man, holding the knife up so the blade pointed at his stomach. He couldn't see his face now from the deep shadows thrown across him. But he could see the ax, the blade rising as the moonlight glinted off its stained surface.

This was it. Now he was going to die for real. He glanced around, hoping to spot Emily again. She was nowhere around. All he saw was darkness, trees, and…

He frowned.

Gale?

She stepped out from behind the Blazer, the shorter of the two shovels he'd packed up in her hand. Thoughts flickered through his mind, questions that he had to ignore. The one that confused him the most was how she was out here and not in his room anymore. Shuffling as fast as she could, she made her way to the big man. She swung. The shovel clanged against the back of the ogre's skull hard enough that the handle snapped in half. Ethan watched the blade spin away. It landed somewhere in the shadows.

The ogre turned around. Gale, holding the broken piece of rod, gasped. Shaking her head, she stepped back as the man moved toward her.

Ethan saw his chance. His window of opportunity was only opened a crack, and if he didn't act now, it would shut again.

Ignoring the pain he felt all over, he pushed himself to his feet. His vision swam, flashed as if the paparazzi were snapping off pictures of him. Though he was standing, he couldn't feel the ground under his feet.

Don't faint, dumbass!

Ethan steeled himself, ignored the sudden nausea.

And lunged.

His plan had been to plant the knife into the nape of the ogre's wide neck. He hadn't prepared himself for just how tall the man really was. The blade went into his back near the left shoulder blade. Ethan put his weight into the strike and still only managed to get the blade to sink in about halfway. He felt the knife's tip scape along bone as hard as concrete.

But the weak attack was enough to distract Mr. Gorley away from Gale.

Groaning, the man reached over his shoulder, patting for the knife. Ethan didn't wait to see if he succeeded in removing it. He grabbed Gale's hand, tugging her until she started moving with him. She tried to match his speed, but she was just too weak and mostly stumbled and tried not fall. If they kept going at this pace, neither would make it to the cabin. Ethan scooped her up, cradling her like a bride, and ran. In his jarring vision, he saw the cabin. It looked as if it had been connected to a strap that was pulling it away from him. The ground stretched and turned ahead of him, fading in and out as he fought to not pass out.

He dared a glance over his shoulder as he mounded the steps. He was prepared to see Mr. Gorley had plucked the knife from his back by now and started his pursuit. But what he actually saw was the giant maniac was right on his heels. As Ethan's feet came down on the porch, the man's boots touched the bottom step. The ax was only a couple feet from Ethan's backside.

Ethan adjusted Gale so she hung over his shoulder, freeing up one of his hands. He heard her moaning in his ear. He knew this position had to be awful for her since his shoulder was pressing into her wound. She would have to deal with it, though.

He gripped the doorknob, hoping they hadn't locked the door yet. When it turned, he let loose with a joyous cackle. The door flew open. He glimpsed Cole and Tina by the chair Zeb had been chained to. Ramona was entering the room, carrying a bucket.

All heads turned toward him.

The women started screaming when he charged inside, kicking the door shut behind him. He let Gale drop to the floor as he started to twist the locks. The door shook in its frame when Mr. Gorley slammed against it. Another wham and the walls of the cabin vibrated.

"Jesus Christ!" Ethan screamed.

He got the rest of the locks in place, crouched next to Gale, and helped her stand.

"Who the hell is that?" he heard Cole shout as the sound of him jacking a round into his rifle resounded through the room.

Ethan looked at his friend. "I think it's Zeb's father."

Cole's face drained of its color.

The walls shook with another hit.

Cole gulped. "Oh, shit."

"The window!" Tina yelled.

Ethan looked over, seeing the broken window Zeb had jumped through. He'd forgotten all about it. "Damn!"

He pushed Gale over to Tina, then ran to the window. He took a quick glance out, then grabbed the shudders and pulled them shut, dropping the hook into the eye. It wouldn't keep the man out, but it should slow him down while they reinforced it.

"Cole," he said as another boom rattled the door. It sounded like he was trying to chop it down with the ax.

"What?" Cole shouted.

"Drag the table over here. Ramona, go into the kitchen and get the nails."

As Cole and Ramona went in opposite directions to retrieve what Ethan had ordered them to, he darted over to where the hammer was on the floor. Snatching it up, he turned back and ran to the window as Cole met him there, holding the coffee table out in front of him. He slammed it against the windowsill, holding it.

Emily's voice floated through his head.

He was big and reeked of death!

The obvious realization dawned on Ethan—Zeb hadn't been the one she'd gone against, after all. It was Mr. Gorley's nose she'd bitten off. That was why he wore that rag mask, to cover the scars Emily had caused.

"Where's Ramona?" Cole said, snapping Ethan out of his troubled thoughts.

Ethan turned to find her. As if on cue, Ramona appeared, rushing toward them with a box of nails. Ethan reached in, pricking his finger on a sharp tip. Hissing at the pain, he tugged out a few nails and began pounding them into the table.

"His damn father," Cole said under his breath. "His..." Cole shook his head. "Damn. We killed the wrong one, didn't we?"

Ethan tried not to think about it. His mind needed to be clear, so he could figure a way out of this. Because he knew it was only a matter of time before Mr. Gorely got inside. Didn't matter how much work they'd done to reinforce the cabin.

He was coming to kill them all.

24.

Reese put her gun away, but kept her light trained on the explorers. After a quick round of introductions, Liz and Bill shared a wild story in exasperated bursts, taking turns, picking up where the other left off. They spoke fast, breathless, like little kids trying to convince their parents they saw a UFO outside. Though Liz wanted them to reach the end of it all, she didn't rush them. She stood in the same spot, listening.

Finally, after several minutes, the concentration in their voices petered out. They stood before her, breathless and sweaty.

"And when you left the house," said Reese. "What were the others going to do?"

Bill shrugged. "Probably nothing good. I'm sure they meant to kill him. Our goal had been to capture him, but this…" He waved his flashlight, pointing the beam into the room. "They're dead. Really dead. Ethan said it was a risk, but I don't think any of us actually believed we were in any danger. This changes everything. I don't think Ethan and Cole realize what they're up against."

Liz stared at Reese before saying, "How did you know to find us here?"

Reese told her how she'd parked her cruiser on the side of the road and saw them leaving. She'd thought it was odd they would be going anywhere at that hour, so on a hunch, she'd followed them.

"Thank God for that," said Bill.

Liz pointed at her. "Your headlights. I saw your headlights."

Nodding, Reese said, "I figured you did, so when you braked, I cut them off real fast." She let out a heavy breath. She could taste the house's mold, could feel the dust coating her tongue. It almost gagged her. She started walking, waving her light around her feet. The floor felt like wet cardboard. If she stepped too hard, she might fall right through to whatever was below. She saw spatters of vomit here and there and moved carefully so she wouldn't slip in the chunky puddles.

"Sorry," said Liz. "I couldn't help myself."

"It's fine. A normal reaction." She stood beside Liz as she gazed into the room. She saw the indistinct shapes of dead bodies along the shadows of the floor. It was hard to tell how many were there. Some had been there for a long time and had decayed and rotted to tattered flesh and bones. The fresher corpses must have been their friends. They were chewed up and mangled, as if they'd gone against a bear. Her eyes made their way to a female corpse in an old, padded chair in the corner of the room. It wore a sundress underneath a flannel shirt that had been buttoned over top. The face was brown and shrunken, the eyes empty and black. The mouth's lips were pressed together, furrowed and desiccated like an old walnut. The puffy hair hung around its face and shoulders like a veil. The whole scene before her did all it could to drown her in shock.

What the hell is going on here?

She'd been a cop in this county for three years now. How had she not known this house was out here? Did any of her colleagues know? Nobody had ever mentioned it. Even when the murders happened last year and they combed the woods up and down in massive hunt for the killer, nobody had come across this place. None of the locals had mentioned the decrepit house in the woods.

How was that possible?

Liz wiped the tears from her eyes. Those that had spilled had left wet lines through the dirt on her face. "What do we do now?"

"First, we have to get back to my car. Then I'll radio for help. I'll get somebody out to the cabin right away, try to catch your friends before they do anything else stupid."

"How much trouble are we in?" Bill asked.

Reese shook her head. "Don't worry about that right now. First thing's first, we..."

Reese peered into the room again. Something had changed.

"What is it?" asked Liz.

Reese held up a finger to silence her. She wasn't exactly sure what was wrong. Whatever the change was, it was subtle. It took her a couple lookovers before her eyes landed on that worn-out chair again.

She studied the corpse.

"No way," she muttered.

Aiming the flashlight at the dead body, the disc of light moved up and down the old clothes, the withered skin. The hair was all wrong now. No longer light-colored and lengthy, it was short and dark. The sundress was gone, as was the flannel shirt. This one was dressed in a hoary tank top and threadbare shorts, as if she'd been a hiker before her death on a trail.

It's a different corpse.

How that could be true, she had no idea. But the realization was accurate. And if that was the case, that meant it had been switched just now, while they were talking.

"What's wrong?" Liz said, louder.

"We're not alone in this house," said Reese. "We have to get out of here. Now!"

She jerked her gun from its holster. She spun around on her heels, ready to lead them away from this place.

Her flashlight slashed the darkness of the hall.

And landed on the female corpse rushing at them, yanking the pulley on a chainsaw that looked almost as big as her as she let loose a shrill scream that thundered in the cramped space. Instead of firing, Reese only screamed in reply, as did Liz and Bill beside her.

The small engine roared as the chain began to spin, spurting hot air in Reese's face, rattling her brain and shaking her teeth. The din was discombobulating, making it hard to focus as she lifted the gun. She pulled the trigger, knowing it was a wild shot. The hallway flashed, the retort of the gun almost silent compared the boisterous chainsaw. The nappy hair on the corpse fluttered as the bullet zipped by. It punched into the ceiling, blowing a chunk away.

The corpse was swinging the chainsaw before Reese had

the chance to take another shot. She saw the whirring blade coming straight for her chest and tried to turn away in hopes of missing it.

She failed. The chain glanced over her ribcage, tearing through her shirt, the tank top underneath, and then the flesh beneath that. There was a grating sound when the metal teeth touched her bone. A burst of blood and sparks clouded in front of her.

Shrieking, Reese spun away, throwing herself into the open doorway. She staggered onto a dead body, the stiff legs kicking her feet out from under her. She landed on her side, sinking into the mushy pile that remained of a man's midriff.

Still screaming, Reese rolled onto her back. To her surprise, she hadn't dropped her gun in all the commotion. She used her forearm to rub the dead man's blood from her eyes. Through red streaks in her vision, she saw the chainsaw push into Bill's stomach, ripping through the clothes and flesh as blood and chunky glops sprayed all over. Liz stood close by, screaming while her face was splashed and slapped with gore.

"Get out of the way!" Reese yelled.

But her voice was inaudible through Bill's cries, through Liz's wild shrieks, and the tinny rattle of the chainsaw. The female corpse hooted and squealed, jogging in place while the chainsaw blade dug a trench in Bill's torso from his belly button up the center of his chest. The other end of the blade poked out his back, spinning and coated in thick matter that clung to it.

Reese had to take a shot. She knew she might hit Liz, but if she didn't try to shoot the corpse, Liz was dead for sure. And then Reese would be the next one to feel the chainsaw's violent touch. Again.

Reese aimed. It was hard to see much from the thick paste in her eyes. She squeezed the trigger. This time, she thought the bullet was on the mark. The chainsaw stopped grinding as the corpse spun around. The blade ripped free of Bill's torso, throwing him against Liz. They tumbled backward, bounced off the wall, and fell to the floor.

The corpse turned around, revving the chainsaw a few times. Its shriveled face tilted, the parched hair dangling to the side as she studied Reese. She raised the massive tool so Reese could see just how big the blade actually was. Reese spotted the path the bullet traveled on the corpse's withered hand, spewing blood down her fingers. How much of it was her own and Bill's, she had no idea. One thing she knew for sure, she'd wounded her. It didn't appear the bullet had gone through her hand, only grazed her.

But it had been enough to inflict pain and prove the corpse was a person costumed in the rotted skin of another. The dress fluttered around her ankles, showing glimpses of bare skin between the bottom and the tops of her boots. The skin was the color of milk, blotted in dirt and grime.

This realization did nothing to help Reese feel any better because she had to stop the feral bitch, and she needed to do it right away.

Reese pointed the gun at the corpse again, training the sites on her face. Just as she was about to fire, the corpse made an abrupt turn and dashed into the darkness, away from them. She heard the puttering saw making its way up the hall. There was a loud banging sound that probably had been the front door being knocked open. Then the puttering was outside, fading with each passing second. Soon, Reese couldn't hear it at all.

Gasping, Reese sat up. Pain surged through her side and into her chest. She checked the wound and almost screamed when she saw the damage. The flesh and fabric were in bloody tatters that had coiled like braided hair.

That bitch had gotten her good. Reese might not even survive a wound like this.

Liz's sobbing pulled her attention away from her own injury. She looked over to see the blond woman sitting on her knees as she leaned over Bill. She held him in her arms, screaming at the ceiling while sobs tore through her.

Bill was dead. He'd been nearly sawed in half.

Liz wore his blood like suntan lotion. Clumps had matted her hair, plastering strands to her forehead and cheeks.

Tears poured down her face, washing away the crimson spills while she continued to scream.

25.

The window was as secure as they would be able to make it. Cole tugged on the table. It didn't budge. Ethan had put nails up and down both sides to keep it there. The table was long enough that it covered the entire window. That was a good thing, but it would only hold for a short time. It would be nice if they could hammer something else across its middle to act as a brace. But they didn't have that luxury right now, or really the time for the work.

Gorley would get inside the cabin, eventually.

"What next?" Tina asked, grabbing Cole's arm.

He hadn't even noticed she'd come over to where he and Ethan stood by the window. "Take Gale upstairs. Secure yourselves up in..."

"Oh, shit!" Gale had sat down on the couch, but jumped to her feet, wincing at the pain it caused her stomach. "Damn. Damn!"

"What is it?" Ethan said, going to her. He put a hand on her shoulder to keep her upright.

Gale shook her head. "I'm such an idiot. Upstairs. How I got out. The window's still open. If I could handle climbing out like this..." She moaned. "Then he can handle climbing in, easily."

Ethan turned to look at Cole, his face losing all color. "Where do you think he is?"

Cole listened. Silence drifted through the cabin. Nobody spoke. Nobody even seemed to breathe. The vigorous hammering at the front door had ceased a short while ago. Probably so Gorley could snoop around the house for another way inside.

And if he saw that window...

Cole turned around, staring through the living room to the stairs. He felt a grip on his bicep and turned to see Tina gazing up at him with watery eyes.

"What are you doing?" she asked.

"I'm going to check upstairs."

"I'm going, too," said Ethan.

"No. One of us has to stay down here."

"Then you stay, and I'll go."

Cole looked at Ethan, silently pleading with him to not make this any more difficult than it needed to be. Ethan must have heard his thoughts because he stopped arguing and nodded.

Tina grabbed his arm, pulling him. "Don't go. Don't!"

"Tina… Please."

"Then fine. I'm going with you."

"You just heard me tell Ethan…"

"He's not your wife. I am. Where you go, I go. Bottom line. Can't nobody *make* me stay down here anyway."

"Just take her," said Ethan. "By the time you're done fighting about it, he might be inside."

Cole worried that action had already happened, which was the main reason he didn't want Tina up there with him. Still, knowing all this, he knew even more that it would be pointless to keep resisting because she would get her way. And Ethan was right that this was already taking too long. He tried to pin down when he'd last heard the pounding at the front door. It had been a few minutes, at least.

Gorley could be anywhere.

"Fine," said Cole. He looked at Ethan. "Got your rifle?"

Ethan grabbed it from where it was leaning against the wall.

To Tina, Cole said, "Come on."

He checked his rifle to make sure it was ready to fire. He kept his finger near the trigger in case he needed to shoot as he headed for the stairs. Tina was right beside him, pressing close enough their elbows rubbed together as they walked.

Reaching the stairs, he stepped in front of her. "I'll go first."

Surprisingly, she didn't argue, though he could tell she was holding in her disputes. If Gorley was up there, he wanted to be between that big bastard and his wife.

There was a light switch at the bottom of the stairs. Cole used the barrel of his rifle to flip it. Light fell onto the stairs from the fixture at the top. Cole headed up with Tina right behind him. They didn't bother being discrete because there wasn't time for it. They weren't trying to keep the element of surprise anyway. The window needed to be closed and locked.

Damn, Gale. Sneaking out like that.

But if she hadn't sneaked out, Ethan would be dead now. Ethan said Gale had saved his life.

"Paying him back," she'd said. "It was only fair."

She could have kept going, saving her own ass, and leaving Ethan to die in the process. It would have been what most would have done in that situation. Cole felt even more respect for the gal.

In the hallway, Cole turned on the other light. This bulb looked as if it were on the verge of burning out, only spreading dim luminosity throughout the narrow hall. Ethan's room was at the end of the hall. The door was closed. Light showed in the crack between the bottom of the door and the floor.

Cole stared at that bar of light for several seconds, looking for any kind of flitting shadow that suggested somebody was inside.

He saw nothing.

"Come on," he whispered.

Nodding, Tina walked with him to Ethan's door. Cole stepped back, pointing at the doorknob with his left hand. Tina stepped forward, leaning against the doorframe just to the side of the door. Reaching out, she gripped the doorknob. She looked at Cole, waiting on him to give her the signal to open it.

He did.

Tina turned the knob and flung the door wide. Cole rushed in, keeping the rifle pressed against his shoulder. He looked one way, then the other, turning a circle. He saw the bed, the sheets bunched at the bottom of the mattress. He dropped to his knees, leaning down so he could see under the bed. Nothing was there, nor was there enough space to fit a man Gorley's size. He stood up, darted to the closet. There was a folding door that had been left partly open. He used his boot to push it all the way back.

Only empty hangers hung from the pole inside.

He turned around, let out a breath. He lowered the rifle.

Tina peeked her head in. "All good?"

He nodded. "Seems to be." He looked over at the open window. The curtains fluttered inward from a breeze.

Tina walked across the room. "I'm going to shut this."

"Good idea."

She flung the curtains out of her way, gripped the window with one arm, and pulled it down. Then she locked it. Keeping her hands on the frame, she lowered her head. "What are we going to do?"

Though Cole knew what she meant, he still asked, "Which part?"

"All of it." She looked at him. She'd scrubbed off the eye makeup while he'd been helping Ethan wrap up Zeb's body. There were still faint dark smudges as if she were recovering from a pair of black eyes. "We're in deep shit. Not just with that guy out there, but *after* him, you know. We get past this part, what's next?"

Cole didn't want to think about that right now, and told her so.

"You can't ignore it," she said. "How much trouble do you think we're going to be in?"

"Does it matter?" he asked. "We killed Zeb and this other bastard is next. Far as I'm concerned, I'll be able to sleep guilt-free." He knew that wasn't true. Worse was, he could tell Tina also knew it.

She was right, though. They weren't going to get away with anything. It had been stupid of him to think they would. At the time, he couldn't have cared less if they'd gotten caught. He supposed that it still didn't matter much to him, but those stubborn sentiments were quickly fading.

Shaking her head, Tina turned her attention back to the window. Cole didn't like her standing in front of it like that, making herself an easy target. It was dark outside, which turned the glass into a mirror, hiding whatever was outside from her view.

"Why don't you get away from the window, huh?" Cole said.

Tina started to nod but stopped. Her eyes narrowed as a frown appeared on her face. "What...?"

Before she could finish the sentence, the window shattered as a pair of thick arms reached through the soaring shards and sharp chunks. The arms were hairy, flexing as they hugged around her back, pinning her arms to her sides.

"Tina!" Cole yelled, lifting the rifle. His finger tickled the trigger, wanting to squeeze it and let loose a hail of bullets. *Needing* to do it. The digit trembled against the cool, smooth curve. Couldn't. He would peg Tina for sure. He couldn't use the gun right now.

So, he started to run toward her. His legs felt as if they had been filled with dough and were expected to lift feet that seemed to weigh fifty pounds each.

"Help, Cole!" Tina let out a shriek that was cut short when she was yanked forward. Her forehead bounced off the frame, killing her cries. Head bobbing, she looked over at Cole. Her forehead split, blood dribbling down into her eyes. "C..."

Another hard pull and her forehead struck the wood again hard enough to break through it. Her thighs collided with the lower half of the frame, halting her momentarily before her back snapped. Her legs flew back as did her head, touching together as she shot through the window folded in a way a body never should.

Cole screamed. He tried to fathom what he'd just witnessed, but all he knew for certain was his wife was gone. Where she'd been standing was now only a spread of jagged glass on the carpet and sawdust swimming above it. No longer caring what he shot, he stopped running halfway across the room and raised the rifle again. He was already firing before even leveling the barrel at the window. The rifle kicked his shoulder as bullets tore into the window frame, blowing out more chunks of glass. Wood shavings floated all around as bullets ripped apart the windowsill.

The gun clicked. He pulled the trigger a few more times to the same result. He dropped the magazine, reached into his pocket, and retrieved the other one. He popped it in, cocking the rifle. His ears screamed from the rifle blasts, but he could still faintly hear the pounding of feet on the stairs. They padded up the hall, slowing as they approached the door.

He didn't wait to see who it was. He darted over to the window, the glass crunching under his boots. He saw blood, Tina's blood, oozing down the snapped wood, dripping onto the sill. He looked through the spiky hole in the window and saw only darkness. Nobody was on the roof. A trail of blood led from the window to the edge and vanished over it.

He jumped off. Took her and jumped.

An image of Tina bending in half flashed in his mind.

She's okay. She's okay.

He knew she wasn't.

She is! She has to be!

"Tina!" he yelled through the glass.

A scream fired back as a retort, chilling Cole's blood and making him shudder. It was Tina. Now he knew she'd survived that, if only long enough to endure whatever awful retribution Gorley did next. Cole began to weep as he listened to her screams turn to thick gurgles before fading to a single, shrill moan. Then tranquility returned to the night, bringing with it the steady chorus of crickets.

Wanting to cry out for her again, he could only mouth her name. His voice was lost behind the sobs.

"What the hell happened?" Ethan's voice. It sounded garbled through the steady whine in Cole's ears. He might have permanently damaged his hearing.

He didn't care.

"T...Tina. She..." Cole tried to point at the window, but he could barely lift his arm.

Ethan started walking toward the window.

"No!" Cole yelled. He rushed over to Ethan, putting his hands on chest. "Stay away from the window! That's how he got her."

"Got her? He got Tina?"

Cole nodded, then shook his head. "He killed her. Just now. She's dead."

Ethan looked at the window. "Damn it."

26.

Liz held back vomit as she daubed Reese's grisly wound. She used the deputy's uniform shirt, folding it into a compress, and pushing it against the mangled injury. It looked like a bowl packed with raw hamburger and threadbare ribbons. She tasted hot, sour bile at the back of her throat and swallowed it back down. "Hold it there."

Hissing, Reese nodded. She put her hand on her shirt.

Thank God I don't have to look at it anymore.

Liz stretched out the uniform sleeves, letting them dangle like hoses. Then she reached them around Reese's midriff, letting them hang over her breasts. The white tank top she had on was stained with red spatters. Sweat had turned the undergarment translucent, showing hints of her dark bra underneath. Liz stepped around Reese and tied the sleeve cuffs into a knot under her left arm and pulled the knot taut.

"Ow!"

"Sorry," Liz said.

Reese let out a heavy breath, then let go of the shirt. It held. "Th-thanks."

Liz nodded. She shone the flashlight on her craftsmanship and frowned. Blood was already trickling out from the bottom of the compress. "It's bad."

"I know."

"You need a doctor."

"I know that, too." Groaning, Reese stood up.

They were in the living room of the old house, away from Bill's body. Liz hadn't wanted to leave him back in the hall, near those other bodies, but she knew there was no other choice. It wasn't as if she could carry him with her.

Liz looked down at herself. Even in the dark, she could see the darker stains of Bill's blood all over her front. She could feel the cool viscousness of it seeping through her clothes.

"Where do you think she is?" asked Liz. Liz wasn't exactly sure what was underneath that corpse getup. Could've been a man, a boy, or even an ape for all she knew. One thing she noticed, though, was the legs had been shaved. Sure, that didn't mean anything either, she supposed.

"Out there somewhere," said Reese. "So long as she's not here."

Liz turned around, aiming the flashlight out the front door. She saw nothing out there. Only the trilling sounds of crickets could be heard outside. Her scalp felt as if tiny legs were scampering all over. She brushed the top of her head. It was fine.

"You got your gun?" asked Reese.

"Yeah." Liz patted her back, feeling the hardness of the handle through her shirt. She'd tucked it into the waistband of her shorts. "I wish I had the radio."

"That radio's done for."

Liz nodded. It had been in the bag when the chainsaw blade ripped through Bill's torso. Everything in the backpack was destroyed by the spinning chain, including the radio.

"Okay," said Liz through a groan. "We're going to start walking."

"Are you sure you can?"

"I have no choice. We need to get back to my car, so I can call this in. We need backup."

"Yeah." Liz wondered how the others were fairing. How would Ramona handle the news about Bill? How would any of them handle it? Then a thought struck her, one she wished would have come to her sooner. "Do you think she's on her way to the cabin?"

"Why?"

"She heard us talking. Heard everything. And there's no way she's not connected to him. She might be heading there right now to help him."

"I'd say that's a good possibility, which is why we need to get moving."

Reese started walking toward the door. The beam of her flashlight jittered around her feet. She moved slow and sluggish, but at least she was moving. Liz was worried that she'd have to assist her all the way back to the cars. So far, she looked okay.

Outside, Liz waved her flashlight this way and that. Everything looked okay. The air was crisp and fresh, much better than the stuffy dankness inside. It was easier to breathe out here and held a sweet scent that made her think of fresh rain.

Reese stayed to the left, her flashlight in one hand, her gun in the other. Liz left hers tucked behind her back. She could feel it nudging her as she walked, rubbing her skin. Though it was uncomfortable, she wasn't going to move the weapon because she didn't feel like carrying it.

They reached the trail. Reese shone her light on the ground. "She went through here."

Liz saw the footprints making a hasty retreat up the hill. They went all the way to the top and most likely on over to the other side. Maybe it wouldn't be a bad idea to have the gun ready. She tugged it out of her shorts. The grip was slick in her sweaty hand. She wished they could have borrowed Bill's backpack.

Then she remembered it was ruined.

Oh, good job, Liz. Think about that.

Liz felt tears burning her eyes. She took a deep breath to hold them in.

Damn it, Bill.

It had been a terrible idea to come out here. Terrible and stupid. And now Bill was dead. Ramona was a widow now, a childless widow. And so many of their friends had been killed already. Might even be more before the night was over.

Might even be Ethan.

"Are you okay?" Reese asked.

Liz nodded. "Peachy."

Reese stared at her a moment, then turned away. She must have decided not to say anything more.

Neither spoke for a good part of the trek. They swept their lights back and forth, keeping their focus on their own side of the skinny path. Sometimes they accidentally nudged each other, which caused a quiet hiss of pain from Reese. Each time, Liz muttered an apology.

Nothing seemed to be stirring out there in the dark. The woods were mostly silent except for the occasional rustle far off in the trees that sounded much too light to be a person. Most likely it was a forest critter causing the disturbance, spooked by their movements and running for cover.

Besides, the corpse girl's footprints were still heading the direction they were going. For all she knew, they were being led right into a trap.

Reese groaned, then slowed down. "Damn."

"What's wrong?"

"Damn thing hurts."

"You were nearly sawed in half, so consider yourself lucky."

"I thank my lucky stars."

"Could just thank your ribcage. It kept you alive."

Reese was quiet a moment, then said, "Sorry about your friend. I didn't say so before and should have. I feel like a bitch for complaining about this after what happened to him."

Liz didn't know what to say. It wasn't like she was actually *friends* with Bill, but she supposed she liked him. She knew him through Ethan, same as she knew the others. But she was still sad about what happened to Bill, and she knew Ramona would be devastated when she found out. Especially when she remembered the last words she said to him before they left.

"Well, you were wounded," said Liz. "I think you're justified to complain a little bit."

"I suppose." Reese let out a tight breath, as if she were trying to work through a stomach cramp. "We're almost at the cars."

"I was thinking we were. I'm glad, too. I'll feel better once I'm in there."

"I was thinking you should just ride back with me. No way should we separate at this point. Hard to tell where that crazy bitch got to."

Though Liz didn't exactly relish the idea of leaving Ethan's Jeep out here, she didn't make any disputes. It was probably safer for them both to be together, watching each other's back.

"Let's pick up the pace some," said Reese. "We're almost there."

Liz thought she recognized the area they were walking through. It was hard to be certain, though, since all of it looked the same: Trees packed close to the trail, solid black stuffed between the trunks and piled under the limbs all around them. They could have been walking in the wrong direction this whole time, and she would probably still think they were going the right way.

Every so often, she checked for footprints. She saw them, still forging ahead.

A few minutes later, Reese stopped walking. A barrier of trees was just ahead, a tight gap segregating them into different clusters. "No...way..."

Liz came up beside Reese, aiming her light in the shadowy blotch in the middle. It glared off the front end of the Jeep. Smiling, Liz said, "We made it."

Reese didn't move. She stood on the verge of the trail, head moving slowly from side to side.

"What's wrong?" Liz asked.

"I parked right beside you."

Liz looked over. She didn't see the deputy's vehicle. "Where?"

"There." Reese aimed the flashlight at the empty spot beside the Jeep.

Liz walked over to the trees, pointing the flashlight past the Jeep, moving it one way then another. The Jeep was alone. "What the hell?"

"She took my damn ride."

"What?"

Liz followed the cop onto the dirt road. Reese waved the light all over as if she might somehow locate the car hidden in a different spot. She walked a little ways up the road, swinging the flashlight to either side. "Shit!"

"We'll just take the Jeep," said Liz. "I should probably be the one to drive anyway. You're hurt."

"I can't radio the station from your car."

"You can use my phone." A sinking feeling tugged at her

stomach. "Shit." Though she knew it wouldn't be there, she patted her pockets for her phone. It was still at the cabin. Maybe in the kitchen? She thought that was where she'd had it last. She'd been outside when Bill had told her they were being sent on an errand. She looked over at Reese. Her face was cloaked in shadows, but she still saw the frustration through the dark. "Doesn't matter. There's no signal out here anyway. We can call when we get back there."

Reese groaned so hard that it almost sounded like a growl. She kicked the road, stirring up a cloud of dust around her knees. Then she stomped back in Liz's direction. "That's what we'll have to do then. When we get there, I'll…" Reese paused at the rear of the Jeep. "You've got to be kidding me."

"What now?"

Reese stepped around from the back, the light aimed down at the tire. Liz followed the path of the beam down to where it glinted off the rim. The tire was a flat ribbon underneath it.

Liz felt panic try to seize her. She strained all her muscles to keep herself from running away. "That's okay," she said, trying to keep her voice calm. "There's a spare…"

Just as she started to say it, she saw Reese move the beam to the front tire. It was also flat. A puncture wound to the sidewall was the reason for it.

A chill scurried up Liz's spine.

Don't freak out. Don't freak out.

Nothing would be made better if Liz lost her head right now. Nothing. But it seemed so easy to do in the moment, almost reasonable. If she just let her mind go, she wouldn't have to be a part of this insane nightmare any longer.

Keep calm.

While Liz tried to steel herself, Reese crept closer, aiming the flashlight into the Jeep. The light bounced off the glass, hitting Liz's eyes. She turned away as Reese opened the door. The dome light came on.

Reese looked inside for a moment, then heaved a sigh. "This Jeep is toast."

Liz walked over and peered through the open door. The inside had been pillaged. The instrument panel was smashed, wires and odometers dangling like electric guts. The steering wheel had been slashed repeatedly, looking as if Freddy Kruger had tried to steer with his gloved hand. The seats were ripped, the stuffing and springs showing between the torn leather like innards.

Liz's mouth went dry. When she swallowed, it felt as if a dry sock was lodged in her throat. "What now?" Her voice sounded weak and raspy.

Reese didn't answer right away. She scanned the area, waving the flashlight ahead of her. She stopped moving when she was facing the opposite direction, where the road continued on. "The junkyard."

"What?"

"This road should connect to Craven Trail which runs behind the old salvage yard. You probably passed it when you came in this morning. I meet the other deputy there every night before I go on shift."

Liz remembered seeing a junkyard, but it had looked abandoned. "Is it even open?"

"Sometimes. It's not a full-time business anymore these days. But it has power. And a phone, which is what we really need. Plus, it's closer to us than the cabin is right now."

Liz couldn't believe how far out into the woods she and Bill had gone. If they were closer to the junkyard, then that meant they were almost on the other side of the mountain, near Gale's place. "What about Gale's cabin? Couldn't we go there?"

Reese shook her head. Her face was washed in moonlight except for the dark spots of her eyes and mouth. "We'd have to walk all the way back to the crossroad, then hike up. I'm not in any shape to do that. Would take us longer anyway. Otis's junkyard would be a straight shot to Craven, then a right. We'd hardly have to mess with any hills going the route we'll be taking. It's our best shot."

"They have a phone? You're sure?"

"Yes. They have a phone. We call them when we need wrecks towed away. I'll get us inside and call the station. Plus, Dixie, Otis's wife, will probably have a pot of coffee on. I could use some."

Liz could go for some coffee herself, though she didn't like the idea of hiking off in the dark to the junkyard. But she supposed it didn't really matter where they were heading because they would still be hiking in the dark wherever they went, and with that crazy girl out there. She doubted they had anything to worry about from her, though. She was most likely on her way to the cabin right now. Might even already be there. The longer they stood here debating where they should go, the worse it looked for Ethan and the others.

They had no idea she was coming their way.

"All right," said Liz. "Let's do it, then."

"Wait," Reese said, leaning into the Jeep. "Guess she missed this." Reese put her gun in the holster, then reached into the Jeep. When she came back, she held out a bottle of water to Liz.

Liz's tongue tingled at the sight of it. She tucked the flashlight under her arm and took the bottle. While Reese fetched a bottle of her own, Liz twisted off the cap and took three heavy swallows. She forced herself to stop. If she guzzled, it might make her sick.

Reese chugged her water halfway down. In a breathy voice, she said, "Got any more of these?"

"No. These were from this morning. I guess Ethan and I forgot about them."

"Damn." She took another swallow, then put the lid back on. She slipped the bottle into her pocket. "I'm ready."

Liz shoved her bottle in the small pocket of her shorts. She nodded. "Me, too."

Leaving the Jeep behind, they started walking.

27.

Ethan returned downstairs. Ramona and Gale stood together by the fireplace, Ramona held the hatchet and now Gale was armed with Tina's hammer. With wide eyes and trembling lips, they looked like a pair of little girls waiting in the principal's office to hear their punishment for doing something wrong. Ramona watched him, her eyes pleading for information.

Ethan paused halfway in the room. He didn't want to say anything at all but knew he had to. "Cole's...upstairs. He's watching the window."

"All that shooting...?" said Gale, wincing.

"That was Cole."

"What happened?" asked Ramona.

Ethan took a deep breath, then looked at Ramona. "Tina's... gone."

"Gone?"

He nodded. "She's dead."

Gale closed her eyes. "It's...I...my fault. I ..."

Ethan shook his head. "No. It's not your fault."

Before Gale could say more, Ramona jabbed her finger at Ethan. "Tina was fine a minute ago. That can't be right. She was *fine.*"

"I know."

"She went upstairs and was fine. What happened?"

Ethan still wasn't exactly sure because Cole hadn't made much sense when he'd tried explaining the events. "I'm not sure. But that guy...Zeb's dad—he did it."

Ramona's mouth trembled as she tried to breathe. She turned away, shoulders bopping as her throat clucked. When she faced him again, her eyes were red and glassy. Her face was wet with tears. "I can't believe it. I..." She plopped onto the couch, the arm holding the hatchet going limp. It dropped between her legs. Hand gripping the hilt, the hatchet blade stabbed into the floor. She looked off to the side, staring at nothing.

Gale sat beside her, putting a trembling hand on Ramona's shoulder.

Ethan labored to hold in his own sobs.

I got Tina killed. Probably the others, too. Probably us.

All of this was his fault. He'd convinced them to do this. Sure, it hadn't been hard work doing so, but it had been his idea, all of it. They were only out here because he'd made them believe they would succeed.

I warned them, though. Warned them all. They knew the risk.

Did they, really? Had he known, for that matter?

He didn't think so. He supposed it had all almost been like a game from the start. Like when he and Cole were kids and would go into the woods to hunt for Bigfoot. The excitement that they might find something buzzed through their veins while they also felt tranquil inside, because deep down, they knew they wouldn't find one. That was how it had been out here, too. He'd even found himself having fun more than once, especially when they were hurting Zeb. But it had left him empty when it was over.

And now Cole had lost his wife and daughter within a year.

This needed to be finished. The situation had gone so out of control, Ethan would never be able to fix it. The police needed to be brought into things. It was either call for help or allow more of the people he cared about to die.

He wondered where Liz was, if she'd even made it to the campsite. Had that monster out there intercepted her and Bill somewhere in the woods?

Were they dead, too?

Ethan felt something tear deep inside of him, opening a space to allow more sorrow to pour in. He fought back another bout of tears that wanted to come. "I'm calling the police," he said.

"Thank Christ," said Gale.

Ramona blinked. She shook her head as if coming out of a trance. "What did you say?"

Ethan slid his cell phone out of his pocket. He checked the screen. On it was a picture of him with Liz in Colonial Williamsburg. They'd visited the area a couple months back because it was a place neither had been to but had both wanted to see. That had been a good trip, overall. There were even moments when Ethan found himself forgetting about what his life had become, only to remember and feel more guilt because he'd allowed himself a glimpse of getting past it.

He checked for a signal. No bars. Holding it up, he walked back and forth trying to find a strong enough signal to call out. "I've caused enough trouble. We need help."

Ramona shook her head. "We can't call the police. They'll... they'll know what we did."

"At this point, it doesn't matter. Tina's dead. We need to put an end to this before more are killed."

Ethan walked over by the window, standing next to the table that had been hammered against the frame. He had half a bar here. It would have to do.

He dialed 911.

The phone tried to connect but was having trouble. Turning to the side, he held his arm out.

"Connect the call, damn it."

Something crashed through the table.

Wood exploded all around Ethan as the heavy object rammed his arm. The collision spun him around, flung him forward. He hit the floor and rolled, losing his phone in the process. When he came to a stop, the side of his face was resting against the hardwood.

Tina's head smacked down in front of him. Her face was frozen in a silent scream as her lifeless eyes stared into his own. She lay on her stomach, her head twisted toward Ethan.

Ethan screamed.

Ramona screamed.

Gale screamed.

Ethan rolled away from Tina's broken body. She looked like a doll that had been horribly abused by a demented child. Her arms and legs were loose and bent in odd directions. The middle of her back was a bloody hole. Flaps of her shirt dangled around the wound like party ribbons.

"He threw her through the damn window!" Ramona shouted.

Ethan looked around for his phone. He spotted it on the floor near Gale's feet. He didn't bother getting up and instead crawled over to Gale. He snatched up his phone. There were no bars over here.

"Shit!"

"Is there another way to call?" Gale asked. "Do you have a landline?" She didn't take her eyes away from the window. Holding the hammer up, she looked ready to whack anybody who might get near her.

Ethan shook his head. "No. I had it disconnected years ago."

That was stupid of me, he realized. When he put the plan in place, he should have had the phone reconnected. If anything, it would have been a nice backup for when things went awry.

He glanced over at the corner of the room, where Bill's equipment had been moved to. "Yes!"

Ethan stood up. He turned to Gale and Ramona. "Guard that window."

Ramona, sniffling, nodded. She wrenched the hatchet from the floor and stood. "Got it."

As Ethan hurried over to Bill's equipment, he heard the heavy pounding of feet on the stairs. Cole was coming down. He'd no doubt heard the commotion.

He wished there was a way to cover up Tina before his friend saw her. There weren't any blankets down here. There might be some towels in the closet behind the stairs, but it was too late for that now.

"What happened?" Cole said. "I heard..."

"Don't look!" Ramona said.

Ethan dropped to his knees. He pulled the laptop over to him.

"Buh-baby...?" said Cole.

His old friend stood beside Ramona, staring down at the floor. From where Ethan was, he couldn't see Tina, but he knew she was there in Cole's line of sight. He also remembered the mangled condition of her body and felt terrible that Cole could see her like that. It was probably causing flashbacks of Cole's daughter in the morgue when they'd had to go identify the bodies.

A fresh surge of rage pumped through him. For a moment, he was tempted to grab his rifle and march outside to find that bastard, but he thought better of it. They needed the police.

"What are you doing?" asked Gale.

"I'm going to access the Panic Button. It'll send out our location to all the authorities with a distress call. Bill said this was our worst-case scenario button. And we've gone far beyond that. I might even be able to add some text."

"It'll work?"

Cole began to sob, and Gale had to raise her voice at the end of her question.

Nodding, Ethan said, "Yeah. So long as we have Wi-Fi, it'll get the message out there. All it needs is to connect online, then I can send out the call."

"Thank goodness for that," said Gale. "At least we have that in our favor."

Then the lights went out, dumping darkness all over them.

28.

"What the hell just happened?" said Ramona, her voice rising in pitch.

While Gale and Ramona tried to talk over each other, Ethan looked at the computer screen. The brightness had dimmed since the power mode had switched over to battery. Down in the corner of the screen, the Wi-Fi icon had been stamped with an exclamation point. "No, no, no..."

"Bastard killed the power," said Cole. He sniffled. "Knew it was coming, which was why I suggested a generator back at the meetings."

Ethan slammed the laptop closed. "You don't think he would've found a generator, too? Damn piece of machinery louder than a plane? We'd be in the dark regardless."

Cole didn't respond. The dark shape of him moved across the room. A zipper unzipped, followed by rustling. There was a click and a thick beam of light bladed through the dark. "I have another one here," said Cole.

Cole walked over to Ethan, holding the flashlight down to him. Taking it, Ethan stood up. He grabbed his rifle from where it leaned against the couch. He didn't know what to do now. He hadn't anticipated there being more than one killer. It was something that should have been taken into consideration and he hated himself for not contemplating it. "What now?"

Cole sniffled again, then wiped his eyes on the shoulder of his shirt. "I think we need to stop hiding in here. We're just making it easier for him. He's got two ways in now. And he's systematically shutting us down. Making us afraid."

"It's working," said Gale. "I'm scared shitless."

"That's what he wants. It drives him. I'm tired of letting

these fuckers win." His head turned to stare in the direction of where Tina was sprawled on the floor. "I've lost too much already."

Ethan didn't like where Cole's conversation was heading, which was why he wasn't surprised when his friend announced he was going outside.

"Don't do it," said Ethan. "We need to hole up here. That's always the big mistake, the way to make the tide shift in the wrong direction. We're safer in here."

"Oh, yeah? Tell my wife that."

Ethan tried not to feel the sting of those words. "I'm sorry about that," he said. "But the last thing she would want is for you to run outside and get yourself killed on her behalf. I say we just stay right here, together. Each one of us keeps an eye on any possible access in here. He can't sneak up on us if we're watching. Wait for daylight, then we make a break for your Blazer."

"He's probably made it undrivable by now."

"Then we walk. When it's daylight. We can see him coming."

"Your idea is better than mine?"

"I didn't say it's better. Safer, maybe."

Cole was about to say something, but Ethan cut him off.

"Listen, brother, I want to kill him, too. But the only thing I want more is to make sure nothing happens to you or anybody else. Liz and Bill are still out there somewhere, and I'm scared shitless that they're hurt or worse."

Ramona sniffled. "God, we shouldn't have sent them away. We probably killed them by doing so."

Sighing, Ethan didn't allow himself to think about that possibility. "We have to be smart here."

Cole stared at him for a long moment, then huffed through his nose. Lowering the rifle, he nodded. "Sounds like a plan."

Ethan felt relief wash through him. He reached out, patting Cole's shoulder.

Cole raised his head. "A plan for *you*. I'm going out there. Anybody tries to stop me, I'll knock them on their ass." He turned and started marching toward the front door.

Ethan groaned. "Cole, don't—"

"Ethan, I love you like a brother. But right now, shut up. Stay in here with them and keep an eye on all corners of the room. Be *safe*."

That had been his way of insulting Ethan for not wanting to go the same route as Cole. Ethan decided not to argue with him anymore. His mind was made up and with such resilient stubbornness, Ethan knew he wouldn't be able to dissuade him.

Ethan walked over to the door, reaching it just as Cole started snapping back the locks. He pulled it open a crack, peeking through the narrow opening. The porchlight was out, cloaking the front of the house in darkness. But the moon threw down enough silvery spread to show nobody was out there.

Ethan grabbed Cole's arm. His friend's head whipped around, eyes tight slits.

"At least be careful out there."

Cole smiled without mirth. "I'm always careful." He opened the door wider and stepped out.

Ethan watched his friend go out into the dark. Somehow, he felt it, deep inside, that he would never get to have one of those late-night, half-drunken conversations with Cole again. He was going to lose his best friend. He felt a hollow space form in his heart. He forced those feelings away, piling them in the corner with all the other repressed emotions he'd been trying to avoid.

Ethan leaned against the frame, shouldering the rifle. He held the flashlight in his right hand, letting the barrel rest on the cylinder and held both as tight as possible. It would be hard to not let the rifle fly back if he had to fire. The recoil might even bust the Maglite, but since it was made of metal, it was possible it would be okay.

"Let me help you." Gale's voice. She had walked up beside him and reached out. Her fingers curled around the shaft of the flashlight.

"Thanks," he said, letting her take it. It was much easier to hold the rifle now.

She kept the flashlight trained on Cole's back as he paused on the sidewalk, looking this way and that. He held the rifle and flashlight in a similar fashion as Ethan. Each way he turned, the blade of light raked across the trees in the background. Ethan checked those spaces for any sign of Mr. Gorley.

"You hear that?" said Gale.

Just as Ethan was about to ask her what she was talking about, he heard it too. A faint howl that, at first, sounded like a coyote. But the way it lowered and rose in volume on a continuous loop, he quickly realized it was not an animal at all.

A siren.

"I hear it!" said Ramona. "Is that the fire department? Ambulance?"

"No," said Gale. "That's the cops!"

Ramona let out a gleeful cackle. "Thank you, God!"

Ethan listened. Sure sounded like it was getting closer. Probably on the long driveway, heading up the mountain to the cabin. How did they know to come here?"

As if reading his mind, Ramona said, "Think Bill and Liz got help?"

"I..." Ethan shrugged. It seemed the most logical conclusion at this point. A part of him maybe even believed so. The other part of him, the louder section in his subconscious, didn't trust it. He felt a hint of circumspection but knew he shouldn't because help was coming. He'd been about to call them himself before the power had been knocked out.

They've come to help us.

Why did he feel so uneasy about this?

Cole had paused in the yard. Facing the driveway, he lowered his rifle. The light shone down by his feet. He was washed in moonlight, making him look like a black-and-white photograph. Looking over his shoulder, he said, "Sounds like the cavalry is coming."

"You better get back in here before they think *you're* the killer and shoot *you*."

Lights appeared at the bend in the driveway. Blue and white swirled above them, washing the trees in a pirouette of colors.

The lights landed on Cole. The engine revved above the scream of the siren, the speed increasing.

"Cole," said Ethan. The dread in his stomach ceased him with an icy grip. "Get in here, now!"

"Good idea," said Cole, backing up.

The police cruiser was an SUV. It rocked and bounced when the tires left the driveway, making the lights sway from side to side. The engine rumbled again as the tires dug into the ground. The oversized vehicle was coming even faster now as it cut across the front yard, homed in on Cole.

It's going to hit him!

Ethan had no idea what was going on. He didn't think there was any way Mr. Gorley could have fled and attained a police cruiser while he was gone. Mr. Gorley was still somewhere out there as well. Did that mean whoever was driving the SUV was with him?

Ethan didn't know, nor did he really have the time to dwell on such matters.

Gale stomped her foot. "Move your ass, Cole!"

Cole hollered, then turned to run. He went a few feet before stopping and spinning back around.

"What are you doing?" cried Ethan. "That's not a cop!"

"I know!" said Cole, raising the rifle.

Opening fire, the rapid bark of the rifle was almost concealed by the tumult of howls from the siren. Ethan could hear the crackling punches of bullets hitting the windshield. Cole became a dark silhouette in the glare of the SUV's lights. It wasn't slowing down. Cole wasn't moving out of the way. And if Ethan had counted correctly, Cole's magazine was about to be empty.

So, Ethan raised his own rifle. Tried to find a shot that wouldn't risk hitting his friend. "Move, Cole!"

No way could Cole hear him over the tumult of gunfire, the SUV, and the siren. The box-shaped truck was only a couple feet from Cole now, the lights swallowing him as they stretched from either side of the yard. Just above the din, Ethan could faintly make out a shrill laughing that seemed to be coming from inside the cruiser.

Then there was a sickening crunch as the dark shape of Cole seemed to spread, puffing out like a thick black mist all around him. The SUV tore through the mass as Cole went down, vanishing underneath the blocky vehicle as it bounced over him without slowing down.

Ethan began to scream, bringing the sights on the dim space between the headlights and rack on top. He opened fire, hearing those punching sounds as the bullets struck glass. The laughing became louder, rising in pitch and fervor until it switched to a howl that sounded painful.

I hit you!

But the truck was still coming. The engine roaring as it sped toward the porch. Any moment, the front tires would crash through the railing.

Move, Ethan!

Ethan spun around, swinging the door shut in one motion. Now, the light was blocked out, and the cabin filled with darkness once again.

"Brace yourselves!" he yelled into the dark, hoping the women heard him. "Get to safety!"

As he started to move, the rifle was plucked from his hand. He turned just as the door swung open again, and he saw Gale bathed in swirls of light as the engine roared through the opening. She lifted the rifle and started firing. Each shot kicked her shoulder back, throwing her graying hair around her face.

"Get away from there!" Ethan yelled. But the roar of the truck was too loud now, filling the inside of the cabin like the turbines on a plane. He could feel the vibrations running all through him.

He took a step forward, prepared to snatch Gale away from the doorway. The cabin felt as if it had been knocked sideways. Everything shook. The floor shifted under his feet as the front of the cabin exploded in a fury of bright lights and wood projectiles that swallowed Gale in one explosive swoop. Pieces of lumber whacked Ethan hard enough to lift him off the floor and throw him.

When he landed, the walls came down, burying him in darkness once again.

29.

Ethan wasn't sure how long he was down before he began to hear the warbly sounds of screams. He opened his eyes and saw nothing but inky black. Moving his head, the darkness shifted on him. He felt the solidity of it adjusting around him, sliding with his movements.

I'm buried.

He was under a pile of rubble. His mouth tasted dry and powdery. Through the ringing in his ears, he could hear the drone of a motor. *A boat motor?* He remembered there was no way that was possible. His thoughts were sluggish, but he knew enough to realize he was still in the cabin. It was a tiny motor, though, but loud enough that it drowned out the screams.

Screams? Why did he hear screaming?

As he started to wonder about the possibilities, recognition kicked in.

Ramona.

She was screaming, but why? Didn't matter. She needed help, and he had to get up.

Pushing himself upward with his hands, his back lifted the debris on top of him. Dusty air wafted against his face as his head cleared the mound. Wood clambered as it fell behind him. He still couldn't see much because of the dirt in his eyes, but the cabin was filled with harsh light. Shadows combed back and forth with the buzzing sounds of the motor.

He blinked until his eyes somewhat cleared. He stood up, kicking what remained of the wall away from him. He saw the front door slanted at an angle on a pile of wreckage to the right. It was intact, the solid tongues of the locks extended from the side. It had held up just fine. It was the rest of the cabin that had been destroyed. He glanced over, saw the huge chasm where the front of the cabin had once been. The SUV filled most of the space, leaving small gaps on either side. The rack had been busted in the crash. One side had blinked out. The other still rolled behind cracked plastic, throwing blue and white against one side of the living room. The driver's door hung open, the cab devoid of a driver.

He staggered. His feet slid on loose boards as he moved toward the buzzing sound. He tripped over a jutting piece of lumber and landed on his stomach. Looking up, he saw Ramona. She was on all fours, crawling across the floor. Her shirt was ripped down the side. He could see her bare arm, the streaks of blood trickling down. Her bra strap hung halfway down her bicep, revealing the slope of her breast. There were small cuts on her pale skin that looked as if they had been drawn with red ink.

Then he spotted the *thing* approaching her.

What in God's name is that?

Ethan stared, unable to move, as the thing stalked Ramona. It took its time walking behind her. Bending at the waist, it shambled like a zombie.

Looks like a damn zombie!

The skin was withered and rotten. The hair that swung around its shoulders was frizzy and pallid like old webbing. A ragged dress fluttered around its emaciated legs.

That *thing* had been driving the cruiser?

Ethan needed to help Ramona, but he felt as if everything had stopped working in his body, except for his eyes. He had no idea where Gale was, but he remembered watching her vanish in the debris storm as the SUV plowed into the cabin.

Move it, damn it!

Getting to his knees, he grabbed a piece of wood that might have once been part of the doorframe. It was skewed on one end, flat on the other. That was where he gripped it, the same way he would hold sticks as a kid when he pretended they were swords.

Though he was dizzy, he managed to get upright. The zombie girl walked behind Ramona, nudging her rump with the toe of her boot. Each time the boot touched her, Ramona let out a squeal and flinched.

Ethan stumbled toward them. As he moved, it felt as if the cabin tilted underneath his feet. He started weaving to the right, so he corrected himself and began moving straight again. He held the sharp tip toward the zombie's back.

He shoved forward.

The zombie turned around, swinging the chainsaw at him. Ethan pivoted back, sucking in his stomach just as the whirring tip whisked by. As the zombie girl continued to turn, Ethan lurched, bringing the sharp piece of wood down.

And missed completely. The tip sliced only air, which threw off Ethan's balance. He tilted to the side, all his weight shifting in that direction. Next thing he knew, he was on his back and staring up at the ceiling.

This was not the place he needed to be. His intention had been to get up. But he found that to be harder than he'd thought. His body screamed at him in pain. He was sore all over from the night's excursions and having a cabin dropped on top of him. It slowed down his progress, made his movements lethargic.

It also allowed the zombie girl the chance to correct herself. She looked down at him, head tilting as she approached. The frizzy mane hung to one side. Her finger twitched, triggering the saw to rumble. Ethan felt the heat of the motor, felt the wind of the spinning chain. The stench of gasoline burned his eyes.

He looked up at the hideous face. Even in all his wild fear, a rational thought somehow lingered.

No way was this really a member of the undead.

Because it had eyes. Real eyes. Behind the black crevasses of the dead face. They stared down at him, so blue they looked almost white inside the decayed rings of eyeholes.

A mask.

Almost. A dead woman's face, but a living one was underneath it.

A living person that was bleeding from a spot below her left shoulder.

That's where I got her.

The chainsaw dipped closer, inches from his chin. It revved, spitting hot air into his face. It rattled his cheeks, made his lips flap. He moved his head from side to side, trying to get out of the saw's path. There was nowhere he could go. He was trapped. The zombie girl started to bend lower. Ethan knew she was about to strike. Her arms started to straighten as she angled the saw toward his neck.

Hot air blasted his Adam's apple. Soon, he'd feel the sharp teeth tearing into his flesh.

The saw jerked away as the zombie girl bolted upright. Tensed up, her head shot back showing a band of smooth neck behind the apron of dead flesh. A scream came from behind the deadened folds of lips. She turned slightly, shoulder sagging to show the hatchet jutting from her back like a lever.

Ramona, standing behind her, bared her teeth. Her hair was a mess. Her face was painted in dirt and blood. She gripped the handle and tore it from the girl's back, eliciting another scream from her.

The chainsaw suddenly dropped, filling Ethan's vision on its way down. He knew wouldn't be able to catch it, but he didn't want it to crush his skull in either. Throwing up his arms, the cube body bounced off his forearms, sending jolts of pain up into his shoulders. The loud tool bounced next to his hand and shut off.

The zombie girl staggered back a few steps, patting over her shoulder for the bloody wound. Her arm wasn't quite long enough to reach it.

Ramona stepped forward. Reaching out with her free hand, she palmed the dead face and pulled it away. It jiggled in Ramona's grip. A pair of straps hung down like an untied bonnet. The frizzy hair was attached to it, hanging over Ramona's hand like a veil.

The face underneath was female. And young. In the wash of headlights, she looked no older than sixteen. Her dark hair was glued to her cheeks with blood. Snarling, she stared up at Ramona, swaying as she hugged herself.

Another damn kid.

Ethan couldn't believe it. Two teenagers. And Mr. Gorley.

"You bitch..." the girl said. Then she lunged, arms held

out. Her fingers were oiled in crimson. She loosed a growl that sounded as wild as the woods.

Ramona must have expected the attack. She easily stepped aside and swung outward with the hatchet. The girl saw it coming. Her mouth dropped open in a look of startled shock. She was moving too fast to stop, so her boots skidded across the dusty hardwood.

Then her head collided with the blade, killing her cries instantly. Ramona released the hatchet to allow the girl the freedom to stumble backward, swaying as she tried to find her balance again. The lower tip of the hatchet blade was in her skull, the handle extending over her nose like a snout while the upper tip jutted like a shark fin in a sea of hair. Blood sluiced down her face, dousing her neck and clothes. Her head bobbed like a drunk on the verge of passing out.

Then she dropped to her knees. She reached out as if trying to catch herself. Missed. And landed on her side.

Ethan remained on his back, relishing the momentary element of peace. He looked up at Ramona, saw the wild look on her face starting to dissipate. She noticed his staring. Blinking, she started to resemble her usual self again.

"I did it," she said. Ramona wiped her mouth with the back of her hand. "I don't know why...but I knew it had to be me."

"What?"

"That killed her. It *had* to be me."

Though Ethan had no idea why she felt so strongly about that, he nodded as if he understood. Rolling over, he pushed himself up to knees.

Ramona wiped her mouth again. "Bill's dead."

"You don't know that."

Ramona nodded. "I do. I can...*feel* it." She rubbed her chest above her left breast. "Here. It's empty there now. I think I felt it when it happened but didn't want to admit it. I suddenly felt all alone. I'd bet all I have that *she* did it." Ramona nudged the girl's shoulder with her foot. "That's why it had to be me who killed her."

Ethan wouldn't allow himself to consider it. If Bill was dead as Ramona believed, then that probably meant Liz had been killed too. Even slightly considering the possibility caused a strong sense of loss to nearly rob him of what strength he had left.

"Who do you think she is?" Ramona said.

"Probably related to Zeb, like the other guy."

"Looks too young to be his mother. Sister?"

"Does it matter?" Ethan looked around.

"I guess not." She let out a breath. "Think Gale made it?"

Ethan looked over at the SUV, the piles of rubble in front of it. She was probably pinned underneath the vehicle and most of the front of the cabin. He shook his head. "No."

Ramona sniffled. "Damn." Ramona looked around. "We need to get out of here. The whole place is probably about to come down on us."

Ethan stood up. His lower back felt tight and sore. He looked around, avoiding looking at the girl on the floor. The cabin was destroyed. Now that the commotion had settled down some, he could hear the faint groaning of wood, as if too much weight was pushing down on what remained of the support beams. Ramona was probably right, the cabin might collapse.

He returned to the front of the SUV, standing in the bright glare of the headlights. He checked the tires and saw that none were flat, though the front axle was probably broken from the way the left wheel tilted almost all the way up. That left the Blazer, if it hadn't already been rendered undrivable by Mr. Gorley.

Shit.

Ethan had almost forgotten about the big man.

"We need to find some weapons," said Ethan.

"Aren't there some in the Blazer?"

"Yeah. But I don't want to go out there empty-handed. The big one is still out there somewhere."

Unless he snuck in upstairs already.

Ethan looked up at the ceiling. Could he be up there?

"Do you know where your gun is?"

Ramona's voice startled Ethan. "No. Lost it in the crash. Gale had it."

Lost her, too.

He shook his head and felt hot tension above his ear. He reached up to rub the sore spot. It felt wet. He checked his fingers in the light and saw they were dabbed in blood. He wondered how bad the wound was. Didn't matter. There was no time to mess with it.

There wasn't any time to waste looking for the weapons, either. The whole cabin might come down on them while they searched. There had been some guns in Cole's bag, but whatever had happened to it, Ethan had no idea. He wasn't going to fret with trying to find it, though. He didn't know where Mr. Gorley was. Whether he was upstairs or not, he was nearby, no question about that.

Ethan's gun was in his bag in the Blazer. That would have to do. He turned and looked at the floor near where the girl was splayed.

Screw it.

He walked over to her and grabbed the chainsaw. It was still warm. He could smell the burnt aroma of oil wafting from the motor. Blood and stringy bits were stuck to the saw teeth. Strands dangled like old gum.

Ramona used her foot to push the girl onto her back. The hatchet jutted from her hairline. Blood had doused her face and spilled onto her neck. Gripping the hilt, Ramona pulled. The blade tore free with a squelch.

The girl moaned.

"What the...?" Ramona jumped back. She looked at Ethan. "Did you hear that?"

Nodding, Ethan stared down at the girl. The wound in her head was a thin hollow that oozed blood. It had split the upper rim of her forehead, separating the hairline. The wound looked painful but not enough to be a killing blow.

Damn.

The girl's hand twitched, fingers curled. She was waking up.

Ethan went to grip the pulley for the saw. Seeing him, Ramona shook her head. "No, she's mine. Remember? Has to be me."

Ramona dropped to one knee, raising the hatchet above her head with both hands. From the angle of the blade, Ethan could tell she was aiming for the girl's neck. This time, most likely, the idea was to behead her.

Ethan felt like they were wasting too much time, but he also understood that Ramona needed to finish it herself. She'd convinced herself this girl had killed Bill, and Ramona wanted justice.

"You're going to die for real this time," she said. The hatchet began a downward swing.

The girl's left arm shot up. Ethan glimpsed a small knife in her hand. The blade punched into Ramona's side just above her hip.

Ramona's eyes widened. She let out a gasp as she lurched. The hatchet slipped from her hands.

Sitting up, the girl snatched the falling hatchet from the air. Before Ethan even had an inkling of an idea what was happening, the girl had spun the hatchet around and as she swung it upward, she said, "You should've finished me off, whore!"

The blade chopped into the side of Ramona's neck. When the girl pulled it back, blood gushed from the wide break in the flesh. Ramona's head canted to the side, the neck flesh tearing like rubbery paper.

Ethan screamed as Ramona stood, stumbled around. Her mouth moved as she croaked and gasped. She bounced off the wall, corrected herself, then shuffled back in Ethan's direction. She reached out as if asking for Ethan's help. He could do nothing but watch. His arms felt lifeless, his mind tilting as he looked on in shock.

Ramona's face was nearly turned upward as if it had sprouted from her collarbone. Her eyes lolled this way and that, spinning like a slot machine. Blood shot from the gulley in her neck, splashing the girl who was now laughing like a child playing under a sprinkler. She stuck out her tongue to catch the blood and gore as if it were red snow.

Ramona took a couple clumsy steps to the side before dropping onto the floor. Her body spasmed for several long seconds before going still. Ethan continued to gaze down at her as he tried to catch his breath. It felt as if a leather thong was tightening around his throat, and the air was slowly being squeezed from him.

He glanced down at his hands, saw the chainsaw was still there. He went to pull the cord. In his mind, his hands made swift movements and got the chainsaw sputtering and spinning within the blink of an eye. But reality set in, and he realized he'd barely been able to lift his arm before the girl snatched the chainsaw from him.

"That's mine," she said.

He was too tired, too numb to try any other means of defense. She could have the damn thing for all he cared.

The girl stepped up to Ethan, raising the hatchet to her face. Blood slid down the blade. She stuck out her tongue, lapping at the sticky red. "Tastes good."

Ethan felt as if he might pass out.

"Nina!"

The gruff voice boomed in the silence of the cabin. The girl's smile faltered. Rolling her eyes, she said, "What, Daddy?"

"Stop playing with him like that."

"Sorry, Daddy."

In a softer tone, the man said, "You okay, darling?"

"My head hurts. My shoulder, too. And my back. She hacked me and this numb-nuts shot me."

The wound on her head looked dirty. Blood leaked from the slit. Her flannel shirt was ripped where the bullet had entered. The frayed tips were doused in dark fluid.

"I bet they do, sweetheart."

"Where's Zeb?"

"Dead. They killed him."

"I was afraid of that," said Nina. "Those other two came to the old house with a cop. I heard them talking about how they caught Zeb. I knew it was him they was talking about because of the mask. I tried to get here in time to help. Figured you'd be here, too. I didn't make it, I guess."

"I was too late."

"What the hell was he doing out messing around tonight for anyway?"

"Don't know. Guess he couldn't help himself. Saw all these

people out here and had to do it."

"Weren't the ones at the camp enough for him?"

"Guess not."

Ethan tried to comprehend what all he'd just heard. Others at the old house? Cop? Was she talking about Liz and Bill? Who was the cop? The campsite must've been Group B. Probably the kids, too. Just as he'd feared, they were all dead.

"Why were you playing at that old house anyway?" said the deep voice. "You could have been hurt and killed yourself."

"I wasn't playing. I was putting the bodies there till we could take 'em home. I got one of 'em that showed up, but the others got away."

"That's not good," said the voice. "We gotta find them."

"They ain't getting out of here. I smashed the other car and took this one." She pointed at the SUV. "They're trapped in the woods."

"They got feet, don't they?"

Nina shrugged.

"Then they have a way out if they can walk."

Ethan glanced over his shoulder and felt a scream tickle his throat. Mr. Gorley was approaching, each step sounding like a mallet striking the floor. He still wore the crudely designed mask of rags that covered his face except for the greasy hair and single eye that were exposed. "You'll have to find them, darling. If you feel up to it. But not until after you're patched up."

"I'm *fine*, Daddy." She swayed on her feet. Mr. Gorley grabbed her arm to settle her. She gave him a bashful grin. "A little dizzy."

Mr. Gorley stepped around to the front of his daughter, putting his hands on her head. He made her tilt to the side while he studied the wound. "You's lucky, girl." Next, he checked the bullet wound near her shoulder. "Went clear through. Bleeding's slow. Yep. You's damn lucky." He made her turn so he could see her back. He whistled. "Probably scar up good. Lucky as hell, sweetface."

"Don't feel lucky. Feel like shit."

"You'd be dead otherwise. Like Zeb. I ain't about to lose another youngin'."

Nina seemed to blush. "Daddyyyy." She shook her head. "What we gonna do with this one?"

Mr. Gorley turned toward Ethan, towering over him by at least two feet. His head was like a boulder that had been placed on top of a body constructed from a mountain. Thick arms hung on either side, bare and hairy under the overalls and sleeveless T-shirt. "He's coming with us."

"Why?"

"I want to take my time with him. He's the one killed Zeb."

"I want a piece too, then. You cain't kill 'em till I get back."

Mr. Gorley nodded. "You'll get your turn. We all gonna get some of him."

"You killed my little girl," said Ethan. He hadn't planned on speaking at all until he heard the words as if a stranger had spoken them.

Mr. Gorley's head turned slightly to peer at Ethan. "I've killed lots'a little girls. Yours don't mean nothin' to me."

Ethan felt heat bubble in his chest. "You're lying."

"Am I?"

Ethan smiled. "She damn near got you, didn't she? Your eye and nose. She did that to you."

Mr. Gorley stared at him. He raised his hand to the rag mask, stroking his covered nose. "She got the nose. Sure. My eye been gone a long time. She looked just like you. Ain't no denying that girl's yours. I wonder if you gonna beg me like she did. I got pick-tures of her. I'll show 'em to you before I kill you. Let you see just what all we did to her."

Ethan was running at the big guy before he even realized it. Reaching out, his hands formed into claws that wanted to tear out his other eye. He saw the amusement appear in that lone eye, though the smile that probably accompanied it was hidden under the rag.

His shins struck something hard, stopping his legs completely but doing nothing to slow down the movement above his waist. He pitched forward, crashing to the floor at Mr. Gorley's boots. Rolling over, he saw Nina straightening up, bringing her leg back to her while she unleashed a wild cackle.

She'd tripped him before he even reached her father.

Mr. Gorley raised a finger to his face, tapping where his mouth should be to shush her. The crazed girl obliged.

Ethan's ears burned with embarrassment. He took a deep breath. Tilting his head back to look at Mr. Gorley, he said, "I doubt she begged anywhere as much as Zeb before we broke his jaw. Then he couldn't do anything but cry like a bitch—"

That was the last thing Ethan managed to say before Mr. Gorley's boot shot toward his face. It filled his vision before a blast of pain rattled inside his head.

Then darkness fell on him.

30.

"We're here," said Reese, scampering over to the chain-link fence. She ran with her shoulders bunched around her ears, softly grunting in pain with each step.

Liz looked at the fence. Towering above them, it stretched on in either direction. The top was covered with spirals of barbed wire. A sign hung on a chunk of sheet metal that had been placed over a section of the fence.

Keep Out.

"No way in hell we'll be able to climb over that," said Liz in a winded voice. She aimed her flashlight upward. The light glinted off the razor-like barbs. She could feel their cold sharpness slicing her open.

Reese shook her head. "You're right. We'll find another way in."

"How?"

"Even if we have to burrow underneath like gophers, we'll get in there."

Reese's statement did nothing to help ease the mounting tension Liz felt in her chest. They walked alongside the fence, making their way uphill. On the other side, wrecked and abandoned cars sat in rows of pale empty shapes under the moonlight. Tendrils of fog drifted up the dirt aisles, curling over the vehicles.

After they'd walked for a few minutes, Reese stepped over to a section of fence. "Here we go."

Liz looked down where the bright disk of the flashlight beam spread along the ground. There was a small gap where the ground sloped upward. The bottom tips of the chain didn't quite reach the dirt. "We're not going to fit through there."

"Not yet. Hold my light."

Liz slipped her gun into her shorts, then took the light. She aimed both beams at the fence. Reese slipped out her nightstick, wedging the tip into the section of fence that was clamped to the pole. Since there was space at the bottom, the fence bowed easily enough. Wiggling back and forth, the nightstick began to stretch the links. Biting her bottom lip, Reese groaned as she pulled down. There was a rattling snap as the fence broke loose from the clamp. It sagged around the pole as if a bubble had formed between the chains.

Huffing, Reese looked at her nightstick. "Damn. Scratched it to hell."

"It worked."

"Yeah." She tossed the nightstick over the fence. Slipping her fingers through the gaps, she gripped and pulled upward. The small opening grew. "That good?" Her voice sounded strained.

Nodding, Liz hurried over to where Reese stood. She slid the flashlights through first. Then, getting on all fours, she scurried through the gap. The tips of the fence scratched her skin, plucked her shirt, pulling it taut as she worked through to the other side. It plopped free. "Made it."

Reese let go of the fence and sank to a crouch. "Hold it for me."

Liz used both hands to pull the fence up and still wasn't able to lift it as high as Reese had, but it didn't matter. The cop dropped flat on her stomach and squirmed under the fence without touching it. When her feet made it through, Liz let go of the fence. Her hands stung, feeling as if they had been pinched with pliers.

Reese found her nightstick and slipped it back into the clip on her belt. Then she grabbed the lights, holding out Liz's to her.

Taking it, Liz mumbled a thanks.

"Come on," said Reese. "The house is on the back part of the property. We'll try there first. If nobody's home, we'll break into the main office."

"How do you know they'll even have a phone that works?"

"See?" Reese pointed at the power pole farther up the yard. A sodium light glowed on top, throwing down insipid light along the ground. "Power. They'll have a phone, too. Or at least a CB radio. Let's go."

They walked along a path between two long rows of hollowed cars. The windshields looked painted black and smeared with dewy dust. The cars seemed to stretch on all around them in endless numbers.

The silence was heavy out here, making the crunches of their footsteps on the dirt even louder.

Reaching an intersection, Reese paused. She pointed her flashlight straight ahead, then right. Her bottom lip was clamped under her teeth. "Shit."

"What's wrong?"

"I can't remember which way to go. I think it's straight, deeper back, but I'm not sure." She put her hand to the makeshift compress on her side, grimacing.

Liz noticed the blood on her fingertips and felt sorry for the deputy. "Are you okay?"

Reese laughed without delight. "I'll be fine." She let out a deep breath. "Straight? Okay. Let's keep going straight."

"If you say so. I have no idea."

"I think it's straight," she said with a quiet voice. "We came in on that side, so we have to keep going this way." The tone of her voice suggested she wasn't quite sure what direction they needed to go.

They forged ahead, moving at the same measured rate they had been this whole time. As they made their way farther back, Liz felt soft springiness brushing against her bare shins. She looked down. The grass was high here, nearly reaching her knees. That meant nobody had traveled this route in a while.

Reese must have realized this herself because she uttered another curse word. When they reached another intersection, she turned right without announcing it.

Liz followed. She aimed the flashlight all around them, spotting more and more scavenged cars walling them in.

They walked a while longer before Reese paused again. She took out the water bottle and sipped. Though Liz wanted some water, she didn't drink any yet. She continued aiming the light all around. She saw no sign of a house or any sort of structure that might be habitable.

"What kind of house?" said Liz.

"Huh?" Reese lowered the bottle.

"The house. What's it look like?"

"I don't know. A house. You'll know it because it'll be the only goddamn house out here."

Liz sighed. "Fine."

"Sorry. I'm just getting pissed. I'm all turned around."

"Do you feel okay?"

"I'll be fine. The sooner we find the house, the better, though."

"Are you experiencing dizziness?"

"I haven't stopped."

"You're probably bleeding to death."

"That's great news."

"You can't keep going on like this."

"What choice do I have?"

In the moonlight, Reese's skin looked pale and sickly. She needed medical attention. That reminded her of Gale. She wondered how the older woman was doing. She wondered how any of them were doing. Had the corpse lady made it to the cabin yet?

Most likely. And you two are just wasting time out here.

Liz was half tempted to leave Reese here and go the rest of the way herself. But she figured it would be a better idea to have the deputy with her in case she ran into the owners anywhere.

"Let's go," said Reese.

Nodding, Liz walked with the wounded deputy. She noticed their pace was even slower now. She kept getting ahead of Reese and would slow down so she could catch back up. This went on for several minutes before Reese pointed her flashlight to the left.

"See that?"

Liz followed the path of the beam to a small shelter. It looked like a lean-to that had been erected against an area where the fencing branched outward. Two tarps hung down in the front like a curtain blocking a stage.

"I don't know what I'm looking at," said Liz. "A do-it-yourself storage area?"

"What?" Reese shook her head. "Jesus. No, the house is over *there.*"

Liz looked past the structure and saw a dark block atop a slope. It was box-shaped and pale under the floodlights that seemed to be blazing from the top of poles all around. The corners were drenched in darkness where the illuminated spread didn't quite reach. No lights shone in the windows from what Liz could tell. She saw no dim flickering that might suggest a TV was on.

It's late. Everybody's probably asleep.

Didn't matter. So long as the phone was in there like Reese claimed it would be.

Without speaking, they started walking again. They approached the shoddy structure. Liz noticed the narrow gap between the tarp flaps where they didn't quite touch. She felt nervous, just as she had back at the antiquated house when she'd crossed in front of the kitchen doorway. It was murky on the other side, which meant there was plenty of concealment for somebody to hide amongst.

Liz aimed her flashlight at the tarp, angling her wrist so the beam stabbed between the flaps. The light gleamed off a round emblem on the other side. She saw white and blue colors and lettering inside a circle.

A BMW logo.

She froze.

Her back felt as if spiders were crawling under her shirt. "Oh…shit." Liz started walking toward the tarp without even realizing she was about to. It felt as if she were stepping on pads of cotton from how lightheaded she suddenly was.

She heard Reese talking to her, saw the deputy's flashlight sweeping over the tarp. Liz knew she should respond, should say *something* back to her. But her thoughts couldn't form anything complete. Her voice couldn't issue any sound.

She saw her hand reaching out to the tarp, saw it trembling as the fingers gripped the flimsy sheet. Reese came up behind her, placing her hand on Liz's shoulder. She heard that voice

again—the confusion, the rising anger at being ignored.
Please don't let this be what I think it is.
Liz yanked the tarp. It fell away with a whispery rustle.
Raising her flashlight, Liz pointed it at the car that was hidden
inside. "Oh, damn..." Her knees folded. She started to drop.
Reese snatched her back up by her elbow.
"What the hell is going on?" Her mouth nearly touched Liz's
ear. "Liz! What's wrong?"
"Th-that's Martin's car."
"Who?"
"Martin. Bill and I wondered why we didn't see their cars
parked in the space back near the campsite. Jesus Christ. They're
here. Look." She pointed the flashlight at the dark shape beyond
the BMW. "That's George's Honda back there."
Reese let go of Liz and stepped forward. "You're sure about
this?" Before Liz could respond, Reese waved off her question.
"Of course you're sure. Damn it to hell. Why are they hidden
in here like this?" Reese groaned. "We need to get out of here."
"I agree."
Reese spun around, looked at the house. "Oh, shit."
"What?"
Liz turned around and gasped. The house's front windows
now glowed with light. The front porchlight clicked on,
spreading coppery radiance across the grass. Light appeared
in the front, widening as the door opened. A black silhouette
stepped out, vanishing when the door swung shut. A blade
of light was slashing back and forth on the side of the house,
jostling as it started toward the hill.
Whoever that is knows we're here!
Reese must have read her mind. "She saw us."
"Who is that?" said Liz.
"It's probably Dixie Gorley. She'll know why those cars are
here."
"And *you* don't?"
"Of course I do. Damn it. I can't believe this." She glanced
over her shoulder, then faced Liz again. "Get in there."
Reese shoved Liz into the shelter. Her rump hit the front of
the BMW, knocking her legs out in front of her. She sat down on

the hood, then slid down. She dropped her flashlight during the movement. It blinked out. "What the hell are you...?"

"Keep that light off and shut up. I'll handle this. If this goes wrong..."

"You think it might?"

"*If* it does, I'd rather her not know you're here." Reese gripped the lip of the tarp and lifted it. "Hide, Liz. Now!"

Liz snatched the flashlight from the ground just as Reese covered the entrance with the tarp. What little bit of light that had managed to leak in here was snuffed out. The air smelled rubbery, with a hint of dust and motor oil.

She took several deep breaths to calm herself. It didn't work. Her heart sledged inside her chest. She could feel its rapid hammering in her throat. She held up her pistol, thumbing off the safety. That helped a little. Just having the gun with her made a lot of difference.

She hated leaving Reese out there alone, but that was how the deputy wanted it. Still, it didn't mean Liz had to be happy about it.

"Who's there?" said Reese.

"This is my damn property, I'm asking the questions. And I suggest you get that light out of my face."

"Deputy Reese, Kassier County Sheriff's Department. That you, Dixie?"

"Reese? Shit, woman. I almost shot you. What the *hell* are you doing out here?"

Dixie Gorley's voice was somehow delicate and squeaky, though the tone was annoyed and angry. The pitch made Liz imagine a pixie or a floating fairy on the other side of the tarp talking to Reese.

"Looking for some answers," said Reese.

The grass crunched as footsteps came closer. "What kind of answers? I think I'm looking for some answers myself. Damn. I can't believe it's you out here."

"It's me."

"You're hurt, dear." The voice, like Reese's, was right outside the tarp. "What happened to you? A chainsaw wouldn't have done that would it?"

Shit. How'd she know that? Was she the one who'd been dressed in that dead skin?

Reese let out a breath that sounded quivery. "I'm going to have to ask you to put down the shotgun."

Shotgun?

Liz didn't like that she couldn't see what was happening out there. Crouching, she waddled to the right. As she moved, the thin gap in the tarp became visible. She could see Reese's back in the wedge of space between the two tarps. The white tank top looked gray. Blood and sweat had left stains here and there.

"I saw flashlights out here. Thought you was an intruder. Are you alone? Could've sworn I saw two lights."

"Just me."

"Well, that's good, at least. I really hate this, Reese. I really do. I've always liked you."

"Dixie? Put it down."

"I take no joy in this, just so you know. And Nina hated that she had to slice you up like that."

Reese started to say something as her body shifted. Liz glimpsed the deputy's arm rising, the handgun extending.

Her voice was cut off by a loud boom that lit up the night in a flash. The shed's rickety walls shook around her. Dust rained down from above. A hole appeared where Reese's back had been. Blood flew all over, pelting Liz's face in hot droplets.

Biting her lip to hold in the scream, Liz rubbed the thick fluid out of her eyes. Moonlight shone through the new space in Reese's back. Liz glimpsed movement on the other side, a gun barrel hanging down as smoke curled from the tip.

She saw female hands holding the weapon, the nails painted a crimson shade.

31.

Ethan jerked awake. Confused, he couldn't tell where he was. It felt as if he were being tossed around inside a massive dryer. Underneath him bounced and shook, triggering a wave of nausea. His head started to pound from how hard he had been kicked.

He remembered Mr. Gorley's boot but not much else.

His stomach twisted like a wet rag.

Don't throw up.

The bouncy floor gave him a hard jolt, throwing him onto his side.

Where he came face to face with Zeb's head.

Ethan opened his mouth, ready to unleash either a hell of a scream or a gallon of vomit.

Then he heard music—an acoustic guitar and something that might have been a harmonica. The tune was a bluesy number, overdoing its depressing key. A country song. A girl's voice started to sing along about losing a dog and a boyfriend on the same night when they ran out on her.

Nina.

Another bounce and Zeb's head rolled close enough to Ethan that the crooked jaw brushed his lips. Ethan felt the scratchy stubble of a sprouting beard, felt the crusty blood wipe across his mouth. The severed cranium had come loose of the tarp and now rolled freely like groceries spilled from a shopping bag.

He eased himself onto his back. After another wave of dizziness passed, he noticed moonlight was spilling into the cramped space above him. It was a rear windshield. He recognized it right away.

I'm in Cole's Blazer.

Nina's voice went high, horribly cracking as she tried to match the voice of the woman singing the sad song. She failed. Nina did not have a natural knack for vocal abilities. What she managed to produce was something that sounded like a drunk version of Gwen Stefani trying to be Crystal Gale.

Ethan spotted two more bodies in the second row of seats. From the flattened, trodden head on one, he assumed that was what remained of Cole. The one next to him must have been Ramona from how the dark bulge of her nearly severed head above her left shoulder jutted like a tumor that had sprouted beside the stumpy neck. The other indistinct shape leaning against the window as if watching the night roll by must have been Tina. He didn't see any sign of Gale but figured she was still underneath the rubble of the cabin. It would take time to get to her body.

Ethan felt another pang of regret for what he'd caused.

Ethan quietly sat up, making sure he didn't touch the tarp that was wrapped around Zeb's body. Any slight contact would cause it to rustle. There was no doubt Nina would hear that, even if she continued to wail like a dog being tortured to the songs on the radio.

He brought his legs up, hugging his shins so his knees were under his chin. It helped to somewhat steady him on such a bumpy ride. The position also helped relieve the pressure in his stomach and ease the cramps, which he was grateful for.

He looked between the two dead friends in the back seat to the front. He saw the back of Nina's head. Her hair hung down in a mess. The instrument panel painted her in green light that made her pale skin look almost alien. Through the windshield, the headlights tore twin paths through the darkness. On either side of the road, trees were compressed together into a woodland fortress.

The song mercifully ended.

"Oh, baby," said Nina in a thick voice. It sounded as if she'd been crying. "That's a good 'un. Damn that girl knows me. She wrote that *for* me. Damn ol' damn."

Another song began to play. The twangy guitar plucked a melodic strain that caused Nina to moan. "Shit on me, here comes another one."

This time, the voice was male and deep, almost clucking when he sang about the love of his life. Nina pitched her head back and bellowed along, not even coming close to matching the man's tenor. Ethan wondered if she were doing it on purpose because he didn't think anybody could sound so terrible by accident. But somehow Nina was exceeding all expectations with her dreadful performance.

He looked out the side window. All he saw was black with the occasional flash of gray trees zipping by. They could be anywhere in the mountain right now. He assumed that Nina was going to stash the Blazer somewhere, maybe drive it off the mountain.

No. They want to torture me first.

Most likely, she was driving them all to a secondary location. Probably a nice, secluded place where they could dispose of the bodies, the Blazer, and have the privacy to do all the vile things they planned to do to Ethan.

This deep in the mountain, she could spit at a place ripe for those conditions. That meant she wasn't looking to find one. Nina already knew where to go. They might show up at any moment.

He had to get rid of Nina. Somehow.

Sure, it sounded so much easier than it would be to accomplish. He could sit here and think of endless scenarios where he would succeed in this plan of action. But putting them into motion in real life was something else completely.

Static crackled, followed by a high-pitched hum that reminded Ethan of old sci-fi radio serials. Nina groaned, then turned down the radio. He heard her rummaging around up front, then she raised something that looked like a brick to her mouth.

"Nina? Come in." The static buzzed and cracked.

Mr. Gorley's voice.

It was a walkie. Older than the model Cole had supplied them with for the weekend.

Cole.

Ethan felt fresh tears form at the thought of his friend. He avoided looking over at his ruined body as he leaned back to get out of sight if Nina happened to look in the rearview mirror. He heard the click of the backwoods girl pressing the button. The static vanished. "What, Daddy?"

"I got the deputy's car hooked to the rig, towing it back now. Your ma rang me on the CB and said somebody was sneaking around the yard with flashlights. She was going to go check it out. Haven't heard back from her."

"Think she's all right?"

"Hell if I know. She better be."

"Shit."

"You can get there quicker than me."

"I'm on it, Daddy. Think it's the people I saw at the house?"

"Probably so."

"Damn. I should'a killed 'em all when I had the chance."

"Just get home and finish it. I'll be there soon as I can."

"Yessir."

The static came back for a second before fading away. He heard the thumps of Nina tossing the walkie onto the passenger seat. She sat there in silence, the only sound now the rumble of the engine rising and falling as she worked the gas pedal.

Then the silence was devastated by a sharp scream. Ethan jerked. He bit down on his lip to keep from letting out a scream of his own. He looked up front and saw Nina's head flailing back and forth as she screamed and growled and spat. Keeping one hand on the steering wheel, she used the other to punch the passenger seat, the dashboard, the steering wheel, and then finally settling on slapping herself repeatedly in the face.

"Way to fuck it up, Nina!" Another slap and a guttural scream. "Your fuckin' brother's dead. And your mama might be in trouble now because you didn't kill 'em all!"

The girl's losing it!

Ethan wasn't sure what Mr. Gorley had been talking about. But the way it sounded was that somebody had made it to wherever their home was.

Towing…

Ethan felt a gasp at the back of his throat.

The junkyard.

It had been there for as long as Ethan could remember. Yet,

he'd never once met the owners of it. He wasn't even sure if his father had even known them.

The Gorleys.

He remembered now seeing it on the faded signed in pale lettering that had once been green on a piece of sheet metal.

Otis's Junk and Salvage.

That was where they were going.

He had to do something.

He wasn't sure if Cole had any weapons stashed in the vehicle, but his bag was up front. Probably in the seat beside Nina. Even if she hadn't noticed the gun, it was no good to him right now. Ethan wanted to let out a frustrated scream of his own, joining Nina in the tantrum she was still displaying from the front seat. He took a quick glance at her and saw she'd settled on slapping herself repeatedly in the face—hard swats that knocked her head back. The Blazer swerved, nearly crashing into a tree. She managed to whip the big truck back, inches from colliding with the trunk. The quick, harsh motion sent Ethan tumbling back onto Zeb's tarped body.

Nina stopped screaming. "What the hell's going on back there?" The Blazer slowed to a crawl. He heard the seat squeak as Nina shifted her body, probably to look toward the back. "You awake back there?"

Ethan remained still, draped over Zeb's body in what he hoped looked like an unconscious position.

"All right, then," said Nina.

The brakes squeaked when she lifted her foot. The Blazer started moving again.

Ethan realized he'd been holding his breath and slowly let it out. Each time he blinked, he saw bright splotches in his vision. His brain felt as if it were pushing against the backs of his eyes. Was it swelling? How hard had Mr. Gorley kicked him? He wondered if he had a concussion. If somebody had one, did that person wonder about it? Wasn't that a scientific fact or something? If you had a concussion, you thought you were fine?

That's insanity, dipshit. Insane people don't know they are.

Yeah, he figured he had a concussion based on how jumbled his thoughts continued to be.

Ethan tried weighing his options. He concluded that he had *none*. So just lying here seemed to be the best idea for now. Besides, he didn't much feel like doing anything else for the time being.

At least Nina seemed to be calmer now. She was no longer screaming or abusing herself. After another beat, the radio was cranked again. An upper-tempo hoedown yee-hawed from the speakers. Nina soon joined in, her voice squealing like bad brakes.

Ethan moved his head so he could put his fingers in his ears. Nina's vocal range was set to high, and it was like a spike grinding in his skull. As he started to turn, he felt a hard nudge against his cheek followed by a dull stinging sensation. Reaching up, he tapped the throbbing spot. It felt wet. He was bleeding.

Confused at first, he quickly realized what had happened.

The machete.

When he and Cole had wrapped Zeb up, the machete had been added with him. Ethan had planned to dispose of it with the boy's body.

It was still there. Ethan almost smiled.

Reaching into the tarp, he patted around. His fingers tapped sticky blood, tattered clothing, and the cold side of the machete. Carefully, he slipped his hand higher up until he felt the grip. His fingers folded around it, his arm aching as he squeezed.

Now he would have to wait for his chance to use it.

32.

Liz dived to the other side of the BMW. She hit the dirt just as Reese fell back through the tarp. Her sprawled arms tore the flimsy curtains down with her.

Looking underneath the car, Liz saw Reese's head turn to gaze at her through the shadows. Mouth moving, it looked as if she were trying to tell her something. Then she took one last quivery breath that made her spasm a few times before going still. Her stomach was a splattered mess. Her intestines were strewn all over, ripped and shredded from the gunshot.

Liz saw a pair of bare calves tucked into baby doll shoes step into the shelter. The skin was so smooth and glossy, Reese's flashlight glinted off them from where it landed on the ground. "Hated to do that. I always thought you were good people, Reese. Just had to come sticking your nose where it don't belong. You did this to yourself. No ma'am. I didn't kill you, you did. Reese killed Reese."

A clacking sound resonated from the other side. Two empty shells bounced off the ground.

She's reloading.

This was Liz's moment. Dixie had no idea she was in here.

The shotgun snapped shut.

Liz didn't wait another second. Liz sprung up from behind the BMW, stepping over to the hood, bringing the pistol up and out toward the area she figured Dixie would be standing. As her finger started to squeeze the trigger, she noticed nobody was there.

A single shot was fired. The recoil bounced off the cars, hitting her ears like a detonated grenade. The dark interior filled with a writhing orange light. In the corner of her eye, she glimpsed movement. Turning in that direction, Liz saw a short, dainty woman smiling at her. Her grin was wicked and somehow adorable all at once as it pushed her cheeks up to form deep dimples. Her hair was the color of coal and hung around her smooth face in a style that could have been on a crime fiction novel from the '50s.

"Hi, dear." That squeaky voice seemed wrong on such a sinister, yet gorgeous face.

A double-barrel shotgun raised.

"Shit!" Liz cried, dropping to the ground. Just as her head dipped down behind the car's roof, the shotgun roared. Liz felt the huff of air as the buckshot sailed over her head.

Another shot boomed, shattering the window above her. Glass sprinkled down into Liz's hair. Dropping onto her stomach, she squirmed under the car.

As Liz wormed her way to the other side, Dixie reloaded. She heard the dusty scratches of Dixie's shoes as she ran around the back of the car. Liz pulled herself out from under the car next to Reese. She pointed the gun just as Dixie's head appeared on the other side of the trunk.

The shotgun raised. "Gotcha!" Dixie said, her smile dropping when she saw Liz already had her in her own sights.

"Nope."

Liz fired.

And missed.

The bullet hit the rear windshield, punching through and sending cracks in all directions in the glass.

Laughing, Dixie shouldered the shotgun. "Boom!" She fired. Her shrill laughter was drowned out by the gunshot.

Liz rolled away and Reese's head exploded from the blast. Dirt and brain matter splattered against the side of Liz's face. Screaming, Liz got to her feet. She'd lost her flashlight and water bottle at some point.

But she still had the gun.

She could have been empty-handed, though, since the blood had glued her eyes shut and she couldn't see where she needed to fire.

Not knowing what else to do, she ran forward. She knew

she made it outside the shack because she felt cool air on her sweaty skin. Running, she dug at her eyes with her free hand. She expected to hear another boom and feel something like a sledgehammer pounding her back.

Nothing happened.

How many shots had that been? One? Two?

Liz was pretty certain it had only been one.

She got her eyes cleared in time to see she was inches from an old van. It was too late to stop. She slammed into the side and rebounded off. Feet flying out in front of her, her rump pounded the ground. The landing jolted her. Hot pain shot up her spine and into her neck. Her arms felt as if sand was flowing in her veins.

She looked around, realizing she was in the high grass. The fuzzy tips reached over her shoulders, tickling her neck as they swayed in the gentle breeze. Peering over her shoulder, she could only see the top corner of the shack because of the weeds blocking her vision. She was surprised by how far she managed to run before her collision with the tarnished van.

Getting to her knees, Liz poked her head above the weeds. She spotted Dixie on the path, slightly turned away from her as she scanned the cars. Her short size made her look almost like a teenager from this distance. Her full figure was an hourglass shape against the moonlight shining behind her.

Liz didn't let her eyes linger too long. Keeping one knee planted, she brought her other foot forward and placed it flat on the ground. She pointed the gun, setting the sights on the middle of the curves. Holding her breath, she only felt a slight ping of hesitation about pulling the trigger. She wasn't afraid of shooting the woman, but she didn't much care for doing it like this.

Beats her shooting me.

Liz slowly let out the breath she'd been holding. Then she squeezed the trigger three quick times. The gun jerked in her hand, moving further to the side with each blast. She wasn't so sure about the last two shots, but she was confident the first one had been lined up perfectly.

Lowering the gun, she saw that Dixie no longer stood on the

path. She looked this way and that, not finding her anywhere. *She must be down.*

Liz slowly got to her feet. In her rising vision, she saw the weeds drop away and the path come into view. She expected to find Dixie sprawled on her back, a bullet wound in her chest. She saw Dixie, all right, but the petite woman was crouched, legs spread with her short dress hanging between her thighs. The shotgun jutted from her crotch like a massive, duel-tipped cock that spat fire and hell.

Dixie loosed another wild laugh, then fired. Liz felt heat zip by her, then a massive hole appeared in the wall of the van beside her.

Issuing another scream, Liz turned and ran for the front of the van as another boom resonated behind her. She heard the metallic punch of the buckshot on the van, folding the metal inward. The van rocked as if it had been slugged with a giant fist. *That was her two shots!*

Liz spun around, bringing up the pistol. She spotted Dixie standing in the path, slipping out two more shells from the bandolier strapped across her torso. It was slid between her large breasts, pulling the dress taut over the mounds.

Dixie had already opened the pipes when she noticed Liz was about to shoot. "Fuck!" Dixie yelled, then ran for the hatchback car to her left. Liz fired. The bullet smacked dirt where Dixie had just been standing. She followed Dixie in the sights of her pistol, ready to fire again. The spright woman was too fast. She ducked behind the car before Liz felt confident enough to take another shot. If she had a belt of ammunition like Dixie had, then she would have unloaded at the woman, blowing holes all through the car with hopes at least one would be on the mark. But she didn't. She needed to use her supply wisely.

Liz turned and bolted to the other side of the van. She pressed her back against it while she tried to catch her breath. The metal was cool and hard through her tank top.

What was she going to do? She couldn't allow herself to become pinned like this. But she also couldn't risk making a break for it. Dixie was close enough that she wouldn't have any trouble hitting her out in the open.

She looked around. She saw the pale humps and juts of dead cars all over the land.

Go through there?

That was also risky. Trying to maneuver through such a foreign obstacle in the dark would be hazardous. Hard to tell what all was on the ground, what she might trip over, step on, or fall into.

"Hey, girlie!" Dixie's voice sounded like a cat screeching. "Did you kill my boy? Otis said our boy's dead! Did you do it? If you did, then come out here and let's settle this. If you didn't, I'll let you go."

Liz assumed she was talking about the man in the mask back at the cabin. Did Ethan and the others kill him? Liz didn't know, but she figured they probably had done it. And it wouldn't matter to Dixie if Liz had been involved or not. She'd already killed Reese and would have no qualms about doing the same to her.

"Yoo-hoo!" Dixie called, closer now. "Where are you, sweetness?" A clucky, squeaky laugh followed the question. "Well, your silence says all. So, you're gonna die, bitch. For my boy!"

Liz's throat tightened. She could feel every ounce of her body trying to make her run, but her feet felt cemented to the ground. If she waited too long, she would be trapped here for sure. She had the gun, but what good would it do if Dixie started blasting at the van again?

Again, she thought of Ethan. She wondered if he was okay. Would she ever see him again? Earlier, she'd been convinced she would never be able to even look at him after all this was over. Now, it was all she wanted—to feel his arms around her, squeezing her. He always called himself her gorilla because of his hairy arms. She wanted to be there right now, embraced in his hairy arms so badly that she trembled.

Then get out of here. Survive this. For Ethan.

"For Ethan," she whispered to herself.

Forcing herself to move, Liz slid down toward the front of the van, keeping her back pressed against the side. She felt the sharp pokes of the folded metal from the buckshot's exit and winced. She lifted her back just enough so she wouldn't be sliced on the metal fangs. Getting tetanus right now would not help her in any way.

She supposed the best course right now would be to just start running and hope for the best. She had no idea how far back this junkyard reached. From where she stood now, it seemed endless. Reese had had some sort of a cognitive idea of how to maneuver out here, but she was no longer here to help.

And Liz was alone.

Alone.

Liz hated being alone. Especially in an instance as dire as this one.

Well, you're not alone, honey. The crazed woman of the junkyard is out there somewhere, armed to the teeth with a double-barrel shotgun.

And she had a gun of her own. She held it up, reassuring herself that it was still there to assist her. It wouldn't last forever. She'd run out of rounds eventually, sooner than she would like.

Get moving!

Liz reached the front door of the van. The dusty window was just beside her. She thought about peeking through the dirty glass but was afraid of finding Dixie standing at the other window, her shotgun perched to fire.

So, she sank to a crouch and waddled under the window. As she neared the front, she saw a narrow pole jutting at an angle from the wheel closest to her. Had she decided to just bolt for the other cars, she would have tripped over it.

Slightly crouching, she examined the pole. It was attached to a jack that had been positioned underneath the wheel rim. The tire was long gone, leaving behind a small, corroded disc and the tattered spiral base of shocks.

She took a few labored breaths to steel herself. Then she poked her head above the side of the van. Gazing across the hood, her eyes searched the dark junkyard. She expected to hear the retort of a shotgun moments before the slug took off a chunk of her head. But it never came. She stared at junked cars of all makes and models, becoming small, indistinct shapes the farther back in the darkness they went. Fog hovered above the roofs like a protective layer.

There was no sign of Dixie. She scanned the cars, the tapered, dark sections between them for any sign of movement at all. She saw nothing.

Maybe Dixie had gone another way, planning to ambush her from behind. Liz looked behind her, toward the other end of the van. She saw no evidence of Dixie lurking down that way. But the crazy woman had to be somewhere, probably closer than Liz realized.

It was time to go.

Liz took one last deep breath, then prepared to run.

Hands grasped each of her ankles and jerked back. Liz managed to emit a grunt before she plunged to the ground. Her chin hit the dirt, then skidded back along the coarse earth as she began to be pulled under the van. As she moved back, she saw her gun bouncing on the ground in the opposite direction away from her.

"No!" Clawing at the ground, Liz tried to find something to latch hold of.

Behind her, she could hear the maniacal, squealy laughter of Dixie. "You're gonna die, bitch! You're gonna die!"

The twin barrels of the shotgun raised toward Liz's face. She saw the sight tip jutting between the black holes.

"Shit!" Liz flung her head aside as she pushed the barrels away from her. Just as her hands shoved, the barrels boomed, exploding fire, and flinging back toward her. The hot metal of the twin barrels smacked her cheek, stinging and burning all at once.

Dixie's yells sounded as if they were coming at the end of a long, clamoring tunnel. The gunshot might have destroyed Liz's hearing. What wasn't squealing seemed to be warbled like an old reel-to-reel on the verge of dying.

Liz was up to her hips under the van before she even realized it. Shrieking and bucking, Liz threw herself forward. She knew Dixie had spent both shots and, thankfully, missed. Reloading under the cramped confines of the van would be tough. This was Liz's moment to get away. Grab her gun. Then come back and unload the rest of the clip under the van.

She held on to the ground, digging her fingernails into the

dry earth, and pulled. She slipped back out, her rump coming out from under the van. She put her knees into the dirt, feeling the coarse flakes scratching her flesh.

Dixie's hands slapped and pawed at her thighs, moving up to the small of her back. She felt sharp flashes of pain as fingernails raked her skin. Dixie must have tossed the shotgun so she would have both hands free.

Another sudden gouge on her flesh and Liz moaned in pain, losing her traction in the dirt. She was pulled back, her fingernails snapping one by one. The skin around her fingertips peeled back in thin strands.

Tears filled her eyes, blurring Liz's vision. Why was it so hard to get away from this lunatic? Even with Liz fighting as if her life depended on it, because it did, she still didn't seem to be a match for Dixie. The woman was feral in her attacks. All her movements came in frenzied bursts that had no pattern for Liz to adapt to.

Liz tried to roll onto her side, but the undercarriage of the van stopped her. She was further underneath than she realized.

"No! Let me go!" Liz shouted other ignored demands at the crazy woman. She saw glimpses of Dixie's crazy eyes, flashes of her evil smile that seemed to fill the lower half of her face.

Liz grabbed a handful of dirt and flung it at the face, momentarily reveling in the satisfaction of seeing the grits fill her big blue eyes. But Liz's joy was quickly replaced by agony as grits of dirt seeped into the flayed tips of her fingers.

Dixie's crazed laughter turned to anguished screams. Her hands released Liz's legs and went for her eyes, rubbing and digging to clear them of the dirt. Liz repeatedly kicked out as she crawled out from under the van. Here and there, she felt the solid connection of her feet against Dixie's face.

Liz managed to twist around. She saw the jack, the angled handle pointing outward. She reached for it. Dixie's hands slapped down on her back, gripping her shirt. Liz's hands closed around the cold metal. She began to pull herself forward. Dixie held on, but the effort was much weaker now. Liz slid along the dirt, wincing at the burning she felt through her shirt. Then she was no longer moving, the collar of her shirt pressed against her throat. She heard the soft ripping sounds of the fabric stretching, but it still seemed like a vice on her neck that was cutting off her air.

She pulled even harder. The grainy dirt nicked her again. She knew her skin was probably streaked in ruddy abrasions. She didn't care. She wanted to be out from under this damn van and didn't care how many scratches and bruises she came away with to ensure this.

Her hands started to slip on the pole. She squeezed tighter, pulling herself one more time. Her shirt ripped open in the front, releasing her breasts covered under the bra. Air smacked her sweaty skin. For a moment it felt glorious. As did the slack she now felt around her throat. She was able to breathe again. She almost felt a smile somewhere on her tear-streaked face.

Then the pole twisted back toward her.

Liz realized what she'd done at the same moment she heard the rusted groan emitted from the jack beside her head.

Shit...

The van plummeted.

Liz managed to roll onto her back as Dixie sprung forward. They were next to each other making wild attempts to escape when the van smashed down on them both, crushing them against the ground.

Liz's chest was flattened. She felt her ribs break apart and explode through the flesh around her stomach, each jagged tip ripping through. Blood jumped from her mouth in the same instant she felt blood from Dixie's mouth splash the side of her face.

Silence drifted over the junkyard as Liz watched the cloud of dust that had stirred up float away into the night sky. As it cleared, she saw the stars twinkling like sparkly freckles.

What had happened?

You know what happened. You just fucked up so bad.

Liz looked over to where the jack sat, the pole still jutting. She saw the front end of the van now sagged over to one, sitting uneven on the ground. The jack was now in front of the van, shoved there when the van dropped at such a strong force that had allowed for Liz to accidently crush herself.

Stupid idiot, Liz. Damn idiot...

She couldn't breathe. Couldn't move. To her surprise, though, there was no pain. That was a good thing, she knew, but it did nothing to alleviate the cold fear she felt swarming all over her. If Ethan somehow made it through this, he would be alone again. Liz wouldn't be there with him anymore. A deep emptiness opened inside her, filling her with a heavy sense of loss. She already missed him. She would always miss him, even in death.

Because she was dying. Any moment now, she would be gone forever.

Liz looked over at Dixie and let out a cough that shot more blood from her mouth. Dixie was on her stomach, the edge of the van pinning her to the ground just below the nape of her neck. She noted how much flatter it looked than a normal neck should look.

Dixie noticed her and smiled. Her teeth were slicked in red as if she'd brushed them with cherry syrup. Runnels of blood spilled down her chin. Her face was powdered in dirt, making parts of it darker than its natural olive hue.

"Damn...girl..." Dixie tried to breathe in but only managed to produce a dry wheeze that turned to a cough. "You killed us both..."

Liz almost laughed because Dixie's comment was accurate. She felt a smile tug the corner of her mouth.

Dixie strained to say, "What's...so funny?"

"I didn't...mean to... It was...an accident."

Dixie looked as if she wanted to laugh, too.

Neither of them got to, though.

33.

The brakes squealed softly as the Blazer came to a halt. The music clicked off. Though the reprieve from Nina's merciless singing was welcomed, the silence seemed odd and suspicious.

Ethan remained splayed across Zeb, keeping the machete hidden underneath him. He felt anxious, his nerves stirring inside like a bag of nails.

Nina started humming, killing the quiet. He heard the seatbelt latch click, then the safety harness whirred back and smacked the molded paneling. The door opened, causing the dome light to come on. Ethan screwed his eyes shut, concentrating to keep his breathing slow and steady.

But Nina didn't seem to be coming around to the back. The soft crunches of her footfalls were moving forward, away from the Blazer. Keys jingled followed by the rattling of chains.

She's unlocking a gate.

That meant they were at the junkyard.

Hinges groaned as the gate was rolled back. A moment later, he heard Nina's feet moving on gravel again. Her humming became louder as she returned to the Blazer. Climbing inside, she swung the door shut. The light was extinguished, and the Blazer popped back into gear.

When they started moving again, Ethan opened his eyes. He wasn't sure what he should do next. He felt a mild temptation to crawl up front and shove the large blade of the machete through the back of her seat.

He'd never make it up there without Nina spotting him. Not only did he have to clamber over a row of seats, but he would also have to sit on Cole's lap to try anything. He didn't want to do that, didn't want to see his old friend up close in his mangled condition. Ethan wanted to go without that image. Plus, he didn't know where Nina was taking him. He would be lost in here, with no idea where to go amongst the interminable maze of dead cars.

Be patient.

He was fine with this because it meant he could keep lying here a while longer. His body ached all over. Each subtle movement of the Blazer sent a wave of dull pain through him. His head throbbed, pulsated as if a damaged heart had been implanted inside his skull. The skin of his forehead felt tight and tender, so he figured a welt had formed there. And he was bleeding somewhere behind his ear. The hair on the back of his head was sodden and sticky with blood.

No, I'm good here for now.

Nina continued to hum as she steered the Blazer along. It rocked and shook over every rent and hollow on the path. Ethan rolled back and forth but never allowed himself to move too far from the machete. He wondered if Liz was out there, lost somewhere with the relics and wreckage. He hoped so. He needed to find her before anybody else did. Soon as he'd dispatched Nina, he was going to find Liz and get the hell away from this awful place.

The Blazer slowed to a stop before the engine shut off.

He needed to take care of Nina before Mr. Gorley's arrival. As unpredictable and feral as Nina appeared to be, her father was much worse. Ethan hadn't forgotten how he'd plucked him from the Blazer and thrown him aside like a garbageman hefting a trash bag. The man was stronger than any person Ethan had ever known.

Nina let a small groan slip out. "Damn." She shifted in the seat, then groaned again. "I hurt all over."

Ethan was glad to hear she at least was feeling a modicum of the effects of her injuries. A hatchet to the head and back, combined with a bullet wound would have stopped most people, permanently. But not Nina. She was still going with a force that seemed supernatural. Much like Zeb, her body somehow didn't operate like a normal body.

He couldn't take that lightly. But he also couldn't allow

himself to doubt he could beat her. If he questioned himself there, he would fail. His timing had to be just right. She would come back here and start unloading bodies. That's when he would strike.

He listened as Nina climbed out of the Blazer. The light returned inside the cab. Outside, Nina started humming again. Her feet crunched on gravel as she made her way around to the back of the truck. Ethan's stomach buzzed. His heart pounded in his chest. Each heavy thump sent a jolt of agony into his skull. His hand gripped the hilt of the machete even tighter.

There was a click and the gate opened with a soft squeak. Another sigh, followed by "How the shit am I gonna do this?"

And that was when Ethan flopped over, swinging the machete, and thrusting it outward. In his hasty movements, he glimpsed the machete's slanted tip soaring straight for Nina's chest. He saw the exhausted frustration on her face switch to a shimmer of panic that only lasted a second before her expression turned into a smirk as she easily sidestepped his attack.

The machete shot right past her.

Laughing, she gripped his wrist and yanked.

Ethan let out a startled yelp as he was jerked forward. His chest pounded the edge of the Blazer. The brutal landing momentarily stunned him. He watched the machete leave his hand, wrenched loose by Nina's tugging. She did a little twirl that caused her dress to flutter out around her pale legs. As she spun, he glimpsed bare buttocks and a thick tuft of hair before the dress floated back down.

Still laughing, she clasped the machete in both hands. It was a heavy weapon and caused her to crouch slightly as she struggled to keep it steady. The blade protruded like a diving board in front of her.

Ethan stared up at her. He gripped his hair with both hands and tugged at his scalp. He'd blown it. How the hell could he have screwed up so badly?

Nina, raising the machete, let out a cold laugh. "You gonna be trouble no matter what, ain't you?" She shook her head. "Daddy's going to be pissed at me, but hell, he already is anyway. I can't risk you gettin' away. And after that shit you just pulled, I know you'll try again. And I'm not in the mood to play around no more."

Ethan figured he would have kept trying until he was no longer able. Which, from the way it looked, would soon be the case. All his chances had been used up. There was a scrap of relief he felt somewhere inside about that. The knowledge that he would finally be with Emily soon also brought him some comfort. It had been teased so many times already tonight, only for it to be stripped away at the last moment. He hated to leave Liz behind, though. He loved her and wished he could be with her right now.

At least she would be spared seeing this.

Nina gave another one of those dour laughs. "Nighty-night," she said, bringing the machete down.

Ethan prepared himself for the blunt impact.

But the blade hacked into the Blazer's rear gate suspended above Nina's head. It chopped into the hard plastic. There was a sizzling pop that shot sparks and flung Nina to the ground. Moaning, her body performed a few twitches as her dazed eyes fought to find focus.

Ethan stared down at her, dumbstruck.

What the hell just happened?

The machete was still imbedded in the gate, jutting like a lost king's sword in a stone. A hot rubbery smell wafted toward him. Then it clicked. She'd sliced into the wiring under the paneling and got a shock for her efforts. He knew the jolt wasn't enough to kill her, or even really take her out of commission for very long.

But it granted him a moment, albeit brief, to get the advantage.

Ethan rolled out of the back and dropped to the ground. Landing in a squat, he looked over at Nina. She was already coming around. She'd managed to get on her stomach and was trying to push herself up onto her knees. She wasn't quite there yet and kept dropping back down, emitting a cuss word each time. Her eyes still looked cloudy, as if they were trying to focus on something far away.

Ethan didn't hesitate. He grabbed her by the hair and hoisted her up to her knees.

She groaned. "Let go of me!" Her arms swung limply at him. Her hands bounced off his torso like the playful swats of an infant.

Holding her face near his waist, he tilted her head back to look up at him. "Were you there?"

Nina's face pinched in confusion. Fresh blood started to spill from the gash in her head. "W-what?"

He gripped her hair tighter, tugging hard enough to make her scalp bulge. He had the urge to rip it from her skull.

Nina hissed through her clenched teeth. "Knock it off!"

"When my girl was killed. Were you there?"

The smile that formed on Nina's face nearly made him shiver. "I'm always...there." She let out a wild, insane laugh that didn't seem to be about to end anytime soon. "She was a squirmer. I love it when they wiggle like that."

Ethan wasn't in the mood to hear her say anything else. She'd given him his answer. He felt zero reluctance when he spun her around and flung her against the rear bumper. Sitting against it, her legs were stretched out in front of her. She seemed to still be groggy from the shock she'd received, which worked in Ethan's favor.

Her head fell back on the bumper, the raven-black hair spreading inside the Blazer like spilled oil. She continued to wail a witch's cackle while Ethan reached up and gripped the gate with both hands. Seeing what he was doing elicited an even wilder laughing fit from the crazed woman.

Ethan silenced her when he slammed the gate down on her head. Her body twitched and convulsed, unable to move from being pinned by the rear gate. Lifting it up, he saw the first hit had been enough to cave the front of her face inward. Dented in the middle, it looked like a flattened Halloween mask. Her eyes had been shoved back into her skull, leaving the brims of her sockets with plenty of space.

Though it was clear that she was dead, Ethan felt no satisfaction. So he swung the gate down again, delighting in the crunchy splatter of her head splitting apart. He didn't fret with examining the damage this time because he wasn't finished yet. He swung down again. And again. He kept banging the heavy gate against Nina's skull until there wasn't enough substance left in her head to hold her upright. He raised the gate one last time. As he was about to bring it down again, she fell over. Her devastated head smacked the ground like a sack of chicken fat.

Huffing, Ethan staggered back. It was then that he noticed the heavy spread of blood all over him. From the stomach down, it was running off him in rivulets. He had no idea why he felt the urge to do so, but he rubbed his hand over his stomach, lathering it in Nina's blood. Then he smeared it over his face as if it were sunscreen. It was cool and sticky and started to feel itchy on his skin right away.

What the hell's wrong with me?

He couldn't let Liz see him like this. He couldn't let *anyone* see him like this.

Disgusted with himself, he left Nina behind and walked to the front of the Blazer. He saw the tip of a rag sticking out from under the seat. He snatched it, grimacing at the oil stains and dead pieces of grass clinging to it.

No worse than a dead girl's blood.

He wiped his face. It didn't feel as if he'd gotten any of the blood off him and had only succeeded in smearing it over the areas he'd missed the first time. He was about to wipe it again when he spotted something from the corner of his eye.

He turned around and stared out into the junkyard. The Blazer's headlights were still on, cutting twin paths into sloping darkness that seemed to go on forever. He saw the small wood-built house to the right. Light glowed from the windows. The porchlight was on, as was the set of sodium arcs all around the yard like they had been expecting a plane to land.

The headlights bore through all that, hitting an area farther down that he would have missed had the light not glinted off something metal on the ground. To the right of the unknown object were the dark shapes of what might have been bodies.

He saw the blond hair and immediately knew it was Liz.

Dropping the rag, he started running up the path. He was over halfway there when he realized he could have taken the Blazer and drove the distance. It was too late now. He was not going back to get it.

Wanting to call out to her, to tell her he was coming, he knew it was pointless. He already could tell she was in no shape to respond or even hear him.

No. Please, no!

He approached an old van that '80s glam metal bands would have used for touring. It was tilted at an angle, leaving the left side flush to the ground. Poking out from underneath it like a pair of Halloween decorations were Liz and another woman that Ethan assumed was the mama Nina had been screaming about during her meltdown in the truck. The hair draping her face matched Nina's in length and color. He looked past her to where Liz was splayed.

Blood had pooled around his girlfriend, soaking the dirt and grass all around her. The strength drained from his legs, and he dropped to his knees. His chest felt as if cold hands were trying to compress it into a ball. It made his breaths sound sharp and squeaky.

He took her hand into his and gasped at the gelid feel of her flesh. Suddenly he was back in the hospital a year ago, in that cold waiting room with the detective and doctor when he'd learned his daughter hadn't survived surgery.

Now Liz was gone too. She was with Emily, where he wished he could be. He would give anything to be there now, in the middle of an endless embrace with them.

Tears flooded his eyes, distorting his vision. He was thankful for it because it made it hard to see the horrid condition his girlfriend was in. He hadn't been able to tear his eyes away and the tears granted him that.

He fell back onto the ground. Something prodded his spine. He didn't care. He stared up at the smeared dots of stars and sobbed.

34.

Ethan sobbed at the sky until his back could no longer handle whatever was jabbing him. Sitting up, he reached behind him. His fingers patted something cool and hard on the ground. He picked it up and brought the object around so he could see it.

Liz's gun.

He remembered when they'd gone to the gun range so she could help Ethan learn to how handle a firearm. He'd known then that he wanted to be with her forever.

And forever was over, he realized.

He pulled the gun to his chest, hugging it as if it were a part of Liz. In a way, it was. It was all he had left. He held it out and released the magazine. Catching it, he saw there was a round at the top. He turned the magazine sideways and counted the remaining bullets.

Six.

Sniffling, he rubbed his eyes on his forearm. They felt tired and itchy. He put the magazine back into the Glock. A brief temptation to put the gun in his mouth came from nowhere. He doubted it would be any easier for him to end his life, but he also recognized that everything he'd been fighting for was gone. It was over. His life had started to end the moment he knew Emily had succumbed to the wounds she'd sustained from these merciless fuckers.

And it had been a slow death for Ethan. One that had dragged on and on, haunting him with the tease of release from his personal torments, only to leave him drowning in them again. Even if he made it out of here alive, he would never truly live again—the walking dead in a life of hell.

One shot by his own hand would take care of that.

It really would.

He sniffled again. His mouth tasted like saltwater. He just wanted to be done with it all.

But he had one thing to do before he could even think about his own fate.

Mr. Gorley had to die.

Ethan was the only one left to make sure that happened.

A few minutes later, he was back at the Blazer. He dug around until he found some water Cole had stashed in a small thermal bag under the passenger seat. He had no idea how long it had been there, nor did he care. It tasted wonderful as he chugged the bottle empty.

He shut off the headlights, then dug through the Blazer some more. He found his .41 in his bag where he'd left it. He also located a hunting knife in the glove compartment. He figured Cole's rifle would have been in the Blazer somewhere, but he didn't find it in any of the places he checked. He still avoided the middle row, making sure he didn't glance at where his friend was seated. For all he knew, the rifle was in Cole's lap. If it was there, it would stay there. He had no intentions of seeing him, even now.

Ethan set the knife and .41 on the hood. He'd already stuffed Liz's gun in his pocket. It was small and slid right in without any trouble. The .41 would be a different story. He crammed it in the waistband of his pants, leaving the handle jutting outside his shirt so it would be easier to retrieve.

Then he grabbed the knife. On his way to the back, he nudged the door with his hip. It shut with a dull thump. He made his way to the back, stepping over Nina on the way. He wanted the machete. It still protruded from the paneling of the rear gate, just below the glass. The surge of electricity should have blown the fuse powering this section, but he didn't want to take any chances of shocking himself.

Reaching up, he grabbed the gate and began to shake it. The machete quickly came loose and plunged. It stabbed into the earth, trembling.

He decided to leave it there while he did the next part. He wasn't exactly sure when the idea had struck him to do what he was going to do, but it was there in his brain, a sick temptation that he couldn't ignore. In fact, a part of him was even looking forward to it.

He walked over to Nina, crouching next to her lifeless body. He grabbed a handful of clumpy hair and pulled her head into his lap. Then he used the hunting knife to carve into the flesh of her face. He had no idea what the easiest way to this was, so he started by her chin, sawing up to the ears, moving behind them and tracing the hairline all the way around her brow to the other side. It had worked in *The Texas Chain Saw Massacre*, he thought, so it would probably suffice in this moment as well. Finished with that, he angled her head the other way and picked up where he left off until he'd sliced all the way around, even going down into her neck a little.

The squishy sounds didn't bother him. From years of cutting meat at the restaurant, he had become quite skilled with fileting. And Nina's face, to Ethan, was like the cold skin on a chicken. But when he pulled the face away from the head, he noticed that underneath wasn't smooth like a chicken. Nina was lined with rigid sinew and muscle. Seeing the under mechanics of her face was enough to disgust him.

But it didn't stop him.

He put her displaced face on her chest. Then he pulled her dress up. The legs underneath were pale and smooth, the color of milk. She wore heavy boots and nothing else under the garment. He didn't want to see any of that. All he wanted was a morsel of the fabric. He used the knife to cut off a strip, then he covered her with what remained of the dress.

Now he had all he needed.

He put the face against his, cringing at the cold paste squishing against his skin. The old blood held the face against his own as if it were a crimson adhesive. He opened his eyes and saw that part of his left eye was blocked by icy skin. He adjusted the mask a few times to get it right. Satisfied, he took the strip of dress and tied it around his head and the forehead of Nina's face.

Finished, he gave it a few tugs.

The face remained fixed there as if it had been there all along.

Standing, he slipped the knife through his belt. Then he grabbed the machete.

He was ready.

As it turned out, he didn't have to wait long. He heard the rumble of an engine nearby. Light appeared in the distance, swishing back and forth across the dark mass of night.

Ethan took a deep breath. His mask made it difficult to pull in much air at all. He'd have to deal with it, though.

He scurried off to hide just as the tow truck bounded over the hill.

35.

Otis Gorley was not usually a man that demonstrated much emotion, except when it came to his family. As much as he hated everything else in this shit-stain of a world, he loved his wife and kids. Knowing that he would be burying his oldest kid tonight had left him feeling an odd combination of melancholy with an overpowering numbing sensation. He knew he was sad, but there was a wall that had formed around him that prevented him from accepting the full effects of his loss. It would break eventually, he knew, allowing all those emotions to flood in and drown him. But for now, he was okay with the emotional shield. He didn't need to be bogged down with hurt and sadness right now. There was still so much to do. So much had gone wrong tonight.

So damn much.

As he steered the truck onto the gravel drive of the junkyard he owned with his wife, Dixie, he tried to comprehend what had inspired Zeb to go after those people on his own. The last thing Otis knew was that Zeb was supposed to help Nina with hauling the bodies away from the campsite. There had to be a piece he was missing that would help him understand. They'd known the others were at the cabin. And they'd known they had come bearing arms. A lot of fucking arms. They were equipped like the damn military. Nina had spotted them coming in during one of her treks through the woods and had watched them for a while, reporting back to Otis on the walkie what she was seeing.

"Leave them be," Otis had told the kids when Nina came back home. "Don't mess with them."

"But they came out here to get us, didn't they?" Zeb had asked.

Otis knew they had. He also had figured out that the people at the campsite were a part of it all. Even the damn forest critters had probably come to the same conclusion from how much those "campers" reeked of incompetence.

"Can't we at least kill the other ones, then?" Nina had asked.

"The campers?"

She nodded and looked at him with those big, supplicating eyes of hers. Nina had that way with him. Never had he once thought he could love a woman as much as he loved Dixie, but Nina had come along and proved him wrong.

"Sure," he'd said. "Plus, it'll show them others we mean business, and they best stay away."

That had been the plan: Kill the people at the campsite in hopes it would deter their friends from fulfilling their plans.

It probably would have worked, too, if Zeb wouldn't have gotten overzealous.

Damn kid. Head full of rocks.

A tear spilled over the rim of his solitary eye. He blinked it away before more could join it. He felt a stinging sensation near his left shoulder blade, then remembered he'd been stabbed.

It hardly counted as a stab, really. More like a prick. He didn't even notice it unless he moved a certain way. Otis was going to do way more than *prick* that bastard tonight. He planned to skin him alive, bit by bit. Let the son of a bitch watch them dance around in his skin for a while.

Otis smiled at the vision it produced.

He saw Nina had left the front gate open, just as he'd requested. He drove through, put the truck in park, and hopped out. He walked back to the gate and pulled it shut, winding the chains and padlocking them in place.

For a moment, he thought he felt eyes on his back, watching. He turned around, staring out into the junkyard. His truck grumbled, spurting thick plumes of exhaust into the air. The law's SUV was up on the flatbed, covered with a tarp in case anybody happened to be out driving tonight while he was heading back. As usual, he saw nobody. The roads were dark and empty, as if the small speck of town was all that remained on this shitty planet.

And that was how the junkyard should be as well. But it wasn't. He was being watched. The hairs on the back of his neck still stood on end. Something wasn't right. It made his skin buzz with a nervous awareness that he didn't like. "Nina? That you, girl?"

No answer. All he heard were the trills of insects barely mending with the loud chugging of his truck. He doubted his daughter would be trying to sneak up on him right now. The timing was all wrong, and she should know he wasn't in the mood for games. She was a nut, but she wasn't an idiot. Most of the time.

Nope. That's not Nina.

Then who was it?

Standing at the back of his flatbed, Otis continued to look around. He saw nothing but jettisoned vehicles swathed in silver moonlight. In the pale glow, they looked as if they had turned to stone.

The odd feeling passed just as strange and sudden as it had come on.

Whatever had been watching him was gone now.

He headed back to his truck, trying not to admit to himself how he'd almost felt...spooked.

I don't get spooked.

The hell he didn't. The goose flesh on his hairy arms was proof that was a lie.

He gripped the bar inside the cab and hoisted his bulk up into the seat. He swung the door shut with a rusty groan. He saw himself about to lock the door and stopped. He shook his head. No way was he going to do that now. He'd never felt the need to lock himself inside anything. Besides, nothing was out there that would want to get in here.

Right?

Still, he knew *something* was off. And that was a feeling he did not like. Whenever his internal warning system flared up like this, it was never inaccurate.

Then what was it?

Could be lots of things, he realized. Something could have happened to Dixie. Or Nina.

Or both.

He started driving. He wouldn't allow such worrisome thoughts any kind of space in his mind.

A few minutes later, he was on the main drive into the junkyard. His house was up a distance on the right, where the driveway branched off. He could go straight or to the left to access more sections of the junkyard. He figured stopping by the house first was a good idea. Make sure Dixie had handled all the intruders. Nina was probably out at the pit, setting up things for tonight's festivities with Ethan.

He was almost at the driveway when something flitted in front of the truck. It darted out from the right and vanished in the darkness on the verge of the drive. The headlights momentarily washed it in a wobbly glow. It moved fast, and he barely had time to notice because he was caught so unprepared.

He stamped the brake. The truck came to a rocky halt, the tires grinding on gravel.

"Nina?" he muttered.

He shook his head. Damn sure looked like her, but the clothes were all wrong.

What the hell was she up to?

Throwing the gear into park, Otis grabbed his industrial flashlight from the floorboard. It was a bulky instrument, with a large, bumblebee eye for a bulb and a massive battery affixed to the bottom. When he clicked it on, it was as good as any helicopter spotlight in the dark.

He aimed the light out the window. A bright tunnel parted the darkness like a glowing stream. He saw the Blazer parked up ahead, just past the house. The rear gate was open, the interior light on and spilling light onto the ground around it. The headlights, also on, ignited a wide swath of the ground in a bright smolder, which made it easier to see what was on the ground next to the vehicle.

He saw the body and knew right away who he was looking at.

"No," he whispered.

Otis shoved the door open. He slid out of the truck, reached back in, and grabbed his ax. With the flashlight in one hand and the ax in the other, he started walking toward the Blazer. As he moved, he heard scampering around him, hidden somewhere in the tall grass. Once or twice, he aimed the light only to catch the weeds swaying as if something had just fled from that spot. He knew his own imagination was screwing with him, which was odd because that usually never happened. He hated this feeling. He was the hunter, the fear-inducer. It was not supposed to be the other way around.

In the bouncy glare of the flashlight, he saw Nina's legs. Her dress was furled around her thighs. Her boots were scuffed and dirty, crossed at the ankles. The fresh scratches looked almost black on her pale skin.

"Baby girl?"

Not even a flinch. His insides went hot and mushy.

Please. Not two kids. Not two kids...

But his silent prayer could not be answered. He saw Nina was too far gone for saving. She lay on her side, bent at the waist with her head tilted back as if she were looking over her shoulder.

What was left of her head, anyway.

It looked as if it had been squished into pulp. Her face was gone, carved off and taken. Her eyes were bulbous and round, staring unblinkingly from a face of trodden red muscle and sinew. He noticed the blood splatter all over the back of the SUV. It trickled over the edge, sprinkling the ground below in crimson.

Tears turned his vision blurry.

"Oh, shit, baby girl..." His voice came out in choked sobs. "Not you, too."

He began to howl. Anybody listening would find it strange that such a large man could produce such small, tormented sounds. But Otis was a simple kind of guy, wore his emotions on his sleeve, and had a big heart that always seemed to be breaking.

He swung the ax, chopping the air. Spinning around, he swung the ax again, and again. He saw Ethan in his mind, saw the ax whacking through him and devouring his diminutive frame.

He saw the man's daughter, begging for Otis not to kill her. She had been luring him in last year, waiting for him to get close enough to grab her.

And when he lifted her up, she'd used that moment to lean in and bite off his nose.

He saw her again, chewing his nose and spitting it out. He swung his ax again, the blade chopping through the memory and causing it to go away.

Finally, he brought the ax down. He stood there, sobbing for several minutes before he managed to regain control of himself. He used his dirty sleeve to wipe his eye dry. Blinking, he looked down at his daughter again. He was about to say a few words for her when he noticed her arm. It was splayed out to her side, as it had been when he'd first arrived. What he hadn't noticed until now was that her index finger was pointing away from her.

Confusion washed through the anguish. He doubted she'd done that herself. Whoever had done this to her was leaving a message for him. He turned, tracing the path of her finger, where the Blazer's headlights shone into the junkyard.

And saw Dixie.

"No!"

His daughter momentarily forgotten, Otis ran. For such a large mass, Otis moved as if he was nubile and sleek, unlike the almost fifty-year-old, three-hundred-pound man he really was. The ax bounced near his side, the blade catching the light and reflecting it against the cars around him.

He reached Dixie in a matter of moments.

"Oh, no...Babe."

His eye spewed more tears. He dropped to his knees. The ax head pounded the ground in front of him, the blade cutting into the soil. He rubbed his eye dry and stared at his wife.

His dead wife.

She'd been crushed alongside a stranger that had also been killed. The intruder she'd told him about, most likely. No doubt in his mind that she was a member of the party from the cabin.

This was what he was meant to see. Whoever had killed Nina had done this and wanted to make sure Otis didn't miss it.

"I'm sorry, sweetie," he said through gasping moans. "I should've come home when you first told me you saw them running around the property. I should've been here...I..."

Otis heard it, the soft whisper of someone slinking through the tall grass. The subtle noise would have gone undetected to most, but Otis had become proficient and intuitive through the years to isolate any type of unfamiliar sound in his junkyard.

He tilted his head, aiming what was left of his nose toward the wind. He let the scents of the night waft into his nostrils. He smelled the familiar smells that were always there. He was able to distinguish the unknown woman's fragrance from all the others and tuck it away. He filtered the others until he caught a whiff of something else.

It was also familiar, but not as well-known as the others. He'd smelled it several times back at the cabin.

Hello, again.

The man, Ethan, was trying to take him by surprise.

Otis almost laughed, but he couldn't. He had to keep up the act of the distraught husband and father, which wouldn't be hard because he was one. Still, a smile tugged at his mouth. He wouldn't have to go hunting for the man who'd done this. The stupid shit was coming right to him, and all Otis needed was to sit tight.

He gripped the ax tighter, slightly lifting it so the blade came free of the ground. Clods of dirt dropped off like rabbit pellets. With his other hand, he reached out and stroked Dixie's coal-black hair. Even in death, it still felt soft and smooth. He loved playing with it, running his calloused fingers through its length. Especially those nights when he couldn't sleep, and she would lay her head on his chest so he had easy access to it. The sleek feel of it, the way it always smelled clean and fresh, would put him at ease enough for sleep to come.

Ethan was closer now. Coming around the rear of the van, moving in stealth.

Otis continued to pet his wife, whispering words to her that he knew she couldn't hear. It made him feel better to say them, though, and he knew had she been able to understand, she would have appreciated his romantic prose.

Ethan was a few steps away. Otis had to admit, the guy was doing a good job of being discreet. Had he been trying to surprise anybody else, he would have succeeded. The fool just didn't know what he was up against. The fool thought he did, but he was so wrong.

This one's for you, baby doll. For Zeb and Nina.

Otis slipped his fingers out of Dixie's hair and lowered his head as if he were overcome with emotions. He kept that façade going, drawing Ethan closer. He heard the soft rustling of clothing as Ethan raised his arms.

Otis caught a whiff of a machete.

Don't think so, pal.

This was the moment Otis had been hoping for. Just as Ethan's daughter had done to Otis, he was luring him in. The man planned to strike him down with one good chop to the back of the head. Split his skull. With a blade like that, he would have no problems.

He heard the quiet intake of air as Ethan started to swing down.

And that was when Otis spun around, bringing the ax around to strike.

He froze when he saw Nina's face gazing down at him, pale and pasty as if it had been smeared in sour cream. Ethan's eyes glared through the ragged holes where his daughter's eyes should have been. Those eyes were filled with hate and malice.

He wore his daughter's face…

Otis missed with the ax, and even if he had managed to hit him, it wouldn't have been a critical injury. The sight of his daughter's face sagging and limp like sliced ham had stunned him, almost immobilized him. But because he'd been prepared and in the process of swinging, he'd managed to move his head free of the impact zone.

But he didn't come through unscathed. The machete chopped into his collar bone, plunging down in his chest and separating his shoulder from the rest of his body.

The pain was excruciating, unlike anything he'd ever felt before. Though in that moment, he was thankful for it because it shocked him out of the haze that had been bogging down his reflexes.

He'd dropped the ax from his right hand. But his left hand had no trouble snatching it back up. Ethan was still twirling from the momentum of his hard swing and was in the process of tilting sideways, exposing the side of his midsection to Otis. It wouldn't be a good hit, but it would still be a hit. Otis thrust the ax up at an angle. The blade whacked Ethan above the hip, bouncing off and bringing a spray of blood with it. The groans Otis heard coming from behind the dead lips of his daughter's face were like a choir of angels to his ears.

As Ethan started to go down, Otis began to stand. Though he was wobbly, he figured he had a good bit to go before succumbing to his wounds. He couldn't play around with Ethan too long.

He needed to get back to the house as soon as possible.

36.

Ethan realized he'd messed up the moment Mr. Gorley started to turn around. All this time, he'd thought he was being discreet in his advances and was about to perform an easy kill, but the large man had been pretending to be incognizant while just waiting for his own moment to attack.

Now that Ethan had been struck with the ax, the pain he felt had woken him up. Thinking clearly for the first time in a while, he realized this course of action had probably been a poor choice. Adding that with the fact that he'd selected to wear Mr. Gorley's dead daughter's face over his own, he'd made a lot of poor decisions in the last several minutes.

He had guns. Why hadn't he just unloaded on the big man when his back was turned?

Because my dumbass wanted him to see me.

Ethan was a bigger idiot than he originally thought.

The ax hadn't hurt at first. Sure, he'd felt the blade hit him. But the pain hadn't been intense, so he'd thought it had only been a tap and nothing more. When he looked down and saw the blood jumping from the triangular gash under his ribs, he realized how wrong he was.

At least he'd managed to wedge the machete in a pivotal spot in Mr. Gorley. No way could somebody survive a hit like that.

And yet, Mr. Gorley proved him wrong once again by starting to get to his feet. The machete was still imbedded in the top of his chest, the tip pointing behind him while the handle jutted from above his right pectoral.

For a moment, Ethan didn't know what to do. He thought about running away, climbing into his Blazer and driving off. Then he remembered Nina had pulled the keys from the ignition and that meant he'd have to find them. There was the tow truck, but Ethan had no idea how to drive one of those. Besides, he needed to finish this once and for all, no matter what happened to him.

You have a gun, idiot! Two of them.

Ethan reached behind into his pocket, felt the gun's handle, and snatched it out. He brought it around the front of him as Mr. Gorley stepped closer. Ethan had wanted his .41 but had grabbed Liz's Glock by mistake.

He pulled the trigger.

Mr. Gorley's stomach spat blood as the bullet went in. The large man let out a groan and snatched the gun from Ethan's hand. He tossed it over his shoulder and stepped even closer.

"You're dead meat," said Mr. Gorley.

Oh, I know it.

Ethan slapped at his back, trying to get the other gun. Mr. Gorley saw what he was trying to do. He gripped Ethan's shoulder and yanked him close. Reaching behind his back, he jerked the gun free of Ethan's pants. The site scratched the small of his back when Mr. Gorley pulled it out.

Laughing, Mr. Gorley flung that gun away, too. "Got anymore, pussy?"

Ethan shook his head. "That's it." Then he reached out and gripped the rag hanging from the lower half of the giant's face. He pulled it free and unveiled a horribly scarred face. The nose was a crater that hadn't healed properly. A large scar traced a line to the ragged hole of his missing eye. Though the socket was hollow, the brow still furrowed as if it could have stared the murderer's anger straight at Ethan.

Mr. Gorley growled, his brown teeth bared between trembling lips and a bushy beard. Ethan jumped back, letting out a cry of his own. His stemmed from a terrified place that seemed to be growing larger than all the bravery and insanity he'd managed to drudge up a short while ago.

The silent stalk-and-slash mindset he'd had was long gone. Now he was just scared and couldn't think straight.

He flinched when Mr. Gorley palmed his face. When he

pulled his hand back, the face he'd tied onto his head came with it. The air was cool on his sweaty face, allowing him to breathe better.

Then Mr. Gorley's fist went into Ethan's stomach hard enough to lift him off his feet. When he brought his arm down, Ethan came down with it. The air Ethen had managed to suck in had been knocked out of him. Now he strained to breathe, struggled to think, and gave up on trying to move.

He lay on his side underneath the big man and stared up at him while he held the face in his left hand. His good eye was soaked with tears. A few trickled down his face, vanishing in the shaggy hair of his beard.

Shaking his head, Mr. Gorley let his arm drop. He stared up at the sky and screamed.

Ethan pulled in a thin draft of air. His throat made a flat, quacking sound that brought Mr. Gorley's attention back down to him.

"Shit...on me," Ethan said through a wince.

Mr. Gorley dropped the face on the ground, then picked up the ax. Ethan hadn't even noticed it was there. If he had, he would have tried to use it himself.

"Enough of this horseplay bullshit," said Mr. Gorley. "Time to get serious."

Ethan couldn't believe that had been nothing but a scrimmage to the killer. How he was still standing and moving about was a mystery to Ethan. But one thing he'd learned from the other Gorleys was that they *could* die. Even this big monster could be killed, though Ethan had no idea what would do the trick. This man was responsible for the deaths of too many people Ethan cared about. He'd spilled the seed that had spawned nightmares.

Mr. Gorley stepped over to Ethan, holding the ax with his left hand. His right arm swung limply by his side like a rope. The machete was still there, too deep for Ethan to try and pull out.

Ethan shot to his knees and jabbed his thumb into the bullet hole in Gorley's stomach. He pushed until his second knuckle touched the man's shirt. Gorely let out a cry of pain and Ethan was glad to finally hear something like that.

Gorley shuffled backward, swaying on his feet. It seemed the blood loss was finally catching up to him. Ethan gripped handfuls of the man's shirt and pulled himself to his feet. Gorley started to lift the ax again, but Ethan tore his bloody thumb from the bullet hole and jabbed it in Gorely's remaining eye. It felt like a small, plushy ball as it slid back. There was some resistance at first, so Ethan pushed harder, growling with the exertion of it all. The eye pushed past the blockage and thick liquid shot out.

Gorley dropped the ax so he could cradle his eye. "You... bastard!"

Ethan didn't even think about what he did next. His body was moving as if it had been pre-programmed for this. He grabbed the ax from the ground and swung it at Gorley's chest. The blade hacked into it, turning Gorley's cries into gasps.

Ethan jerked the blade loose and swung again. This time, the blade punched into his stomach. While Gorley screamed, Ethan wriggled the blade back and forth, splitting the wound even wider. When he yanked the ax back, blood dumped from the rent, soaking the crotch of his pants.

Gorley was no longer screaming. His breaths came in short spurts. He swung at Ethan uselessly, not even coming close to connecting the blow. His legs folded and he dropped to his knees. He coughed a few times, then spat a wad of bloody phlegm onto the ground. "Shit...I'm fucked up."

Ethan moved in, raised the ax, and prepared himself for the final hit. He wanted the blade to go into his face, halving his skull as the blade tore through.

But Gorley surprised him again by dodging the swing.

Ethan tumbled over the big man's shoulder as he brought the ax down. One of the blades stabbed into the ground. Ethan saw he was about to land on the other blade jutting upward. He managed to spin around and land beside it on his stomach. He turned and his nose rubbed against the cool surface of the ax.

Then he felt a hand grip his hair and pull his head up. "No!" Ethan tried to resist but could do nothing to stop his head from being moved to the side and angled right above the protruding blade. He could hear Gorley laughing behind him.

"Now I got you..."

Ethan bucked and thrashed, swinging his elbows back in hopes of either hitting or knocking Gorley away from him. Nothing seemed to be working. Ethan decided to stop trying to overpower the killer and go in a different approach.

He whipped his head from side to side. Gorley's grip didn't slacken, nor did he expect it to. He just continued to pull until he heard a sound like fabric tearing and felt a hot rush of pain on the back of his head.

Ethan fell over and rolled away from the ax. When he turned around, he saw Gorley was holding a hank of his hair attached to a flap of skin. Gorley barely managed to emit a holler before his face smacked down on the blade, killing his cries.

Both arms dropped and didn't move. His neck was bent upward, the ax blade buried deep in his face and holding the mass of his weight.

Ethan stared at the big man's back, checking for any signs of movement. It remained flat, unmoving.

Mr. Gorley was finally dead.

They all were dead.

Ethan dropped to the ground and panted. A strange stillness seemed to drift over the junkyard. It was almost tranquil, the kind of peace that Ethan would have loved to experience in a different situation. He wasn't sure how long he stayed that way, but he was sure a lot of time didn't pass before his injuries stopped allowing his rest.

Sitting up, he let out a groan as his side throbbed with pain. He checked the damage and saw it hadn't started looking any better since the last time he checked. His shirt was doused in blood and the wound in his skin was almost black. Blood had spread all around it, spilling down his stomach.

He didn't think it was going to kill him, though.

Ethan turned his head, feeling the back of his skull flare up with dull pain. He didn't want to touch it and receive the confirmation that he was missing a large chunk of flesh and hair back there.

He looked back at Liz. She was on her back, face pointing up as if she'd been enjoying the serenity with him moments ago. In a way, he supposed she had been. He only wished it could have been for real.

He felt nothing about the deaths of the Gorleys. But the loss of his girlfriend, his friends, and his daughter was something he doubted he would ever recover from. He had no clue what he would do next. He supposed contacting the police was the appropriate thing, but he didn't look forward to it. There would probably be jailtime for him. He'd broken a lot of laws, he was sure.

And he wasn't surprised to find he didn't much care. Nothing really mattered anymore.

He was so lost in his thoughts that he didn't notice somebody else was out here with him. Somebody that, like him, was still alive.

"What'd you do to my family?"

Ethan jerked at the almost pitiful quality of the voice. He turned his head to find a little boy, no older than ten, standing a few feet from him. He held a pump-action shotgun to his small shoulder. The barrel was pointed right at Ethan.

Oh, shit. Not a kid.

The kid wore pajamas that looked as if they had been made specifically for him. Probably by the woman underneath the van with Liz. They were checkered and seemed to be a one-piece. He had on boots that looked much too large for his small feet.

Ethan looked down at Gorley, turned, and looked at the woman he'd heard Gorley call Dixie. Then he faced the kid again. "They killed my family."

It was the kid's turn to look around. He did so with his big eyes, moving from one side to another, keeping the gun trained on Ethan.

"Are you a Gorley?" Ethan asked.

"Huh?" He blinked, bringing his attention back to Ethan. His hair was shaggy and hung almost in his eyes, much like Zeb's hair had been. In fact, he looked like a smaller version of Zeb entirely.

"Are you a Gorley?"

The kid gave a terse nod. "Rusty Gorley."

"Rusty. I'm Ethan."

"Did you kill them?"

Ethan stared at the kid, who looked almost innocent in his baggy pajamas and overlarge boots. *Almost* innocent. The way he held that shotgun made Ethan think he was anything but. He didn't even seem to be scared.

But what really gave him away were his eyes. It was the same look he'd seen in Zeb's eyes—the empty, almost vacant stare held on by a thread of brutality. If this kid wasn't a killer, he soon would be.

"Do you know the stuff they did?" Ethan asked. "To people? Like my daughter? And my friends?"

The corner of Rusty's mouth twitched as he seemed to struggle to keep a smile in check. "Know? I get to do it, too."

"Thought so."

Ethan didn't want to kill a kid, but he supposed it was something he would get over pretty quickly. He also thought he could probably reach the kid before he even had the chance to fire the weapon. After all, he hadn't heard the kid jack a shell into the chamber. He would have to do that before he could even fire. Ethan would be on him before then. He had zero doubt about it.

Ethan got to his feet, groaning as fresh waves of pain rippled through him. He was tired and hurt all over and did not want to keep doing this. But if this kid was involved with it all, then he wanted to make sure he died, too.

"You asked me if I killed them?" Ethan asked. Rusty nodded. "You're damn right I did. And it's your turn now."

Ethan took a step forward.

Rusty stepped back. "Now, Dusty!"

Confused, Ethan turned to see a kid that looked identical to Rusty rush at him. He held a scythe over his head while he let out a feral scream. Ethan froze at the sight of the other kid, Rusty's twin brother, no doubt. It wasn't just that the sudden appearance of him had caught him by surprise. It was the evil expression that somehow mutated the kid's features into something that looked almost inhuman.

Ethan didn't even try to defend the attack. The scythe blade struck him down, slicing right down the middle of his torso and splitting it wide. Ethan dropped to the ground and rolled onto his back.

He looked up as two identical heads peered down at him. Two sets of smiles appeared on the faces. Dusty lifted the scythe and ran his little tongue along the blade.

"Pa's right," he said. "Fear does taste good."

Rusty looked at his brother. "My turn?"

Dusty nodded. "Yep. You won the coin toss. You get to do it."

Rusty let out a clucking laugh. "Finally! My first!"

Then he raised the gun, bringing the barrel into Ethan's line of sight. It was a black hole that blotted out his vision.

"Can't wait to see the brains splatter all over the ground."

"Me too!"

Ethan had no idea who had said what. Not only did they look alike, but they sounded like the same person. And he would never find out because the darkness that obstructed his vision lit up with a fiery boom.

The quick glimpse of brightness was the last image Ethan would ever see.

37.

"**M**s. Bedford?"

Gale stared at the TV mounted on the wall in her hospital room. A soap opera was on, the volume muted. She had no idea who was who or what was being said. She didn't care, either.

She glanced over at Detective Wilcox. He'd pulled up a chair beside her bed and sat, leaning forward, his elbows on his knees. It had been almost a year since she first met him back at her cabin. He'd come by to interview her after the Emily Bowers incident. His hair was almost completely white now, and his face made him look as if he'd aged ten years in one.

Gale sighed. It caused her ribs to ache. "I already told everyone what I know."

Wilcox, holding his notepad, nodded. "Yes, but you haven't told me, yet. Last you said before zoning out was about the police cruiser smashing into the cabin."

Nodding, Gale said, "That's the last thing I saw. I woke up in here after that. The doctors said I'd been here three days. That was a week ago."

"You were really banged up. Lost a lot of blood."

"Correct. You should be a cop with intellect like that."

Wilcox didn't smile at her joke. "So you heard nothing else? Saw nothing else?"

"Not a damn thing."

"And you had no involvement with Ethan Bowers and his crew?"

"Not at first, as I said. They brought me back to the cabin after I was attacked. I helped them a little bit, then." Gale looked directly at Wilcox this time. "How much trouble am I in?"

Wilcox puckered out his bottom lip. "Do you need to be in trouble?"

"I'd rather not be."

"Then let's not focus on that."

Gale figured that was as good an answer as she would get. "Have you found Ethan yet?"

Wilcox shook his head.

Gale's throat tightened. "Found anybody?"

Another shake of his head. "Just the cabin. It seemed to have fallen in on itself. No cruiser, but the tire tracks all over the yard corroborate your story. Definite evidence it had been towed away, which probably caused the cabin to collapse. We checked the junkyard, found nothing. Whoever took the cruiser is long gone. And we don't believe it was Deputy Reese, though she's still missing as well."

"What about *my* cabin?"

Wilcox tucked his notepad in the front pocket of his shirt. Leaning back in the chair, he let out a long breath that rattled his cheeks. "No bodies. The girls' parents have filed missing person reports, but so far, we haven't found any trace of them other than the blood all over your floor. It's a match for the podcast girls."

"They're gone. Ethan's gone. His friends are gone. A deputy's gone. The killers are gone."

Wilcox lifted a shoulder in a half shrug. "Seems that way. Long gone, most likely."

"You checked the junkyard? The Gorleys? That kid was Zeb Gorley. The big man was his father. Probably the whole family was involved in this mess. You looked there, right?"

Wilcox nodded. "They fled. The house was cleaned out. But there was evidence of…violence in the junkyard. But what it was, we have no idea yet. A lot of blood. An old house in the woods had been set on fire, but by the time the flames were extinguished, it had burnt to the ground. Investigators are still combing the scene. So far, they've found traces of bodies there. Maybe that's where the other bodies were stashed, too."

Gale nodded. She figured they wouldn't find much of anything at all. The Gorleys got away, and any evidence of what happened went with them. Gale wasn't sure how this was possible, but she knew it was fact.

And from the defeated look on Wilcox's face, he seemed to know it, too. "This shit keeps happening out here," he said. "And, frankly, I'm at a loss on how to stop it."

"Maybe it's over now."

Wilcox gave her a sorry smile. "You think so?"

Gale snorted. "Not a chance."

"What are your plans when they let you out of here?"

"Go home."

"And that's it? You got somewhere you can go stay until this blows over?"

"Will it blow over?"

Wilcox stared at her.

"That's what I thought," she said. "And, no, I have nowhere to go. No kids. No siblings. My late husband has a sister in Florida, but we never talk. So, I'll go home, clean up and reinforce the place, and hope for the best."

"Don't you worry you might be in danger?"

Gale thought back to what Ethan had said that day in her living room. He'd told her that she was a part of this now. She supposed since she was most likely the only survivor, she would remain a part of this.

Gale cleared her throat. It still felt sore from the tube that had been crammed down her esophagus while she was unconscious. "They haven't gotten me yet."

Wilcox nodded. "Don't know if that's stubbornness talking or if you're just the bravest person I've ever met."

Gale started to laugh, then felt pain all over that quickly stopped her.

"Sorry," said Wilcox, standing up. He put a card on the tray beside her bed. "You need me, call. Doesn't matter what time."

Gale nodded. "Thanks."

"Take care of yourself," he said, heading for the door.

Gale settled her head into the pillow and watched him leave. She was glad to be alone again but also hated that nobody was in here with her. She thought about calling the nurse in for another game of Uno, then decided against it.

She stared at the TV.

Most likely, she would get to leave in a few days.

Then what?

Gale had time to figure it out.

But one thing was for certain. She would need more than the double-barrel to protect her because she had zero doubt that somebody would come for her eventually.

And she would be ready.

About the Author

Kristopher Rufty lives in North Carolina with his three children and pets. He's written over twenty novels, including *The Devoured and the Dead, Desolation, The Vampire of Plainfield, The Lurkers,* and *Pillowface.* When he's not spending time with his family or writing, he's obsessing over gardening and growing food.

For more about Kristopher Rufty, please visit his Website: www.kristopherrufty.com

He can be found on Facebook, Instagram, and Twitter as well.

Novels

All Will Die
Anathema
Angel Board
Bigfoot Beach
Desolation
Hell Departed (Pillowface vs. The Lurkers)
Jagger
Master of Pain (with Wrath James White)
Oak Hollow
Pillowface
Prank Night
Proud Parents
Seven Buried Hill
Something Violent
The Devoured and the Dead
The Lurkers
The Lurking Season
The Skin Show
The Vampire of Plainfield

Novellas

A Dark Autumn
Last One Alive
The Night Everything Changed

Collections

Bone Chimes

Curious about other Crossroad Press books?
Stop by our site:
http://store.crossroadpress.com
We offer quality writing
in digital, audio, and print formats.

Printed in Great Britain
by Amazon

35274453R00169